SCATTERED

A TIME TRAVEL NOVEL BY

KATHERINE BENFANTE

The views and opinions expressed here in belong to the author and do not necessarily represent those of the publisher.

This novel's story and characters are fictitious. Certain long-standing institutions, agencies, public offices are mentioned, but the characters involved are wholly imaginary.

Author Photo credit JRW Designs

ISBN 978-1-961093-16-4 (Hardcover Book)
ISBN 978-1-961093-17-1 (eBook)

Published by Silversmith Press—Houston, Texas
www.silversmithpress.com

To mom, my biggest cheerleader
for this book and everything

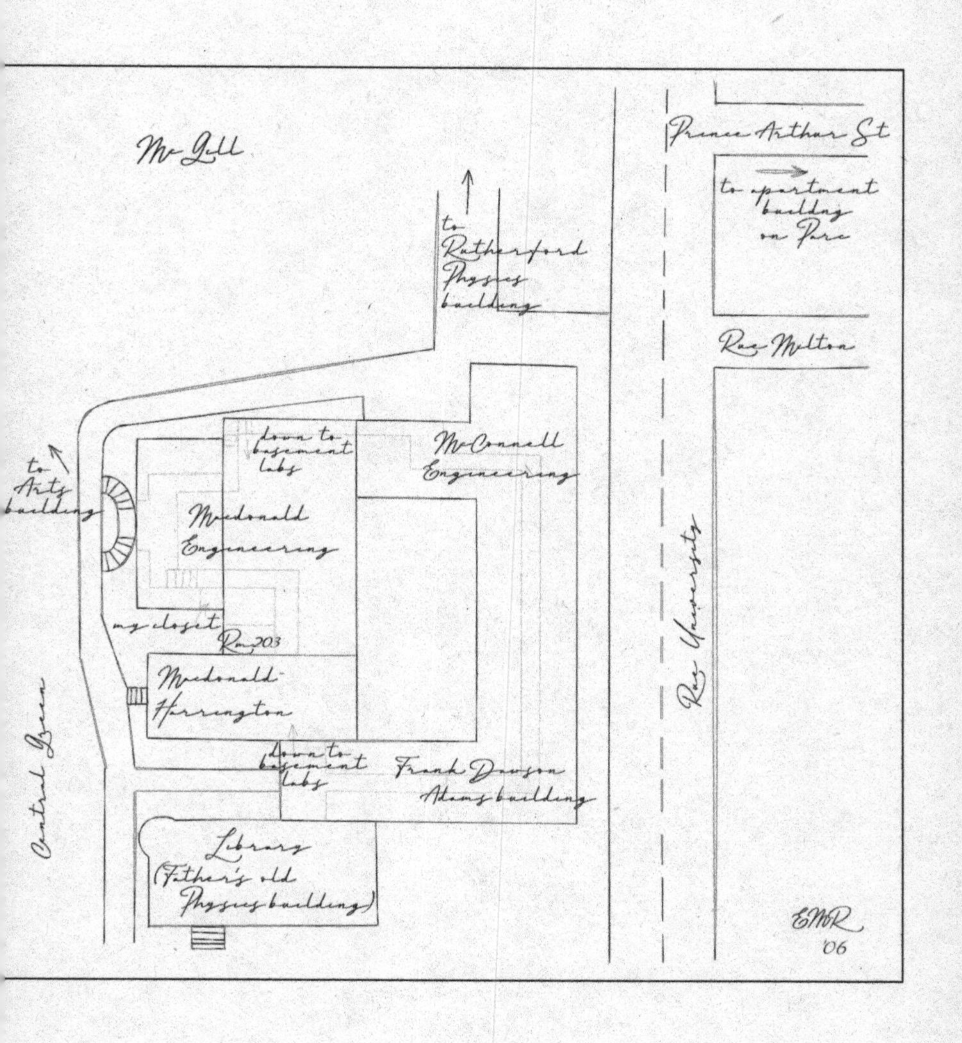
McGill
to Rutherford Physics building
Prince Arthur St
to apartment building on Parc
Rue Milton
to Arts building
down to basement labs
McConnell Engineering
Macdonald Engineering
my closet Rm 203
Macdonald-Harrington
Rue University
down to basement labs
Frank Dawson Adams building
Central Green
Library (Father's old Physics building)
EMR '06

1

Sunday, August 19, 1906
Montreal, Quebec, Canada
Eileen Rutherford

Walking lightly on my toes to avoid Mother's ears, I sneak back into our house and hear excited voices inside the parlor. *Fantastic, I'm not too late to eavesdrop on their discussion.* Listening in on my father's meeting with his student researchers is a weekly thrill for me which I won't let be diminished by Ralph Fowler's presence today.

As I move my right hand up to crack open the double doors, my mother steps into the hall from the kitchen, startling me into a little jump. In her arms is a walnut tea tray loaded with our large China teapot, milk and sugar, and a plate piled with shortcake biscuits and whole strawberries.

"Eileen! Do you know how long you were gone? And your skirt—twenty years old and you still come home with a hem rimmed with dirt!"

I shake off a few specks of brown from the ivory muslin. "I was busy discussing *MacBeth* with Emma at the

Mont Royal promenade, Mother. Our British Literature class starts next week, and we want to be prepared."

"You can't be seen today of all days looking like a lady who doesn't take care of herself. Oh, never mind that now. Please bring the tea in for them before it gets cold, then come back to the kitchen."

When I push the door open with laden arms and step into the parlor, nobody pays me any attention besides a small smile from Father and Ralph—who is clearly distracted enough to momentarily ignore the conversation around him. I don't dare let my eyes meet his, but rather keep my gaze to either my father or the floor, although I can feel Ralph's eyes following me as I step silently to the coffee table to set down the tray. He can't very well start a conversation without interrupting the ongoing discussion all around him. I'm glad for that small complication. I can listen in on the powwow in relative peace. Except for the fact Ralph's eyes sear my skin like a sunburn, it feels like any other Sunday. Today they're ironing out technical details of the "scattering experiments"—as Father named them—they've been working on for the past few months.

My father is Ernest Rutherford, the brilliant physicist and chair of the Physics Department at McGill University. He's still young, but he has more acclaim than most of his colleagues, like the Curies in France, and maybe even more than his mentor, J.J. Thompson. I'm astonished at the way his brain works, especially his incredible intuition that's led him to make so many discoveries in the last twenty or so years. From my visits to his labs and listening in on his Sunday afternoon teas, I think his work ethic helps too.

"The mica sheet can't be too thin, Ernest, or we'll never be able to mount it in the chamber. It'll flake apart when we touch it. There's no alternative than to keep it as thick as it is, but it's microns thick, if that," argues Frederick Soddy, his top research assistant. Last Thursday he and Father showed me the mica sheet through which radio-active particles travel. It's mounted in front of a small lead chamber, completely enclosed except for a thin slit on one face that holds a radioactive lump of radium.

"Yes, but the scintillations on the screen are simply too fuzzy at this point to be sure of what we're seeing. The screen looks as if you lobbed the dregs from your teacup straight at it. We must do better!" My father pounds his fist into the palm of his other hand for emphasis as he thunders his signature encouragement.

I would've loved to have seen last Thursday what he's describing, but I can't be in the lab when they run the scattering experiment, which they run in pitch darkness anyway. They need darkness to see what the physicists call "scintillations"—a phosphorescent dot on a screen, coated in zinc sulfide, which curves nearly three-hundred-and-sixty degrees around the mica sheet. Those scintillations mark the path of the radioactive alpha particles, a recent discovery by Father and Mr. Soddy describing positively charged emanations from a decaying radioactive source.

"Ernest, if you consider the emanation rate of the alpha particles, we should be seeing a clearly defined, constant glow on the screen. This fuzziness along the edges that flickers a bit . . . it's all very curious and doesn't at all fit with the theory," Mr. Soddy says.

Essentially, my father and Mr. Soddy explained to me they're trying to describe the makeup of an atom—the smallest indestructible amount of matter. They hypothesized they would see a thin line of scintillations exactly mirroring the shape of the slit. Father taught me that's because negative charges moving around the atom are balanced by the positively charged substrate. But for months they haven't gotten the clean line they expected.

Once I make my rounds with the teapot as slowly as I can, I know it's time to return to the kitchen. I catch Father's eye to wink my thanks; he beams at me, his lips pressed together and corners of his mouth turned up with happiness that I care about his work. It's at those moments I feel my heart tethered more tightly to his.

How I want to be a permanent member of that group instead of an "illegal" hanger-on! I've always wished my classes generated this vigorous of a discussion.

But Mother is waiting for me in the kitchen. She immediately puts me to work helping her prepare dinner. Her hands are full dressing an enormous leg of lamb to barbeque, a specialty of her and Father's home country of New Zealand. The barbeque pit is already set up in the backyard—our makeshift enclosed coal fire grill is a shortcut to the traditional slow-cooking, in-ground barbeque pit. She puts me in charge of helping get the vegetables prepared. After I finish, I wander into the back garden to cut enough daisies for a generous table centerpiece.

"That's lovely, Elie. Thank you for thinking of flowers for the table," Mother praises me as she walks over to wrap an arm around me. "I'm sure Ralph will enjoy these too."

I can't stop my face hardening, and a scowl replaces my joy-filled expression in a flash.

"Mother, did you and Father invite Ralph Fowler to dinner? When did this happen? Why didn't you tell me?" My voice squeaks higher than I thought possible.

She looks genuinely surprised and turns straight at me to reply. "Why, Eileen Rutherford, I thought you'd be happy. He's been courting you for some months now. And ever since he began teaching in the Mathematics Department, your father's taken quite a liking to him. He's such pleasant company, and three is really too small for a barbeque, after all."

"That's why you bought such a large leg of lamb."

My mother looks only slightly guilty. "I thought you'd assume Ralph would stay for dinner at this point. Why wouldn't he?"

"Why would he?" I retort in amazement. "Does he have a standing invitation now?"

This time my mother's expression is one of slight alarm. "Elie, I don't understand why this is a problem. Ralph Fowler is a kind man, a wonderful guest, and a friend of your father. I don't think I have to add that he's particularly smitten with you; I know you don't express your emotions clearly, but you don't complain when in his company either," she answers. Her reaction to my quick and defensive questions is genuine, but I can tell she wants to believe what she said.

I have absolutely no counter to that; Ralph is indeed a fine man, just not one I believe I'm capable of falling in love with. If I have, however unintentionally, led Ralph and everyone else to think my polite attentions to him have been in fact signs of my deep interest in him, then I can't outright deny what she has said. Moreover, this isn't the time or place to have an argument with my mother, what with there being a handful of esteemed men down the hall and dinner with a guest forthcoming.

"I guess I'll put on fresh dinner clothes in a while," I say with a simple nod at half-speed and half-vigor.

"Wear that light-blue dress with the little ruffles down the front and the ribbon at the waist. That'll bring out your eyes nicely." She's content with, if wary of, my sudden calm and alacrity in relenting to her argument.

Again I nod, though I'm determined to choose an ill-flattering dress instead.

Dinner passes slowly, if somewhat better than I had dreaded. Despite a cooling breeze blowing across the dining table set up in the garden, I'm not able to breathe when his eyes meet mine. The pressure of being pushed into the welcome arms of a man I haven't even a faint swelling of emotion for suffocates me. At least the scientific conversation and food distracts me. The barbeque is delicious, and I would inhale my succulent lamb and crispy potatoes if I possessed less manners. The meal takes me back to my childhood when my mother used to often cook her traditional dishes rather than fare from Britain and Canada, where I've spent my entire lifetime.

While eating and conversing politely, I practice what I had devised while dressing: to act civil tonight toward Ralph but display no emotion that can possibly be conceived as encouragement of his affection. This is my only hope to sway Ralph—and my parents—I've either changed my mind or never felt strongly for Ralph in the first place. My father surely wishes me to be with Ralph, but I also hold out hope he loves and respects me enough to want me to choose what I think is best. Of all people, Father understands the need to sow your own seeds in life and listen to your inner guide. That belief, as now, settles my nerves.

Throughout the meal Father plays The Great Ernest Rutherford and peppers Ralph with questions about his research plans at McGill; apparently he hadn't gotten to ask Ralph anything specific earlier at tea. Ralph politely and patiently explains several hypotheses of statistical methods he plans on expanding upon with his new colleagues in the mathematics department. My father is completely absorbed and is posing experiments with radioactive materials with which he can test Ralph's theories.

Trying to keep my face expressionless and emotionless, so as not to give an inch to Ralph, I'm inwardly dying to join in and interrogate Father on how exactly he's planning to test statistical methods in his work. I've always been naturally curious to hear what my father finds interesting in the realm of nuclear physics, and I genuinely find Ralph's theories fascinating even though I can't follow everything he explains.

"Now Mr. Fowler," my mother interjects for the third time, clearly bored by all the science talk. "Have you been to the theater at all since you've arrived in Montreal? Ernest and I enjoyed a show last month at—"

"Mary, Ralph doesn't have time for the theater! He's got important work to do! Great men can't waste all their time at teas and social dinners, can they, eh?" Father claps Ralph on the back, not taking Mother's bait. His brain, when exposed to matters dealing with physics and most sciences, closes down to all non-scientific comments, unlike Ralph's. He's been trying almost as hard as Mother to steer the conversation to include myself, which to him necessarily means the high level intellectual discussion has to end.

Mostly, Ralph keeps trying to ask me about my upcoming school week. He knows I take literature classes at the Donalda Department, in the all-female

Royal Victoria College at McGill. I answer blandly to each inquiry to thwart any attempt he might make to meet me after my classes. Humorously to me, Father actually saves me from having to divulge many details by interrupting with questions of his own, much to my mother's evident annoyance.

At one point, Ralph asks, "Miss Rutherford, you'll be able to get a nice reprieve from all of this physics talk during your poetry classes, won't you?"

Behind my placid face his insinuation that somehow I don't enjoy scientific discussion or worse, can't comprehend any of it, causes my jaw to clench.

"Well," I begin, trying to come up with a diplomatic answer, "the study of the written word can often be a strenuous and very technical process. I suppose it may actually be analogous to physics or mathematics in that regard. However, there is nothing 'new' to discover, per se, so the advancement in the subject may merely be to reinterpret a work—hardly as earth-shattering as discovering elemental decay."

Ralph's thick eyebrows arch, but he recovers well. "That's true. I wouldn't have thought literary analysis and scientific experimentation have much in common, but I may be wrong."

He may have been about to expand upon this vein of thought with me a little further, but just then Father jumps in, to my relief.

"Yes, yes, my dear boy! And that's how Frederick and I first came across the decay phenomenon with thorium back in 1899, I believe it was. It takes a dedicated application of the theory, sometimes recursive, to find patterns such as what we found. But she's right, it is a very technical process, and never easy or straightforward. You must always dig deep, and always question what you are doing to make sure you have considered everything!" His passionate voice reverberates against the back of the house and the white spruces lining our yard.

And so begins a discussion on the scientific method. On this note I'm happy to let my mind wander out of the conversation. Father, content to discuss work matters with Ralph, monopolizes the conversation. He normally wouldn't do so if the guest wasn't such a fascinating subject to him. My mother first scowls at my father, then starts nagging him about his usual messy eating habits—dribbling lamb *jus* onto the yellow tablecloth, dropping potato bits into his lap. I try not to roll my eyes at her constant harping.

At the end of the night I bid him an uninterested good night and make my excuses for needing to prepare for my classes early the next morning. As I turn away a faint wash of alarm and something else—hurt, perhaps—fills his expression, and guilt weighs me down heavier than the dessert dishes in my arms. The distance between us is ballooning, though his dejected face dampens my satisfaction.

I do not want to injure a kind man, and yet. . . .

Ralph's comments to me tonight and his general inability to see me as having intellectual value replay in my head like a needle stuck at the end of a record. In spite of his polite inquiries about my classes, I know Ralph doesn't see any point to my pursuits with the other women students at McGill. The previous week he had said to me, after starting to tell me about his research, "But you don't care about that, Elie. Women needn't be bothered with subjects like mathematics and statistics." Despite what I'm sure was an insulted frown on my face, a few breaths later he tagged my studies as "for recreation."

He's the sort to be perfectly content with a wife who sits at home and takes calls in the morning and cleans the house in the afternoon—and later, cares for his children. Not that I don't plan to bear and raise children, but I do take exception to not being free to pursue studies as I please.

What I want to get out of life from those studies is anyone's guess at the moment. All I know is I want to make a mark somehow in the world, like Father is doing. Unfortunately, my status as a female prevents me from chasing the highest of heights, but I figure if Marie Curie can be a famous nuclear physicist and do something as fantastic as discover entire new elements, then I have the prospect to do something significant with my life as well. While I have no idea yet what that significant thing might be, I know I can't achieve anything if I marry a man who'd rather close doors to it.

2

Friday, August 24, 1906
Elie

At the end of our Friday classes at four o'clock, Emma indulges me in stopping by Father's office to see if he's ready to leave early for home.

We walk from our building to the physics building in silence, paying no attention to anything around us except the clatter of carriage wheels on the street and our footfalls on the bricked walkway. I'm completely unprepared for what happens next; I don't even hear him approaching.

"Miss Rutherford? Is that you?" asks a voice behind us.

I freeze immediately and a cold bath of dread drenches my insides. *Why does he have to mar such a nice afternoon*?

Emma puts her hand on my forearm and turns to me with concern, knowing the man behind me is the last person I want to spend time with. Her gaze passes a silent reassurance to me, as if to say "I'm here for you; don't worry."

"Don't leave me," I whisper to her out of the corner of my mouth as I spin slowly to face Ralph Fowler.

A jubilant smile is wide across his face; he looks so happy for this chance meeting. His expression of hopeful elation would be too much to bear if Emma hadn't been at my side for support and distraction.

"What a surprise seeing you here! How are you, ladies?" He greets both of us with a polite, small bend at the waist.

"Quite well, thank you. We're on our way home. You remember my friend, Emma Chase?" I reply, then look down. Hopefully this will end the conversation quickly so we can be on our way home. It's probably smart not to stop in and see Father, lest Ralph want to pop in and say hello also.

"Miss Chase." Ralph nods and smiles at Emma. I'm surprised he recalls her name, since I'm sure they hadn't talked extensively when they met—a consequence of him trying to monopolize my attention that night. He then clears his throat quickly, and either summons the courage to say something or tries to decide exactly what to say. Finally he says, "Actually Miss Rutherford, I'd like to walk you home. And you as well, Miss Chase, of course."

"Oh!" A split-second cry bursts from Emma; apparently I'm the only one who expected Ralph to say that. I step in and smoothly give my hastily crafted excuse, hoping for the best.

"Thank you, Mr. Fowler, that's kind of you. But we're going in the opposite direction as you, and we're only fifteen minutes from home, really."

I'm not finished, but Ralph quickly interjects, "It's no matter. Like you said, you're only fifteen minutes out, so it's not too much out of my way. Besides, it's not often a gentleman gets to walk with two charming ladies at his side." He winks at Emma, who good-naturedly offers him a smile.

"Yes, that's true, and I would hate to deprive you of our company at your arm, but to be honest we're in the middle of discussing a reading for our British literature class, which we'll be tested on in class next Monday." *God is going to strike me down for lying like this. . . .* "I really would like to go over the last points with her before helping my mother with dinner; if you're on your way home, Father can't be too far behind." I give him a rueful smile to help sell my story.

Ralph's face falls a little, but I can tell he believes me. I doubt he cares about my studies, but he certainly won't want to upset my father by making me late if I have to talk with Emma beyond the time it takes to walk home. *That's a nice touch, blaming my need to get home on Father.*

"Aha, yes of course. I can see I did interrupt you ladies. I apologize and do wish you a pleasant evening." His gentlemanly manners are so good it's hard to begrudge him anything, had the previous circumstances been nonexistent. Then he adds, looking at me only, "Perhaps I can escort you safely home another day."

I blanch inside but try to act calm. Looking at Emma, whose cheeks and ears are genuinely blushed, I smile kindly and murmur a vague "thank you."

Ralph raises his hat slightly in a farewell greeting, then his footsteps grow fainter and fainter in the opposite direction we were walking. I've dodged what would surely have been another uncomfortable conversation in which I would have had to avoid his suggestive overtures and make up some sort of silly story to get me out if need be.

Once we're out of range for Ralph to overhear us, Emma exclaims quietly, "Quick thinking, Elie. That was close!"

"I wasn't sure we were going to get out of that one."

She laughs. "There's nothing a little white lie can't fix, right?" Her eyes twinkle with a devilish light.

"Surely, but I do feel a bit guilty for sneaking away from him, especially since he has *such* manners, as always . . . but you! I saw you blush a bit when he tried to charm us. You're not falling into his grasp, are you Emma?" I tease her playfully and nudge her with an elbow.

Emma blushes again, to my surprise, but laughs it off. "Hardly! He's no more my type of man than he is yours, Elie. But I can't help but be flattered if a man calls me pretty and is kind enough to first offer such an escort and then politely take a falsely concocted rebuff. He took it so well, I can't help but feel his kind heart showing through."

"That's what makes this situation difficult. How can a girl turn down a man who acts so graciously?"

We muse in silence for a few minutes, until Emma concludes, "I guess if it doesn't feel right, it isn't right, and there's nothing you can do about it."

"It might be that simple. But I don't know; I haven't been in love to know what 'feeling right' actually does feel like!"

We giggle together at the absurdity of it all, then chat more about Ralph until our discussion circles back to our school semester. The classes we take as sophomore students aren't as detailed or strenuous as those which the men attend. Even so, all fourteen of us dedicated ladies take our classes very seriously. We only learn literature, art, history, health, music, and home economics, but we're able to use the full library at McGill—which thankfully includes books on calculus, biology, physics, chemistry, anatomy, astronomy, and every other subject I can lay my hands on.

Yet none of those books compare to time spent in my father's laboratories during my ample free time. I even know which labs house each experiment he and his colleagues have set up, where the precious radioactive materials are stored, which man in the Workman Labs blows the best glass tubes for holding a vacuum, and best of all, I understand how some of the experiments work. My mind wanders to thoughts of their scattering experiment as we reach the physics building.

"Why don't you go on home? I might be a while with my father." I give my friend a quick hug of thanks.

She gives me a quick kiss on the cheek and squeezes my arms, saying, "Don't worry, Elie. It will all work out. I have a good feeling despite all this business with Ralph. You'll find the right man when you least expect it."

"Thanks, I needed to hear that. And you will too."

Yet even her reassurance can't quell my worries. I suppose now I need to speak with Father frankly about what's going on and let him know how I'm really feeling before it's too late, before Ralph gets to him and has a serious heart-to-heart request . . . well, to request me. What a dreadful thought! Though I know Father loves me and wants what's best for me, I fear he believes Ralph might actually be that thing.

Pausing outside the heavy oak doors of the physics building, I smooth out my black muslin skirt. I readjust the high collar of my white blouse around my neck and straighten my billowy sleeves. I heft my satchel, heavily weighed down by three books, two composition pads, a spare cardigan, and my lunch from today, onto my shoulder. My lunch of an apple, chunk of pumpernickel bread, and a few small well-preserved sausage links sits untouched because I was too distracted with reading four hours earlier to remember to eat. At the moment growls of hunger make themselves heard over the flap of butterfly wings filling my stomach, but I ignore them to focus on what I'm going to say to Father.

Once inside his building, I decide to check his office upstairs first in case he's there; that would be a more private place to talk than one of the labs. Taking two steps at a time, I reach the fourth level breathing a tad heavier than usual. I turn left and peek disappointedly into the empty office in front of me. I'll have to talk to him in the lab anyway and hope no one else will be able to hear.

I move to walk back downstairs when I hear a brisk rustle to my right. Frederick Soddy emerges from the researchers' office next to my father's, and he smiles instantly upon seeing me.

"Miss Rutherford! I'd been wondering when you'd appear this week. Are you looking for that busy father of yours?"

"Good afternoon, Mr. Soddy. Yes, I thought by chance he might be in his office, but I guess he's downstairs working, eh?" I work hard to clear all the tension from my face so as not to reveal my nerves.

"Yes, he should be in B5 still. He sent me to look for some set of papers he put up here years ago. I'll be surprised if I find it before the end of the year." He chuckles.

"Well, no one ever accused my father of being neat," I concede. For the moment my curiosity distracts me from my mission. "What papers? Do you want help?"

"No need to trouble yourself with this wild goose chase, Miss Rutherford. I'll find them sooner or later.

Your father is busy cleaning up that pile of old experiments down in his lab, and he wants to refer to something he wrote about the magnetic properties of iron after exposure to high-frequency oscillations. He's trying to see if those old buzzards still work at all and are fit to keep. He needs to spool up the big power supply to make sure the wires and connections are still good."

"Oh? Will I be bothering him if I walk down there?" I don't want my chance to talk with him to evaporate.

"You know he'd nearly stop a running experiment for you!" Soddy laughs again and throws me a wink. "I'm sure he'd welcome the distraction today. We were working on the alpha particle scattering experiment earlier today, but the equipment was acting up and losing the vacuum. We started taking that apart but decided we were doing more harm than good once we broke the main glass cylinder, so we switched gears to take a break."

"Oh no! I'm sure my father's none too happy about breaking that glass!"

"No, but your father thinks the glass blower over in the Workman building made a spare last time. We'll be up and running again on Monday."

"Good." I breathe a sigh of relief. "I'll head downstairs. Thanks for the information, and good luck with the search."

The tense anticipation had briefly left me while we talked, but it's returned with full force now as I trod down the stairs. I force myself to put one foot on the next lower step and rehearse my speech in my head. *Father, I have something very serious to talk to you about. . . . Before Ralph comes to talk to you about him and myself, I want to tell you how I feel about the subject. . . . I am convinced that what I want out of life is not what he wants, and I will never be happy with myself if I go down his path, nor will he be happy with life if I'm in his. . . . Yes, he's a wonderful man and I'm sure there's one lucky woman who'll make him a happy wife, but I know I cannot be that woman. . . . Yes, I've thought this through quite thoroughly the last few weeks, actually. . . . No, I don't need more time to consider things. . . .* I'm prepared to both state my case and defend it, if need be.

Once I reach the basement, my mouth is too dry to form words and my legs too leaden to carry me through the threshold of his lab door. I stop two feet from the open lab door.

A deep breath and a step. A second deep breath and a step, then I'm standing silently an inch inside the doorway. In the rear corner of the room with his back to me, Father's bent over an exposed lead box which usually contains the radium source for his scattering experiments. I assume he's emptying it after the glass cylinder broke. I can barely see the box's thin slit staring at me around my father's torso.

There are no windows in the room, but the brick-walled space is dimly lit by only half of the four equidistant pendant lights suspended between exposed piping and electrical cables running along the ceiling. They cast flickering, overlapping shadowing across equipment strewn across utilitarian oak tables pushed against the back and side walls of the room. Electrical wires snake around the various components circling the room from a routing point at an enormous metal sided box—the power supply Mr. Soddy referenced. Old mismatched wires, some stripped at the ends and others with their outer insulation sleeves cracked to expose the copper cores, loop about each other and twist at certain junctions looking like thrown spaghetti.

I stand in place for almost a full minute watching my father work while trying to calm my nerves and letting my eyes adjust to the low light. He hasn't seen or heard me enter. He strides toward an experiment I don't recognize and separates a few tightly wound coils of wire from a tangle of black wires which have the metal cores exposed at their frayed ends. Turning to the large metal box connecting all the power cables, he sighs at the array of dials, switches, and open ports for attaching cables.

"You worked when I had you at Canterbury," he mutters, fussing with the dials. "Only like New Zealand air, do you? Ah, we'll sort you out soon enough."

During my past visits to his lab, Father has explained to me what that and the rest of the equipment does. The box houses a current source whose high frequency can be tuned via a knob in order to measure its influence on the magnetic properties of iron. There are other high-frequency, alternating-current generators with wires and metal rods protruding from openings at odd and painful-looking angles. Robust glass tubes, miraculously surviving years of what were probably rough storage conditions, if their present state of organization is any indication, are connected to a high-energy light source. The energy sources are capable of producing x-rays aimed directly through the tube's length, in which the rays' effects on ionized gases are studied. Along the opposite wall, the tiniest experiment is a detector for electromagnetic waves. It has what my father calls a magnetizing coil of small bundles of iron wire. When alternating current electricity passes through rods connected to the coil—a solenoid—its magnetic field can be deflected, as measured by a magnetometer. Even miniscule oscillations in current, Father has explained, can be accurately measured. It's neat and tidy; it *was*, for now the wire leading from the solenoid to the coil is broken and seems to be looped into one of the high-frequency generators.

The most curious piece of equipment, in my opinion, is an apparatus used to measure time intervals accurately. Apparently it can distinguish between a hundred-thousandth of a second, which I can't fathom. Mr. Soddy told me the average human reaction time is about a quarter of a second, which is twenty-five thousand times slower than such an interval.

How incredible! Its actual function is to measure the rise and fall times of current through a pair of circuits using a falling weight and levers. The circuitry and levers are miniature, but precisely machined and assembled. I imagine it whirring with electricity, the levers ticking away at their stops as current flows in and out of the two circuits. Despite the haphazard organizational state of all its components, I can almost feel it come to life, if only fed a surge of power.

Father's humming quietly to himself, oblivious to me and completely absorbed in whatever he's tinkering with next to the box on the table. The only other sounds I hear are a faint clanking of tools and muted conversations coming from the closed doors of the other laboratories, plus a dull electric buzz. The noise seems to come from B5 itself, but I can't see from where exactly it's emanating. A small, curious part of my brain lingers on the machine's buzzing for an instant, but my emotions quickly push out those thoughts.

I can tell my father's deeply engrossed again in the lead box because he's barely moved except to pick up a screwdriver and rag. I almost don't want to disturb him—maybe it's simply apprehension of his reaction—but I know if I don't talk to him now, it'll either be too late or I might not be able to summon the courage again. I shuffle silently into the room, fearing the uncomfortable conversation. My legs are still a pair of barges, but I manage to move five feet. My father still doesn't hear me, and I suddenly realize why.

The electronic buzzing I've been hearing is much louder inside the lab. Once I see the red lamp flickering on the bulky box's front panel, I conclude the noise, uneven in tone, is definitely coming from the power supply. I hope none of the wires are shorting each other and causing the power supply to sound like it's on its deathbed. To me, it sounds like an opera singer with a sore throat at the end of a long aria—it almost hurts my ears. I assume the ill-sounding vibrations are characteristic of a high-frequency, alternating-current power supply, although its slightly erratic-sounding pitch doesn't seem perfectly healthy.

Under the wires leading from one side of the power supply are a few thick coils of copper, and in front of that lay the remains of yet another broken experiment. I trace the wires back to the device used to measure time intervals and beyond to the rest of the equipment. It looks like the wires are merely routed to main electric lines running along the walls. I don't want any of my father's experiments to get too tangled, so I step forward to push away the time-measuring device and move the copper coils from under the power cords.

In the split second it takes me to make contact between my left palm and the surface of the copper coil, I feel an incredible surge of energy pulse up my hand. My whole body pulses in the same rhythm as the audible buzz of the power supply, and it jolts every organ my skin and bones manage to hold together. I see, for the briefest of seconds, a tiny but distinct flash of yellow light wrap around both the large copper bundle and my hand, then it fades as quickly as it appeared.

I'm now in total darkness. The buzzing and electric vibrations have ceased altogether. A surge of nausea weakens my knees. I clap one hand to my stomach and another to my mouth. My skin perceives a distinct change in the atmosphere around me. I move a tiny step to make sure there is still ground below me.

It's still there, but my heel makes a sharper click on the floor's surface than it did ten seconds ago. I know instantly something incredible and momentous has occurred, but beyond that I have no idea what just happened. Disoriented, I suddenly shiver alone in the dark.

3

Friday, August 25, 2006
Montreal, Quebec, Canada
Will Hertz

It's incredibly noisy outside, and I silently will them to *shut up.* I understand they're trying to have fun. Hey, I was a freshman once too—pardon me, I was a U0 once (it's hard to get used to the Canadian lingo, even after five years)—but do they have to yell and sing quite so loud? I honestly don't remember orientation being *that* rowdy out on the McGill green, unless I was a tad more intoxicated during that initiating pub crawl then than I realized.

Alain, my friend and fellow graduate student here in our shared office, enters and answers my thoughts. "Nope. We were definitely *not* that loud and obnoxious, sober or drunk. I would have rather hid somewhere on campus than do whatever it is they're doing. Is that singing? While wearing bright-orange hard hats?"

"Actually, we did the same damn thing they're doing, sadly. Same nerdy drinking song, in fact,"

I remind him. "But maybe we did it with a bit more self-respect, huh?"

"Or a bit less beer, more likely. At least until later in the night, eh Will?"

I groan as my friend and dependable, brilliant lab partner recalls my first alcoholic experience; it didn't go as smoothly as I had hoped—for me or the front stoop of our dorm building. It's as to be expected in a province where the legal drinking age is eighteen, in retrospect. Thankfully, Alain was one of the few to see me in my less-than-spectacular moment and has been good enough to keep that quiet, even after this long. That's one of his character traits I value: knowing when to keep his mouth shut.

"Hard to believe I was that inept five years ago."

He shrugs. "Eh, you grew out of it. Now look at us, working away at the daily grind like old men. The semester hasn't even started yet, and we're sweating in this oven of an office—if you call this old room an office—getting as much research work done before Monday when we'll have classes and homework and teaching assistant duties piled on top of this. *Merde*. . . ."

"Hey, what part of this life isn't awesome? Dream research on a cool project in the best city, working under really smart physicists?" I remind him. Heck, I have to pinch myself still, and I'm halfway through our two-year-long project for our masters physics research. In addition to the research work this semester, I'll be a teaching assistant—TA—for a class taught by each of the professors who head the research: Topics in Classical Mechanics class for Dr. Anna Davidson and Introduction to Quantum Physics for Dr. Kevin Nagar. "The heat and long hours make up for getting to work under Kevin and Anna."

Alain groans, splaying backward in his desk chair dramatically. "Ugh, don't mention her name. I can't. . . ."

I shake my head slowly. "Still?"

"She's . . . I can't. . . . All I see is her—"

"—In your dreams?" I ask, trying not to grin.

"You have no idea, *mec.* . . ."

"Have you tried therapy? Hypnosis? Drugs?" I suggest, working really hard now to keep a straight face. "Or dating someone your own age to distract yourself?"

He closes his eyes and moans lowly. "Why does she have to be the way she is? Why . . . so—"

"—Tempting?" Hard not to grin right now, but I manage to hold back a laugh.

"She's so perfect, and all summer in those dresses, it's hot—"

"—I'm sorry, *it's* hot or *she's* hot?"

"Oh shut up, Will." Alain sighs and rubs his temples. "Ugh, this is *terrible.* Why does she have to be our advisor?"

"You mean, why does she have to be the best-looking female on campus?" I say quietly.

"Yes! Honestly, why can't she be a fat, frumpy, old dog that makes me want to toss my dinner every time

I see her? At least I wouldn't act brainless in front of her."

"Agreed. It takes you ten minutes to refocus after every time she talks to you. You're killing our productivity, man." He knows I'm pulling his leg as I cross my ankles atop my desk and lean back in my chair.

"How do you do it? You're like Teflon to her . . . *je ne sais quoi.*"

I shrug, staring at our office door ajar. After a few seconds' reverie, I shake my head of her image. "I'm not blind, you know. But she's our *advisor.* Off limits, man. And she's kind of the same age as my mom, so. . . ."

He half laughs, half sighs. "That doesn't help me. I can't stop. . . . No other girl I meet compares. . . . It's torture. . . . You have no idea." His head is buried in his hands now and goes on for a minute longer bemoaning his torment.

"Hello, gentlemen," says a woman who suddenly fills the doorway while knocking. "Alain? What poor girl are you crying over?"

Anna's pixy grin exposes two rows of blindingly pearlescent teeth. A petite woman with the face and body of someone you'd expect to see on a dance stage, Dr. Anna Davidson's looks belie her demeanor. Anna, as she prefers to be simply called, is a demanding professor and researcher who you try always to impress and never to disappoint lest it release her ferocious criticisms, but her brilliance and track record let her get away with it. I've been working under her supervision—besides the Modern Physics and Relativity class of hers I took third year—for over a year, and I learned quickly to put my best foot forward under her watch. Maybe that's why I only see her in a professional light.

Alain, on the other hand. . . . His eyes have peeked above the hands still covering his reddening face, frozen in shock. I know exactly what's running through his brain: *how much did she hear?!*

I too am frozen momentarily, until Anna's gaze turns to me.

"That bad, huh?" she says.

My eyes shift from her to him, unable to suppress a grin this time. Alain's eyes could not be wider, now in fear of what I'll say.

"He, uh . . . seems to find himself . . . enamored by a particular . . . bartender," I say smoothly. I'd never rat on a friend, but sometimes it sure is fun to tease Alain.

Anna throws her head back, laughing, and doesn't see Alain's shoulders relax. "I was going to suggest you boys cut out early. It *is* still summertime officially. Go enjoy some sunshine like those noisy freshmen outside. Or a pub?"

I check my watch: 3:47 p.m. It isn't happy hour yet, but that usually doesn't deter froshies.

"Sounds like they've already been," she mutters.

Alain, whose color is still somewhat pinker than normal in the cheeks, laughs nervously.

"Maybe you ought to be careful what you find in pubs though," she says with a wink to us both.

"Going to the pubs already, are we?" A male voice—Dr. Nagar, or Kevin, as he told us to call him once we became his graduate researchers—comes from the hall. A moment later a head sparsely populated with hair pokes into the doorframe a foot above Anna's.

"Well. . . ." I look sideways at Alain, but he's trying so hard not to ogle Anna that he hasn't yet processed what she said. No way can I get his attention now.

Kevin turns to me wearing his typical serious professor face. "Will, that strength calculation we were discussing yesterday on the titanium parts of the optics train assembly—I'm going to need that today, actually. Where are you on it?"

While I flip to a page in my notebook, Anna cuts in, "Kevin, I was about to head out, and I suggested these boys do the same. Last day of summer, you know."

"Is it?" Kevin's brow furrows as he checks his watch, a stainless steel exposed gear affair.

Anna shakes her head at him in amazement, an amused smile spreading on her face. "Well, I'm about to go in any case. I promised my husband I would take him somewhere nice tonight for his birthday."

"Have a good time," I say. I don't look over at Alain, though I can guess his reaction.

"Yes, I like to take time out to go on a nice date every once in a while. You boys should try the same thing sometime—all three of you," she suggests. Patting

Kevin's shoulder on her way out, she adds, "Don't keep them too late, eh?"

He sends a pleasantry her way as I exchange a hopeful look with Alain. I know we'd both like to start our weekend soon, but I'm already resigning myself to finish whatever Kevin needs. I lean over our shared wooden work table, scarred with decades of scratches and gouges, scanning the pages of my notebook for the scrawled sketches and formula he referred to yesterday.

Freed by the spell Anna always puts over him, Alain speaks first. "So . . . are we all heading out soon?"

"Sure, boys, but get me that value first, Will. I need to send it off today to the team in Arizona," Kevin says.

"Wait, wasn't this vacation week for the guys in Arizona? Are they even in today?" Alain interjects before I can answer Kevin.

Kevin shakes his head. "No, they're out until Monday, earliest."

"So why . . ." Alain trails off.

Kevin looks puzzlingly at us both, not understanding—ever the dedicated, single-minded physicist.

Luckily for him, I don't mind getting work finished and out of the way.

"I'll get it to you before we leave, professor," I say, glancing at Alain to shut him up.

Kevin gives us his trademark thumbs up and "thanks, boys" before heading out.

As soon as he's well down the hall, I burst out laughing. After a minute, so does Alain.

"*Enfant de chienne!*" he swears at me. "I thought you were going to spill the beans to her. God, I looked like such an idiot. *Tabarnak!*"

I spare him an answer; at least it could've been worse. And it provided pretty fair humor on this sweaty, still afternoon. Granted, we tend to have a pretty good time, along with our other friends who share our office and lab space no matter if we're hard at work or ribbing each other.

True, it sucks the main lab I'm working out of at the moment is in the ancient Macdonald Engineering building rather than the sleeker, newer Wong Physics building; heck, even Rutherford Physics has better facilities than here, and they have A/C. Unfortunately, I chose to start my masters research the same month the powers-that-be decided it was the perfect time to begin renovations on the Wong building. As a result, lab real estate was at a prime, so whoever could be pushed into Macdonald was. I'm one of the lucky five physicists crammed into an "office" room on the ground floor. I'm thankful to be working with my close friends, though I feel isolated from the rest of the physics students. I think the department justified sending me to work in the engineering labs because of my double major in mechanical engineering and physics; I know my way around them and am friendly with all of the professors. And since Alain transferred from mechanical engineering to physics in the beginning of his second year, he isn't a complete stranger around here either.

Despite our cultural and language differences, we bonded due to our status as outsiders—and also because physicists have been accused of being a different human species. Alain's pure French-Canadian, but if it wasn't for his thick colloquial accent, I'd have sworn he walked straight out of the Bohemian streets of New York City's East Village—an insanely intelligent avant-garde nerd replete with tattoos and old sandals worn three seasons out of four. I'm the straight-laced, four-eyed conservative type, pure rural American, and my bad French—still, after five years here—reflects that. Thankfully, Alain brings life to any party and any class we're in together, and I'm his voice of reason and savior when he wants to do something stupid—like investigate the rickety fire escape of our freshmen dorm after four hours of Molsons and cheap whiskey.

Knowing he'll snap out of it in a few, I leave him to stew about his own failure to act professionally and reread my notebook page's strength calculations, half-finished. Like him, I'd like to get out of our stifling office and at least pretend I have something more interesting to do until Monday morning.

Nah, Will. Face it, the most interesting thing in your life is your work, and at least that comes with good friends. Still, though; sometimes the weekends are long and—*and lonely lately, don't deny it*—Monday can't come fast enough.

4

Friday
Elie

The first thing I notice is the metallic tinge in the air. It smells exactly like a fresh thunderstorm—or Father's lab after a few hours' experimenting. I know immediately I'm catching a whiff of ionized air, and it catches me off guard. The air shouldn't be ionized since Father isn't running an experiment.

All this is running through my head at lightning speed while I stand in the dark, too shocked to move even the tiniest muscle. As the ionized air dissipates, my nostrils are overcome with the musky scent of aged books and brick. A new chill flows around me, as three seconds ago my body was stifled by the summer heat, but now it's as if I'm being shoved into an icebox. It's an odd and uncomfortable—no, unnatural—sensation, especially because I'm sure I'm not in an icebox. My eyes are finally adjusting to the surroundings. Relieved, I see I'm not in the dark, although there aren't any windows in the room. Bookshelves, tall and narrow with a thin, metal structure, line the walls; I can't imagine how they can support the weight of the books. Filling the center of the tidy ten-by-twelve room are two pairs of little desks with their backs connected to each other. They look like they're made of wood but are shoddy and Spartan. However, no one's sitting at them. In fact no one is here at all, and the silence is eerie. The buzzing I heard earlier has been silenced.

I've been distracted by so many sensory piques it only now sinks in that I have no idea where I am. *Why isn't this Father's lab? Wasn't I just there? And where is Father?* My heart, thumping in my chest at an increasing pace, reveals my panic. The blood flow must help to finally activate my muscles because I step tentatively toward one of the desks. Taking rapid, shallow breaths, I spin my head around as I shuffle forward on the thin, grey rug and brace myself on the closest desk, taking in what is no longer Father's lab. As soon as I'm near to touching the metal frame separating the two desk backs, a rainbow of electricity arcs from my fingertips. My hand springs back, and I rub the tingling fingertips.

Where did I get that static charge? Did I black out and wake up in another room in the building, one that I've never been to before? Am I dreaming right now?

I need to get my wits about myself. I inhale deeply a few times and take stock of my body. I don't feel sick at all; in fact, I feel exactly like I did when I walked into Father's lab a few minutes ago. My satchel is still slung over my shoulder; patting it lightly, I know my squishy cardigan and bagged lunch are still inside. I'm satisfied there's nothing wrong with *me*; I decide there's nothing to do besides try to get back to Father. He can't be too far, I reason.

The dark bricks are oppressively heavy overhead as I pass beneath the doorway. There's surprisingly little beyond save a short, low hallway which opens up into an equally low-ceilinged room not bigger than perhaps ten feet square. The base of a staircase lines one wall; the others are lined by a locked door and three large, white, machine-like blocks. These look more complex—perhaps a foreign design—than any I've seen in the physics laboratories or in photos my father has shown me.

I'm not too concerned about what's in this room, although it's unsettling in a way I can't define. I peer up the stairs and gingerly touch the metal cage lining the space in the center of the staircase. I know I need to search the floor above, since I've apparently seen all there is to see on this one. *I assume this is still the basement, but why are the rooms suddenly different?*

The dark wood staircase is worn and creaks under my weight with each step. It looks as though a herd of hippos have battered it since it was installed. I'm unconsciously trying to be silent, but the aged stair treads groan in misery. Finally, at the foot of the stairs I'm met with silence again.

It's unnerving.

As I spin around, my eyes meet a view I've seen a hundred times. It's the sandstone fireplace of the foyer in the physics building, and on the opposite wall are the heavy, dark doors opening to the half-moon portico.

Releasing the breath I held, at least I know I'm still in Father's building. *But what in God's name happened to the basement, and where is everyone?*

Knowing something isn't quite right, but hoping I merely passed out a bit ago, I head toward Father's office; perhaps he's there, waiting for me? I hike up my skirt and take the stairs two at a time, pushing my heels hard onto the treads until I reach the fourth floor. The wide hallway is still flanked by several wooden doors but are now attended by a small bookshelf on wheels, double panels of door-sized metal inset into the wall about half a foot, and what looks like an antiseptic metal drinking fountain. On my left is a room filled with high bookshelves, nearly identical to those I saw in the basement. Father's office no longer exists, nor Soddy's, nor anyone else's, and Father's certainly not here.

I weave through the large rooms and their endless bookshelves. Walking to the window-lined wall at the far end of the largest room, I inspect the books along the way—*Optics*, *Theories of Physics*, *Engineering Practice*, *Engineering Design*. Now it's obvious where I am: a library. But how the physics building was transformed into a library in the span of five minutes, or however long I passed out, I cannot answer.

"Where *am* I?!" No one is around to hear me, of course; I meet silence with a grunt.

The next fifteen minutes are spent exploring the rest of the floors, up to the attic-like sixth with its dormer nooks and down to the second. They're each a little different. Some have more desks than bookshelves, and two have long rooms with rows and rows of tables and chairs. This is definitely a library for serious studies, and it seems either a science or engineering library, or both.

And still, each room is as devoid of other human beings as a street at midnight. Perplexed, I decide to descend to the ground floor. Making cautious footfalls on the drab grey rug, I slowly make my way to a low counter of sorts. Behind it are rolling carts lined with neatly ordered rows of books, stacks of paperwork, and a little table and chairs pushed up against a window. These items are all indicative of a library I am familiar with, but there is so much that is unfamiliar, such as the large, light-grey box plopped atop the metal counter and the flat-ended, probe-like instrument in front of it. It's like an alien world. Even the air has a distinctly foreign smell to it down here; it's pungently laced with chemicals. Harsh sulfur-like notes invade my nostrils with malarial ferocity.

I realize I've been standing in front of the counter—I assume the librarian's station—for more than a minute. And yet no one has appeared. Perhaps she's occupied elsewhere in the building? An office room, maybe? I would have thought I'd have seen her *some-where* on *one* of the floors below I wandered about. The lack of other humans is starting to eat away at my brain, cruelly numbing the rest of my senses. My heart claws its way up my throat, but I keep breathing deeply to calm my rapidly fraying nerves.

With great effort, I lift my sandbag legs and move toward a big room off to the right. High-ceilinged with tall, thin windows dotting two of the perpendicular, adjoining walls, this room is also dead silent. More large, light-grey boxes—a dozen or more—perch atop spindly wood and dark metal tables with bright-blue chairs tucked up against them. I am entirely at odds with understanding what these boxes are, as well as the similarly-colored slabs in front of them, and examining it all makes the hair on the back of my neck stand up. My muscles are seconds away from propelling me backward, somewhere safe—wherever that may be at the moment—when my eyes zero in on a brightly lit screen of one of the grey terminal boxes. The words *Montreal-Gazette*, the city's newspaper, catch my eye, and I recognize what looks like a colorful newspaper article. A group of men in suits smile from the main photo below the headline "World Leaders Discuss Nuclear Security at G8 Summit."

Nuclear security? What on Earth is that? I bet Father would be interested in knowing about it; it sounds like something to do with physics.

I scan the rest of the page, then my eyes travel back to the date under the headline: Friday, August 25, 2006.

The 25th? But I could have sworn today is the 24th, unless I wrote the wrong date all day in my classes. . . .

Wait! 2006?! I give a little shriek, and with lightning speed, my head jerks up and faces the brick wall in front of my face, then slowly lowers back down, resting back on the date.

I stare a very long time, but the date does not change. There is no way to comprehend this. There is no possible way it can be 2006. I live in 1906. This is Montreal, evidently, but not 2006. *How can I be one hundred years into the future if I'm still here?*

My brain crunches inward at all angles. Invisible anvils smash it smaller and smaller until there's no way to make a thought anymore—and now the muscles have won. I'm running back through the short hallway, past the librarian's post—and suddenly, with intense clarity through the foggy animal instincts leading my body, I'm into the expanse of a lobby with dark stone walls. I see double doors off to my immediate right; light fills the stairwell beyond them, and something pulls me toward that brightness and out of the dark lobby. Hair flying behind me, I push through the heavy oak doors and race down the wide, shallow treads. Down half a flight, then around a corner, down the other half a flight, and through a white-walled hallway with a red-brick arched ceiling. Turning left, then right, then back left again, I keep running through the maze-like hallways. My shuffling steps echo in the space, making it seem like more than myself is fleeing madly.

Suddenly this empty, winding tunnel looks much more dodgy than anything I saw upstairs, and I can't run any further down the hallways. I admit to myself I have no idea where I am or where I am going. Stopping abruptly, I stand to catch my breath, slightly, then step slowly backward to where I came.

My safe point is the wide stairway; I can't make my body walk back up, and I won't re-enter the tunnel. I am stuck, stunned, and scared. Exhausted, I slump onto the bottom stair and crumple into a little ball, my head safely burrowed into my skirt.

I'm in too much shock to do much of anything except pretend this isn't happening, fool my brain into imagining myself back in the basement of the Macdonald Physics building as I know it, secure as always and ten feet from Father. It doesn't work, of course; my mind is flipping through the images it saw since . . . the "incident." Like a record played and replayed, the rooms and walls and windows flash in front of my closed eyes.

Assuming, of course, the newspaper's date is correct—and it's almost impossible for me to believe it as truth and to even repeat in my head the date of August 25, 2006—then naturally the building would have undergone significant renovations in one hundred years. Even transforming it from science labs to a science library, apparently, would be possible. After half an hour of hiding, I can think a little more logically, and I compare the main stairwell I used to ascend from the library basement up to each floor with that which I'd climbed countless times in my past to get to my father's office on the second floor. They are, of course, identical, save a few details.

I alternate between thinking about my situation in a composed manner and bordering on spontaneous explosion of my nerves. Finally, knowing I can't stay curled up on this step forever, curiosity gets the better of me. I want to know for sure where I am. Maybe I can find someone to say hello to, to help me, to explain what's going on.

I half crawl up the stairs to the ground floor and through the double doors. The library—the physics building—is to my left, and a large doorway, flanked by its weighty, opened doors on either side, marks the line where the building should—used to—end. Now it opens into the dark lobby to my right. All I can see are the floor and walls of dark slabs of black stone flecked with gold glinting in the mottled, very late afternoon sun trickling through the glass windows and doors.

I step cautiously into the lobby and peer to the right—down a long and empty hallway—and out the entrance to my left. Instantly, I recognize the central commons of the McGill campus outside; I can even see the old limestone façade of the physics building—the library—from here. Relieved, I'm sure now this is the Macdonald Physics building I know from 1906. A big part of me wants to run outside to the lawn, to be free and to see the familiar again, but I still want to find out a little more of what's inside here first.

Instead of taking the long hallway, I cross the lobby to two sets of double doors, one on each side of me. I take the doors to the left. Down a ramp I walk, gazing at pen-and-ink drawings of unorthodox angular buildings; these line the entire twenty-foot hallway, which opens up into another hallway. This one isn't tall nor lengthy. This time, I know immediately where I am: the bottom floor of the Macdonald Chemistry building. In my time—*is that what I should call it?*—the chemistry building is separate from the physics building. They must have built a link between the two at some point.

I know my way around this building, having been here a few times with my father to pick up this material or that, but I don't know its layout nearly as intimately as I do the physics building. By the time I explore this small bottom floor and the basement work area below it, I've realized how little the structure has changed and how much junk—dusty, rusty old machines and half-finished contraptions—has accumulated; it looks like a century of odds and ends.

I sink to the floor, my body shaking with wracking sobs. The striking—decaying—visual laying is too much to bear. Never have I felt so abandoned, out of place, confounded, and alone. That's it—I am alone. Not only do I find myself in a solitary predicament, it's a predicament which is singularly unique and terrifying.

Am I the first person to travel in time?

I'm going batty; this cannot be possible. I cannot have read the newspaper date correctly. There's no way it can be 2006. Yet I read the date twice, carefully. And this aged building and discarded detritus seems to corroborate it, however unbelievable it seems—but my mind is too stressed to process this information. There is only one word going around my head.

"Why?! Why did this happen?!" It pops out with much force and more volume than I thought myself able to muster.

And just like that, my brain shuts down. Me, who Mother is always accusing of being too headstrong and making independent decisions before thinking, cannot deal with all of this right now. With tears flowing like a waterfall down my cheeks and chin, my chest convulsing with sobs, and my eyes squeezed as tightly as I can close them, I crunch once more into a little ball. Safely tucked into a corner of one of the smaller basement rooms, I cry violently, hoping to wake up from an awful dream.

5

Friday
Will

Alain's staring out our one office window, itching to pack up, I'm sure, but he's nice enough to wait for me to finish working. While I plug in values for variables in a pair of equations, he's lost in space—thinking of Anna, no doubt. Then he spins in his chair.

"Say, Will, speaking of women—"

"Were we?"

"—what's going on with you? It's been awhile, *non*?"

"Not too long," I say a bit too quickly. "Montreal's short on worthy women."

"Ha! Right. Do you think there'll be anyone worthy at a ladies night somewhere tonight? It's not Wednesday." Montreal is famous for its $1 drinks for ladies at almost every bar on the island every Wednesday night, so the bars are usually chockfull of buzzed and drunk college girls, leading to my personal rule of bars any night but Wednesday.

"Worth a shot, Al. We can go once the froshies clear out. I need the Young's Modulus value for that titanium alloy Arizona is using. It was on that pamphlet from them. Have you seen it?" I'd look up the material properties on the internet, but the alloy is specially developed for this project, so none of the information is published.

"I swear I just saw it," he mutters as he searches the work tables.

On his side are notebooks filled with equations to process the measurements of gamma ray fluxes. Random papers are piled around his laptop, notebooks, and part drawings. We've been trying to design a new housing for the optics train of the project McGill partners called VERITAS, or Very Energetic Radiation Imaging Telescope Array System. This particular task uses more of my background in mechanical engineering than pure physics knowledge, but I don't complain. The overall project is a phenomenal opportunity, and if our advisors want to leverage my skills in mechanical design at the moment, I'm okay with that. I'm also helping Alain apply some of the gamma ray theory. We're proud to work on one of the more in-depth projects in the department.

Last year we primarily worked on the design of the detector, contracted out to us from the head of the project in Amado, Arizona, which is north of the border with Mexico. Unfortunately none of us grad students have gotten to see the installed detector array yet. It's actually an array of four telescopes over thirty-six feet in diameter. They sense gamma rays emitted during showers of electromagnetic radiation and ionized particles in the upper atmosphere. Our two faculty advisors have been involved for over five years now, first as conceptual advisors and theoretical researchers and now as system integrators. All along they've had their graduate students conduct background research and development of the infrastructure and emission analysis.

Alain and I both considered ourselves beyond lucky—not to mention grateful—when Kevin and Anna sought us out during our last year as undergraduates, wanting to take us on as masters students to help with VERITAS. At that time I realized I had to earn an advanced degree somewhere in order to get even a decent job in the field of physics, but I wasn't sold on staying at McGill. Their offer sealed the deal for both me and Alain.

And now here we are, sweating in a dank office whose walls have seen ten decades of engineering breakthroughs.

The space tightens when the other three physicists with desks here, Nico, Shavash, and Jean-Phillipe, walk in after an afternoon spent up the hill in the physics building, stealing time on expensive equipment we don't have in our old engineering labs downstairs. Gulping water to rehydrate, they crowd around my and Alain's desks squatting nearly in the center of the room. Everyone has a laugh at Anna's earlier comments to us, which I recount while continuing my search for the missing pamphlet. Nico nudges the usual scattering of papers, tools, and reference books aside to perch on the corner of my desk. Shavash, the lone girl in our office, frowns at his imposition and pulls her chair over. Jean-Phillipe—JP to us—stands like a sentinel in his trademark stance: legs spread about two feet apart, hands clasped together behind his head, and his face cocked at a slight, contemplative angle. He gives the impression, as always, of a tall, sturdy guy holding down the floor.

"Nico, got a question for you." I glance over to his shelves on our communal bookcase. Its shelves are stuffed with textbooks, scribbled-on paper, a vernier caliper, spare lab supplies, and old experiment prototypes; the overflow has nowhere to go but his chaotically messy desk he oddly thrives on.

A concerned expression covers Nico's face; I'm instantly confused. "Mr. Hertz, I'm sorry. It's not normal, it doesn't happen to every guy, and yes, you really do need to get it checked out."

For a few seconds, I have no reaction. Then I chuck a dusty crumble of scrap paper from the bookcase at his head. "Haha, guess I walked right into that one. Seriously though, do you remember the Young's modulus of the array's titanium alloy?"

"What am I, Mr. Google? No, sorry. And I'm pretty sure Kevin took the one pamphlet we got and cataloged it in the library already," Nico replies, his sarcasm fading.

I groan loud enough to interrupt the others' conversation. I'm close to finishing my task for the day, and much as I want to start my weekend, this won't take long. "I guess I'm off to the library. I won't be long, then I'll be ready to leave. Anybody need anything?"

"A cup of coffee would be great. And I could go for a bagel," quips JP.

"*Oui*, but I'll take an espresso, one sugar please," adds Alain.

I roll my eyes at my friends and coworkers. "No, I meant from the library, you dolts!"

"Yeah, we know what you meant. But the caf is on the way, Will; you've gotta need some coffee too, I know it. You're a thirsty guy." Alain's pulling his trademark persuasion routine. Well, he's trying, though I know they're half-joking.

"Right, the caf is smack dab on the way—" the cafeteria is in the McConnell Engineering building, on the other side of our building, "—or perhaps I can walk down to Sherbrooke Street and go to Tim Horton's. Would you like that better?"

"Ooh," gushes JP, honestly excited. "They have iced cappuccinos! Screw the hot coffee. And while you're there, nix the bagel and grab—"

I crack up and walk out of the room before JP starts on a long list of donuts to pick up. The great thing about working with these guys is their sense of humor and love of fun despite all being incredibly intelligent. The bad thing about working with these guys is their lack of seriousness for all times except when necessary.

The maze of hallways in the four interconnected engineering buildings—McConnell, Macdonald, Macdonald-Harrington, and Frank Dawson Adams—are no longer as confusing as they were five years ago. The two older Macdonald buildings were built at the turn of the last century and had meandering halls, rooms hidden in nooks, and multiple levels, including the basements all with different layouts. Unfortunately, the other two engineering buildings were built in the 1950s adjacent to the original structures, but the floor levels don't exactly match up, let alone connect at every level. I can now manage to avoid dead-ends, mostly because by now I've tried every path combination.

Today I take a direct route—no stopping at the caf—to the black granite-walled lobby where the humble doors of the most powerful library on campus are found. The turreted Schulich Library appears nondescript from the inside, its original stonework architecture hidden behind modern drywall and endless bookshelves. With pride I recall it was once the Macdonald Physics building, best known in its heyday for housing the labs of the great Ernest Rutherford. Even through three renovations and a fire in the 1920s, the building has kept some of its turn-of-the-century charm.

Today the building is a tomb. I must be the only person besides the librarian inside the library, and my taps on the keyboard of the card catalog database echo jarringly. I jot down the area where the pamphlet is supposed to be on the fourth floor and decide to huff it up the stairs. I plod up the square, enclosed stairwell cooled by original sandstone walls. It's quiet and peaceful, much better than the usual struggle it takes to squeeze past anyone on the stairs.

At the crest of the steps to the fourth floor, I inhale the scent of aged books and even older stone. One of the best things about the Schulich Library is it smells less like a used bookstore and more like a warm house you want to curl up and read in—which is exactly what I've frequently done here during my five years. I navigate easily to the pamphlet and pluck it off its resting place on the bottom shelf. Kevin's messy, block-letter printing is scrawled across the inside cover: "PROPERTY OF MCGILL PHYSICS DEPARTMENT, APRIL 2006; PROVIDED BY JAMES T. GREGORY, VERITAS PROJECT. PLEASE RETURN TO THE PHYSICS DEPARTMENT IF FOUND." Apparently, the professor didn't originally anticipate entering the information into the library stores but was no doubt prodded by Anna, ever conscientious and organized—and ever the atypical physicist.

Instead of checking out the pamphlet, I memorize the value of 121.3 GPa I need and file the paper back into its spot. On my walk out of the room I can't help slowly scanning the shelves for something new or interesting; something in classical physics catches my eye. A thin, red-spined book titled *Famous Physicists of McGill* sits shyly at the far left end of its shelf at eye level, pushed in a bit behind the massive book beside it.

I have no idea who was famous at McGill besides Ernest Rutherford, so I pick up the little book and wander over to my favorite reading and studying spot. At the end of a bank of arched windows is a two-foot-deep wood bench running the length of the wall. Many hours between classes were spent fondly here in my undergraduate days, leaning against the brick wall, feet extended straight out on the bench, staring outside at the trees and center lawn when my eyes needed a break. So I settle my limbs in comfortably and thumb through the book while an A/C vent blows down on me.

By far the fattest section is about Rutherford's life: his discoveries of radioactive half-life, radon, the proton, and neutron; his redesign of the atomic model to show a dense center nucleus; his work with wireless communications, radar, and sonar; and his race to be the first to split the atom in 1917. Most of these milestones I'm aware of, especially those leading to the Rutherford Model of the atom because his gold-foil scattering experiments are legendary at McGill. A little known fact I discovered three years earlier, while extensively researching Rutherford's life and work for a physics paper I wrote, was that he didn't actually do the experiments with gold foil while at McGill, despite our professors repeatedly making the claim. During his years here, from 1901 to 1907, he wasn't very far along on his scattering experiments at all. The mica sheets they used here yielded inconclusive results, and he and his graduate researchers later at Manchester didn't have their "eureka" moment until 1909 or publish the theory until 1911. However, the experiments at McGill did lay the groundwork for the hypothesis. Sometimes for a matter of pride a small legend can grow into something a little more exciting, I suppose.

Engrossed in the background story of the great physicist's life, I lounge in my nook for ten lazy minutes. I skip over the tidbits the author included about Rutherford's family life, as I've read about them before: his homey early life in New Zealand, his quiet wife Mary, and his daughter Eileen. She supposedly grew into a bit of a rebel whose tendency to bring wine to public picnics—*oh, horror of horrors*—earned her mom's disapproval and chiding. I'd rather read about the physics, not his footnote-in-the-history-books daughter and his son-in-law, so I shuffle ahead to the next chapter.

A vibration in my shorts pocket jolts me back into the present. It's JP text-messaging me. "did u get lost on way 2 get coffee? or library turned into black hole?" Bad physics joke. But it is a good alarm to get back to work. So I spin my legs onto the floor and return *Famous Physicists* to its resting place, making a mental note of its location.

Three minutes later I'm almost back to our office when I pass the open door of Dr. Nagar's tiny office at the far end of the hall.

"I'll shoot you an email with what you need in a few minutes. I needed to run to the library, but now it's just plug-and-play," I explain.

Whatever open floor space there might have once been around his desk, bookshelves, and guest chair is now perennially cluttered with stacks of milk crates and cardboard boxes. Inside each is a mismatched collection of books, lab record books, years of subject journals, and old experimental equipment; he's as much an experimenter as he is a theorist.

"Excellent, Will, thanks. I can always depend on you."

I nod appreciatively, then bid him a good weekend.

"I suppose I'd better wrap this up in the next hour or so as well," he agrees, squinting at the time displayed on his screen.

I try not to chuckle out loud. I'm picturing his wife, hands on hips and standing over a cold dinner laid out on their kitchen table. Kevin's perennially the last to leave the building.

"Well, see you Monday, Will, eight thirty-five for Intro to Quantum Mechanics, eh?" He wants to introduce me and Shavash, his other TA, for the first class of the semester.

"Right, bright and early." I'm mid-wave when he stops me.

"Oh, Will? Can you do me a favor and close up the labs downstairs?"

I pause, but not too long. "Sure, I'll head down there right now." I want to head back to my desk and finish my calculations so we can go out, not play lackey, but since I am one I do what I'm told.

"Thanks, Will," he replies, not taking his eyes off his screen this time.

Now I wave goodnight and head down to the basement after texting Alain I'll be delayed another ten minutes for my new task. I methodically shut off every light in the labs, even those used by the mechanical engineering department, and close all the doors. It's courtesy in the building that whoever is last around that day, no matter the department, is responsible for closing up shop. None of the doors have locks, since the building's exterior doors are locked at the end of every night by the janitor, but they have to be shut. Finally, I make my way to the south end of the basement labs, having crossed the boundary into the Macdonald-Harrington building. The path to the stairwell up to the ground floor is lined with dusty piles of prehistoric machinery, warped sheets of undetermined materials leaning against the wall, and medieval lab equipment. Once on the ground floor of Harrington, I cross the short, wide hallway into the ramped vestibule connecting it to FDA. I throw open the door and nearly fly into the open foyer—then I gasp in surprise.

I had thought I was all alone, but the second I emerged from the vestibule I see a flash of golden hair disappear in a flurry through double doors across the hall. Those doors aren't ten feet from the library's entrance and lead down to the basement of the library and a tunnel to the Mathematics Department's building about one hundred feet to the south. I stop in my tracks and catch my breath. I've been so single-mindedly focused on getting out of the building I didn't expect anyone else to be around. That girl—I assume it was a girl, since the hair was long—is the first person I've seen in the halls all day. She must have been in the library and was taking a shortcut to the math building; too bad someone else is here so late on a Friday, but maybe she's a professor getting ready for Monday's class.

Hey, if Kevin wasn't already married, they'd be perfect for each other.... I laugh a low chuckle ringed with pity.

Yet . . . why would a professor be running? Strange.

She had nice hair. . . .

Theories on who she might be and visions of her golden hair fill my head until I step back into our office, where JP breaks my thought train.

"Are you ready to go, Will?" he asks. "Alain told me we're going out. Well, except Shavash—she's ditching us for her *boyfriend.*"

JP rolls his eyes at the word, teasing her, as ever.

"Two minutes," I promise him, already writing 121.3 GPa on the top of my notebook page and filling in the rest of my unfinished calculations.

The rest of them chat about their plans for the last weekend of summer vacation as they pack up. My mind can't help but wander as I look forward to a new semester, full of classwork and working with these guys. I'm a physics geek, and I know it and accept it, but at least I'm social, at least I have friends. God help me if I end up like Kevin: brilliant and witty but chained to my books and papers with an unshakeable and slightly unhealthy passion.

Here's hoping, Will, you can make this next semester a bit more lively than just deriving equations all day. . . .

6

Friday
Elie

It's dark, but after what has to have been at least a couple of hours, my heartbeat has finally slowed to almost normal. Enough that I can finally think. Or at least try to think about Father. It might be unlikely he's here, but not improbable. If I can find future him, maybe I can find my way back home—to my present time.

Father. Mother. Emma. Ralph.

A few hours ago I was preoccupied with my life full of them—my family and friends—and now I am ripped from them like a baby from the womb, seeing only unfamiliar things. How silly and small is the worry I obsessed over a few hours ago: how to evade an engagement with Ralph Fowler. Convincing my father to agree with my view was the hardest thing I had tried so far in my life, a life devoid of truly difficult obstacles. Now one scary word looms over everything I have right now: survival.

Thinking of Ralph and Father forces my eyes to close. Wetness tinges my eyelashes and my chest tightens. Such trials, both then and now, and I wonder when I can return and if I'll have the chance to try again to convince Father.

Marriage is the least of my worries now. I try to forget the memory of Sunday's dinner with Ralph. Even now with a century between us, I can't feel happy about causing someone else suffering, though I know it's for my and his own good.

A century between them and me . . . and my classes on Monday. . . . Yet I won't make the classes—I didn't make it to my classes, in the now-past, in 1906?—and Emma will be—was?—worried sick when I don't—didn't—show up. And Mother and Father will—did—know I haven't—didn't—return home that day. My head convulses with confused tenses.

Do they—did they—already notice I'm gone? Surely they must miss me.

My shoulders haunch over my aching chest, full of misery.

2006. The newspaper said today is Friday, August 25, 2006. Without understanding what that date really means, it occurs to me, like in 1906, there probably won't be anyone in the buildings until Monday.

Who would I seek out beyond the campus? A police officer? What could I tell him, I'm a girl from 1906 and could he please help me return home? No one would believe me!

And no one can help me.

No, I must stay in these buildings unless I really must go beyond the campus. There must be a key to returning back to Father. He may be here, and I must search every hall for him, calling in his name. At the very least, I have to search for a way to return home, although the library's basement will be inaccessible until Monday morning. Until then, I can't help be curious to explore the rest of these buildings, now that the shock of spinning through time has dulled.

Women like me weren't raised to develop survival skills, but I've tried in the past hour to put aside my shock in favor of rational thoughts. I still have my knapsack, which contains a bit of food, enough to last me through the weekend if it must. My stomach rumbles loudly at the very idea of being largely empty for several days. I remember seeing what looked like a water fountain in the library, one on each floor, so I know I won't die of thirst before Monday. If I can't locate Father, as long as I can take a bit more serious stock in my surroundings, develop a course of action, and survive physically through the weekend, I'll be able to find someone on Monday who can help me. Until then, I'm trying not to think about what future lies before me, only the here and now.

7

Friday
Will

Finally, Alain and I are leaving campus, the other three having gotten a head start ten minutes ago.

Maybe we'll both end up like Kevin after all.

As I close the door behind us, I remember an incident from hours earlier. "I forgot to tell you, Alain. I ran into Nina this morning. . . ." Nina is Alain's obnoxious ex-girlfriend who's only turned more obnoxious after she dumped him.

"Fantastic. And what vile epithets did she demand you convey to me this time?"

"Surprisingly few, you'll be happy to know. She just glared at me and made sure I told you—"

"—to go to hell?" Alain suggests in a laissez-faire mocking voice. Apparently he's gotten that line from her before.

"She was a little more imaginative than that. She wanted you to know that she's so much better off without you and is glad she's been able to move on so well."

Confusion and disbelief dominate his expression. Shaking his head, he wonders aloud, "But why say all that when *she's* the one that dumped *me*? Isn't it assumed she's better off since she made it so?"

I laugh at the absurdity of it all. I understand that girl less than Alain does. How am I supposed to know why she said what she did? Heck, I can barely wade through my own female problems. "No clue, man. They're from Venus, remember? They don't speak our language."

"But why go out of her way to tell you she's happy now when I would expect her to be?"

"Hmm," I muse. "Maybe she suffered more than she let on. Don't women always cry into ice cream bowls after a break-up no matter what? Some pathetic Julia Roberts comedy comes to mind."

"Hey, she was hot in *Pretty Woman*! Don't you be talking bad about my Julia," Alain teases.

"*Pretty Woman*? When did that come out, like a hundred years ago? If you're stuck on her, no wonder Nina dumped you!"

At that, Alain reaches down for a piece of litter and chucks it awkwardly in my general direction. The weapon misses me by a light-year.

The conversation quickly shifts from his love life to mine—or lack thereof, thanks to a schedule dominated in recent months by nonstop work and lab hours. The last girl I dated did a real mind bend on me, and I really don't want to be reminded of the whole ordeal. My roommate Evan set us up; although in hindsight, judging from his own poor dating record, I'm not sure why I took his recommendation. She was a marketing major at McGill, intellectually stimulating, and full of crazy ideas of where to go and what to do. Things grew pretty intense between us over the next six months. Spending most of our week together, we moved at warp speed. But her crazy ideas turned into her just being crazy. One week she made me think I was the only thing in her world and the next week I was the last thing she ever wanted to see. In the end, she gave me such emotional whiplash I was happy to be off the ride—almost.

I tortured myself by sticking with her that long, and afterward I was a complete wreck as the previous months' euphoria washed over me in reverse. When my life slowed back to normal, I alternated between shutting myself in my room to let the memories torture me and taking long jogs through the city to run out my anger. I ended up settling on a happy, reclusive medium—and I decided to become infinitely more guarded with my feelings. Never again will I let myself be swept away and forget everything else around me. No more ripped open hearts, thank you very much. Three months later, I'm alone with my books and lab equipment, but busy and content. Who needs a girlfriend when you have great friends and you're designing revolutionary works of physics?

* * *

By the time Alain and I drop off our bags and meet up with Nico and Jean-Philippe it's nearly six. While we walk to one of our favorite downtown haunts, Brutopia, Nico and Alain are debating, almost to the point of argument, whether Brutopia's honey wheat beer is better than German Hefeweizen. JP, on the phone with his girlfriend Marie for the first four blocks, is spitting rapid-fire French so fast even my fairly trained ears barely hear anything more distinct than "*non, cherie*" and "*pas de problème.*" I don't want to hear what they're discussing, but I'm so used to hearing French I immediately tune to the words, almost as if it's now a native language for me. Though, as JP is fond of pointing out, while I can understand it well enough, I routinely butcher things like verb tenses and pronunciation when speaking.

Naturally, however, the subject between Nico and Alain eventually turns to physics; it's inevitable with our crowd. Not two seconds after flipping his phone shut and shoving it into his jeans pocket, JP nudges Nico and asks, "Hey, if the universe were to stop expanding tomorrow, but we don't realize until months or even years later, could we accurately calculate the redshift—negative z at that point, I guess it would be—or would we be stuck with an unrecoverable error?"

And now our geekiness is exposed to anyone within earshot. The next thing I know, however, we've all put in our two cents, and the idea degenerates into an in-depth, serious discussion about the age of the universe, its state of expansion, and eventually *Star Trek*.

Our favorite bar is overrun by a thirsty throng of incoming freshmen, so after one round and too many elbows to our ribs, we decide to give up and go back to our apartments on Rue du Parc, east of campus. At least we take the scenic route up Rue Crescent. This street is one of the hippest and busiest streets at night in Montreal because of its volume of bars and clubs—sometimes stacked two or three stories high. Tonight, the new college students are mixing into the usual Friday crowd, and the mayhem spills over the sidewalks and onto the street. Scores of people are squished into every possible square inch of the open café and restaurant patios. No doubt on their way to the newest bar, clacking down the streets in groups are girls in miniskirts and skyscraper heels. Mixed into the younger crowd are sharply dressed couples and men in their workday suits and ties. They fill the higher-class restaurants and cocktail lounges, those with urban-chic minimalist décor and drinks with the price tag of a small island.

We wind our way through the throng of people and end up on Boulevard Maisonneuve, having realized the shopping lane of Rue Saint-Catherine is too crowded to walk down except in single-file. As we head east on this wide, quieter street, the others start in on the bartender's outfit of the night.

"She looked *gooood*," drawls JP. "If I wasn't spoken for, gents, I'd—"

"Ha! You grab anything that moves," counters Alain.

"Mmm, you're right there. It's the brute force method of getting dates . . . works about half the time."

"What does? Hitting on anything with two legs and less hair than your little brother?" I tease JP. I always wonder how he keeps up his borderline dating swagger.

He smirks at all of us. "Hey, you're looking at the only guy here with a girlfriend. And why don't you ask her out, Will? If you don't, any of the hundreds of guys tripping to get to her every night will."

I start to shrug slowly.

"Yeah," Nico chimes in. "Don't tell me you didn't see how she was looking at you whenever you came by."

"Meh," I begin noncommittally as I check for opposing traffic. "It was too noisy in there—how could she have heard me if I said anything? She's nice enough, but . . . I don't know. . . ."

Nico punches my upper arm. "Nah, think of it this way, guys. She didn't try to pick him up, either. It's gotta be Will. Must be those glasses! You gotta lose the glasses, man."

"*Non, non, non*, keep the glasses, Will. Those are hip frames, very stylish. Plus chicks dig guys with glasses—they make you look smarter," JP argues. He's the best-dressed guy in the physics department, so I figure his fashion opinions have merit.

Alain agrees. "Yeah, it's not her fault because of Will, it's Will's fault because of Will."

I raise my eyebrows, taken a bit aback.

"You're too polite to women," he says. "So formal and reserved around them that they don't think you're actually interested in them. They don't pour it on for you. It's like how you're so polite with Anna."

JP and Alain laugh, nodding, but I'm still shocked.

"First, if I'm too polite instead of being a jerk to a girl like you guys are, fine by me," I start, confused about how polite is too polite.

Those two have the decency to look momentarily shamed.

"And second, I'm polite to Anna because she's our advisor and professor, not because I'm trying to impress her so I can ask her out. And she's married for God's sake!"

"But Anna's, like . . . a goddess . . . who speaks our language, Will. Don't tell me you haven't been the least bit tempted!" Nico interjects.

"Okay, okay, I'm not a monk, but I'm polite to Anna because she's *Anna*. I treat her the same way I do Kevin."

"But you're like that to every woman, Will, like you're afraid they'll yell at you if you're not nice, or they'll break if you don't treat them like china dolls," Alain chides. "I'm not trying to be mean, but sometimes they like it if you're a jerk to them—well, not a jerk like JP here, but just *real*. Girls hate perfect guys, Will."

I can't help but picture my dad, always opening the car door for my mom and never speaking badly of her, ever. "What can I say? I'm from the Midwest, guys. Traditional family values and all. I was taught to treat women with respect, and if she doesn't like it, then that's her problem. And hey, if girls like it when their guy is a jerk, how come you've been single for a year?"

"Ooh, touché, *mon ami*, touché. But I'm a little more chill around girls."

"Yeah," says JP, putting his arm around my shoulders in a big brotherly way. "You're, like, uptight with girls sometimes. Always holding the door open for them."

"So?"

"So they want to do that for themselves now. It's a new century, *mec*."

"What you need is a good old-fashioned British girl that expects that kind of thing," Nico says. "Heck, I wouldn't say no to someone with that accent."

At that, I laugh. I actually wouldn't mind dating a nice British girl with a cute little accent, saying things like "*dahnse*" and "*luv-ley*" all day long. But the chances of meeting such a girl are slim to none.

The conversation gets dirty real quick with the guys naming who's on their top five British women—and what, ahem, features earned them a spot on the list. For a good three or four blocks, the conversation goes about the same, as always with my friends. But the night's conversation sticks with me. Even though we ribbed each other, I know what they said about me being perpetually polite to women is true. But if I'm honest with myself, I don't care. Maybe I was raised differently than these guys, or maybe I'm a mama's guy—or maybe I was born into the wrong era, who knows—but I'd rather be known as kind and considerate than earn a reputation as a prick or a heartbreaker.

Finally we arrive at the corner of Parc Avenue and Milton in front of the apartment building where I share an apartment with Evan, a graduate electrical engineer I've roomed with all five years here, two floors above Nico and Alain. JP lives at home with his parents in Laval, but the three of them have decided to spend the night playing Call of Duty. Though I love hanging out with my friends, there are some things I can't stand, and gaming is one of them—and I don't need to become any more nerdy than I already am. Thank goodness my roommate shares my hobby of jogging. Taking a run through the cooler evening air is infinitely more appealing than lounging in front of the TV, and it might clear my head.

Is it true no girl wants to be with me because I'm too nice? Is there any way I could be less nice to a girl? Is that why my ex-girlfriend left me?

Basically, I conclude, there's no girl in Montreal who wants a nice guy like me. We always finish last, isn't that how the saying goes?

Looks like I'm going to have to embrace my inner nerd-dom after all—alone.

8

Friday
Elie

Since it's dark by now, I doubt it's smart to start wandering around outside; I have no idea who or what may be out there. I feel safer the longer I'm inside the buildings I'm familiar with. As a bit more courage winds through my veins, I emerge from my little hiding place and make my way back upstairs. With the faintest of residual light filtering down here, I choose to—cautiously, taking care not to trip—thread my way through the debris in these basement lab areas and corridors.

I'm glad to return to a brighter ground floor, lit sporadically by fantastically brilliant incandescent bulbs. However, my relief is short-lived. Immediately upon re-entering the lobby area I see the tall metal library doors are shut.

Blimey, I must have missed the cut-off time for the library closing!

The realization I squandered my chance to catch the librarian as she left for the weekend while I cried like a little girl down in the basement hits me like a steam train. I cannot believe I was so stupid to forget about the librarian; even though I couldn't find her during my search of the building doesn't mean she wasn't around somewhere. I should've staked out the entrance instead of wallowing in my unfortunate sorrows. Granted, I had good reason to be upset—and naturally I still am—but I pledge right now to stop letting my emotions overtake reason, clarity of thought, and determination to get back home.

There might be a night owl still working in this complex of buildings!

Surely there's someone here who can help me, somehow. With new hope, I start off down the long, wide hallway. Along the way I pause to read a plaque on the stone wall; in gold-plated letters it describes a Mr. Frank Dawson Adams for whom this structure for Mining and Metallurgical Engineering and Geology was built in 1951 and who served as Vice Principal of McGill in the 1920s. My heart skips two beats, I'm sure of it. Reading about events happening in the future—well, *my* future but this present time's past, I guess—violates nature. My head spins, but I keep walking.

Dark, empty classrooms flank the corridors, which jig right and left as the Adams building blends messily with the McConnell Engineering building—which I learned about from a simpler plaque emblazoned with black block lettering stating it was donated eight years after the previous building. I marvel at the expanse of engineering that must have occurred at McGill during the middle of the last century—and then, as if prompted, my brain shouts back, *"Add that to the rest of the one hundred years of occurrences you don't know about!"* I simply cannot contemplate what might have happened in my "absence" . . . but it's enough to twist my innards as if I'm about to be sick.

Clack, clack, clack, clack announces the heels of my shoes on the hard floor. Muted echoes follow against the bare walls of plain, rectangular blonde wood and glass. Every noise is magnified here, as if cruelly and purposefully underlining my solitude. Still, not a light in any room nor any sign of a teacher or student.

Of course, who would want to be at school on a Friday night with a summer weekend looming?

There's the possibility someone is in an office, which is probably on an upper level. To my left are double doors whose pair of eye-level windows reveal a dimly illuminated stairwell leading up and down. I'm tempted to enter, but I see my hallway is about to open up into a larger area, so I press on, etching the stairs' location into the rough floor plan my memory is storing.

This larger area is another lobby filled with a few offices and a closed-off general store and ice-cream shop. I salivate when I catch the sugary scent of the cones wafting through the metal grate barrier. At the farthest end, a thin hallway veers off in the direction of the campus commons, and I have to follow it. With relief I recognize this hallway with its tall windows, at last: the Macdonald Engineering Building. *I know my way around here!* I turn left into a dark, dirty vestibule with a heavy door closing off a large staircase I know leads up to the classroom and office levels.

Like the basement of the chemistry building I saw hours earlier, every surface of this building, which was recently completed, has instantly aged. Yellowed walls match chipped, worn stair treads replete with ancient dust bunnies inhabiting every corner. Thick layers of paint hint at decades of maintenance. The jarring state of things continues to make me nauseous.

All the same, I mount the enclosed stairway and leap my way up to the first floor and its large, grand, familiar lobby. This is what architecture should be. Oversize brass chandeliers—though these, in dire need of polishing, are unlit now—fill the high ceilings lined with dark wood molding, mullion windows at the front façade, niches with stone busts, and decorative wall and door frame tiling.

I pirouette lightly on the limestone floor. It's nice to know some things have endured.

These classrooms are all closed up for the night, but I wander around the main room a little longer, dawdling at the doors and staring inside, then make my way to another hallway at the opposite end of the room. Here I find yet another set of stairs, wide and shallow like all those in Macdonald. Naturally, I keep expecting them to be in near-pristine condition, being only thirteen years old, but here, now, each tread is battered and tired. My heels settle into their worn concave centers.

Another half hour passes by the time I've meandered up and down the familiar hallways of Macdonald's floors. These floors too connect now to the other engineering buildings, and soon I'm completely turned around due to the myriad of stairs, hallways, and building abutments. Still, not a soul to be found.

By now my curiosity is starting to wane; I'll have to explore this further with sunlight and more energy. A few hours' adventure starts to take their toll on my body finally. My stomach growls louder than an angry mountain lion, so much so I jump in surprise; I hadn't felt an ounce of hunger since "it" happened. Despite the hunger pangs, eating is the last thing I want to do at the moment. In any case, I feel it wiser to ration my food. I take an extended sip from the nearest water fountain instead.

It must be past nine o'clock by now, and my eyelids are heavy and my limbs are ready to stop moving. I need a place to sleep, not that it'll be a soft, warm bed tonight. Oh, how I miss home right now! I imagine a filling, home-cooked meal in our tranquil house and my cozy little bedroom with its comfortable quilted bed. It brings pools of tears to the corners of my eyes and pushes a lump up my throat, but I force them all back.

You're stronger than this, Elie. Buck up. It's only been four hours; you can't break down yet.

There will be no bed tonight, nor even a blanket, but I can settle for the floor, if I must. Maybe there's a windowsill I can lay on. I remember the generous upholstered chairs I saw earlier on the second floor of the library and rue its closing. Then I remember the black granite bench facing the library, in the dark library I once fled from. While cold and hard, it was secluded and seemed like it offered some degree of protection—from what, I'm not sure, but I need to be enveloped in security right now. And strangely, though I don't know where he is tonight, it's comforting to know I'll be near Father's old labs—whatever happened to them.

As for what will happen tomorrow morning, or the morning after that. . . . Someone must be here, and even though a harsh voice in my brain contradicts me, I hold out hope Father could possibly be here too. Tears threaten again, but this time I can't hold them back, and they roll silently down my cheek until they splash onto the cold, granite bench. In the silence of the night, I can only hear the echo of those tiny splashes.

9

Saturday, August 26, 2006
Elie

A few dry pumpernickel crumbs tumble from my hand onto my skirt. I pick these up and shovel them into my mouth like a starving beggar. A chunk of bread remains in my satchel for tomorrow, but moments ago I tore into half of what I had with little remorse. I had woken up to the same sounds to which I fell asleep: my stomach verbally threatening to eat itself if I didn't give it food. Better to keep my strength up and consume what little food I have, bit by bit, than to faint of weakness and let my food rot wastefully.

"A cup of tea would be splendid right now," I say. What a wimp I am. Less than one day on my own and I'm already yearning for my creature comforts. I suppose I'm only acting like a normal human, but I wish I was a little tougher.

Buck up, I keep telling myself. *You're stronger than this.*

The lightheadedness accompanying my angry stomach's early morning symphony is fading. Finally, I can think straight. While I chew—slowly now to fool my body into thinking I'm feeding it much more than I am—I'm considering how I'll get help on Monday. Can I explain that I suddenly found myself in the library basement on Friday afternoon, but don't know how I got there? Say Ernest Rutherford is my father, asking to be shown where the physics labs are? If I'm here in 2006, maybe Father is as well, but in a different location. I was in the room with him when *it* happened, so it stands to reason he came to 2006 as well. I'm sure someone will know where he is; someone *has* to.

Though nourished, that's about all my brain can process at the moment. It's not much of a plan, and I'm sure I need to figure out what else to say when questioned. *But I'll worry about that tomorrow. . . .*

My thoughts fade into the ether; I'm distracted but for the solemn quiet enveloping me like a winter blanket. I should be used to the silence by now, but I associate this building with such a bustle of activity that this current state is deadening. Indeed, it makes me lonelier than I already am. Yet again, I almost succumb to tears and wallowing in sadness, but I have to push those emotions away. Forcibly, I stand from my makeshift bed and pack up my cardigan, which served as an ersatz pillow during the night, suddenly eager again to search the buildings. I hope against hope someone has come into the buildings to work.

It takes me much longer this morning to walk the halls than it did last night. Now I take my time, reading all the signs on the wall and room names:

Computer Lab, Spectroscopy Lab, SONAR Equipment Lab, Computing Center.... I don't understand a technical word longer than "equipment." I might as well be on an alien planet right now; I can't decide if this is disturbing or exciting.

Room after room I peer into, trying to make sense of their purpose. I find two gigantic, plain auditoriums in the new McConnell Building, but besides those there are no classrooms in any other buildings above the ground floor, just labs and offices. Machines, for lack of a better descriptive word of what they might be, fill the most interesting labs, whose walls shared with the hall are fully glass. With sun shining through the large banks of windows to illuminate their contents, I can see almost everything in each lab, to my delight. I stare into each for minutes at a time, taking in each detail and imagining what might go on in each lab, were it full with researchers and students, even though I can't fathom how most of the equipment works. My thoughts all come back to how much Father would be interested in seeing all of this. *Has he already*?

Each hallway of each floor keeps my mind distractedly churning as I snake my way through the interconnected engineering buildings. More than once I get lost. A tidal wave of relief washes over me when I return to Father's physics building—pardon, the *library*—accompanied by lightheadedness and loneliness again.

Collapsing onto a slotted wooden bench in front of the lobby windows, I lie down on my side and cradle my head in my hands. I shake a little as my emotions do battle.

"I'm so alone; I'm all alone here," I whisper in despair. "Where is everybody?"

I think of my parents immediately. They must be sick with worry. My mother is probably searching our house and nearby parks for me in vain, and my father—if he's still in 1906—searching the McGill Buildings.

Well, you're in the right place, Father, but not the right time, I think to myself bitterly.

During my wanderings, my subconscious has admitted he probably isn't here with me, or else he would have found me and I him by now, I reason. Where else would he have gone, if he's also in 2006?

Of course, I have no answers, since I have no explanation for why I'm here either. I suppose if I was somehow transported to the old physics building basement, Father could have been sent to some other building—or some other year, who knows—but that makes less sense than him being sent to the same room as I was since we were a mere few feet apart last night. If I appeared in what used to be Father's labs, then maybe I was sent to the exact same physical location, yet one hundred years to the day into the future. That would imply Father, if he was transported along with me, would have been ten feet in front of me when I came here last night. But he wasn't, unless I'm thinking about this incorrectly, and he's in the same spot but one hundred years to his *past*. . . .

This is all too much for my brain to contemplate right now. It starts to hurt in addition to being dizzy. My eyes turn up to a clock near the library doors, and I'm shocked to see it's nearly two o'clock. No wonder I'm lightheaded—my body is telling me it needs food! That I can do, and then I'll take a rest. . . .

* * *

Though re-energized and feeling much calmer, I'm down to the apple and a small chunk of my pumpernickel bread still in my satchel. Relaxing on the bench, I glance again at the clock: 2:41. With a sharp pang of sorrow, I remember I had agreed to meet with Emma at two thirty in the Royal Victoria Library to research a Yeats work for a paper due in our poetry class.

So much for that. *I'm sorry, Emma.*

I picture her in the library right now, pulling books off the shelves and looking over her shoulder, expecting to see me arrive and getting angrier with me as the minutes pass. I have half a mind to run over to this Royal Victoria Library, but I know it'd be fruitless. She won't be there; I'll have to apologize when I get back home.

Assuming I can get back home.

Out of sheer boredom at this point, my feet begin walking back down to the basement labs. Perhaps it's because of my previous affection to McGill basement labs, or perhaps the older, dustier, *used* feeling of all the items down here remind me of my era. All of this creates the sensation of getting something done, of making things, of figuring out how things work. In my head I hear Father's booming voice echoing off the walls: "Let's see some results!" And here, I'm sure, many results have been seen over the years.

After twenty minutes of prodding multiple work-stations and their tools and test equipment, I don't see much that could pass for a physics lab. It all seems very mechanical, and there's even a small wood shop with lathes, mills, and drill presses.

My feet drag along the dirty cement floor with my heart not far behind. Father's presence is merely a memory in these buildings. Nothing familiar lies in this basement, aged as it is. Nothing redeems this forlorn expanse of discarded works in progress.

Yet, gazing farther ahead, I spy something curious on the edge of what appears to be a makeshift desk in the corner of a side room in the main lab area. Atop a pile of mechanics books is a bright box of what looks like food of some sort: "Cranberry Morning Granola Bars." I know what granola is, but I've never seen a bar of it before, nor any kind of food packaged as this is. Guiltily, but knowing what little food I have left, I decide who-ever these belong to won't notice a few of them missing.

I glance side to side like a squirrel guarding his acorn store, then press onward with a lift in my step.

Eventually I return upstairs, finding myself at the old enclosed staircase of the Macdonald Engineering

Building. So the buildings all connect via their ground floors as well as the basements. With a sense of accomplishment, I peek around the corner and follow this little hallway past another washroom and water fountain—gratefully using both—and another mechanical shop area. At the end of all this is another stairwell looking very much like a traditional Macdonald design. I muster the courage to investigate this area I've never walked through before, past or present.

At first the area, landing me somewhere on the second floor, looks like everywhere else in this building I've walked through, and I find a little door opening into the main hallway of what must be professors' offices. I don't return to that area, however. I open a little disused-looking wooden door, unlocked, that creaks in pain as its hinges yield to me.

The stench of petrified dust and stale air streams out of the room. I open the reluctant door wider to let in light. The room, stuffed with discarded items, looks like it hasn't been breached in years. Stacked brown boxes fill one corner. A dilapidated desk, one leg missing and a large fissure nearly splitting the thick wood top, lines one wall, barricaded by equally decrepit but probably still functioning chairs. On the opposite wall is an ugly hay-colored chesterfield, rough-textured and spotted on the arms though looking relatively comfortable otherwise. Piled elsewhere in the ten foot square room are odds and ends: a cracked brass table lamp, tottering mountain of ancient books, and yet another unidentified box with switches and dials. Hanging from the ceiling is a metal pull-cord; stepping inside, I impulsively pull it.

Instantly I'm awash in intense artificial light. I squint, then finally see the room's objects properly. It's not too filthy, although it has definitely seen better days. I test out the couch. It squishes obligingly, and I can almost imagine being comfortable atop it if I ignore the faintly sour smell wafting up. I can tell no one's been here in months, if not years; this excites me, because I know I can stay here if I need to.

If I want to.

Perhaps I won't sleep on the same stone bench tonight. . . .

No one would find me here, if I need to hide. I don't know why this train of thought creeps into my head, but I file it away regardless.

Pulling the light cord again and slipping out of the room, I shut the door tightly. Dazedly, I promise myself that room will be my secret. Before I know it, I'm heading down the wide stairway that dumps me into the Macdonald Engineering lobby. Absently, I make my way down to the front doors, and as I'm midway through the portal I pause, suddenly cognizant of my environment again. To make sure I won't be locked out, I wedge my British Literature book between the door and frame on my way out.

Immediately my eye is drawn to movement on the lawn and pathways in front of me. To my surprise, there are several people outside. The campus isn't empty after all! It's been just shy of one day since I've last seen a fellow human being, but it could've been ages. Despite feeling like I've been dropped into an alternate universe—*oh wait, you* have, *silly Elie*—in which I'm unsure what the people are like, I hone in on the students. Two boys are ambling slowly down the path; one is gesticulating with great energy as if explaining something complicated to the other. A few dozen students lounge in the sun or play catch on the great central lawn cleaved by the main road leading from Sherbrooke Street.

Impulsively, I trot down Macdonald's front steps and head straight across to the lawn.

With some relief, I realize I don't have to wait until Monday to see if anyone's seen Father or can help me. It's a chance that scares me, but I must take it.

It's much less hot today, here, than it was yesterday in my Montreal of 1906. *I wonder how it is at home right now, there. . . .* But here I am, long black skirt flowing around my ankles as I walk with purpose to the big field. It's freeing to be out in the open again, but just like the halls I've wandered, these grounds are almost unrecognizable—and it would completely be, had I been without Father's physics building as my reference. I have to remind myself this is what a hundred years does to a place.

Dotting the green are endless maple trees—much taller than I remember them—casting long shadows.

The buildings from my recent memory are crowded on all sides by towering monstrosities squishing the wide open and sparse campus I know into a mass of sky-scraping piled stone. At least I can still see the hilltop of Mont Royal beyond them all, but even her feet are obscured by square-topped behemoths so tall I'm astonished they don't collapse under their own weight. When I sweep my gaze back and forth to take in the panorama, I stop dead in my tracks as I reach the main road—which is indeed a single, solid, homogeneous stone beneath my feet. To my left the downtown of Montreal is . . . gargantuan! There are almost no words to describe its size. It's at least ten times that of the Montreal I know. Gone are the tallest five- and six-story buildings of the city center whose highest points were church spires and the double bell towers of Notre-Dame Cathedral down at the Old Port. There could be no church spires left by now for all I can see. Perhaps they've been squashed like little bugs by the herd of elephantine institutions filling my vision as far as I can see. Twenty, thirty, forty, fifty stories up. I lose count, absolutely flabbergasted.

A minute or an hour might have passed while I stare dumbstruck at this new city. I'd seen the skyscrapers of New York City when my family passed through to take a ship to visit England when I was ten, but this far surpasses the scale of that supposed metropolis. Well aware cities change over time, I never expected Montreal to stay the same, but this skyline is beyond any of my wildest and far-fetched dreams. I wonder what *les Montréalais* do in all those buildings. How much wealth must the city have to expand into such a fortress? I swallow to rewet my mouth which is dry from gaping this long, then drop my gaze to my hands, which are shaking.

I strengthen my wobbling leg muscles and continue down the steps. When I reach the lawn, no one takes notice of me at first. Then as I climb slowly up to the little rise, intending to say hello to the others and ask them about where I am, a few of those lying on blankets stare at me. Their eyes zero in on my blouse and trace down my skirt, and one by one they cock their heads to the side as their faces turn to disapproval, even condemnation. I didn't see this reaction coming, and I stop near the foot of the hill, stunned, then sit down on the grass.

Hunching my shoulders and hiding my face, I surreptitiously turn my eyes to view the others in my peripheral vision. They're still boring holes in my body. I hunch over more, then look again to study them.

The more I look, the more alien they seem. Oh, their faces look the same as mine, but their clothing is like nothing I've ever seen, in Montreal or European fashion catalogs. My cheeks redden to see what they're wearing, especially the girls. With the exception of two of them in extremely short skirts—the hemlines *far* above their knees—they all have on the shortest pants possible, like little knickers baby boys would wear. Women wearing pants? And such short pants! Their tops, barely more fabric than their bottoms, are plain, colored cotton with either sleeves cut midway up their upper arms or no sleeves at all, mere thin strings draped over their shoulders. And fully exposed necks and collars! Surely these girls must be an anomaly. Surely this cannot be an accepted form of attire.

However, the more I look around me—down the lawn and back behind me on the stone pathways—the more I see everyone is dressed nearly identically, and that I am the one sticking out. Even the men all wear the short pants and tiny shirts, or—*gasp!*—none at all. My face burns; I know my cheeks must be cherry-red with blush. I'm mortified for the scantily clad people around me—*have they no shame?!*—but also for myself. Suddenly I'm more concerned with how different I look.

"Hey, hey you!" calls a boy to my right. He was laying on his back with his friend, a girl, sharing a bright blue towel spread on the ground. Now he's propped up on his elbows and regarding me with a rather unkind stare.

Low on courage, I manage to croak, "Heh-hello?"

"Hey, frosh week is over, dude! Did you miss the deadline for wacko dress day or something?"

No idea what he just said. "Uhh . . . umm . . . no, I—"

"Yo, what faculty are you from that they make you dress like such a freak? You're, like, from the 1800s or something."

His friend chimes in. "Yeah, Jane Austen called and she needs her ruffles back!"

My stomach churns like I'm about to retch. *How cruel!* How I'd love to tell him to check his history because he's about a century off—and then to go back home because he forgot his trousers.

"Vous *venez de Québec? L'Europe? Vous avez l'air d'une Européanne, là . . .*" An older boy, seated near the other two and previously engrossed in a heavy-looking book, is asking me in French if I'm from Quebec or Europe, saying I look like a European. He must be from Quebec himself, maybe Quebec City, judging from the accent.

Without an idea what to say to him, I stare back with my mouth open. *Do I make up a story? Do I say I'm from 1906 and desperately want to find my father and mother and go back home, to a Montreal I know and understand?* A little voice inside my head tells me these people wouldn't believe me if I tell them the truth, but I need to say something. I stall.

"*Vous parlez français?*" he asks.

"*Oui,*" I say, nodding.

"*Alors, êtes-vous québéçoise? Du nord, peut-être?*"

"*Non, j'habite en Montréal.*" That much is the truth; I live in Montreal, not northern Quebec.

"Ah," he replies, staring at me a bit more curiously now through the messy brown hair draping down past his ears. Clearly my appearance does not fit his expectations of how a Montrealer should look. The other two students, plus a few more near to where I'm sitting, are listening in and watching the conversation bat back and forth. The boy next asks if it's my first year here.

"*Uhh, oui, c'est ça . . . mais mon père, il est professeur ici.*" I don't know why I blurt that out, that my father is a professor here. I'm flustered. It's technically the truth, but how can I stop this conversation?

"*Ah oui? Cool—*"

What?

"*—mais il est prof de quoi? L'histoire?*" I hear a note of mocking in his voice.

I tell him no, he's not a history professor, but he teaches physics. Immediately I regret this. What if this bloke is a physics student?

"*Fantastique!*" the boy exclaims, now leaning toward me in interest. Next, he says he says he probably knows him and asks his name.

Great, now I've gotten myself into trouble. There's no way he knows my father because he doesn't teach here. Well, he does, but not *here* here, so I can't say that he does.

In fact, what do I say at all?

Everyone is staring now. A few of the boys stop tossing a baseball back and forth.

"*Uh, non, probablement pas, je ne crois pas. Excusez-moi, il faut que j'y aille. C'était bon de faire vos connaissances. Au revoir.*" I say in a polite rush he probably doesn't know my father and that I have to go. Faster than the words tumble out of my mouth, I'm on my feet again and quick-stepping up the pathway.

If I had a penny for every eye fixed on my back at this moment, I'd be instantly rich. I don't dare turn around. Never, not even when Ralph tried to talk to me about marriage, have I wanted to disappear more. I am so out of place, so . . . homesick.

Walking so the bushes lining the north edge of the green hide me from the students' view, I hurry on my way and avoid the glances of those few crossing my path. Taking a roundabout way to the north end of the Macdonald Engineering Building, I look down at my clothes and wonder how I can make them look like those of the girls I saw on the lawn.

I don't want to look like them—as if they are too poor to afford full clothes, or as if they wear only undergarments—but I don't want to stand out so much I'm ridiculed like that again. I unbutton the three tiny pearl buttons at the end of each sleeve, then neatly fold them up to above my elbow. Amazed at how much cooler it is, I smile in spite of how silly I feel. Then I unbutton the front of my collar and fold that down as well, tucking the fabric inside to hide the lacy ruffles. Not knowing if I went too far or not far enough, I unbutton two more buttons below my collarbone.

Why should I worry about impropriety when those girls were nearly naked?

Cooler yet uncomfortable, I hope I won't attract quite so much attention now. I had ventured out on impulse, and the result was a small fiasco. *That's what you get for not thinking ahead, Elie.* For now, I'll stay inside and decide what to do next.

***

In the little room—now *my* room, as far as I'm concerned—I have no idea what time it is, because the hands on the wall clock have been stuck at 8:37 since goodness only knows when. But I have a feeling it's near that time in the evening. Tomorrow is Sunday; I imagine everyone is home and readying for church tomorrow. I know I won't be attending for the first time in a long while, but I can't help that. After today, there's no way I'll risk venturing deep into the city to find a church. Mother used to tell me a little fear would do me good, and now I'm feeling it in spades.

For the past while I've been writing in one of my composition books. I figure I should start writing journal entries there since my actual journal is at home, far out of my reach at the moment. It is cathartic, really, jotting down the sights and sounds and emotions I've experienced in the last day. Like a torrential downpour, everything washes over me for the second time like fat, stinging raindrops, and I feel every surprise, fear, elation, and curiosity again. Somehow, everything's stronger the second time.

The astonishment of seeing the date on the newspaper. The pit of my stomach sinking when I realized

I'd missed my chance to talk to the librarian and was utterly alone. The fear of every dark hallway. The humiliation of looking like a complete misfit in front of the students on the lawn. The intense longing for being in my own home and with the familiar again. The sense of not knowing what to do next, whether to wait and see what unfolds or run around screaming for Professor Rutherford. Those last two are the strongest.

I've come to a conclusion about what my plan of attack should be, if I can call it that. My gut feeling is I should sit tight and observe before telling people I'm from a hundred years ago and am looking for my father. Beyond knowing today's date and the few observations I've amassed since Friday night, I have little concept of the world of 2006. A lot could have changed which I may have no possible way of imagining. After thinking about how different 1906 was to 1806—and realizing no one in 1806 could have described life a hundred years later—I conclude there are too many unknowns to do anything but collect more information first.

What a bland, scientist's answer this is to the problem, but then I suppose I am my father's daughter. Too conservative to go boldly to city hall or the local police for help, and considering the dangers I might encounter along the way, I have no other choice but to play it safe. I can stay in this little room for now, and try to figure out this new world from here. *Then* I'll devise a strategy after I better know what I'm dealing with.

Who are you kidding, Elie? You know the reason why you're hiding away in this room! Everyone will think you're as crazy as a bat in the daytime if you go out and tell them it was August 24th, 1906 yesterday for you and suddenly you found yourself in August 25th, 2006 a millisecond later!

Of course, there is that. I don't want to be thrown into a loony bin for telling the truth. More terrifying than thinking about how I got here is imagining how people will react if I tell them I somehow, mysteriously, time traveled. If they react badly, I'll never get back home. I have no clue how I appeared here—my subconscious has tried riddling it out since I "arrived," although no scientific explanation has magically appeared, like I did—and until I do know, I have no way of returning home.

As I write in my new journal, I find myself devising a sort of survival strategy. A human has three basic needs: food, water, and shelter. Luckily, I have found the shelter, and I also have the clothes on my back. However, they do need a washing, as does my body. That's something I can do tomorrow in one of the washroom sinks. I haven't explored all of the bathrooms, and I'm holding out hope, however slim, that I might find a bathtub somewhere. If not, I'll have to resort to little "bird-baths" from the sink.

Of the first two needs, access to water is no problem. Finding food, however, will be much harder. Right now I am absolutely ravenous, despite having forced down the stolen "granola bar," which was nauseatingly sweet and made me thirstier than I've felt in a long while. If this is what food in 2006 is like, I might be in for a rough ride; I'd rather eat another than starve, however. Nevertheless, I still have my apple and a wee bit of now-stale bread with me to eat tomorrow. As pathetic as it is, I have no choice but to forage for food; perhaps people have left behind something other than the unpalatable granola bars I found. Too bad Montreal's climate is much too cold for fruit trees to thrive.

This is barely a survival plan, I admit to myself, but it's all I can do at the moment. I will spend tomorrow simply surviving, exploring my surroundings more, and searching for clues to my appearance here—and how to reverse it. I might wander outside again, but avoid other people until I've come up with a solid "cover story" of who I am and what I'm doing here.

Somehow I've found the courage to keep moving forward, to take this strange new reality day by day. It's my only choice. *But what will happen when I talk to people again*?

10

Monday, August 28, 2006
Elie

There is no easy way I can describe the sheer pandemonium taking place around me right now. The Adams Building lobby is choc-a-block full of students, mostly pouring through doors and rushing down the hall and into the doors flanking the ends of the lobby, but others stop in the dead center of the floor and block the traffic while they consult papers in a confused, anxious stupor. I have no contemporary reference, of course, but it feels like the first day of classes with a quarter of the students completely mystified about where to go.

Here I sit, like a frightened child, watching the goings-on from one of the benches lining the front windows, the one closest to the corner. It's safer in the corner, here at the place above where I appeared over two days ago. In all my life, I have never seen a cacophony of sights and sounds quite like this. Certainly the Donaldas don't attend class with this unrefined flurry, and I'm fairly positive the men at McGill—my father's McGill, not this—do not either. Shocked beyond all means, I am glued to my seat as I watch everyone around me—trying to look inconspicuous, of course. The events have swelled to a crescendo since eight o'clock when students first started trickling onto campus.

Conversations, laughs, and shouts echo off the walls and building into a great thunder. More spectacular than that is the range of languages I hear; besides the usual English and French, I'm hearing Chinese, Russian, Indian dialects, Arabic, Italian, and some others which I can't identify. They're combining to make a whirl of words even a trained linguist would struggle to navigate.

Perhaps the biggest surprise of all is the presence of not just male students here, but so many women also. Mixed in. Together with the men, as if they're about to walk into the same classroom.

And then they do exactly that.

This single observation has almost paralyzed my brain.

The girls are carrying the same textbooks and are well-prepared with bags filled with composition books, pencils, and more textbooks. I can barely keep breathing in astonishment. *What a change from my classes. No separation between the sexes, it seems. Are we equals? How incredible that all of these students are talking together about their classes.*

"What the fuck, yo?! How the hell am I supposed to find this fucking FDA1 if there aren't any signs in this shit hole?"

My head jerks like a shot toward the origin of that foul language. I've never heard Father's colleagues or students, not even when they've broken a piece of equipment, talk like that. *How could those words have streamed out of that young boy's mouth*? He can't be older than eighteen, and this must be his first year at McGill since he doesn't know where to go. His blue pants are tight from his waist down to his sleek and shiny black pointy shoes, and his black buttoned shirt has tiny silver threads that trace parallel lines up and down his chest and arms; the effect is odd to me.

The boy's eyes, bright blue underneath stiff spikes of his hair, catch mine and he growls defensively, "What?"

I stammer in a low whisper, "No-Nothing." I'm sure he doesn't hear me. I must have been gazing wide-eyed at him in a perpetually appalled stare. It's all I can do to push my lower jaw back up.

"*Freak*," he mutters as he turns down the hall with his friend.

My eyes widen as I sink lower onto the bench. *Is this what people are like here*? Suddenly I'm not sure I know humanity anymore. It's a strange sensation to be alone amongst a horde of people. I want nothing more than to crawl between the cracks of the floor tiles and disappear into the basement, becoming small enough that no one will be able to find me; maybe I'll somehow morph my body back to 1906 that way.

Wishful thinking on my part. Impossible, desperate thinking.

And then, in the form of a perky, smiling brunette comes salvation.

"Hi!" she says brightly, stopping to stand directly in front of me. "I saw you from over there," she continues, pointing to the opposite end of the lobby at the library entrance. "You look like you have no idea where to go. Do you know where your first class is?"

Her question is sincere, her voice caring and helpful. Her kindness takes me aback somewhat, after what that boy said to me.

"I, ah . . . well, I don't really know." *Ugh*, I don't want to sound like an idiot, but I can't think on my feet fast enough to reply coherently. But now my mind is spinning like a top, churning possible stories—believable stories—to explain to this girl what I'm doing here.

She cocks her head at me curiously, as if I've said something really nutty. I put up my guard again, fearful that this girl, too, will call me a freak. Then with relief I see her crack a smile; she must have been surprised to hear my accent.

I breathe deeply. The moment has finally arrived, sooner than I thought it would. I need to decide my path right now. *Do I go along and play like I'm one of these students to try and figure out why I'm here and how I can get back home? Or do I run away and hide like a fugitive on the loose, trying on my own to find my way back?*

Then the most sickening thought comes. *Will I ever be able to find my way back on my own?*

"No, I . . . I don't know where my classroom is."

"Oh, you must be looking for B10, then, like a bunch of other people around here, probably."

I return her smile and nod shyly. Hopefully I'm convincingly playing the part of a novice, lost student.

"Great! I'm going there too, and I actually know where it is. Here," she says, gesturing for me to follow her. "Come with me and we'll get good seats before everyone else squishes us to the front row."

"Thanks." My feet are unsteady, but somehow they manage to step in front of each other, obviously calmer than my ferociously beating heart and shallow, nervous breath.

This girl is already chatting away and coaxing me gently along by my elbow.

"I'm Lindsey, by the way. It's my first year too."

"It's nice to meet you. I'm Eileen, but everyone calls me Elie."

"Elie, cool. There's nothing worse than being late to your first class on your first day, especially one in a big auditorium like B10, right? Can you imagine walking through those huge doors and having to find a seat with 150 people watching you?" Lindsey grimaces and laughs, a mature but very female giggle exuding a rare mix of confidence and humility.

A light bulb turns on in my head. "An auditorium?"

"Yeah, an old one, but pretty big. It's actually in the building through those doors," she explains, pointing to the doors opening into the old chemistry building, "but it's really close. I found it ten minutes ago, but came back up to go to the bathroom."

"Oh! I know that room!" That particular lecture hall is familiar to me, my father having taught a few classes there over the past few years. At least I won't be immediately stepping into the unfamiliar.

"Then you know where you're going after all. Are you excited? Survey of English Literature is supposed to be really good for a first-year class."

Literature! *You stepped into a lucky series of events, missy.*

Now I smile wider and nod in return. "Lucky us!"

"Say, where are you from? Judging by your accent. . . ."

"New Zealand," I blurt automatically. The truth.

"Oh, awesome! You're a Kiwi, then, aren't you?"

"Yes, that's what we call ourselves. After the bird, of course, not the fruit," I tease, trying to relax myself. It seems I'll be inventing my cover story right now, but we've settled into seats near the center of the auditorium; the busy-looking academic at the front—Professor Badgely, Lindsey tells me—is preparing to hush the horde of students before him. It seems I'll have the next hour or so to mentally formulate my ersatz life story.

"Well, I'm from Orangeville, Ontario, but we don't grow any oranges there. Or birds. But how cool that McGill has so many international students. Goes to show you what a small world it is, eh?"

And here I was beginning to think it was actually very, very large. . . .

***

I suppose I had already chosen my path this morning when I had decided to venture into the lobby instead of hiding in my little secret room. I was partly curious to see what a Monday morning was like, since I had figured there would be students milling about on the way to and from classes, but I had also been a little scared my room was actually used. I feared someone with authority—the authority to throw me in jail for squatting or telling ridiculous stories—would burst through the door looking for an old desk but come out with a vagabond girl from another time instead.

I had also started to fear something else this weekend: if I hid, I wouldn't learn anything about how to get home.

Rain yesterday had kept me inside, so my morning and afternoon were spent wandering all the halls again to better acquaint myself with all the passageways. I had finally gotten my bearings no matter where I was, but I sketched a detailed map of everything anyway. I went even further: I marked the location of the most remote washrooms—including one conveniently close to my room, which I felt I'd be able to use safely without attracting unwanted attention. I don't want anyone to find out I'm squatting here, after all. I had played memorization games in my head, studied the windowed labs as best I could, tinkered with bits and bobbles in the basement labs, and read far into my Donalda class texts out of sheer boredom.

By the evening, I had concluded this will be no way to live. I'll be able to live here in secret for a while, but I'll have to figure out a permanent arrangement sooner or later, if I can't get back to 1906 immediately. Not that I managed to concoct a plan for achieving that, of course, but I did resolve to make myself available to every opportunity thrown my way. I figure, naively perhaps, that if I keep my eyes open and keep searching for a way back, eventually the way will open up in front of me and bang: Bob's your uncle! I came here by happenstance; perchance I can likewise return.

Well, it is naïve of me, I know, to imagine it'll be that simple, but I do know I will achieve nothing if I hide in that little room all day. It's a perfectly fine place to sleep and write in my journal at night, but I need to navigate life in 2006 if I am to have any chance of going home. And that's how I managed to trudge downstairs to the Adams building lobby half an hour ago, despite the gargantuan knot twisting Olympic somersaults in my stomach as I had approached the growing crowd of unfamiliar and very foreign faces.

* * *

"He doesn't pause for a second, does he?" Lindsey whispers, leaning over so close our shoulders are touching.

I can't believe she's talking right in the middle of class! My level of astonishment is waning, however;

nearly everything surprises me because everything is very different from what I'm used to, so much so that I'm ceasing to be surprised anymore.

"Ssh," I whisper back discreetly.

"I'm sorry; you're trying to follow him. I'll shut up."

"No. I mean, yes, I'm trying to follow him. I don't talk in class—it's disrespectful." Inwardly I cringe as I'm breaking my own rules of decorum.

"Oh! You're right." She blushes, then goes back to taking notes.

For the past fifty minutes, Lindsey, her roommate—who came in right as class was starting—myself, and 150-some-odd students have been jotting down notes faster than I have my whole life. This Professor Badgely is quite the talker, and I'm writing down every word he's saying. I know I'm not technically *in* this class and I shouldn't bother taking notes, but since I'm playing the role of student, I might as well play it full-tilt. As it turns out, this class is quite interesting—naturally, since I'm taking the same subject in the Donalda Department at home—and I'm fascinated by how this professor teaches it versus Professor Boddington, my British Literature professor back home. Since this class is enormous as opposed to having only a dozen students, there are no intimate roundtable discussions or individual readings aloud, only the professor lecturing straight and asking the occasional question of us. It's an intense method of instruction, but not unenjoyable.

As I sneak a sideways glance at other students, their eyes are straight toward the professor as well while their hands scribble madly on their notepads. It may be early in the morning, but everyone is invigorated by taking their first university class. However, there are a fair few chatting to neighbors every now and then. The hushed tones make a low but distinct background buzz, but Professor Badgely seems not to notice, curiously. If students did this in one of my classes back home, they'd receive a severe lecture, perhaps be kicked out of class for a repeated offense. Trying to drone it out, I concentrate extra hard on the lecture.

In spite of my role playing, I'm finding it effortless to be a student here.

Yet the unusual mix of men and women discomfits me, but it doesn't seem to bother anyone else. In fact, they talk together so casually and sit together so haphazardly that I wonder, distractedly, exactly when this mixed-gender studying began.

More snuck glances, in between scrawls in my composition book, reveals a superficial difference making me as self-conscious as if I were sitting here naked as a jaybird. I am sticking out like, well, exactly like someone who recently time-traveled from a hundred years in the past. There is perhaps one other girl wearing a skirt down to her ankles, but hers is white and layered with delicate eyelets all over while mine is black and heavy and plain. On her feet, like nearly all the other girls, are strappy sandals while I'm wearing my usual low-heeled buckled shoes.

At least my top fits in so I don't look completely dowdy; it's a small, thin white cotton shirt with sleeves ending far above my elbows with the words "Je me souviens," or "I remember," in French, across the chest in dark blue. I found it discarded on the floor of the Macdonald basement yesterday and washed it in a bathroom sink, all in an attempt to wear something which would help me fit in. I certainly would look like such a slob in 1906! Yet Lindsey and her roommate, Isabelle, are wearing similarly graphical shirts. They're both wearing khaki-colored short pants above their knees, which I imagine must be quite wearable during the summer, although I'm appalled at how exposed their legs are. Again though, it doesn't seem to bother anyone else, so this must be normal. Not that I would be caught dead in a casket wearing those, but they do look lightweight and comfortable. . . .

"And that's as far as I would like to go today. I'm sure you all won't complain," says Professor Badgely from the podium. "I don't want to overwhelm you on day one of our semester with too much Eliot and Austen. See you all bright and early on Wednesday!" He bids us goodbye with a wink and a reminder of assigned readings.

"Wow, that was great," Lindsey remarks as we stand up and file down to the exit.

We all agree and chatter on about Professor Badgely's thought-provoking analyses, then laugh a little bit about how intense his delivery style is. I get caught up in the conversation as if I belong with them. This is easily the most relaxed I've been since late Friday afternoon.

"Do you have Intro to International Development in Leacock right now too, Elie?" Isabelle asks once we return to the lobby, her steering our little group out the front doors to a wide footbridge leading to the green. Sunlight, already warm for this early in the day, bathes us, making me suddenly glad I'm no longer wearing my old long-sleeved shirt.

"No," I say automatically. Never having heard of a Leacock Building, I don't have a more convenient answer ready than, "I don't have another class right now."

"Boo! Both of us are heading there right now. Do you have Twentieth Century Novel in an hour? I think it's back here in an engineering building, for some silly reason."

"They must have run out of rooms in the Arts Building and Leacock," Lindsey interjects. "Or else we're slowly driving them off campus. Bummer, though, because there are an awful lot of cute guys over here." Her gaze follows a group of French-Canadian boys approaching the FDA building and giggles. Isabelle joins in, but I was too distracted to hear what Lindsey had said.

I can learn about twentieth-century novels, yes. I recall Professor Boddington once telling me the best way to learn about a society is to experience them through their writing.

"Yes, I do. I can't remember what room that class is in though. Is it there on your schedule, Isabelle?"

"Umm, McConnell 301, wherever that is."

"We'll find it," I assure her, not giving away yet that I now know exactly where that lecture hall is. "You'd both better hurry to your next class."

Lindsey smiles widely and gives me a wave goodbye. "We'll meet you here after our class so we can sit together again?"

I nod with a grateful smile, and I mean it. "See you then. Have fun in class!"

I'm on my own again, now floating out of my heels. What a change in events from an hour ago! I have definitely started down a path which may prove difficult to step off of, but it's oddly comfortable for the moment. The sense of belonging, however deceitful, is too strong to turn down.

11

Monday, August 28, 2006
Will

"We will be dealing with a lot of ideas and theories which you have doubtless heard of before and are excited to learn about; quantum mechanics is literally a building block for the science of physics. We will address radiation from atoms. We will study electron waves. We will learn the Schrödinger equation—"

Low snickers from the back of the room interrupt Professor Nagar. The joke is obvious, at least to nerds like me.

"If you're thinking about Schrödinger's cat, we won't be studying that this term. The question posed, however, is fascinating, and I invite you to discuss it amongst yourselves in your spare time. You might see your TA, Will, wearing a rather humorous t-shirt depicting an unfortunate such cat." Kevin inclines his head toward my seat in the front row of the classroom and winks; I roll my eyes. The deep-set wrinkles around his vibrant eyes squish like crumpled cellophane as his cheeks rise as he smiles.

I always enjoy his dry sense of humor, since usually his playful nature distracts us—his graduate students—from a sticky point in our research. Today, however, I'm a bit impatient and not in the mood. It's 8:40 on a Monday morning, day one of classes, and I'm sitting in front of seventy-five or so nine-year-olds.

Well, add ten years to that, and it would be accurate, although they certainly don't look their age. I guess I forget how young undergraduates are. Being a teacher's assistant isn't the worst task in the world, but this is the third semester in a row I've started off fearing the young skulls full of mush plunked in front of Kevin, Shavash, and I will be nothing but pestering disasters.

I'm always proven wrong. But that's beside the point.

This class is Introduction to Quantum Mechanics, a first- or second-year course Kevin loves teaching; I can take it or leave it, preferring topics like astrophysics and high-energy physics more. And, it's in the Rutherford Physics Building, which means I had to trek farther from home this morning than my usual path to the Macdonald Building. Yes, I'm being lazy, and yes, I'm acting sullen for no reason.

Well, not for no reason, actually. I ran into my ex-girlfriend on my way to campus this morning at the coffee shop, and it's still ticking me off. It was completely harmless, but I still practically pissed my pants out of surprise. She doesn't live near me, so I never expect to see her in my neighborhood. In fact,

I'd like to never see her anywhere ever again. While there were no words exchanged, there was definitely a Look, something between a demonic stare and half-human scowl. Why after over three months couldn't she act normal? And why did she have to make my insides cramp up like the hurt idiot I am?

She still hates my guts, no doubt about it. Evan, standing next to me at the time, agreed and promised to put me under his personal witness protection program for the rest of the walk to campus. Damn it, I just got over this girl and her ridiculous grip on my emotions, and now she had to show her psychotic side again. I've never been good at relationships, but I at least hoped I could put this one to bed and start afresh.

So instead of professionally presenting myself to the physics students, here I am sulking in my seat with my semester started off-kilter. What a great day. I decide I need to change my attitude right now—*forget even her name, Will*—and focus on work. And the students. Next to me, Shavash takes a break from texting her boyfriend to nudge me in the ribs.

Kevin is gesturing toward me. "Here's one of your TAs for the semester, William Hertz, who will teach your tutorial every Monday from 1:35–2:25 . . . and it looks like it will also be in this room, right Will?"

I get up out of my reverie and spin around to stand in front of the class. The room is long and narrow, packed full as typical for an intro course. I try to project my voice.

"Yes, you'll be here in room 225 with me every Monday. I won't be holding a tutorial today, of course, but usually I'll teach a little bit at the beginning—filling in the gaps where Professor Nagar might have run out of time during class or clarifying something if you all have a general question on a topic—and then we'll go over specific derivations and problems from your textbook."

I head to the blackboard behind me and write down my full name, email address, office number in Macdonald, and phone extension for them to copy.

"If you want to contact me directly or need more help outside of the tutorial times, email me or stop by the office I share down in the Macdonald Building—I know it's probably far from the rest of your classes, but I can't help it," I add, glancing sideways at Kevin with a wry smile. "I practically live on campus, it seems, so you're almost guaranteed to reach me somehow. And if you can't, you can catch Shavash, who sits in the same office as I do."

Hopefully I came across as moderately interesting and equally interested in the subject. Scanning the room, I see about sixty bored guys and fifteen pairs of keen female eyes boring holes into mine. Typical.

Professor Nagar tries to prod me into saying a bit about myself. "Will here is one of my graduate students, along with Shavash, working with Professor Anna Davidson on a gamma ray detector built in Arizona in the States. He's very knowledgeable of more advanced physics, of course, but also mechanical engineering."

I take the bait reluctantly—only because I like Kevin; I'm still in a bit of a funk. "Yes, I double majored in mechanical engineering and physics, not because I'm masochistic but because I changed my mind halfway through undergrad. So, while I get to do all the fun stuff for Professor Nagar which deals with astrophysics and high energy detectors and things like that, I also get pigeon-holed sometimes into taking care of the mechanics side of things for the project." Another wry smile aimed at Kevin, but more jokingly this time. "But it's an awesome project, lots of fun, and always something new. I'll try to add in some bits here and there about what we're working on during our tutorials, because I think you'll find it as fascinating as we do, and maybe it'll keep you motivated to stay in physics."

Kevin nods appreciatively; he's told me before how much he likes how I run tutorials, which I like to make a bit more engaging than the standard "let me run through the homework problems and nothing more" template most TAs use. Naturally, though, I do end up helping with homework, which is undoubtedly why most of the class shows up to my sessions.

I sit myself back down, now in a bit better mood, for Shavash to introduce herself. I listen as intently as if it's the first time I've heard her explain her move from Bangalore, India, to McGill for her undergrad in physics, how her specialty and project work are similar to mine, and the offer to help the other transplants from the Asian continent to settle into a new life in Montreal.

For the remaining thirty-five minutes of class, I listen to Kevin finish his standard beginner's talk on quantum mechanics and a personal spiel on his background and research before he starts with chapter one's material. I work hard to focus on what he's saying—not that my being present is anything more than a courtesy rather than being required—instead of what occupied my head earlier. By 9:22 Kevin has dismissed class a few minutes early, and Shavash and I are the first ones out the door and on our way to Macdonald.

The walk down the hill takes more navigation skills than usual. We're the proverbial salmon swimming upstream as a horde of students charge uphill to get to their 9:35 classes. Eager beavers.

"Ugh, they all need to chill the *hell* out," Shavash complains as she's whipped sideways by a rogue backpack. "There's, like, more than ten minutes until class starts!" The irritation showing through her thick Indian accent is amusing, but I don't laugh at her, smartly—also because the throng annoys me too.

"Agreed. They're like a swarm of bees. At least by next week they should be calmed down."

"Hey, I'm going to run over to Tim Hortons and get a cup of coffee. You want to come?" There's a little outpost of Canada's favorite coffee and donut shop nestled in a basement corner of the Redpath Library, clear across campus—all of the five hundred feet, if that. Shavash ditched her former tea addiction for coffee when she moved to Canada, like the rest of us immigrants.

"Hmm . . . nah, I'm too tired to walk over there. I'll probably make a pot in the office later."

"Suit yourself. I'll be up in a little bit."

"See ya." I wave as we part company; in my mind's eye I'm planning a zigzagging path to take me from this little bit of road leading into McConnell to the front steps of Macdonald. It's not far, but the mass ahead of me will make it seem like threading a needle in a hurricane.

As I walk, jostled every few feet or so, my eyes follow the many tops of shorter heads around me. But then a small glint, a reflection of sunlight perhaps, draws my attention farther ahead along the path.

It's like a pot of glimmering gold at the foot of a rainbow—or in this case, a sea of people.

A hundred yards beyond me, standing at the end of the narrow bridge leading to the FDA building entrance, is one of the most mysteriously beautiful girls I've ever seen. She's what my grandmother would call a "classic beauty," her blonde hair cascading like ribbons of pure gold as they catch sunlight. As she grins her apple cheeks rise high between a small graceful nose, a face like out of an old movie I watched as a kid with that same grandma. I can almost see an aura of happiness and warmth surrounding her like an invisible bubble.

It's her smile that's the most... mesmerizing. Listening intently to two friends standing with their backs to me, this girl has the kindest look I've ever seen. But there's more to it than that. Even from this far away I can tell she's excited to her core about something and relieved at the same time. She seems like the kind of girl you can talk to and she'll perk you up better than any cup of coffee.

You're obviously damaged from your encounter at the café this morning, you dolt. Can you turn off the emotions for a few hours so you can get some work done?

I've stopped walking, dead in my tracks and blocking part of the thoroughfare, but I hardly care. I can't take my eyes off this girl. But just as I wonder if I'd look stupid walking over to say hello, she's turned to the FDA lobby and her friends are leaving in the opposite direction, toward the Arts buildings. *Hmm, so is she an engineer or science student then? With Arts friends? Or her roommates?* Such questions for someone I don't know; I suppose I could follow her into the building, but I'm sure that would freak her out—*yeah, her and me.*

But my curiosity lingers as I reluctantly head left and mount the flight of limestone steps to my building, Macdonald. It's probably the sour feeling my ex left in me and the need to sanitize myself from her presence, but I have to get to know this girl—if I ever see her again, that is. I picture her blissful gaze again and smile to myself.

Her clothes were a bit funny, though. The shirt was okay, a mass-made tee with "Je me souviens" printed across the chest—*is she French-Canadian then?*—but the huge black skirt looked kind of odd. My great-grandmother would have worn it. Maybe she's from northern Québec; from what JP says their sense of style and technology lag behind the rest of North America.

Yanking me, literally and figuratively, from my little daydream, Alain comes out of nowhere and grabs my left elbow from behind as he holds up his baggy shorts on his skinny waist with his free hand.

"Will, *mec*, you won't believe what she's wearing today," he hushes.

The long black skirt? *Does Alain know this girl?* I give him an incredulous, confused stare as I retrieve my elbow from his grasp. "What?"

"Anna, Will, *Anna*."

I let out a breath I didn't know I held.

"Oh my God, Will, she's got this shirt on that's tighter than . . . holy shit, man, her tits are like—"

"Alain! Dude, you can't say that stuff out loud!"

He tries to look sheepish or embarrassed, but I'm not fooled. I don't want to admonish him, but I have to for both our sakes.

"Seriously, man, she or some other prof could be right in the lobby. You gotta watch yourself!"

"Ach, chill man. No need to be uptight all the time."

"I'm not uptight; I'm reasonable. I know she's—" I lower my voice and tone down my language,

"—attractive, but can you imagine how things would be if she heard you say that? Or if some other faculty member did and told her about it, knowing you work for her? They'd think you two were hooking up or something."

I can see my last comment excites him again, but he gets my point and quiets down.

"*Merde*. You're right, Will, as always. But hot damn, if she isn't. . . ."

I smile in spite of myself. "Did she drop by while I was in Kevin's class?"

"Yeah, briefly. She was on the run to get her lecture together for today, she said, but wanted us to confirm some amendments Arizona sent for the measurements they compiled."

"Oh yeah? For the model or real data?" I ask.

"Well, both really. She wants us to try and correlate the Chernekov light reading with our model's projections. But it's more than that; she wants us to extrapolate their data to determine if—oh hell, it'll be easier if I show you."

"Okay. Let's go see the data," I reply, keyed up for a new analytical task after a few weeks of mostly mechanical work. Though I'm finding it hard to walk forward, feeling like half of myself is still with the mystery girl down by the FDA entrance.

12

Monday
Elie

Not knowing where else to go, I spend the next hour in the library. I'm drawn to the fourth floor, where I pick a book at random—*General Physics Theory*—and plunk down on the long wooden window seat I found on Friday night. I have a little view of the lawn from here, which I stare at between half-heartedly perusing the battered physics textbook to make myself look authentic and daydreaming to develop my cover story to explain why I am here.

The book is actually more interesting than I thought it would be, full of brightly colored graphics and tables and equations solved step-by-step. I find myself more and more engrossed in its contents and find it easy to read and understand; reading this versus one of the old texts my father used when he was in school is like writing with the finest fountain pen instead of a feather quill.

But back to my real task. I need to make my story as believable as possible, and I also need to stick to it without fail. I am well aware the second I contradict myself or state something outlandish, people will question who I really am. I absolutely cannot give anyone the chance to doubt me. For all this, I take out the little book I've been using as a diary for jotting down my "official story" as a reference. No mistakes.

I can say I'm from New Zealand. That's an easy enough start, since my parents are natives and have passed the accent down to me. I know all about it, more than anyone else here, surely, and can provide enough rich details to convince anyone. I'll say my parents still live there, and I'm their only child. This way no one can ask to meet them. I decided to come to McGill to experience a new culture. Since we're both in the British Commonwealth, the move was natural. Best of all, being a New Zealander means I have my own unique vocabulary and lifestyle, so any claim of not fitting in can be blamed on that.

My parents can still be who they actually are, to make things easier: my mother is at home but used to teach; my father is a physicist at Canterbury College. He actually used to be a researcher there before he moved to the Cavendish Laboratory at Cambridge and then on to McGill. But should I reveal who he is, in case someone recognizes him? Should I change his name—and therefore mine? By now I've pretty much resigned myself to the fact he's not here in 2006, looking for me, and to show myself as his daughter will surely make people think I'm a few eggs short of a full basket.

My shoulders sink. I sigh. I don't like the truth, but I have to accept it.

So I won't be Eileen Rutherford any longer. I'm now . . . Eileen Newton; that's my mother's maiden name, and the first name that pops into my head. Despite her riding my nerves at times and the probable cause of me being what my mother has termed a rebellious child over the years, the constant reminder of my family is comforting right now.

This will be my first year at McGill since I can still pass for an eighteen-year-old, but regardless, I'm too ignorant of modern student life to be anything other than a first-year. I suppose I should be here to study Literature, broadly, so taking Twentieth Century Literature and English Literature fit in well for me. I need to come up with at least three other classes for me to be enrolled in this semester, as well as where those classes are. This will be difficult; I have no idea what a plausible course of study is for English Literature nor where the classes typically take place. I'll have to either wing it, probe other literature students for their classes, or wholly make something up. Since I'm faking being a student, I'm hoping for large classes to get lost in; if there are hundreds of students, will a professor notice one more? So far, this seems to be the norm at McGill now.

Come to think of it, I do remember hearing a boy in our English Lit class mentioning to a friend he has a Medieval Art and Architecture class today at half past one in the Arts building. I can "take" that class too. I wish the class were medieval literature, romantic literature, or maybe some kind of science, but I quickly resign myself to accepting whatever fortune comes my way. I can't be picky but must make the best of whatever is thrown my way.

Isn't that some sort of survivalist creed? Wouldn't Father say something like that?

I jot all this down in my notebook, carefully, and format the classes into a sort of daily schedule. I have three out of five classes chosen—*found*—so far, and I notice a lot of empty space in my days. I wonder what I can do in those spare hours. Pretend to study? Read about the last century? Figure out if anyone else in recent history has time traveled?

Find a better place to live than a closet?

That last is probably the most important for survival, but I also know that will take money, as will finding more clothes and food. I push those essential, basic tasks to the side for the moment, my aching stomach grumbling in protest, in order to concentrate on my "studies" first to guard my cover.

With minutes to spare before I need to meet Lindsey and Isabelle outside, I quick-step down the narrow main stairwell of the library. Between the third and second floor I press my back against the wall to make way for two approaching boys, deep in conversation.

"It's not him that's bad, it's that the class is *so easy* for me that I'll want to jam my pen into my eye just for something interesting to think about," says the first boy. He's fairly tall, but quite thin with straight dark hair styled in spiky strands. His thick accent betrays his northern Quebec origins. "*C'est pratiquement La Physique 101, tu sais? Bleugh, c'est trop. . . .*"

"Being a teaching assistant for a basic physics class is dull, no question, but at least it's for engineers who know something about physics already, Alain. It's not Physics for Arts students, thank God. And you do have Julien to TA with you." This second boy, whose eyes have been locked on the steps in front of him, is a little shorter than his friend—Alain—yet still far taller than me. There's an easy sort of grace about his very masculine features locking my eyes on him without my trying. His reddish-brown hair loops in short, loose ringlets, as if the boy twirled each strand absently around his finger and let them go one by one. The rectangular, black frames of his eyeglasses rim his eyes like little elfin spectacles that make him seem almost impish yet too sophisticated for glasses.

It takes a lot of effort to look down.

"*C'est vrai.* Kevin wants us both in his first class tomorrow at ten in FDA-1 to meet his students, so I'll find out if at least some of them have brains. Maybe there'll be a hot little froshie in there I can tutor, who knows?" This Alain raises his eyebrows suggestively a few times at his friend, still nameless, who elbows him in return. I caught Alain's meaning quite clearly and involuntarily scrunch my nose in disgusted disapproval.

"Excuse us," the unnamed boy says quietly, cheeks touched with pink above the tiniest of dimples, as he slips behind Alain to squeeze past me on the stairs. His eyes, which I glance up to meet in a fleeting microsecond, are soft and apologetic. Behind the glasses gleam green irises flecked with gold. It could be the lens' effect, but those eyes seem to have endless depth.

My stomach flips in an unfamiliar way.

I feel his eyes continue to search my face as he brushes past, slowly. His left shoulder clears me by a centimeter.

"I beg your pardon," I whisper back in a cordial manner while I flatten myself even tighter to the plaster. I know I'm smiling, blushing, but my eyes don't raise again to meet his. Then they're off, Alain chattering more about the Julien fellow.

Through a fog, my brain files the image of the polite boy and takes mental note of what Alain said about the physics class. Tomorrow morning at ten in FDA-1: there's the science class I wanted to take! I know a little about physics from my father and his work, I reckon, so I should be able to keep pace with the others—I hope. I'd never be able to take such a class as a Donalda.

Carpe diem.

* * *

To my delight, our Twentieth Century Lit class turns out to be fascinating. The hour passes quickly as I learn there have been two world wars fought mainly in Europe, Indian independence from the now greatly diminished British Empire, and a Jewish state created in the Middle East which have shaped writing in the past one hundred years. The only way I can hide my shock at all this is to keep my face close to the notebook I'm furiously scribbling notes upon as I write down major historical topics to research in the library. The other two girls watch me curiously, as does Natalya, the bubbly Russian girl sitting to my left. The other girls met her in their International Development class they had before this.

"I really liked that class, didn't you guys?" Isabelle asks later as we walk away from the auditorium doors toward the exit stairwell.

"Rand is such a serious professor though," complains Lindsey. "He's going to be a tough marker, I'm sure of it."

"Well, at least we'll learn. If a class isn't a challenge, what's the point of taking it, right?" I say.

Natalya chuckles shortly. "*Da*, but a hard class is still hard. And it's harder still if English isn't your first language. *And* he mumbles a little bit," she laments in her thick Saint Petersburg accent.

"Maybe he was tired and not used to talking for an hour straight after a whole summer off," Isabelle suggests, laughing.

"Are you kidding?" says Lindsey. "Professors talk nonstop all year long, just to hear themselves. We're the ones who have a right to be tired. Except you, Elie—how were you writing so fast?!"

I blush, sheepishly muttering, "I like taking notes. And we, uh, didn't spend much time on this period back at home." It can't be a lie if it's impossible to have learned, right?

"Well, I guess you're in the right class. Say, is anyone else hungry? I have three hours until my next class, but I'm absolutely starved right now."

"Me too," Isabelle says. "There's a café on Rue McTavish across from the Leacock building. When I was in *lycée* we would go there for lunch sometimes to see all the cute university boys!"

We all laugh with her, picturing petite Isabelle's long black hair in two braids aside her high school book bag, ogling the much older and taller Québéçois boys. Making our way out of the McConnell building and westward across to the "Arts" side of campus—as the others inform me it's referred to—we examine the students we pass and try to decide if each is an arts or science/engineering major. I contribute nothing, since everyone looks the same to me. Though I'm getting comfortable with the clothing style, I cannot tell what's fashionable and what's "geeky" like the others seem so easily able to do.

Once we enter the cafeteria, housed inside the very open and bright William Shatner Student Center, I fret about my lack of money. I have absolutely no way to purchase a lunch, and fear my jig is up. My worries are assuaged, thankfully, when after shyly turning down the mouth-watering food, at least to my literally starving stomach, by explaining I'll eat the disgusting, small cranberry granola bar I'd stuffed in my satchel early this morning just in case, Lindsey insists on buying me fresh food. Embarrassedly giving the false excuse I left cash at home and don't yet have this debit card thing the others mention, I gratefully accept her offer and promise to repay the favor.

Ten minutes later, I'm trying not to devour my first cup of tea in days and a sandwich of grilled chicken and grilled vegetables like a glutton. It's my first meal of the day, and I'm thanking God for it all. With this distraction, it's hard to concentrate on our conversation of class schedules. I find out I'm the only one of the group taking Medieval Art and Architecture, as well as physics, unsurprisingly.

"You're taking *physics*? *That's* your elective? Elie, do you like torture or something?"

I laugh. "No . . . my dad's a physicist, you see. I know enough about it to take a class, and I actually like physics, believe it or not."

Isabelle eyes me skeptically. "I don't believe it. Who can like physics?!"

Laughing again, I reply, "People like me, I suppose, and—"

"Nerdy engineers?" interjects Lindsey, teasing me.

"*Nerdy* engineers? Sure? I hadn't heard them called that before, but yes, physics is for engineers, and scientists, and very curious people like me. I guess it runs in the family."

"Where does your dad work, Elie?" asks Natalya.

For this I have a ready answer. "Canterbury College, in New Zealand."

"Wow, he must be brilliant."

A lump rises in my throat that has nothing to do with my lunch. "Yes . . . he is."

"Do you miss him?" asks Isabelle.

"Yes, very, very much. He's so . . . far away right now." I try to steel myself more, turning the conversation to the others. "Don't you all miss your families too?"

That works. We compare family stories: Lindsey's family lives near Toronto and plans on visiting for Canadian Thanksgiving in October, Isabelle's parents live outside Montreal, and Natalya shares my grief since her parents and two younger sisters live in St. Petersburg and probably won't be able to travel here for a long while.

"We should have lunch together again tomorrow, but it'll have to be before one o'clock because I have a class from then until two thirty," says Natalya.

My ears perk up. Could this fill the final slot in my schedule? "What class?"

"Renaissance English Literature 1, over in the Arts building," Natalya answers after consulting her own schedule.

"Me too!" I cannot believe my luck! I couldn't have dreamed up a better list of classes, fake or not.

"Excellent! Oh, I'm glad I'll know someone else in my class. It's always difficult for me to walk into a room blind without knowing what to expect."

I know what she means; I tell her so with honesty.

"Great—then we can meet here tomorrow at eleven thirty?" Lindsey suggests. "That's after Isabelle and I get out of Poetics."

"That sounds perfect." I'll be glad not to be alone tomorrow.

"And you'd better get to that Art and Architecture class, Elie. It starts in ten minutes, and you have to get over to the Arts building. But here—" Lindsey tears off a strip of paper from her notebook and writes a series of numbers on it. "Here's my cell phone number in case you can't make it tomorrow."

"Thanks," I mumble, not knowing what a cell phone is. I know what a telephone is, of course, but have no access to one that I know of.

"Do you have a cell? What's your number?"

"No, I don't have one . . . sorry."

"Oh, wow, I thought everyone had one! You couldn't bring it over from New Zealand, eh?"

I shake my head slowly. *Sure, that sounds reasonable. . . .*

"Well, you'll have to get one sooner or later, like that debit card."

"Right," I agree blankly. "Soon. . . . Well, I'd better run, ladies. See you tomorrow!"

As I walk away, they wave goodbye and smile warm, genuine smiles, making me feel human again and a little less bewildered. Those unkind people I met Saturday on the lawn and this morning in the lobby must have been an anomaly; they *must* have, I conclude firmly to convince myself more than anything. I trudge up the central road to the Arts building, grinning broadly at my good fortune to meet four great girls who are almost like friends and get an entire schedule settled on my "first school day." My cover story is forming well so far, but can my luck last, I wonder? It only needs to lead me to my father, somehow, and soon.

13

Monday
Will

"Can *you* figure it out, JP?" Alain asks. He shoves a stack of papers over and slumps back into his chair, rocking it off its front two legs slightly.

We've been poring over Arizona's data for the past half hour and trying to decipher what anomaly might cause our model to predict values nowhere near their readings. The detector seems to be picking up a lower resolution of gamma-ray flux, which is crucial because this can have a high variability, and it's imperative the detector be able to record even the most minor difference in flux levels.

"I'm stumped. There has to be something wrong with our method. Perhaps we're using a simplification that can't be used," I say. "What I don't understand is why the flux is so low. I can see if the value is about ten percent or twenty percent below what we predicted, but this is ridiculous to be half of what we calculated."

"*Ouais* . . . and not only that, it makes us look like idiots to be *so* off. You know Anna would say so."

"Let's hope she doesn't," I say, but I know one conflicting set of data won't make us hapless in her eyes. I glance up from the spreadsheet on Alain's laptop and recognize the real source of his worry.

"Oh, come off it, Al—she won't think any less of you for one inconsistency. Granted, this does seem pretty damn significant, but. . . ."

Sighing, my mind now entrenched deep into space, trying to visualize gamma-ray beams racing toward our detector, I squint my eyes shut to block out the room's harsh fluorescent light.

"There's some big error somewhere here, and I hope it's in this one calculation and not propagated into every part of the model."

"The way I figure it, either Arizona's detection readings were obscured by errant ambient energy—"

"—Which is possible but unlikely," Alain interrupted.

"But still possible. Or, we've failed to account for a widespread source of attenuation between the energy source and our detector. Or, the most probable and most desirable from our perspective, we've made one simple error in the model that affects only this calculation."

Nico pops out from behind his barricade of bookshelves to chime in. "That about sums it up, Professor Hertz. Any suggestions for a course of action?"

I spin around with a wry smile across my lips. "I didn't hear you there! What, first day of school and you have to come in early to impress the profs?"

Nico usually rolls in at about ten-thirty every day, and never before ten; of course, that means he's also here until seven or eight at night and even the weekends, sometimes—a crazy schedule, in my opinion.

"Nah, couldn't sleep last night and decided to pop in early. What else can I do on a Monday morning?" He reaches his arms up in a lazy, cat-like stretch, as if to show he's honoring us with his presence this morning.

Alain cackles. "Gee, work?"

"Nah, that's not what we're here for. We just drink coffee and talk about the girls we'll never meet. And then we go out drinking and see the girls we'll never date," I tease.

"Well, while you boys have been sitting around doing who knows what since the sun came up—"

"Drinking coffee and talking about women, like I told you. We haven't gotten to the booze yet."

"Oh, and Will and Shavash went to Kevin's Quantum Mechanics class. That's something, Nico, because you've done . . . what, exactly?" Alain asks.

"As I was about to say, boys, I got the data from Anna also, and I've been re-deriving the equations and double-checking all our calculations."

Alain and I look quickly at each other, both surprised Nico was so industrious this early in the day. *Oh well, the more brainwaves warming up the room to solve this problem, the better.*

"Excellent," I commend him. "Thanks for tackling that. Are you going to check the inputs into the model as well? Make sure we didn't make a dumb transcription or transposition error?"

"Yeah. . . ." His eyes cloud over as his mind is undoubtedly back to crunching numbers. "I'll get to that. . . ." Then he ducks back into his corner, and the rest of us are left with silence again.

We brainstorm for another few minutes and bat a few ideas back and forth, but it's pretty clear we're getting nowhere. I suggest Alain and I go to the library and search the latest books on high energy physics to see if we missed something fundamental.

"'Go to the library?' Who are you, Hermione Granger?" Alain jokes. "What answer is there that we can't find online?"

"Plenty, cyber boy. We should at least check that big book on essentials of observing high energy emissions we used last year—maybe we missed something—and see if there's a specific text on gamma characteristics that's new in a journal."

"That's a good place to start. I'd go with you two," Shavash chimes in from her desk, looking up from her own calculations and now-empty coffee cup, "but my first Nuclear Physics class is at 10:35. If you're still there when I'm done I'll meet you there."

"Okay," I reply. "We'll text you at eleven thirty if we're still in the library. It's a better option than standing around here and scratching our heads for another hour."

"*Mais... faque là, j'ai pas encore mangé de petit déjeuner.*" Alain, ever the beanpole who eats as much as an NFL linebacker, is whining about his lack of breakfast.

"Here," Shavash says, thrusting a small Tims bag in front of him. "It's a bagel with cream cheese. I was gonna eat it later, but since you'll whine for an hour about starvation unless you eat and never get any work done meanwhile, you can have it."

"Aw, thanks, Shav. You didn't have to—"

She waves him off with a small smile. "Nah, don't mention it. You got me one a few weeks ago. Karma."

She's one of the few people I know who'd do something as nice and unexpected as that—a bit motherly at times, as her boyfriend has complained once or twice, but a great friend to have.

"*Merci!* What a lifesaver you are...." Alain thanks her, then digs into the bag.

I gather my book bag and push Alain toward the door; otherwise he'd be rooted to the spot, devouring his gifted meal. In the four minutes it takes to get to the library, the bagel disappears.

"When's your tutorial for Anna's quantum class, Will?" Alain asks. He's looking up at the stairs between the second and third floors of the library instead of at me; his tone tells me he's thinking more about Anna than the class itself.

"Wednesdays at 10:35, but I'm headed to her first class in two hours. Hey, don't you have to go to Stringam's first class today?"

"*Ouais* . . . Electronics, PHY328. That'll be a fun one to TA." His answer is thick with sarcasm; Alain's strong suit isn't electronics, but Professor Stringham loved him when he took the class a few years ago and wouldn't accept a "no" from Alain.

"Well, at least you have an easy physics class for Kevin as your other TA spot. Mechanics and Waves, right? PHY131?"

"Yeah, it's an easy subject, but it gets boring easily, and there are, like, two hundred kids in that class. It'll be insanity!"

I feel bad for Alain because the large class *will* mean constant pestering by nervous first-years, but I point out how lucky he is to have Kevin as the professor.

"At least you know he'll teach the class well enough that you'll have less confused kids than for Stringham's class. I heard no one can understand what the hell he says half the time."

"It's not him that's bad, it's that the class is *so easy* for me that I'll want to jam my pen into my eye just for something interesting to think about. *C'est pratiquement La Physique 101, tu sais? Bleugh, c'est trop. . . .*" Alain slips into French as we turn the corner on the flight of stairs.

"Being a teaching assistant for a basic physics course is dull, no question, but at least it's for engineers who know something about physics already, Alain. It's not Physics for Arts students, thank God. And you do have Julien to TA with you."

I draw my eyes north from the steps to a girl who has moved out of the way a few feet in front of us.

It's her.

I nearly freeze in the nanosecond it takes me to realize this is her, up close: the same full black skirt, the *Je me souviens* t-shirt, the blond hair of an angel. Her back already flat against the rough brick wall and her face tilted to our feet at a sort of modest attitude, she's pushed her shoulder bag to the side to give Alain and I room to pass.

Through the golden curls I don't hear Alain's full response until his last remark.

"*C'est vrai,*" he agrees. "Kevin wants us both in his first class tomorrow at ten in FDA-1 to meet his students, so I'll find out if at least some of them have brains. Maybe there'll be a hot little froshie in there I can tutor, who knows?"

I'm mortified Alain would say this in front of a noticeably younger student—she could be a freshman for all I can tell. Clearly she heard him, because her nose scrunches a little with obvious disdain. Still, it doesn't mar her features; it couldn't. Everything about her is slight—a button-like curved nose, thin arms and fingers clutching her bag, and a whole foot less of height than my six-foot-one-inch frame—but her stance displays an air of strength, perhaps a touch of defiance. Her hair drapes past her shoulders in a thick curtain of loose waves which shines, thanks to faint streaks of copper, even in the limited light of the stairwell windows—but not as brilliantly as it did outside when it nearly blinded me from afar.

Despite her awkward clothing, she's undeniably alluring and has subsequently tied my tongue into a pretzel. Alain, however, seems to have his mind on the froshies and doesn't notice this girl as he passes her.

"Excuse us," I manage to mumble to her while pausing to follow Alain.

I try, but I can't take my eyes off of her; as she hasn't met my gaze yet, I'm not exactly staring; this is more being mesmerized than being rude. Though she's looking down, her bright amber eyes, round and alert, reveal an intelligence behind them. She has to be smart, I conclude, if she's in *this* library. No Artsies come here.

She's young, Will; don't look at her like that. So what if she's smart? That's not always a good indication. Plus, she does look a bit . . . weird, what with those clothes. Either she's from way out in the country or is too foreign to speak English. That hair is like an angel's hair. God, I'd like to bury my face in it. . . . How is her skin that pale? It's like it glows from the inside. Wicked. I wonder how long she's been out of the sun. Is she blushing? Oh God, she knows I'm staring at her. Look away. . . .

My mind races in the three seconds I study her face, the disjointed thoughts overwhelming my brain and body. I can't help but smile a tad at how easily this girl, this stranger, has virtually intoxicated me in two of the briefest exchanges—sightings, more like.

Her eyes dart up in the quickest of flashes, those apple cheeks reddening more by the second, but still she doesn't quite meet my gaze. The only contact from her is an extremely polite, almost old-fashioned, whisper, "I beg your pardon."

She said "beg" like "beeg," and "pardon" came out like "pah-don" . . . what an accent—Australian? Or was it New Zealand?

I'd ask Alain later, but he didn't hear this girl; he said something about Julien, but I haven't been listening.

I guess I was off about where she's from, except for the foreigner part. Wow, that was really . . . hot. Maybe she is from New Zealand—but definitely not French-Canadian or something weird like Latvian. If she's a science or engineering student, there's a good chance I'll see her again. Hopefully soon, unless she wandered in, lost—

"Yo! Will! Are you listening to me, man? I have no other choice, do I?" Alain has stopped and turned around to face me on the second floor landing, finally noticing I haven't heard a word he's said in the last forty-five-odd seconds.

"Huh?"

"I said, 'I have no other choice, do I?'"

"About what?" But I'm too distracted to really hear what he's saying; a different face keeps popping into my head.

His frown turns into a knowing, mischievous grin as he glances down the stairwell, where the girl's footfalls are finally fading away, then back to me. "Aha," he says, laughing. "Small distraction, *non?*"

I don't even want to know how red my face is as I smirk at him and pretend I have no interest in that girl. But I don't fool myself, and most likely not Alain either. As the friend he is, though, he continues upward and leaves it be.

The library research is a bust, unfortunately, and not just because I can no longer focus on gamma ray attenuation. We don't make it to the end of the class period before we decide we're wasting our time and would have better luck with the stacks of journals in our office.

Our walk back to our desks in Macdonald is filled with Alain mainly chattering about his classes. I try to stay engaged in the conversation, though a different and brief conversation keeps playing in my head. I can't help but wonder when—*if*—I'll ever see that girl again. So much for focusing on work today, though I am trying.

Once I'm sitting in Anna's Classical Mechanics class at twelve thirty-five and waiting to be introduced, I allow my mind to escape again to thoughts of *her*. With the liberty of not having to digest what Anna's saying, I lean back as much as I can in the hard plastic swivel chairs here in McConnell 11, examining every aspect of the girl's expressions, which are singed in my memory.

Stop, Will. Girls are toxic, girls are poison. Stick to physics unless you actually enjoyed that last, prolonged breakup.

Even as I shake my head, I can't clear it. I can't understand why she's so compelling to me; I only know I want to find out more about her. I have an inkling—no, make that a sure sense—there's much more to her than meets the eye.

When I saw her standing outside she was jubilant and excited. But in the library she was nervous, no question, but maybe it amounted to more than first day of university jitters. The way she held her upper body—shoulders held stiffly high and forward, neck still and barely turning when she saw Alain and me—signaled clearly she felt flat-out anxious about something really serious. But those eyes . . . they were intense, fierce even. It's human nature to be curious, concerned even.

And she was beautiful. Dressed a bit oddly, but with eyes like that, hair like that, who cares?

Forget it, Will. Toxic. Poison.

Anna's still talking, but it's not her face I see.

It's your funeral, Will. Don't say I didn't warn you.

Yeah, I'm screwed.

14

Tuesday, August 29, 2006
Elie

I have lived three and half days in the twenty-first century, and the concept itself is still too new for me to fathom despite living it as truth. Even H.G. Wells could not have imagined my recent life to be possible. Sitting in my hidden room—pardon me, my broom closet—on this Tuesday morning is leaving me with perhaps a bit too much time to think on my own. Every event and conversation from the past few days is circling round and round my head.

Yesterday afternoon I endured a steady stream of stares from the other students in Medieval Art and Architecture class. Everyone ignored me except a nice girl from Toronto, Ashley, who chatted with me before the professor started his lecture. Well, she talked on and on about her own schedule without pressing me with questions about mine, but that was fine by me, as I was marveling at how easy coed classes seem to be. Clearly nobody else paid any mind to them being special, and everyone was at ease with each other. I was almost wide-eyed when a boy sat down right next to me without a "hello" or polite request to seat himself. But now I assume this is normal behavior because he wasn't the only male I saw who acted this way. *Are manners completely erased from societal interaction?*

One who certainly didn't have any was a fancy boy sitting behind Ashley and me who asked, with his nostrils flaring in disgust and appraising eyes fixated on my skirt and heels, perhaps the most offensive question I had ever heard.

"Did you buy your outfit at the Salvation Army to save for tuition and books?" he'd asked.

My cheeks had burned as I stared down at my outdated dressing style, as if it could be helped.

"Mind your own business, jerk," Ashley had retorted, her anger as strong as my shock. To me she whispered, "Forget him and his Gino pinstripe shirt and tight pants."

I had recovered enough to ask what a Gino was.

"A guy who dresses like an Italian, but he's not a real Italian, just a wannabe who's trying too hard to look like the real thing."

"Oh," I'd said, not really understanding Ashley's explanation. "Why would someone want so desperately to look like an Italian?"

"Good question," she'd responded, as if I was trying to be funny. Then she'd given the "Italian" behind us as dirty a look as he'd given me, and that was the end of it.

Later during the lecture, I caught a girl staring at me in pure confusion. She wore pants cut scathingly short, barely past her rear end, and a skin-tight shirt barely covering her chest; compared to her I must have looked dressed for winter.

Mostly, I was too distracted by trefoils and flying buttresses to be bothered by the rather rude behavior of those who rather discourteously looked at me like I was a leper. Yet the undercurrent of being the odd fish made me question all my actions and everything I said.

It'll be the small things I'll have to pick up which will help me the most, things like how to address friends, how to dress, what to talk about, and what's now considered rude or not. It seems overall standards and manners are unequivocally lower now, but perhaps my current environment isn't the best indication. Students are young and immature, Father always told me, and I wonder if that's as true now and it was—*is*—for him.

Yet I've managed to find three friends who actually do seem mature and kind—and concerned about me—while also accepting of what must be obvious quirks in my behavior. And they aren't the only anomaly I've encountered. The shortest conversation I had all day yesterday has replayed in my head more than once. Not technically long enough to qualify as an actual conversation, the encounter between myself and the boy on the library steps will not leave my head. He spoke only two words to me yesterday, but it was his sincerity and appraisal of me which I now can't stop ruminating over. I close my eyes, and I can still see his burning cheeks; clearly he was embarrassed by his friend's lewd comment in front of me. Compared to the rest of the brutes around here now, no wonder he stuck out to me.

More than that, his thoughtful, curious expression revealed he thought about me more than how one regards a stranger. Maybe I'm being paranoid, but it seemed he tried to figure out who I am and why I stood there. It was almost as if my façade was transparent to him—and if he gazed a little deeper, he'd be able to see the real me. It would have been disarming if his interest hadn't been so subtle.

And to top it all off, this boy had an absolutely charming, almost impish smile. I can't get that out of my head either.

I wish I knew his name.

And it's occurring to me, as I'm comparing those I've met in 2006 with those I know in 1906, that I've never, ever thought of Ralph Fowler in the same mood as this, though Ralph is ever the gentleman as this boy appears to be.

This is the first time I've thought of Ralph since I've arrived here, and I strive not to again. Shaking my head clear, I brush my cardigan straight, now dismissed from service as a pillow and enlisted as a shirt, hoping I look passable. I would feel awfully odd about this outfit if I hadn't seen Professor Miller, a thirty-something-year-old woman, wear one herself in my Medieval Art class yesterday. She'd fastened all but the top button and pushed her sleeves up to her elbows, so I did the same this morning. Granted, my light cotton cardigan isn't as nice as her fine wool, but mine is undoubtedly more appropriate for the summer weather. At least I washed my hair and body late last night—unabashed in the bathroom once I was sure I was alone—and I look and smell clean, I hope.

It dawns on me suddenly how quickly I've settled into a routine in my little secret corner of the building.

This morning, emerging early from my dim cave at perhaps half past seven, my pupils shrink smaller than a pinhead as the hall's light blinds me. After my eyes dilate back to normal size, I can see again where I'm walking, and this morning I'm simply following my feet. My little couch couldn't help but give me mediocre sleep, so today I'm dragging.

There are two and a half hours before my physics class, an excruciatingly long wait. I need to do something to fill my time. Strangely, the less I consider where to go, the more I find my legs doing the thinking. They shuffle down the wide hall, the shallow Macdonald steps, and the front steps outside. I pass barely anyone, save a few eager yet sleep-deprived professors clutching stained tea mugs. This morning's walk, I fear, won't be as fortuitous as yesterday afternoon's stroll. . . .

* * *

I had wanted to walk off campus to the downtown area, but fear held me back. The city is so large now, and bright, and daunting. What if I were to get lost—then what would I say? What if I make a fool of myself by sticking out too much, then get thrown into a loony bin? What if I can't get back into the Macdonald Building? So far I've propped open a door with a small rock, but I'm terrified of my luck running out.

So I had decided to pass my afternoon mapping this new McGill in my head. I had walked west from the Arts Building, holding vigil at the top of campus as reassuringly identical as the Arts Building I grew up knowing. I expected to only find new buildings—what I didn't count on finding threw me for an absolute loop. I mounted some terraced steps on my way to Avenue des Pins, watching my path carefully so as not to trip. Wedged between the second-to-top step and the low stone side wall was a wad of paper dollars. And when I say dollars, I mean it was an *incredible amount of money.*

I froze when I spied it near my right foot; I didn't want to *steal* anything, but the money was literally wadded up in the corner, forgotten like it was garbage. No one else was around, so I did what any homeless person stranded a hundred years in her future would have done.

I grabbed the money and kept on walking.

And I didn't stop walking until my heart stopped threatening to break out of my ribcage, which was somewhere around two blocks west. I had finally caught my breath and leaned against a nearby tree inconspicuously, shielding my hands from the few passersby on the sidewalk. Unclenching my fist slowly, my head worked double time to count the colored bills crumpled inside. Even now, half a day later, I'm still amazed at how much money unfolded in my hands: $155.

That's more than twice what Father earns per week!

Then, as now, what I felt more than anything was relief, despite the intense guilt of holding what was obviously someone else's money, someone else's *forgotten* money, because money means security. I could buy dinner, a change of clothes, whatever I needed until I find Father and go back home.

That's precisely what I did last night—buy dinner, that is. However, I was completely unprepared for how much of that bundle of cash I would be forced to part with. At a small café, far from fancy, I would have walked out of the place once I read the menu had I not been so hungry by 7 p.m. As it was, my wide eyes and mouth frozen in an "o" were proof I was a stranger in a strange land. This led to a questioning glance from the waitress, but I had managed to pull my expression together quickly enough to order a breast of chicken and a salad—for an astounding eight dollars! *Eight dollars!* Why, no one I know would consider paying more than seventy-five cents for that in the Ritz-Carlton itself.

But the clientele in this café was no higher than the average stranger on the street, and no one else had looked like they were being robbed as they placed their orders. Then I noticed all of the prices were around twenty times what they were in 1906, and I suddenly realized how much of an effect inflation has had in a hundred years.

Suddenly, my $155 felt more like the $8 I spent on my meal. It would be gone before I knew it if I wasn't careful.

As I chewed my dinner slowly, I made a plan to have my basic needs met on the reality it could be days or weeks before I find a way back home. I'd have to visit a grocery store to buy food more cheaply. I'd have to get more clothing than what I came with and a discarded, old shirt. I could buy a second skirt that fits today's styles. But I could also alter my old clothes: my ruffled white shirt could transform into something like the clean-lined, crisp white shirts men and women alike wear nowadays, with the help of an emergency sewing kit which my mother has always insisted I carry in my satchel.

Well, if this didn't qualify as a clothing emergency, I didn't know what would.

So I quickly laid out an alteration plan. I would clip off the high ruffled collar, take in the side seams to fit it closer to my body, and fashion a new, stiff collar somehow from the fabric I removed. My night, and probably the next night as well, was thus all planned out—I would be sewing by the dim light of my single overhead incandescent bulb.

Later, on my walk home, I had found an open shop with merchandise spilled out onto the sidewalk outside their windows. I didn't know what to expect as I moseyed up to the outdoor display, trying my best to look casual for the *vendeuse* standing as sentinel by the store's front door, so I took an evaluative scan of the clothes.

"*Tout est en solde*," she had said to me in a bored voice, too busy poking at a little square object in her hands to actually look at me.

"*Merci*." I thanked her for the news of the sale.

I had spied mostly slacks, but I couldn't fathom why women would want to dress like men. I recoiled at the thought and instead tried to find a simple skirt less billowy than the one I arrived in—the one I've worn for four days straight. I shuffled through a limited rack of long skirts until I found a white one simply bunched into thick rows. When I had asked the sales clerk in English how much it was, she answered in the same dull tone, "That one is ten dollars. Do you need to try it on?"

"Umm . . ." I was still registering the shock of the price at that point. *Ten dollars?!* It took about five seconds to compare its price with that of my dinner, and then I realized the deal I was getting.

She had interrupted me then. "It is a two, *non*? That would fit you fine." She sized me up in a quick glance. I had only nodded, happy to have checked something off my list with minimal effort or conversation.

Once I'd paid the clerk for both the white skirt and a similar grey one with a swirling seam instead of the horizontal bunches, I made my way back to campus and let out the breath I'd been holding for far too long. It had been a relief to know I'd be able to fit in a little better now, albeit thirty-two dollars and nineteen cents—the cost of my dinner and skirts plus outrageous taxes—short of the $155 I had been gifted a few hours earlier.

I had been nervous about parting with the money then, but looking back this morning, I'm happy I did so. Last night the money burned a hole in my satchel, not because I wanted to spend it but because the immoral method of attaining it weighed heavily on my mind. Had I been in any other situation, I would have admonished myself thoroughly and then turned the money in. My, how such a short time has changed me.

***

I could be mistaken as a sleepwalker this morning, had anyone been paying attention to me. I follow a path outside I know by rote. The familiar takes over my body, and I scarcely hear my heeled feet clicking the pavement below. To my left and right are the same homes I've always seen—aged red brick and grey stone edifices fronted with heavy oaken doors, carved pediments, and welcoming steps polished by years of tenants' footfalls. The scene, if I squint my eyes to blur together the rows of cars and mess of added balcony chairs and falderal, looks exactly as it's always been. In fact, any moment now I expect Emma to come bounding out from her street. Or from Rue Sainte-Famille, my father.

I know my mind is playing tricks on me now because, without realizing it, ten minutes later I am actually walking up Ste Famille, along the same path I'd take any day to head home. I keep imagining this is all a dream—my eyes are squinting shut ever tighter, then opening to find nothing changed. I'm still in 2006, and Father is still not with me. Our house—or whosever house it is now—is right there in front of me, the same three-story limestone façade, the same twin dormers peeking out of the steep roof, and the same shiny, white-painted, double front doors. I can see into the room beyond the right dormer, my bedroom, and I long to lie under my heavy quilt and shut out this strange reality.

Slam! From the front door emerges what must be Father. This is our house, after all. He's a tall man, somewhat spindly like Father.

But of course it's not him. It's the current patriarch of the house. As quickly as the suited gentleman trots down the front steps, I am thrust firmly from my childish, hopeful daydream of that house still being the Rutherford house, with my father inside, eating his breakfast of biscuits with marmalade and his favorite Earl Grey tea. Still, though, my legs are stiffly planted to the sidewalk and my gaze is unbroken.

"Good morning, miss. Can I . . . help you?"

The stranger's eyes search me, apprehensively making sure I'm not a crazy homeless person or a robber, I'm sure. *Getting near to the first one though, Elie.*

"No, Sir. Ju-Just admiring the houses here on my way to class. Lovely home you have."

"Yes, thanks." He's still appraising my stance, but can't seem to find anything threatening about me, it seems, except that I'm odd. "Well, nice day," he adds as he heads downtown.

It's rather numbing to know with certainty only I was transported to this century. Why did I think Father would be here, in a house we would logically no longer own? My subconscious beats my conscious delusions away and forces me to believe what I feared all along was true.

For the first time in my life, I'm on my own. Shivers rack my body and leave my skin prickly with goosebumps. A hard knot rises in my throat and tears flood my eyes; I force both back.

But I can't give up—Father would never do that—and need to face the fact I truly need to create a new life for myself. Looking over my shoulder at my old house behind me, I know the path to my old life can only be found by going forward.

***

My PHY131 class is conveniently in FDA-1, the big auditorium in the Adams building. Since this class is more of an introductory physics class than a specialized, advanced course, I'm not lost. In fact, I've understood everything that's been said so far. Professor Nagar is starting out with an explanation of the basic building blocks of matter and the states of matter. Everyone around me is furiously taking notes, but my tutelage as Ernest Rutherford's daughter has prepared me well—despite being an English student.

Now the professor is explaining the history of the discovery of atomic particles, and I'm at the edge of my seat. This was Father's research: radiation, beta particles, and the positively charged particles he hypothesized were in a very small area of the atom.

"First," Professor Nagar begins, "J.J. Thompson in his Cavendish Laboratory at Cambridge University, around 1897, showed that every atom is not indivisible but rather contains negatively charged electrons in a positively charged matrix. This was affectionately called the 'Plum Pudding Model,' or on this side of the pond the 'Raisin Bun Model.'"

I know the former name, the model for which my father hypothesized was incomplete. My staccato breaths are shallow. I know what's coming, but what does a century of reflection say about his experiments?

"Then a former postgraduate of Thompson's, who became the Chair of Physics at this very university, discovered the extremely small and positively charged nucleus present in each atom. Ernest Rutherford—see more in chapter one about his scattering experiments—bombarded a very, very thin sheet of gold foil—"

He used mica sheets first, but I guess only I and his team would know about that.

"—with alpha particles, or positively charged particles, and found a tiny percentage of the particles bounced straight back at the source. Presented in a 1909 paper, this proved the atom is largely empty space, but contains a small and massive area, the nucleus, which holds the positively charged subatomic particles. We now know these to be the protons and neutrally charged neutrons."

My mouth dry from hanging agape, I can barely hold myself together enough to keep from leaking tears of pride onto my notebook. Instead, I finally start taking notes. I want to remember every word of this new world.

"Of course, the university is very proud of this achievement, and McGill is now known around the world as one of the premier laboratories due to the eminence of Rutherford's work. As an aside, I highly recommend reading his book on radioactivity and visiting the Rutherford Museum up in the Rutherford Physics Building, but I believe you need to set up an appointment. If any of you are serious about science, it's a must-see."

My father, a giant in the science world? With a building named after him and a museum in his honor? It's unbelievable everyone around me is listening and writing as if nothing spectacular was said, and it's all I can do not to cry out, weep for joy, bolt into the isles. To behave normally is to be chained.

"One of Rutherford's assistants, Frederick Soddy, discovered in 1913 the idea of an isotope, which is a variant of the common form of an element but varies in the number of neutrons it contains.

"Also in 1913, Niels Bohr—another colleague of Rutherford and member of the Manhattan Project team—refined the explanation of electrons. He postulated they exist in energy levels around the nucleus and can change their orbit state by emitting or absorbing energy. This largely forms our modern model of the atom, with small further refinements that I won't bore you with. Nor are they relevant to this class. If you are interested in things like particle physics and quarks and nuclear physics, however, please feel free to become a physics major and take more of my classes, like Alain here."

Fascinated by the professor's words—already I'm beginning to like this fellow—I barely notice the boy in the front row he's waving toward.

It's the other boy, the spiky-haired friend of the handsome boy on the library steps. He's nonchalantly nodding at us students, shoulders crouching above his torso as he stands for as short a time as possible to acknowledge us.

"This is Alain Proulx, one of your TAs for this class. Stand up again and let them all see your face, Alain. I want them to recognize you when they come to your tutorials, for goodness sake." Though Professor Nagar is scolding Alain, his cheerful nature bleeds through stronger than his irritation.

"Hello, *bonjour*," says Alain. "I'll be your main TA, like the prof said, all semester, so come to my tutorials Wednesdays, 3:35 in the Macdonald-Harrington auditorium. Julien will teach those when I can't, but we're both available in our office when you need extra help. Don't be scared when you see a half dozen other physicists in there working. Macdonald Building, room two-oh-three. Our contact info is on the class outline."

Julien Tremblay introduces himself with a bit more enthusiasm, but I keep staring at the back of Alain's head. So he's the curly haired boy's friend, and possibly in the same program. They might even share an office—which, I realize, is dangerously close to my little hidey-hole. It's only a few doors down, in fact. They might work long hours, or odd hours at least, and could easily see me if I'm not careful with my comings and goings. My stomach churns, almost burning with the weight of my secret life.

* * *

After leaving lunch with my girlfriends—they went to the campus bookstore to buy the course pack for their next class—already I miss them and my physics lecture. Professor Nagar is no Father, but being back in a science environment is a revelation after the past few days. I didn't realize how much I naturally crave being surrounded by electrons and waves.

It's not the science you need, Elie, it's the connection to Father. I don't need a psychiatrist to tell me what my subconscious is making perfectly clear. All the same, my reverie overcomes reality, and before too long my legs have taken me toward the Milton gates again. I'm on the sidewalk with the gates in front of me, the McConnell Building doors to my right, when I spy him out of the corner of my eye, standing and staring directly at me.

It's him, the green-eyed boy, with the noontime rays bending around his short curls. I could forget about him, not risk meeting him and giving away the truth about me, but I'm too curious not to talk to him. As my own legs slow their pace, his begin a steady amble to intersect my path.

As he closes the gap to me, I notice he stiffens and straightens up, swallowing noticeably yet never taking his eyes off mine. Normally that type of reaction would frighten me, but I can feel this man's gaze isn't harmful. It isn't aggressive in the least.

"Hi," he says after a moment's hesitation. "I'm . . . William." His weight shifts onto his heels slightly as he appraises me further. It seems as if he's trying to figure out what to say to me—or rather, what I need. "Do you need help finding your classroom?"

I pause at his question. His formality is unmistakable, and remarkable to me. I can't put my finger on why this is so, for a brief second, until I realize again it's the pleasant contrast he makes against the other men I've encountered so far in this . . . time.

"Hello, William," I begin, unsure of how to answer him.

His eyebrows furrow curiously but his expression relaxes into a look of surprised contentment. That impish smile returns, and it gives me confidence to speak further.

"Well, I'm Eileen. But please call me Elie. All my friends do," I lie—everybody in my past did, my real life. I can't yet count my new acquaintances in the tally. However, this seems like an appropriate way to introduce myself, as I try to make myself appear more comfortable, more normal, and also to evade his question.

"Elie. . . . It's nice to meet you, Elie." His back remains as stiff as the limestone walls he's standing near, but his eyes warm immensely. He hesitates to add, a bit reluctantly it seems to me, "My friends call me Will."

The words tumble out of my mouth before I can reign them in. "You'd like me to call you William though." I make that a statement, not a question, shocking myself in the process. *Have you gone mad, Elie? What impropriety! What possessed you to say that?*

Will—William—looks momentarily taken aback, but the left corner of his mouth turns up the tiniest bit as it had when he passed me on the library stairs. "So I can use your nickname, but you use my full name, huh? And why is that?" He's teasing me, I can tell, but he must already know the answer subconsciously.

"Sorry . . . William." I shrug as I say his full name again. "Will" sounds odd to me—too casual, too easily forgotten. I hope the shock of my words hasn't transferred onto my face.

To my relief and surprise, William chuckles and widens his smile.

"Only my grandparents use my full name—they must have picked it—and I usually hate the way it sounds. It's too long and old-fashioned. But it. . . ." He pauses, looking like he's—unsuccessfully, like me—unable to reign in his own words. "But it sounds right coming from you."

I work hard to hold back a gasp. *Old-fashioned*? William's nothing if not perceptive, unless I really do still stick out more than I realize.

William's expression changes into one of bewilderment. Embarrassed, he looks down to his right. A few seconds of silence later, as if pondering a decision in his mind, he takes a step toward me.

"*Do* you need help, Elie? Finding your classroom, I mean? People seem to have trouble finding their way around the halls in the engineering buildings. They're interconnected and laid out oddly, especially for people from other programs. If that's what you are, that is . . . from another program. . . ."

A bitter laugh almost escapes my twisting lips. *Oh, if only you knew how well I know my way around these halls.* "Ah, no, but I thank you. I had a class earlier and then met up with a few friends for lunch."

William raises his eyebrows, looks down to his right again, then turns his eyes to me. His gaze traces the flow of my hair around my shoulders, then settles on my full satchel. He glances quickly up to my eyes, then back down to the bag. In a cascade of words, he asks, "If you would like to, that is if you're not busy later, I mean if you don't have class later, maybe we can grab a cup of coffee? I'm not doing anything, I mean, I just got out of a physics class myself, and I don't need to be in the lab all day, so. . . ."

Physics? Lab? He works in one of the labs in this building? I wonder what he does. Maybe he knows about Father's labs. There's only one way to find out.

Yet . . . I cannot be seen unchaperoned with another man. What would people think?

My thoughts distract me from answering him promptly. "I have another class in an hour . . . and many, many readings also, already." I cringe as his hopeful smile is fast falling. "But perhaps we can take a stroll around campus now?"

That is of course forbidden as well, but goodness—something tells me, by looking around at the mixed pairs walking around us, society has loosened standards regarding chaperones for women.

"Of course, right. That's fine. Should we walk under those trees, along the path to the front gates?"

"Lovely," I answer with what I hope is restrained excitement. But I can't hold back everything. "And you'll tell me all about what you do in your laboratory?"

William's eyebrows raise in surprise again. *Did I give myself away? Why is William looking at me so curiously?*

15

Tuesday, August 29, 2006
William

I can't believe how lucky I am to be talking with her. She's asked me about my research, what I work on, where my labs are, what they're like—and has listened to what I answered. Every other girl I've talked to has tuned me out after, "I study gamma ray radiation." Elie's response, after a thoughtful pause, was, "Goodness, really? Tell me about your experiments with it!" I don't understand how a perfectly lovely girl who's studying literature and likes art and architecture could possibly listen to—and understand, not to mention appreciate—what an ugly physicist-in-training has to say. Even if she wasn't fascinating in her own right, I'd be enthralled.

Compared to my gibbering, Elie is calm and demure as she tells me all about her classes and her friends Lindsey, Isabelle, and Natalya. Her bright eyes keep flickering with unmistakable coyness, shyness, and exhilaration all at once. I've never known a girl—or guy, for that matter—to speak in such a refined, almost sophisticated manner. I had no idea people from down under act as if they stepped off a turn-of-the-century movie set. It'd be disconcerting if it wasn't so . . . and I squirm uncomfortably as I pin down the word I'm searching for . . . alluring.

I'm trying not to ask too many prying questions, though I'm dying to unravel the mysteries of who she is and where she came from. So I hold back and let silence eventually take over. But I can't stand the dead air, and I end up babbling.

"Another day when there's more time . . . maybe . . . there's a Tim Horton's under that library where you can get coffee and food, but there are better, tinier shops east of here. I stop into one of them for a morning cup on the way to campus occasionally, and sometimes a few of us go there for lunch or an afternoon cup, when we're sick of these undergrad-infested campus digs."

"Oh!" Elie looks mildly revolted at that last remark. I can't believe how callous that sounded.

"I didn't mean it that way, Elie, I'm sorry. I have nothing against undergrads—I teach them twice a week—but after six years of being here, I'd rather be in places dominated by others my own age, not nineteen-year-olds. And it's quieter there."

"It's okay, William. You're allowed a strong opinion or two. I like the quiet sometimes too. It's awfully noisy here, even outside. I can scarcely believe how many people are on the grounds."

"It's a good place to people watch too. It amuses me to see all the people on their cell phones, obsessed with them really. They could be with half a dozen of their friends, but most of them will be more absorbed by that little screen." Elie scans around with me, and I realize it's the first time her eyes have strayed from me except to watch her step; she's the most attentive listener I've ever met. There's something so earnest about her—or naïve.

"It's true. Didn't their mothers teach them manners?"

"Clearly not. Your mom did, though, I see."

She blushes, her pale cheeks mottled like tiny wild strawberries. "One thing my mother did teach me was manners, yes. And how to sew, and cook. It's not as fun as it sounds, I assure you," she teases.

"Very domestic."

"Naturally!"

We share a few moments of laughter, though I sense we're laughing for different reasons. Then I have to confess: "You're so easy to talk to, Elie. We've spent twenty minutes walking already and made a complete circle of the center buildings."

"You too," she whispers. She's rather shy in a way, despite her conversational openness. "I've made friends in my classes of course, but it's a bit different talking to you. We tend to discuss our classes—they're quite exciting—but. . . ."

"And I barely know you. I actually can't believe you're here talking to me when you could be chatting up some young boy in your classes." As I say the words, I hear how lame and hopeful they sound.

"Bah! They're all too into Tolstoy and Flaubert. I read enough of that. Besides, I love physics and find physicists fascinating, I suppose."

I gulp. "I guess I'm the lucky one."

Elie laughs, saying, "Well, my father is a physicist, so it only seems natural to 'chat one up.' You must have a physicist's air about you. Clearly that drew me in." But her grin fades.

"Your father is a physicist? Fantastic! Maybe I've heard about him before. Where does he work?"

"Oh no," she rushes. "You wouldn't know him. He's a professor at our local university."

I'm dying to press her more about what her dad does, but her dismissive tone tells me I shouldn't pursue. It's odd to hear after her being enthusiastic about me being a physicist, but I let it slide.

"Well, I haven't published anything yet—not as the lead writer at least—but hopefully somewhere en route to my master's degree I can get something published in the field of astrophysics or high energy physics."

Elie's eyes glaze over slightly. *Great, now you've bored her with too much physics talk, right when it seemed we were having a great time.* I need to save this.

"But enough about physics, it can be boring—"

"No," she stops me. "It's fascinating, really. I'm used to this talk, though I'm afraid I'm not familiar with those fields of study."

Though momentarily distracted by her manner of speaking, I decide to take a chance and try to find out more about her father.

"Yeah, there are all sorts of specialties, you could say. No doubt that's what keeps a university like this going, with its long history of research. What about your father? What kind of research does he do?"

She pauses. I wish to God I could know what's going on behind those vibrant eyes.

"Atomic physics, radiation, the like," she says in a flat voice.

"Oh?" I'm surprised, and I wonder where he does his work. I thought she was from New Zealand, but what cutting-edge research do they do nowadays? "Does he concentrate on nuclear power plant technologies? Or maybe looking at ways to reduce—"

"Do you know Ernest Rutherford?" Elie blurts out, an unexpected bit of hope edging her question.

"Of course I know who he is. He literally chose the name for gamma radiation, which is what the VERITAS array detects. He did some of his most famous work in the physics world here, and he's one of the best physicists in the last century."

"Oh, of course, of course," she mutters, eyes wide.

"Why are you so interested in Rutherford? Is it because he's from New Zealand too?"

Her face registers shock, then worry, surprisingly to me. Have I hit a nerve?

"You *are* from New Zealand, right? I didn't misplace your accent?" *Let's hope you didn't make a fool of yourself and insult her right off, Will. She could be Australian and mortal enemies of New Zealanders for all I know.*

She's silent for a moment. I didn't imagine hitting a roadblock like this so soon—her being too nervous to answer me, it seems. That wasn't a prying question.

"Yes, I'm from New Zealand. I guess I couldn't hide that, could I?"

I knew it the moment she opened her mouth in the library, but hearing her confirm it makes my head oddly light. Great, she looks my way and it sends me for a loop, then she says something to me and I feel giddy. I'll be as bad as Alain if I'm not careful.

"I got here on Friday night, to be honest," she continues, unaware of my emotional carnival. "I don't have any relatives here, unless there's an ancient link to Fa—er, Rutherford being here a hundred years ago."

"Wow, I didn't realize you were so alone, and your family so far. I mean, I moved here from Michigan five years ago, but that's at least within driving and flying distance. And I have cousins in upstate New York, so I never feel too far from home. But you . . . how are you managing?"

"It's . . . hard already," she says, and I know she's sincere. I hope I don't make her cry. "It felt so all of a sudden that I came. One minute I was at home, and the next, I'm here. . . ."

Suddenly I realize how young she really is and what a terrible roller coaster she must be riding right now. I almost feel like I'm intruding on a private moment, but at the same time I'm intrigued she's sharing with me.

"Will you see them soon? For the holidays, maybe?"

"I don't know. It's . . . so . . . far. . . ."

"And expensive, I'm sure."

"Er—quite."

Elie's looking down at her feet which slow and start pushing the grass blades around. I'm torturing her by questioning her like this, I can see.

"Well, where are you living? Somewhere nice, at least? Do you have good roommates? That helped me adjust when I moved here." My hopeful, bright tone helps at least lift those sky eyes.

"A place to stay? Umm, it's not ideal actually, no."

"You're not in one of the hill dorms, are you? I heard those are more Communist than cheerful."

"No. . . ." she replies, unsure of what I said, apparently. Great, now my jokes are falling flat. "It's just that . . . I—I had a place lined up before I came, but on Friday I found out the landlord re-rented it out because she didn't think I'd come all the way over."

"That's terrible! You should get your money back!"

"No, I haven't paid her yet, which is good and bad. I had to find myself an inexpensive hotel room until I can find another apartment."

"Wow—it can't be that cheap after a few days though, right? But Elie, can't you get into a dorm by now?"

She breathes in, pauses, and says, "No . . . they're full."

"So, technically you're . . .?"

"Homeless, yes. Alone in a new country, poor as a beggar, and without a place to live."

16

Tuesday, August 29, 2006
Elie

"You need to find an apartment soon, right? You can't stay in a hotel forever," William says.

My face flushes when I hear this lie repeated back to me. I hate to do it, but I have to continue lying.

"Sure, it's expensive. . . ." *You can't imagine how affordable a free broom closet is, actually.* "I've been looking for a permanent place." *Not at all at the top of my priority list, really, having my found cash decimated by inflation's claws.* "The process is daunting, though—it being somewhat different from what we do in New Zealand, and there being ever so many more choices here."

William purses his lips for a long moment. "I don't want to be presumptuous—and I know you've made some friends here who can help you—but do you want me to give you a hand in finding a place?"

Do I?! But how would I ever pay for it? Worse yet, how long can I stay in that little broom closet before someone finds me? But how can I refuse him?

"William, that's sweet of you. I hadn't asked any of my other friends for a hand yet. But. . . ."

"But what? I wouldn't mind; it wouldn't be a bother to help you, no worries," he says.

"It's. . . . It's the cost, I suppose. I simply don't know what I can afford, and where. Prices are much more affordable at home." *Living with your parents in their era is so much more convenient.*

He laughs, saying, "It must be near free to rent there, because Montreal has some of the lowest rents in North America, from what I've seen and heard. You can get a good place for five hundred a month, less if you have a roommate."

I gulp. And to think Father only makes $2,500 a year!

"I don't know about that, William, but I do know I'll have to be . . . creative, let's say."

He's silent and stares right through me, his thoughts either miles away or churning like mad. "You know," he begins slowly, "There's perhaps a room in my apartment complex you might be able to rent out."

I can't stop my eyes from widening; I want to hide under my chair. *Surely he couldn't be thinking about . . .?*

"No, not my apartment! Of course not. There's an older lady who lives one floor below me with a spare bedroom. Her place is big because her granddaughter lived there with her while she was at McGill, but she moved to Toronto this summer. I heard the old widow has a lot of money, so I can't imagine she'll downsize into a little studio apartment. If she's still there, she may rent you one bedroom at a lower price than what you'd pay otherwise for an entire apartment. And she's really a nice woman, Jeanne—not too old that she can't get around anymore and funnier than my goofy friend Alain. She's a lot like my grandmother actually. What do you think?"

It's ideal, I want to say, if only I could afford to pay her for even that one bedroom! But living with an old woman could be odd—odder than living in a broom closet though?

"Maybe," I say, wondering how long I can keep up the lie of me affording anything. "I could certainly talk to her and see."

"I can walk down there tonight and ask her first. I used to go over occasionally for tea because her granddaughter . . . well, her granddaughter is best friends with my, er, a girl I knew. Well, we'd all chat, and it was nice. You'll probably like Jeanne a lot."

Unexpectedly, I blush, surprised this man would be so kind as to help me when he barely knows me. Would Ralph do something as kind as this?

"Thank you, William. I'm astonished you'd go to this trouble for me—"

"It's no trouble at all—"

"—but thank you tremendously all the same."

We're silent for a few beats, then William adds, "You're welcome. I'd feel horrible if you ended up paying nine hundred dollars a month just because you didn't know somewhere better to look and no one helped you."

"Well, it's generous of you. I do appreciate it."

"I know; I can see it on your face. I hope it can work out. How about you stop by tomorrow morning to meet her? I'll text you after I check with her when is a good time."

I narrow my eyes in confusion. Text?

"You have no cell phone yet, do you? I'll call your hotel phone. What's the number?"

Flustered, I stammer a bit to cover my ever-growing cocoon of lies. "I-I won't be there much tomorrow morning. I have classes in the morning and don't have a proper break until eleven thirty. I can probably make my way down to your building after that though, as long as I'm back on campus for my one-thirty class. Would that be decent timing?"

"Sure," said William, leaning backward as my words rush to hit him. "That'll be fine, sure. I'll write down the address for you, and I'll buzz you up when you get to the lobby. Good?"

"Good. And thanks, William—I'm a bit overwhelmed right now, as you can imagine. But this will help me a great deal to get settled, you know?"

As soon as I say that, I realize how widely I'm enlarging my lies. The cocoon is closing me in. I have zero money to pay Jeanne—if she decides to offer the room to me. But what will I tell her about me? How will I explain my lack of clothes and suitcases? No personal items? I look like an immigrant sneaking across a border with only the clothes on my back; in a way, that's what I am, only my border was some sort of strange time-warp portal. But at this point, I might as well take the chance; it could turn out to be the greatest blessing I've gotten since getting to 2006. I can't stay in that wretched closet forever, and I can always turn down the room.

But perhaps more importantly, why am I worrying about where to stay, like any normal person would, if all I want is to find a way to transport myself back home?

I know, down where my heart tells me the truth I'm so fiercely shutting my eyes to, that I'll be here quite a while before I manage to make it back to 1906. And however that happens, I may not be able to manage on my own.

* * *

Like yesterday, this afternoon I have a lot of time after my classes are complete but not enough tasks to fill it. My brain replays my earlier conversation with William. When he mentioned gamma rays, I thought, *Where have I heard that term?* It took a beat to recall Father discussing the term, a third form of emanation after alpha and beta rays, with his colleagues during a Sunday pow-wow. He was as animated then as William was telling me about the work he does with the large gamma ray detector. I wish now I'd been able to spend more than half an hour with William—a time span far more pleasant than any I'd spent with someone else—since there are still five hours of daylight left. I'd rather spend these five hours outside than locked in a dim, windowless prison.

More than anything, I'm mostly bewildered by my own attitude toward my living arrangements. Not five days ago I had a life-altering experience and have been looking for my family—misguidedly, I now know—and wishing I were back home. I've had to survive in these past days by developing a cover story to explain my sudden appearance here. I've gone to classes and met friends and actually *enjoyed* both. I've met a young man who has—I admit—beguiled me and provided a link to the past I so desperately crave.

But I wantonly accepted help in finding a permanent place to live. Here. In 2006.

It's almost an admittance of failure, or an acceptance of the situation as unchangeable. Certainly, I can't fathom how I'll magically transport myself back to 1906 any more than I can fathom how I got here in the first place. I'm in uncharted territory, but my failure to understand the mechanics of what happened has perhaps forced me to plant my seeds here and at least try to make this a life. The opposite choice would be to hide away in that closet during the day and find my way home—somehow—at night, a truly sad prospect.

I've become a full student, but I'm not even registered, for goodness sake! How will I keep up this charade?!

Earlier, at lunch with my new acquaintances and at "Renn Lit," as everyone calls it, I found myself fitting in seamlessly with the rest, since they're all new to this school as well. It wasn't as hard to chime into the conversations as I imagined it would be. True, we have a hundred years between us—in language, culture, and shared history—but I have the advantage of being foreign; anything strange I do or say falls under the guise of being a New Zealander. It's a remarkable security blanket I'm using shamelessly.

Taking these classes offers so much more than what being a Donalda student does. I used to envy the men studying at McGill and wonder what it would be like to be in a technical program. Now, I can finally experience what they had, albeit with both men and women in the classes. Fundamentally, this experience has been engrossing—and what I believe I've been searching for in my studies as a Donalda—that it's almost shielded me from the disorientation and pain of being misplaced into an unfamiliar time.

Almost. The more time I have to myself, the fewer distractions I have from my thoughts and memories of family and old friends. These are the difficult times, the evenings alone. These are the times I envy Lindsey, Isabelle, and Natalya, who all have a dorm full of people to spend time with.

Perhaps soon I'll have a roommate, aged as she is. It'll be *someone*, and perchance a few other McGillians live in William's apartment complex as well.

I decide to fight the melancholy by heading up to a sunny spot in the Schulich Library to immerse myself in a few books in lieu of lounging outside. Well, first I suppose I should tackle my class readings for the literature classes and the text reading for physics. I have homework for the physics class as well, which of course I'm excited to do. *If ever there was a bookworm, Elie, it's you.*

The fourth-floor bench with its bank of windows will become my favorite study spot, I realize. For a while I gaze at students milling about the center green, catching the last warm rays of the day. Then I pull out my readings—photocopied from the girls since I haven't bought my course packs yet. I don't know how I will either, knowing they cost upwards of a hundred dollars apiece! But I'll worry about that later this week; I need to plan how to somehow come up with the funds. My leftover "found" cash certainly won't cover all the books.

On the plus side, I found a copy of my physics textbook on the fifth floor, so at least I have ready—and free—access to that. I spend the next hour breezing through the first chapter and even answer nearly all the end-of-chapter questions just for fun. Only five were required for homework. Sighing, wishing there was more physics work to do, I return the text and return to the other readings. These take me longer, but I find them equally fascinating. In particular, the first reading from Monday's Medieval Art and

Architecture class is a panorama from Romanesque to Gothic churches. I smile as I read it, thinking the revival architecture on McGill's campus is as good an education as the reading.

As I lounge, despite enjoying my readings, loneliness darkens my mood like the rising night. *How much longer can you endure hiding out like this, alone, making do with a substitute life lived out of a broom closet?*

17

Wednesday, August 30, 2006
Elie

I'm going to need another notebook soon, at the rate I'm going. My sole composition notebook, already a quarter-full of notes from my 1906 classes, is flooded with a tsunami of scrawls. I suppose if I weren't such a fervent student, I wouldn't have this problem.

"Is your hand crampy too?" Isabelle asks me as she orbits her fists around her wrists. She's been writing as diligently as I've been during our Twentieth Century Novel class.

"It feels as if it's been in a fight."

"Mine's still trying to recover from Badgely's literature class this morning. Three classes in a row is tough."

"I'm glad I don't, though having three classes spread throughout the day is a bit disjointed. But I guess it gives me time to read in between."

"Or eat lunch," Natalya suggests. "Speaking of, will you come to the dorm cafeteria? I'm sure they'll let you come if you bring your lunch."

"I'd love to, thank you, but I actually have a meeting right now."

"Ooh, sounds formal. What's it for?"

"To look at an apartment. I've been staying at a hotel the last few days, and I need to find a permanent place to live." The line is sounding more and more normal the more I say it. To their shocked faces, I explain the situation as I explained it to William yesterday—though spare most details of him. "So I really do have to run, I'm sorry. Can I meet up tomorrow with you all? I can meet you up at the dorm if you'd like, as long as you show me how to get there."

"Of course," Lindsey reassures me with a warm smile. "We'll make this our daily lunch group. But good luck—I hope you get the place!"

I thank her as class finishes and part from them with a wave, and I'm soaring as I make my way down Rue Prince Arthur toward du Parc. Five days here and already a group of friends to have lunch with every day! It makes me miss my old friends suddenly, as I wonder what they're doing right now—or did do, or whatever the time equivalent is. But all the same I know I'm blessed to have met these three girls who are all easy to talk to and fit in with. It's hard to blend in to the twentieth-first century, but they do make it a tad less difficult.

The sheet of paper from William has been burning through my bag all night and morning, and I clutch it now to reread the already-memorized address.

3563 Rue du Parc, #15B, but I need to press the #15B button on the panel in the lobby to be let upstairs, he said.

The building is enormous, and I recall passing it on the way to my family's house—rather, what was our house—on my walk yesterday morning. Rather than a humble brownstone, this monstrosity looks like a few dozen plain brownstones were piled atop each other, the highest area thirty stories high, with no regard to uniformity or symmetry. It's garish, bold, and embarrassing to look at, but I decide it's certainly a building that belongs in 2006, and I reluctantly embrace it, promising to forget its façade by the time I enter my Medieval Art and Architecture class later this afternoon.

I enter the lobby and steal a fleeting glance at a bank of steel doors before finding a large panel of labeled buttons. So far, the instructions are easy to follow. I push the square button for #15B, but nothing happens. Ten seconds elapse. Wasn't that supposed to open a door? I press the button again. Five seconds elapse, and I start to panic as if I've done something terribly wrong, and worse, will never be able to figure out the intricacies of life here. About to despair, a crackling man's voice spreads through a mesh to the left of the panel, sending me jumping back a step.

"Elie, it's William. I'll meet you outside the elevator up here. Take it up to the fifteenth floor, okay?"

I understood everything though tripped on the word elevator, but that was obviously crucial. I've heard of one, certainly, but never ridden in one. Where is it?

The walls are lined with all sorts of strange panels and several doors, some metal and some not, but none of folding doors I saw in pictures. I suppose I can take stairs up to the fifteenth floor—if my lungs survive—

"Elie, are you there? Press the 15B button again and hold it while you talk."

I do as I'm told, saying, blankly, "Where's the elevator?"

A long moment's pause makes me realize I've asked a profoundly ignorant question. Bloody hell!

"The elevator, Elie, it'll take you up . . . it's . . . okay, stay there. I'll be down in two minutes."

I flop down on a bench in a miserable heap next to an array of small metal boxes. I shake my head with embarrassment, though I can't imagine how I'd deduce what an elevator is without actually knowing what it looks like. Depressive thoughts swirl around me until I remember why I'm here. *You need a place to stay, Elie; pull yourself tidy else you'll be doomed to that wretched closet until God knows when*. The determination to find a decent bed and bathtub push me to sit up straight and smooth the worry creases from my forehead.

With no warning, a clear *ding* sounds from the wall of steel doors, and one of them slides open to reveal a compact box beyond.

"Elie," William says as he emerges from the opening, "hi. How are you?"

"Fine, thank you. And yourself?"

"Good, yeah. You just gave me a little chuckle there. Do they not have elevators in New Zealand?"

"Umm. . . ." *Am I the only person alive in 2006 who didn't know those metal doors were the elevator*?

"They don't have stairs in their skyscrapers, do they?" he teases.

"We, ah, call it something different—a silly name."

He nods slowly; I'm not sure if I fooled him. "What do you say, the 'lift,' like the British do?"

That's a much more reasonable term than what I was going to say: an "ellie," which is the first thing my brain thought of—and the silliest name I could possibly create, and cheaper still since it's my nickname. Saving face, I nod.

William shrugs, then gestures for me to follow him. "Makes sense. Okay, we'll go right up to Jeanne's floor."

I step into the metal—suffocatingly tiny—box and turn toward him. His face is a mere foot from mine; I stare at my heels, pressing my shoulder against the far wall. After a moment wondering what will happen next, a firm jolt pushes me toward the floor, and my knees buckle a few inches.

"Elie, you okay? First time taking an elevator?" William is teasing me again, but this time it's definitely half-loaded with suspicion.

"No, no," I say quickly to cover. "I wasn't expecting it to be such a jerk."

He pauses, still with a curious look, then grins and says, "You mean such an impulse?"

"Uh . . . well, quite."

"Never mind, it's a physics joke, a bad one."

I'm saved from further indicting myself as the elevator sounds another *ding*, apparently as a warning, since the floor jolts back down and we stop.

"Here we are, the fourteenth floor. Jeanne's at 14K. Walk straight out, yep, follow the hallway, and it's on the right."

Slow, deliberate steps precede Jeanne opening her front door. A vibrant woman with a head full of shoulder-length, wispy, white hair says in a low voice, "Ah, here's the girl. Elie, I presume?"

"Good afternoon, ma'am. How do you do?"

"I'm doing just fine, young lady," she answers with a small laugh. "Please, call me Jeanne. And hello, Will. Please, please, come in both of you, and I'll bring you a cup of tea I put on the boil a few minutes ago. No need to plug up the hallway like a gaggle of geese."

William gives me an amused half-hidden smile and a wink as he gestures me to enter before him. In front of us, Jeanne beckons us to follow with tissue paper hands.

Southern light floods the apartment, which resembles a jungle what with its overflowing pots of pothos, aralias, palms, and spider plants. It could be a greenhouse if not for the generous white couches and modern kitchen open to the living room. White painted cabinets and steel appliances gleam with the midday light. Underfoot, a plush Persian carpet softens the room, and together with the abundance of crocheted blankets draped over the furniture make me feel at home already.

"Thank you, Jeanne. I really appreciate you agreeing to meet with me. Your kindness—"

"Of course, dear, of course," she assures me as she hands both of us a blistering mug of orange pekoe. "Will here told me about your journey here and being unsettled, and I couldn't have that. And perhaps your being a pretty young girl made it natural for him to try to convince me—"

Now it's her turn to throw me a wink, and I see William's ears develop a crimson tinge.

"—but it didn't take me long to say yes. It's been terribly quiet here since Stephanie left for her new job, and I could use the company in addition to helping one in such need as yourself."

I nod slightly, trying hard to conceal my elation and not quite knowing if I should respond yet. I take a few hot sips to calm my elation.

"You're too nice, Jeanne," William steps in. "I'm sure Elie'll be as great to live with as your granddaughter."

"Of course, of course. Now tell me, Elie—Elie Newton, correct?"

"Yes, ma'am—Jeanne."

"Good. Now tell me, how long have you been in Montreal?" she asks, glancing over at William as if to corroborate the story he told her.

I relay the story which I told William yesterday.

"And where was that place you tried to rent?"

"Ah, Rue St-Marc," I improvise, hoping there actually is an apartment building there now. Actually, I hope St-Marc is still there, and still named so.

"And the apartment wasn't ready for you? Was that the problem?"

I get the feeling that rather than having forgotten the story William told her, she's testing me, perhaps to make sure I'm not a lunatic—though at times lately I've wondered if in fact I am—because I'm certain I told him something different. The interrogation is more grandmotherly than demanding though.

"No, it was ready, but simply rented out to someone else. I—"

"Oh!"

"—believe she thought I wouldn't actually turn up. Maybe if I'd sent advance money. . . ."

"You poor dear, Elie. All alone in a new country and nowhere to live."

"Quite. A bit disorienting. . . . But I kept my wits about me and walked to the first small hotel I could find. It's affordable enough for a few days, but I don't believe I'll hold out much longer before becoming flat broke." *Though I really will be soon enough, since I can't afford to pay you rent.*

"Goodness. Well, Will here was right to ask me if my spare room is free. That's just awful and not what a first-year student needs to start off her studies at McGill. That university is demanding enough as it is without personal dilemmas muddying things, eh, Will?"

"Yeah," he answers, raising his eyebrows in a sigh, as if he understands fully. "So you'll let Elie live here?"

She turns back to me, a peaceful smile on her face showing the slightest shadow of uncertainty. "Well, I can't see why I shouldn't. . . . Tell me, Elie, do you smoke?"

"Of course not!"

"Are you the type to bring blustering, bickering friends over six at time?"

"Why, no," I say. "I don't have that many friends, and they're all quiet girls besides."

"Do you stay out until past midnight all weekend?"

"I'm afraid I'd rather be in bed sleeping well before the wee hours of the morning."

"And do you play that raucous hip-hop boogie music high enough to rattle the door frames?"

My bewildered stare answers that question sufficiently.

"Well then, my dear, test passed. You seem like a delightful young woman and completely sensible. But don't be too quiet when you're here, else I'm likely to forget about you!" She laughs, and I realize she could be quite the roommate. Her eyes tell me she's excited to have me stay with her.

"Thank you, Jeanne," I say, smiling widely. "I'm rather thrilled to have a nice place to stay." *Yet the money, Elie. Where will you find more money?*

"Yes, thanks, Jeanne. I might even introduce Elie to some proper music so you won't forget she's here."

"No you won't, Will! But back to necessities, Elie. We need to suss out the rent. What can you afford to pay each month? Now, I don't know if your parents are sending you money, but I imagine you don't have a job lined up yet—if you do intend on working here."

"Well . . . they'd sent me over with some cash," I start, unsure where I'll finish this. "I don't have a job, no. I'm sure I could find one soon, and that will help me pay you."

"Aha. Well, Will could probably point you in the right direction there, couldn't you, Will?"

"Yeah, sure. Elie, I can look around and see if I find anything that fits student hours."

I smile a grateful thanks.

"But now, Elie," Jeanne continues, "I'm an eighty-year-old woman. A spry eighty-year-old, I've been told, but getting slower every day it seems. You can guess it's easier for me to manage this apartment than a sprawling house, but it still takes a lot out of me."

I nod slowly. I believe I see where she's heading and can't believe my luck.

"I'm in all sorts of women's clubs around the city, and that's far more fun than pushing a mop and scrubbing a toilet. Now, I don't intend to make you into my maid, you understand, but I'm sure we can work out an exchange of sorts until you're ready to pay an acceptable rent." Jeanne's thoughtful gaze is still grandmotherly, and I can tell she'd rather take care of me for the benefit of having company rather than make money.

"Well, I'm certainly no stranger to a broom and mop."

"Nor am I, dear, but at my age. . . . Well, let's see. I'd be glad to give you the roam of the place and feed you, that's expected. How about you help me with the cleaning—the floors and bathroom and dusting and sorts, though I do have a dishwasher so you're spared there—and pick up a few of the groceries from time to time? I don't eat much at my age, and I can't imagine a rail of a girl such as you does either. How does that work for you?"

"I believe I can manage that," and I truthfully do think so—as long as I can secure a small and steady cash flow for groceries.

"Good! And once we see how that works out, we can adjust from there. No need to rush to change things if we're doing well."

"I'm ever so grateful, Jeanne. This means the world to me, really it does."

At the edge of my peripheral vision, I spy William suppressing a wide, beaming grin.

"Yes, I know dear. I'm delighted to help out a young student who's been wronged, and I can tell already we're going to get on very well. I should've known that Will only knows the nicest people in Montreal," she says with an amused voice. Clearly Jeanne is one of those elderly people who's too old to think it improper to speak exactly what's on their mind. "And I think he won't mind a bit to have you living so near."

"Jeanne!" Now it's more than William's ears that are red.

"Oh hush, I know you're only trying to be nice." Jeanne's playing it like she's teasing, though I do wonder, but only briefly. I'm too busy worrying what kind of job I could do and how I can do that while figuring out how to get back home.

We spend the next half an hour eating chicken salad sandwiches and fruit salad Jeanne prepared before we arrived—*I'm sure I'll quite enjoy her cooking*—and chatting. The more we talk, I realize how closely I connect with her. I can't tell if it's her age, her birth being not too far from my time, or merely her wit and warmth, but I know I'm going to love living here.

Additionally, I find myself really enjoying William's company as well. He speaks so naturally to Jeanne, and I can tell he's much more mature than other men in this era. In fact, not many men of any era truly enjoy talking with grandmothers. William, though, speaks as comfortably with her—and warmly, I note—as he does with me.

Finally we move to say our goodbyes, as both William and I need to get back to campus.

"When will you be back to move in, Elie? Tonight, or will you be checking out of the hotel tomorrow morning?" Jeanne asks.

"Oh, I already canceled my room for tonight, on the chance you'd say yes." The lies are piling like snowflakes in a blizzard, but there's no way to stop now.

"Smart girl." Jeanne winks at William. "Well, come back any time tonight. Here's your key now, actually, since I promised my friend Millie I'd stop over at five today for a quick visit. Will you need help bringing your things up, or can you manage?"

"No, thank you." I chuckle as I take the door key. "I don't have much with me. I'm sure I'll be fine."

"Oh, dear. Have a good afternoon, kids. Be good, Will—and I'll see you tonight, Elie dear."

Despite the relief of having a warm, clean bed tonight, my brain is aflame with the story I have concocted and must keep up with. Trying to stop my hands from shaking, I clutch Jeanne's key so tightly it threatens to cut my palm.

18

Wednesday
Elie

My hour-and-a-half class is as fascinating as Monday's was, but I'm concentrating on Professor Perraux much less than I should. Thoughts of how much I fancy living with Jeanne distract me greatly from the designs of trefoils. My right hand is, of course, still diligently taking down notes and sketches.

I do realize the trials that living with an elderly woman can create, although she certainly doesn't seem a hapless sort of woman. Jeanne seems more active socially than my own mother and livelier than some women half her age. Strangely, I feel a kinship to her. That and a deep gratitude for providing me a comfortable place to live.

If only I can live up to my end of the financial bargain.

A few minutes before three, the professor puts down his pen and shuts down the "projector," that amazing device projecting a picture from a flat paper up onto the wall screen; it's times like these I have to restrain myself from exclaiming out loud and asking those sitting near me what I'm sure are ignorant questions about technology. But now class is over, and I can look forward to the big move tonight.

I walk down the stairs toward the Arts Building lobby, and as I take the bottom step—

"Ooph!" The girl walking in front of me cries out as I trip and bump not-so-lightly into her, sending her flouncy curls every which way.

"Oh! How clumsy of me—are you all right?"

"Ugh, yes, I'm fine—Elie! Gosh!" It's Lindsey, her cross eyes instantly relaxing as she sees I'm the culprit.

"I'm so sorry, Lindsey. I'm an oaf in a skirt. Naught an ounce of grace was passed down from my mother."

"No worries. You're allowed once or twice," she says with a laugh. "Although I had you pegged for a ballet dancer with your build."

"I wish! I of course wanted to be a ballerina when I was younger, as did every girl my age. But. . . ." I shrug. *Goodness, only professionals train to be a dancer. Not just anyone can take classes!*

"Yeah, me too. But my skill didn't get me past first-grade classes. Anyway, how was your class?"

"Good! And that woman Jeanne is as sweet as can be, and said yes!"

"Congratulations! Is it expensive?"

I pause, wondering how much I should tell her.

"No, pretty cheap in fact. She's over eighty, so what she really wants is help around the place—cleaning and such—in exchange for lower rent."

"Sounds like indentured servitude!"

"She was afraid it came off that way, but I don't see it as that. Her granddaughter used to live there and helped her keep the rooms up, so I suppose she's glad to have me do the same. It's like living at home, to be honest."

"I guess . . . but if we come over one day and see your back broken over a freshly scrubbed toilet, we're calling the authorities."

"I'm sure I'll thank you for it!"

She laughs in return, then coyly turns to me and asks, "And what about that boy, William? How is he?"

Trying not to blush, I answer airily, "Oh, fine."

"Oh? Just *fine*?"

"He's a nice man, that's all. He knew a neighbor with a room, and—"

"Aha. Just a nice guy helping a girl. That's what they always have as their heart's desire—goodwill." Lindsey's look to me says *you can't possibly believe he doesn't have other motives.*

"Well . . . potentially he likes my company. I'm not sure. But I'm not completely thick; I know men have certain thoughts on their mind. But this was a particularly goodwill gesture, yes."

"Ha! You're a tad naïve, Elie, but I believe you. But don't let him pull a fast one on you."

"I'll be sure to club the dodgy fellow if he tries!"

"You say the funniest things sometimes, Elie. Anyway, I've got to run to my next class. See you tomorrow!" She waves quickly as we part outside on the lawn.

Funny things I say, eh? I cringe, wondering how I can sound more mainstream.

I make my way back to the Macdonald Building and into the hallway leading to my little nook. I pass some open and some closed doors, hearing student discussions behind both. By now I've gathered that the graduate engineering students have these rooms as offices. One week ago I walked through this hallway and these were professors' offices. *One hundred years ago*, I remind myself. Amusingly, what hasn't changed are the large classrooms in Macdonald; the same wooden bench desks and long chalkboards are still there.

It's easy to sneak into my closet since the hallway's deserted. It's just as easy to pack up my meager belongings: my sewing kit, the folded cardigan I wore Tuesday, my old and dodgy black skirt and the new white one I wore yesterday, and my altered white shirt. Placing the clothes in the shopping bag I acquired is really all it takes to pack up my life; everything else is already in my satchel. It's pathetic, really, how little I have here.

If I'm honest with myself, I've survived pretty well with only my wits and a few items. I have my books, the clothes on my back—plus a few extras—a needle and thread, and a fistful of money. We'll see how far the money will get me, but I fear it won't be much farther. Thank God for Jeanne and her kitchen, but I'll have to buy food to help supply it. I certainly can't starve, but I also can't afford to keep going at my current rate. Somehow, I'll need to find income, even if it's a few dollars a week.

No, a few dollars a week won't cut it. I need to get a serious job. William said he could help me, and hopefully he has a lead on a job. I'll do anything to survive—I'll have to—as long as someone will hire a woman like me.

I should feel lighter laden than when I first arrived in this room, but in a way the whole Macdonald Building's weight seems mercilessly perched on my back. Gladly, though, I pull the light bulb cord and turn my back to my little hole. *Hope we never meet again, closet.*

Jeanne said she'd be out by five in the evening, and I want to make sure I get to her apartment when she's gone. I don't want her to see me arrive with naught but few belongings; they don't really fit my cover story. So I have over an hour and a half to wander around before then. My legs take me up to a little park I—used to—love, up on Jeanne-Mance Street. It feels appropriate to go there now and do a little reading for my classes.

***

By the time I reach the lobby of my new home, the clock on the wall reads five minutes to five o'clock. Perfect timing. Mimicking William's motions from earlier—push the square button next to the elevator door, walk in when the doors separate, press the button marked "14," nonchalantly accept the jolting motion of upward transport, and walk out when the doors separate again—I manage to arrive at Jeanne's apartment and look like I belong here.

I do belong here.

The key works, to my relief, and upon entering it actually feels like I'm coming home. Actually, it's like entering a luxury hotel after staying in that musty dust convention I called a broom closet. Late afternoon light falls between the plants' leaves and stripes me. The air is clean, and the place is spotless and inviting.

The room Jeanne pointed to this afternoon is ajar now. It takes zero prodding for me to immediately set up camp. It's not overly spacious, but it amply holds a single-sized bed with a padded headrest. *That'll be comfortable for reading in bed.* Next to it is a plain wooden table with a large lamp. Filling the opposite wall is a long, low dresser illuminated by an equally long east-facing window above the bed.

Cautiously, reminding myself I'm not an intruder, I open the top drawer to pack in my clothes. The drawer is full! In fact, they're mostly full. Sweaters, slacks, cotton shirts, loose cotton pants in bright colors and patterns, small cotton shirts like all the young girls are wearing, socks, and even underclothes lay in six of the nine drawers. I'm flabbergasted. Did Stephanie not take her clothes with her to Toronto? Did she not want them? What is she wearing now?

Then, before I can stop myself, a surge of envy and desire shoots through me. I want all of these clothes.

No, I want my dresser full of clothes back at 152 Rue Saint-Famille, but this can do for now. But I can't steal these clothes.

But I want them. I need them, actually.

They're not yours, Elie. Pack your things in an empty drawer and leave the rest for Jeanne to sort out. And I do just that.

The rest of the apartment, save Jeanne's bedroom, begs exploration, and I give in to my curiosity. The living room is starkly sparse compared to that of my parents, but it does create a serene welcome. Next to the bank of windows, a plush chair nestled under an overgrown fern looks like an ideal reading nook.

As soon as I nestle into the cozy chair to test its comfort level, I hear a hesitant knock on the front door.

"Elie?" a familiar voice calls. "It's me. Are you here yet?" William.

Propriety suggests I shouldn't let him in since I'm here alone, but . . . I can't leave him outside the door without being rude. I could have sworn he heard Jeanne say she'd be gone around five o'clock too.

"Ah . . . just a moment, William." Politeness—and some raw, unknown desire—beckons me to the door.

"Welcome home, Elie," he says as soon as I pull the door open. In his outstretched hands is a small pot of lavender. The tiny purple blooms smell divine.

"Thank you. Is that for me?"

"Yeah—it's a sort of apartment-warming gift. I figured you needed a plant of your own to keep up with Jeanne's greenhouse. Maybe it can live in your bedroom."

"I love lavender, though I've only seen the fresh plant in books. Hopefully I can keep it alive."

"I'm sure Jeanne will make sure of that. She's a better gardener than Martha Stewart, trust me."

"Aha," I say, puzzled. "Jeanne's out, or I'd ask you to come in."

"Actually," William starts, drawing the word out, "I was going to ask if you want to come up to our apartment. You know, meet my roommate Evan and such. Just for a bit, until Jeanne gets back."

Come up to your apartment?! Do you have no sense of propriety?

I have no idea how to answer that; I'm incredulous he even suggested it—unchaperoned and barely having met.

"Elie? Do you?" he asks again.

"I-I couldn't, I shouldn't."

An innocent crinkle of confusion distorts his face. "Why not?"

"We-We only just met, William! We barely know each other, for goodness sake!"

"We'd only hang out, Elie. What's the big deal?"

"That's not—That's not how I was brought up." I don't know how to explain basic rules of etiquette to him. *Have social norms changed so much since 1906 that a man can openly invite a woman to his house and not cause a scandal?*

William hesitates again, embarrassment and surprise clouding his face. "Okay . . . I'm sorry I asked."

I match his hurt face with regret on mine, though I still can't comprehend how I could reasonably visit his apartment. Even worse, it's irritating William suggested it at all.

"Please, William, I need to go. Jeanne will be back soon, and I need to unpack." Another lie, and cruelly told at that as I slowly close the front door before he has a chance to respond.

There's silence on both sides of the door. Eventually slow footsteps tap down the hall, then I return to my new bedroom and flop down on the bed. Exhaling, I ponder again what on Earth William was thinking to invite me upstairs. Then snippets of conversations with my new friends replay, the bits where they talked about going places alone with a friend, boy or girl.

There are no such things as chaperones anymore, Elie. That's in the past!

So William wasn't being forward; he was perfectly reasonable. It was a welcoming gesture, and I swatted him coldly away. I moan with remorse.

Outside my window, high above the eastern horizon, a waxing half crescent moon stares down at me. The same moon stared at me in 1906, but not for the first time in the past six days have I felt at once such a similarity to my physical past and yet such a cultural distance.

19

Friday, September 1, 2006
Elie

The slacks are nearly unbearable. The clinging, the resistance to bending, being enveloped like a sausage. It's a ridiculous way to dress. And to think men have to wear these *pants,* as I hear them called instead of slacks, all the time. At least women still have the option in this century of wearing skirts.

But in the interest of fitting in, I acquiesce and bear it. Really, I'm grateful to have them, and the rest of the clothes which once belonged to Stephanie.

"Oh, those things are still in the bureau?" Jeanne had said when I mentioned them to her later on Wednesday night. "Dear me, I meant to donate those. I wish Stephanie had done it before she left, but. . . ."

"You mean she doesn't want the clothes?" I was incredulous, hopeful.

"No, she took everything she needed. Her parents do spoil her tremendously, you know, so she's always had more than what she needed. But they're still perfectly nice clothes! If you pile them into a box,

Elie dear, we can take them out first thing tomorrow morning. You can throw in her toiletries from the bathroom drawer as well."

"Oh no!" I couldn't help exclaiming. To waste them would be a sin, and worse for me because I would desperately love to wear them. "Do you think. . . ."

I had to quickly come up with a plausible story of why I'd want—and need—the clothes.

"Jeanne, do you think I could keep them? My parents were going to ship the rest of my clothes to me, you see, but I'm sure they haven't yet. This would save an awful lot . . . if you don't mind, of course."

Her eyes had become brilliant as lamps when she realized how much she'd help me. Clearly, I was beginning to deduce, Jeanne loved being grandmotherly, and I was bloody lucky for it.

So one of the most trivial yet most practical problems had disappeared, and now I find myself with more dressing choices than I've ever had. When I dressed myself this morning, I managed to look quite modern in my new blue jeans and white tee shirt, despite Stephanie's clothes hanging off my frame a bit much. I made do and tucked the shirt into my waistband. In my opinion, I look horrid, plain, and too masculine. I actually wished I had a lady's maid to check me to make sure I look appropriate before I left the apartment, due to my limited idea of what is "normal" now.

Well, if I show up somewhere looking odd, so be it. Live and learn, Elie—be brave.

Brave I am being, I know, but that didn't stop me from crying softly into my pillow—the flowery-smelling, cloud pillow—late last night, as I have the last seven nights. I should be feeling relief and calm and happiness at my newly stable situation, and I do, but I can't shake the frightening disorientation of not knowing exactly how I arrived here and if I can ever return to my old life.

And my family.

I laid awake for many minutes last night and wondered how they were faring without me. I hope they're missing me—I know they must be—but not knowing what's going on has been torturous. Being so far from my reality is searing me, but it's finally less lonesome. With the girls and William and now Jeanne, a life is starting to take shape around me.

Yet, that life is like a fragile shell that will crack and break around the volcanic yolk of my real, unresolved, enigmatic life.

Despite the upheaval, my Friday manages to be quite pleasant. Thanks to my Art and Architecture class running one and a half hours on Monday and Wednesday, I have no afternoon class on Friday. Neither do Lindsey, Isabelle, or Natalya, so we decide to take an exploratory walk after lunch.

"The view from Mont Royal is beautiful and quite breezy this time of year," says Isabelle. Much as I'd love to swap stories with her, of course I can't chime in with my long—outdated—knowledge of the place.

Dutifully sticking to my cover story, I play like an interested tourist—much like Natalya—and follow the crew up the mountain trail.

At the summit, an icebox breeze momentarily cancels the early September solar burning. Mont Royal is the one place in the city where you can reliably cool yourself down—unless you're wearing jeans apparently. With no air circulation up my legs and the thick weave heavy on my skin, I can't fathom why people wear these in September. Winter, perhaps.

"Elie, you're sweating!" exclaims Isabelle when she sees my damp forehead and watery beads rolling down my jawline. She offers me water from her bottle.

"I beg your pardon; it's absolutely disgusting, I know," I say in a pant. "I'm melting in these jeans. I can't wait to be well shod of them and back in a skirt!"

Lindsey laughs. "Yes, you're quite a fan of them. I say wear them—they're more feminine anyway. I suppose that's what girls wear in New Zealand, eh?"

"Yes, all the women, typically." *Rather, all the time, of course.* "This is my first pair of these things, and I can't understand why they're so bloody popular around here."

Isabelle shrugs. "Meh, it's just what people like. You don't have to follow trends. I wear skirts too; don't worry."

"In Russia only the old women in babushkas wear skirts. It's too cold, so us younger people are more practical and wear pants all the time," Natalya says. "It's not like warm New Zealand!"

"I suppose," I answer. "I'll wait 'til fall strikes, then."

We laugh and lollygag more at the plateau park, pointing at landmarks across the horizon, then walking through the wooded trails while we dissect our professors. Around three o'clock we head back down the mountain, walking down the stairs at the top of Rue Peel at des Pins. Down the hill we head, along the shaded eastern side of the street, until we hit Maisonneuve Boulevard. Isabelle wants to pop into a shop at the corner with Rue Stanley.

I absently troll through the racks, purposely not reading the price tags for fear of heart attack, but the other three try on several items. I feign interest as they parade the clothes; secretly I'm comparing my new wardrobe to what's in stores now. It seems Stephanie dressed somewhat plainer than this, but I suppose that'll help me blend in better. Again I count my fortuitous stars.

We leave the store, sans purchases, and walk south down Rue Stanley. Natalya is describing the old Tsarist palaces in Saint Petersburg, where she used to live. Though I'm fascinated, particularly by the architectural bits, a store on the left catches my eye.

A used book shop sits humbly between a parking garage and a cheap-looking shirt shop. In my mind I hear Professor Nagar telling his students to read Ernest Rutherford's books. I bet a shop such as this is the best place to find them, as I assume his works aren't popular in the mainstream. I can't imagine how they'd be interesting to anyone but me.

"Girls?" I interrupt Natalya as politely as possible. "Do you see that used bookshop across the street? Do you mind if I take a quick spin 'round it?"

They agree, and into the cozy shop we go, its blinds pulled mostly down against the late afternoon sun and its teetering shelves choc-a-block with tomes of all conditions.

"*Bonjour*," greets a rather elderly man sitting behind a tall cashier's desk. From his remote post in the corner of the store, his low voice rumbles clear across to the front door.

"*Bonjour, monsieur*," I respond in my New Zealand French accent.

"Good afternoon, ladies," he returns, knowing at once we're not local francophones, then turns right back to his task.

"Charming fellow," Isabelle whispers in my ear.

I shoot her a wide-eyed look, then mingle amongst the towers in search of the science section. The other girls follow me. It seems they think I'm heading toward an art or literature section because they look confused when I finally find the area marked "Physics and Biology" in the rear corner opposite the owner's desk.

"What in God's name are you looking for here, Elie? A bit of light nighttime reading?" Lindsey asks.

I blush but decide to tell most of the truth. I say I'm looking for a book by Ernest Rutherford to supplement what I'm learning in physics, as suggested by my professor. "I figure it'll most likely be here if anywhere."

"Hmm," Natalya says. "Sounds like you're really interested in physics. You sure you're really in the right major? Should we have you tested?"

For a moment I don't realize she's teasing me, but I recover and laugh it off. "Very funny. Perhaps I'm a bit too interested in it, yes. . . ." *You don't know how interested.* "But all the same, it's probably a good read, or at least I'll give it a go."

Suddenly the owner's large frame, even when stooped, covers our corner in shadow. "Can I help you find something in particular?" His eyes tell me he's bored and doesn't expect four youngish women to be big spenders in his shop, but that his curiosity and sense of obligation brought him over.

"Yes, sir, thank you kindly. I'm looking for a book by Ernest Rutherford, the physicist. Do you have . . .?" I trail off, realizing I have no idea what any of them are titled, nor how many Father wrote during his whole career.

"*By* Rutherford? We certainly have some written on him, but I don't have any written by the man himself. They'd be very old, you realize?"

"Yes . . . I imagine they would be. But your front window says you have rare books. I rather hoped you'd have one." I try to keep the desperation out of my voice, and instead it sounds accusingly stern.

The man stands up straighter. "Well. It does say that, yes. But we tend to focus on the more popular rare books, I'm sorry to tell you."

"Aha." I believe this man just told me my father wasn't important enough to have his books in this shop. That stings right into my chest—though I do see his point. Physics, no matter how popular to science devotees, is not something most people devour. I must be a special case, judging by my friends' opinions.

"Have you tried the McGill libraries? I'm sure they would have them. Perhaps the science library, even?"

"No sir, I hadn't thought they'd have it, actually. I assumed it'd be too old." I laughed. The irony of the situation amuses me. Father's books might have been in front of me the whole time!

Lindsey interjects, "Are you sure you wouldn't be able to get a copy here, in case the library doesn't have one?"

"I can make inquiries and keep my eyes open for such books, but I'm sorry that I can't put much time into obscure chases. I'm quite busy running this shop by myself now, what with the other owner not able to work anymore."

As he begins to shuffle back to his desk, Lindsey puts on a pout—clearly irritated by the old man's unwillingness to help me—but I rather see an opportunity instead.

"Sir," I stop him. "Did you say it's you running this shop alone? You must be awfully busy. Are you open only on the weekdays?"

"Hmph, I wish. No, we're open seven days a week, but it's getting harder for me to do it. I'll run myself into the ground like Claire did if I keep going like this."

"You could use some help, then?" I push, wondering not for the first time lately where I've summoned this forwardness.

"Of course I could use some help, but it's hard to find people who appreciate books and understand them. Seems it's only us old-timers who enjoy it and can handle it. Unless. . . ." He looks at me a second time, head cocked and appraising me.

"I could," I confirm. "How much help do you need?"

"*Bof*," he half-dismisses me. "Would a young lady like yourself really want to spend your weekends and nights in a dusty rot shop like this?"

"It's not rot, it's history. I love reading, and I'm an English student besides. It's sort of natural to like a place such as this, you know." *And I'm used to old things, though probably older than most everything in this shop.*

He ponders my response. I stand up straight to make myself look taller and hopefully older, more mature—as if I need that—with my chin tilting up a few degrees. My three friends stand on either side of me with wry smiles.

"Well, I don't suppose you'll do it for $7.75 an hour. I can only pay you minimum wage to start."

"That's more than enough." I swallow. "When can I start?"

For the first time, the man's grumpy jowls turn up into a semi-grin. "We have a deal then, Miss . . .?"

"Newton. Elie Newton."

"Elie, Bernie Wolfersheim. I suppose you can come by tomorrow at eleven—that's when we open. Oh, and don't spread the word around that you're working here; I'll be paying *under the table*, if you understand, at least to start." He lowers his head and his voice.

"Under the table?" I repeat, not understanding the term.

"Meaning I won't put your wages through Canada Revenue Agency, so I don't want anyone snitching."

Isabelle pokes my ribs. "He stills pay minimum wage, even without taxes taken out. It's a steal!"

I nod toward her, then Bernie. "Fantastic, sir. I'll see you tomorrow morning. And how long should I expect to be here?"

"Call me Bernie. I'm not an officer in the army, for God's sake. And you'll be here until six in the evening, so bring a lunch."

"Fine, Bernie. Goodbye then—and thank you," I say, trying to be as courteous as possible to this slightly rough old man.

"Yes, we'll see how it goes, eh? Eleven sharp tomorrow," he says as he turns back toward his desk.

We walk out of the place, and the rest of the girls congratulate me.

"Well done, Elie! Way to sniff out a job," Isabelle says.

"Yeah, well done you," Lindsey adds, "But what an ass he seems!"

"Lindsey!"

"Well he is, you have to admit."

"Maybe. But it's a job, and I need the money. Plus, it's a bookshop. How bad could that be?"

"Good, as long as you don't have to work next to him."

"Hopefully not after the first day." And I do hope that's true. I have a job, but what have I gotten myself into?

20

Saturday, September 2, 2006
William

The morning is quiet, as it usually is in our apartment. Evan is lounging like a zombie on the couch, per usual at this weekend hour. For a guy as intelligent as he is, he can stare blankly at the same spot for entirely too long; I like to think he's silently solving differential equations, but somehow I doubt it. I'm trying not to make too much noise in the kitchen as I set up the coffee pot to brew and toast an English muffin.

"Hey, Alain's coming up in a while. We're going to run through some numbers for work, but we'll be quiet. I don't want to wake you from your daytime slumber," I tease.

"Mmphf, yeah, eh? Ugh, I need to get some work done too," Evan says with a strong dose of reluctance. "Say, what are you guys doing now anyway? Isn't it a full moon now? Can't that gamma ray collector not read during a full moon?"

"Yeah, it's inactive for the full phase, but it was just a new moon. We're still trying to jive some anomalies in our model with their recent readings. We think we've made a logarithmic assumption somewhere that's throwing our curves off."

"Mmm, you don't want your curves thrown off," Evan agrees; I roll my eyes at his double entendre. "Say, why exactly can this VERITAS thing not measure during a full moon? How does it mess up gamma rays?"

It's early, but I can't resist teasing him. "Oh, is it time for a physics lesson? Did I miss that on my schedule? Hold on, let me find my little chalkboard and solar system model." I feign walking toward my bedroom.

"Haha, very funny," he says as he rubs sleep from his eyes. "I'm serious. That multi-million-dollar thing has to shut down just because it's a full moon?"

"It's actually fairly simple—even you could understand it. Just kidding, man. In all seriousness, during the five to six days the collector shuts down, the background level of light and reflected emissions is too high. It decreases the sensitivity of the detectors and fouls up the readings. And it also can have decreased sensitivity under cloudy skies."

"Hmm, interesting . . . so basically it's an ornery old woman?"

"Basically."

"But wasn't there a big storm out in the Southwest last week?" Evan asks. "How could you guys have readings from VERITAS if it was cloudy? Maybe there's your data problem."

I ponder that, trying to match the order of magnitude of the deviance from last week's data to weather-related bad data we'd seen previously. It might be a long shot, but it's worth investigating, or placing a call to the Arizona team at least.

How is an electrical engineer possibly right about this? "Huh. You could be right. . . . We'll take a look at it. Thanks, man!"

"Always here to help. I don't stare at the wall all the time."

"Really? I couldn't tell. Oh—there's Alain's knock."

"Don't let it get out, though. I can't have people think I do good work only to have them turn around and give me more work."

"I'll remember that," I say as I open the door for Alain.

"Ciao, bro. Evan, what's up?"

"Alain, hey." Evan has clearly slipped back into his groggy mode.

I lead Alain into the kitchen and pour us both a mug of coffee. After I prep my breakfast, I usher us both into my room where we can work without disturbing Evan. Sometimes I treat him like he's fourteen rather than twenty-four.

We spread out our sheets of printed data and notes, my cheap "wood" slab desk being spacious enough to seat us side by side and fit my laptop and our coffees. I open my mouth to start in on Evan's theory of weather derangement, but Alain holds up his hand to stop me.

"Will," he says, leaning back in his chair and crossing his long, outstretched legs. "That girl you like. . . ."

Like a scene right out of a Foghorn Leghorn cartoon, I give Alain a double take and say, "What? S-Say what?"

"That girl you like, the Frenchie from the library steps, remember?"

Of course he means Elie, who looked like a francophone based on her clothes. Alain doesn't know she's from New Zealand, but I also didn't think he realized I had a thing for her.

Truth be told, *I* didn't realize it until now.

"Uh, the girl from the library, yeah, I remember her, but why would you say I like her?"

He play acts a little bit, scratching his chin and contemplating the ceiling. "Let's see, you nearly drooled when you saw her, you had to concentrate as hard to talk to her as I do around Anna, and you've been ditsy the rest of the week. Clearly, she's been the only thing on your mind; ergo, you like her."

"Aha." Caught in my own school-boyish behavior. "Red-handed guilty. She's really pretty, you've gotta admit, but she's easy to talk to too."

"Oh, so you've talked to her since then, eh? *Fabuleux!*"

I nod, then pause, waiting for the expected interrogation and obsession over my interest. What comes instead takes me a bit by surprise.

"Well, *mon ami*, do you know she's an engineering student?" Alain's eyes have a mischievous gleam I'm not sure I trust.

"Um, I'm pretty sure she's an Arts student, an English major."

"You'd better check again because she's in Nagar's physics class, the one for first-year engineers. I saw her Tuesday at the first class."

Stunned, I try to remember exactly what Elie told me about her classes. She's taking a literature class, a Renaissance literature class, something about modern novels, and an architecture class. That's four, which would leave space for a final course. Why she'd take a class as difficult as physics is beyond me, but her dad *is* a physicist.

"You're sure it was her?"

"I remember that hair, yeah. She *is* beautiful, I'll give you that. I thought it was funny that you fell for a young physics student. Had to get off your high horse first," he says with a grin.

"I haven't fallen for Elie. We've just become friends—that's it, and all," I say. "And hey—why didn't you tell me this until now?"

"Whoa, Will, stop the accusations. I didn't think she was anything, but you've been in such a fog this week. I couldn't figure out what your deal was, but then I remembered how strange you acted when we saw that girl in the library, and I knew I saw her someplace else. It took 'til yesterday to realize it was in Nagar's class," Alain explains, and I relax.

"Hmm. You're sure it's her though—Elie Newton?"

He shrugs. "I don't know her name, but I can check the class list."

"Maybe . . . sounds like a stalker move, though. I can ask her the next time I see her."

"Ooh, look who's planning dates with her! You're finally moving on from the last girl." He punches my arm.

I stifle a gruff laugh. "Hardly. She's a friend. I helped her find a place to live. She moved in with Jeanne downstairs, actually."

"Sounds like a built-in date. . . ."

"She's just a friend, seriously. Anyway, bust out the file and let's run through these numbers."

Do I really believe that, her being no more than a friend? I'm certainly not going to tell Alain how I feel, mostly because I haven't sorted it out yet, but also because his teasing and gossip abilities are unparalleled. Well, whatever it is I need to figure out on that front, I need to figure out our VERITAS data first. I'll think about Elie tomorrow.

***

By Sunday afternoon, I can't take it any longer. I'm so curious about Elie taking a physics class I have to ask her. Before I know what my legs are doing, they're leading me out my apartment and down a flight of stairs. But as soon as I raise my hand to knock on Jeanne's door, I hesitate. After Elie's dismissal of me on Thursday, I'm not sure she actually wants to see me again. She'll think I'm a nut job for barging in unannounced, but then again how else would I get a hold of her? She doesn't have a cell phone, I don't have her email address, and I don't really know where to meet up with her on campus without looking like a stalker.

So I knock on the door. Jeanne's familiar shuffle sounds come through, and I'm saved from seeing Elie at the door right off. A moment later Jeanne's relaxed, kind face greets me.

"William! What a surprise! You're lucky to catch me; I'm about to run out and visit with a friend of mine across town."

"Hi, Jeanne," emerging from her hug. "Actually, I was looking for Elie. Is she in?"

"Oh, she's at work, dear. She won't be back until after five, I'm afraid," she says.

"Work? Already? Where?" I'm so shocked, I can't form full sentences. Elie really can't stop surprising me.

"It's awfully quick, eh? She came home Friday evening and told me she had a job at a used bookshop downtown. Quite fortuitous, I understand."

"I wonder what shop," I muse, more to myself than to Jeanne.

"You can ask her tonight if you'd like. Why don't you come over for tea after dinner? Seven thirty will be about right," she says.

It's really luckier than I'd hoped, having an invitation to come over from Jeanne. "Thanks, Jeanne. You don't mind?"

"Of course not, dear. Any friend of my Stephanie is always welcome here, and now any friend of Elie is too. I know it's been awhile since you were here with her best friend—I'm sorry, I know you don't like being reminded of her—but I still like having you over for tea, Will."

Smiling more at her kindness than the memories, I recall the many evenings I spent in Jeanne's apartment, sipping tea or playing Scrabble with the three of them. As much as I regret dating Stephanie's friend, the best thing it gave me, oddly enough, was a friendship with Jeanne.

"I appreciate that, Jeanne. I hope things are working well with Elie."

"Oh, yes, very well. She's so quiet I've already forgotten she's moved in, but she's pleasant to talk to, and approachable too. It's quite a refreshing change from my former lonely life here, I'll tell you that, my boy." Her face has brightened at the mere mention of Elie, and I know she's already had quite an influence on Jeanne.

"Glad to hear. I had a hunch you two would get along like long-lost friends."

"It is quite like that, yes. Now Will, I'm going to be late if I don't skedaddle now." She hauls her pocketbook onto her shoulder and follows me out the door as I thank her again for the invitation and promise to see her later.

In five hours I'm back at Jeanne's apartment, though it's felt like ten. I didn't make much progress on my homework for my high energy physics class, but I figure I have until Tuesday to finish it—though I've been forming a better idea for what to do on Tuesday afternoon. Hopefully, I'll be able to concentrate on the work by tomorrow night; yesterday and today I've been restless and distracted—like Alain said, I guess.

Not four seconds after I knock on the door, Elie's pulling it open to let me in. Her smile is full of joie-de-vivre.

"William! Hi—come in for tea," she says, pronouncing both "hi" and "tea" liltingly with two syllables. She ushers me in with a wide sweep of her hand.

"Thanks. I see you're settling in well. Looks like you own the place already."

She giggles, more an overjoyed laugh than that of an immature schoolgirl.

"Yes, I suppose I have. Jeanne's awfully nice to be with."

I nod, then give Jeanne a kiss on the cheek when I enter the kitchen.

"Oh, Will! Be careful—don't make me spill our tea!"

"Sorry, sorry. Here, let me take that tray in."

We settle down on the white couches, and Jeanne pours us tea in her delicate, flowered cups. She and Elie take milk in theirs; I like my mine plain. Jeanne's laid out a small plate of red grapes and digestive cookies, and I munch on some of each while I listen to the two women chat about how well their weekend has passed. It's increasingly clear to me what a smart match this was; I'm so relieved. The last thing I'd want is for Elie to be stuck with an old lady she doesn't get along with, but I suppose even that'd be better than throwing money at a hotel room or finding a lonely studio apartment in a country you just moved to.

"And the room is perfect for me," Elie continues. "I went to bed with a wedge of moon filling my window and woke up this morning to the most peaceful sunrise streaming through. It's incredible being up so high and seeing so much of the city from there."

"Yeah, this building is pretty fantastic for that. I have a west view and love it. And it was a thick waxing moon, yeah. Full moon'll come in six days," I say.

I'm sure she really cares about when the moon is full, idiot.

"Aha, interesting."

"Ha," I laugh with self-deprecating sarcasm, "I'm sure it is."

"No, no," Elie insists. "It gives me . . . bearings, I suppose."

I have no idea why she'd say that; it's not like she needs to track it for work like I do—she's really an intriguing girl, to care about the moon phase—but I don't want to pursue this path with Jeanne here. It's suddenly too personal.

"So, Elie, Jeanne said you're working at a bookshop downtown?"

"Yes, it's a really charming little place, Odyssey Books on Stanley. I can't believe the nerve I had to push for the job, especially when there was no advertisement for one," she says, then goes on to explain how she happened upon the shop and then persuaded Bernie to take her on so he could work less days a week.

"It's not much of a place, but it's chock full of books in and around and on top of every bookcase. Bernie's method of storage is certainly curious, not to mention his organizational choices."

"Sounds like a mess. Can you make sense of it?"

"Oh, it's a clean place, but a bit chaotic. Some major subjects he breaks down into the most minute subcategory, but others are a mass of small topics—some lined up by author's last name, some by topic. It needs a major overhaul," Elie laments.

"But dear, he's how old?" Jeanne asks.

"Goodness, he must be over seventy."

"Oh! Well, at his age perhaps he doesn't have the energy to reorder every shelf, no matter how compact the shop is," Jeanne says, as if she understands his plight perfectly.

"That's exactly why I'm ideal help for him. He can't or may not want to put the effort toward doing it, but I can barely stop myself from tidying up every inch." Elie laughs. "I hope I haven't confused things so much that he'll curse me on Monday morning!"

We laugh with her, joking about a confused old man in his own store who comes in on Monday to find the place unrecognizable and named "Elie's Odyssey."

"Maybe you should take your time with the changes, Elie," I suggest. "Sometimes the less-than-young don't like change too much."

"Oh, I haven't done anything drastic yet—just put things back in alphabetical order that have been rustled through by customers and put some lost items back where I think they belong. I do have ideas for changing a few areas though."

"You'll talk to Bernie first though, won't you dear?" Jeanne asks.

"Of course! He's not the most effusive fellow though. I can tell I don't upset him per se, but on Saturday he was there during my whole shift and almost testing me with roughness. But by the end of the day I got the feeling he was relieved I can take some hours off his load."

"That's wonderful, dear. Was anything confusing for you by being different from things in New Zealand?" Jeanne, ever concerned, puts her tea down to hold Elie's hand.

Elie hesitates and reddens a bit. "Well . . . I didn't understand the payment system well. I-I didn't get the *credit card* thing." She emphasizes "credit card" like Dr. Evil naming a "laser."

"Do you mean the machine to run the cards, is it different here?" I ask.

"Er—sort of. Y-Yes. I'd never seen that . . . kind of it before. Poor Bernie had to explain the whole process like I was child; he must have thought I was the daftest person. Thankfully, by the afternoon, I got the hang of it and didn't look like a newborn baby every time someone tried to pay for a book with something other than money."

"Well, a credit card is also money," I say.

Elie's eyes narrow and forehead wrinkles in doubt. "Yes . . . I suppose. But all that's cleared up, and I'm good to go now. And even better, there were definitely some slow periods in the day when I could get some reading done for my classes. Bernie suggested that at one point—and pulled out a book himself around four o'clock."

I can tell she sees the job as pretty much ideal for her, and I can't say I disagree. "How many hours a week will you be working?"

"Quite a few," Elie confesses. "Although I'm sure I can handle it. I'll be heading over a bit after my last class on Friday, at one, and work until eight in the evening. Then he gave me all the Saturday hours, eleven to six, and most Sundays, from noon to five."

Not many undergraduates would take on that many hours, even if they're taking Arts classes. I'm amazed, and I shift my body backward into the cushions as if hit by a shockwave.

"That's your whole weekend, Elie! That won't do much for your social life." Another second later, I realize I don't really like what it'll do to my social life and how I might want to have her in it.

"He's right, Elie," Jeanne chimes in. "I know you need money, dear, but I don't want your grades to suffer if you spend too much time at a bookshop."

"True, it is a lot of hours, but I can do some work while I'm there. And Bernie seems to need the break. I don't mind it—I'm even excited by it—and yes, the money is a bonus."

"If you're sure, Elie," I shrug. "As long as you have some free time at night, that'll be fine—for homework, I mean." I don't mention the plans my subconscious won't stop spinning.

"I'm sure, yes."

Our tea is gone by now, as is the plate Jeanne set up. She stands up and winks at me, then places the dishes onto the tray and ambles back to the kitchen.

Now it's just Elie and I alone on opposite couches. Even with Jeanne in the next room, and it open to the living room at that, the space feels immediately tighter. I remember how she felt Wednesday night about not wanting to be alone with me. We both shift in our seats and look out the expansive windows at the deep mauve, gold, and sapphire shades of dusk.

"Listen, Elie," I begin, "I'm sorry about the other night, when I invited you to our place. I don't want you to get the wrong idea of what I meant."

Her face turns the slightest shade of pink, then she waves my words away. "Thank you for apologizing.

I'm sorry to have shut the door in your face. I-I think I misunderstood, yes."

If it wasn't for her smile telling me we're fine, I wouldn't be sure we were on the same page. Yet I let it go and change tack. "So . . . your classes are going well?"

"Yes, quite. They're simply amazing, to be honest. I'm not used to this openness and informality in my instruction, but I find I'm learning more than I ever have."

"Oh—I had no idea Canada was so different than New Zealand. But you make it sound almost primitive there," I say, then instantly realize I've offended her. "I didn't mean to imply New Zealand is in the Stone Age. But sometimes you make it sound like it's stuck in the turn of the century."

Elie stiffens, eyes unblinking. She's nearly paled and obviously speechless—*great job offending her again, Will. Just stop talking now.*

Or not.

"I'm sorry, Elie. I didn't mean to say that. I know you love your home." Maybe that will save face.

She shrugs, surprisingly, and says, "No, it's quite all right. I've never heard anyone put it in those words is all. Things are a bit old-fashioned, you could say. But. . . ."

Elie's trailed off, I guess not sure what else to say. I don't know either—although thank God she has enough class not to admonish me—so I change the subject.

"Well, ahem, I heard from my friend Alain you're taking a physics class."

"Your friend . . .? Right, Alain Proulx, from Professor Nagar's class. He's the teaching assistant, isn't he?"

"Yeah. So, you *are* in the class?"

"Yes, Tuesday and Thursday mornings at ten. The professor's fantastic. I've already learned so much, and it's only been a week!" Her voice has raised and quickened with excitement.

"Oh, good—yeah, Nagar's great." I'm tempted to tell her Nagar is my mentor and the leader of the VERITAS program, which I had already told her about, but I'd rather hear her talk.

"But why are you taking a physics class if you're majoring in literature?"

"Oh, it's only for fun—an elective," she says, dismissing the class as if a homemaking course from middle school.

"An elective? Most people who major in engineering dread that class, and no one else ever takes it. Why would you?"

"Why not? I like physics, even though I'm not a science student."

"I guess. . . . As long as you enjoy it." Now that I see Alain was right—and she really does like the class on top of it—I'm ready to take a chance and act on my hunch. Remembering her asking me about Rutherford a few days ago, I ask, "So I don't suppose you'd like a tour of the Rutherford Museum over on campus, would you?"

"Would I? Definitely! Professor Nagar mentioned it's up in the Rutherford Building, and I wanted to check it out but wasn't sure exactly where it is and when I could go." Elie's almost breathless now and as wide-eyed as ever.

"We can go as early as Tuesday afternoon, if you're up for it."

"Absolutely. I'll be ready."

"I'll need to give the curator a call because he usually gives tours by appointment only. If he can't be there, maybe he'll let me take you around myself. I know the experiments almost as well by now."

"As long as that doesn't put you out, William. I don't want to burden you with taking a silly literature student through a physics museum, as keen as I am to see it."

"You're not silly, Elie, and not a burden. Besides, as a physics student you have every right to visit." I'm about to say I like spending time with her, that I want to get to know her better, but hold back. I'm sure Alain would be pressing me to push myself on her, but I know I have to play it cool for once—maybe be friends for a while. Maybe things will work out if we start out that way.

"I appreciate you chaperoning me there. I'm sure you'll be a perfect descriptor of the exhibits," she says with a small grin.

"I'll try, at least. Anyway, I'm sure we'll have fun. I can meet you at the Prince Arthur gate after your class, say two thirty?"

"Perfect! I'll be there."

We hear Jeanne finishing her fussing in the kitchen, then drying her hands on a towel. As she starts walking toward us, I stand up.

"Leaving already, Will?" Jeanne asks, disappointment and fatigue mixing in her voice.

"I should, Jeanne—schoolwork, you know. Thanks for the tea."

"Anytime, dear. You know you're always welcome."

I hug her goodbye, then say quietly to her, "And thanks for taking good care of Elie here. I think she needs it."

"It's nothing, dear, but she's doing just fine. That girl is made of something tough, that's for sure."

I squeeze her shoulders softly, then turn to Elie, still seated, her long white skirt making her disappear into the couch. "See you Tuesday, Elie."

"'Til then. . ."

21

Tuesday, September 5, 2006
Elie

"This is really the experiment that got the ball rolling for him, success-wise. It's a bit obscure and underappreciated now," William says, pointing to an unimpressive conglomeration of coils and traps inside a glass case.

"Aha," I say, more from recognition than being awed. I've seen this lay in Father's lab for years and heard him explain it proudly to me—once in exaltation after he set it up and again a few years later when I was intelligent enough to understand its significance.

"You know about this?" One of his eyebrows is cocked.

"Yes—er, I read about it, a long time ago, back home." I chide myself for letting my thoughts show so clearly. I need to be more nonchalant if I'm going to hide from William how much I know about Father.

"The national hero back in New Zealand, I see." He shrugs. "Anyway, it's not much to look at, but at the time it was remarkable. Rutherford managed to measure a time interval of a hundred-thousandth of a second, which was incredible back then. It's purely mechanical of course, though now we can't conceive of doing this with anything less than an electrical device. It's a far cry from an atomic clock, but it was its ancestor, you could say."

"Right . . . time intervals . . . interesting. . . ."

"Your eyes are glazing over." He laughs. "Moving on!"

"No, no—I was lost in thought. Please continue." At his use of the word "time" I connect my own time travel with Father's experiments. I hadn't thought before of him working on anything to do with time. *Was one of his apparatus capable of sending something through time? Perhaps by accident?*

"*Oh*-kay. Though it's weird he developed something like this when you consider how much his later experiments had to do with nuclear physics, this was his background. It seems almost juvenile, but in reality it was as impactful as anything else he conceived."

I nod mechanically, following along after him as he leads me past the display cases with their orderly labels and logical layout. It's all here, all the work I knew Father to have completed up until August 1906, but it looks so *old.* It's dusty, faded, slightly rusty, and unmistakably tinged with age. That's what shocks me the most as I tour the museum, not the fact that Father has an honest-to-God museum—albeit just two small rooms—devoted to his legacy. William's only shown me half of it, but my initial impression still lingers. I've stepped temporarily back into the past, *my past*, by entering this museum, except this past looks ancient instead of holding my contemporary memories.

Suddenly the gravity of being wrenched through one hundred years of time feels very, very real, and the time very, very lost and gone.

William pauses and looks at me, but I can tell his thoughts are purely on Father's achievements. "When you think about everything else Rutherford either worked on directly, contributed to, or oversaw—from sonar and radar to splitting the atom—"

"I beg your pardon?" I ask, startled out of my own reverie.

"Splitting the atom. It was Cockcroft and Walton who were credited, but they were directed by Rutherford, who no doubt guided them extremely closely."

I stand open-mouthed—dumbly, I'm sure. "I-I didn't—"

"You didn't realize he was involved with that, eh? Yeah, no one ever credits his work, unless they're physicists or really understand the history."

Luckily for me, William doesn't understand it's really that I can't conceive of splitting the atom itself rather than Father's role in it. The more I'm seeing in this museum and hearing from William, the more I realize what a prolific and famous scientist my father is.

"That's simply amazing. . . ."

"It was, yeah. And of course it wouldn't have been conceivable if he hadn't discovered and described the positive nucleus via the gold-foil experiments here in 1905 to 1906," William continues.

"Oh?" This time I manage to keep my jaw from slacking right down to my pink silk top.

"Not only were they ground-breaking, but they became—as I'm sure you know—what he was most famous for."

To think—my disappearance was around the same time Father was embarking on his most revolutionary discovery! I was there to see it!

"His legacy was already being established by the time he began those trials, first with mica sheets and then with a slice of gold foil only a few atoms thick. After his death, he was more singularly remembered for steering researchers down the right path regarding the nucleus overall. Men like Niels Bohr, who actually studied and worked under Rutherford as well, owe their success directly to Rutherford's prior work."

For me, these facts are earth-shattering, mind-blowing, and dearly personal. This is my father he's talking about, and in the past tense too. As William let out the words "his death," I literally felt my chest tighten and cramp. Suddenly an anvil is crushing me into the floor, making me avail all my strength to keep upright. His *death* . . . Father is *dead*, in this reality, in this world, where I'm standing right now.

Of course he should be, in William's lifetime, because no one could live so far into their hundreds, but the miniscule but existent kernel of hope I'd kept alive that he was somehow here in 2006—even though all rational thought told me over and over it couldn't be true—is now as gone as my entire past life. Somehow, cruelly, I am to go on while he is unmistakably dead.

"And here in these smaller cases are just some letters and mementos and such of his. It's boring compared to the setups, so we can go right to his later and more exciting experiments over—"

William stops short when he sees I'm not following him, but I can't help myself from reacting to the letters.

It's the handwriting that catches my eye—and my breath. I reach up to grasp a note, but the glass is there to protect and preserve his words. There, as if it was lifted just yesterday from his writing desk, is a letter from Father to Otto Hann. It's yellowed and wispy—very fragile—but it's *his.* My first finger strikes the glass, and it's as close to Father as I've felt since I left him.

"Elie?" William is standing a few feet from me, awkwardly watching my frozen expression. "Elie? Are you okay? Is it really that interesting?"

"I—it's—" I croak, then swallow, but my mouth is so *dry,* and there's a fat lump that won't wash down. I crane my head closer to the glass, partly to read the letter better but mostly to shade my face from him. I can't let him see my face.

Why did I think I could keep it together when going through this place?

"Elie, what's wrong?" William takes a few steps toward me and reaches for my arm.

I use my other hand to erase a small teardrop from the corner of my right eye, my emotion betraying my attempts to bury my reactions.

"I'm fine, I'm fine. This is all incredible." I laugh quickly, more to fool my senses into changing their direction than anything. "It's so old, and all right here for anyone to read. Wherever did they find all these objects?"

He shrugs, apparently relieved I'm just engrossed in the exhibit. "From his estate, I guess. His stuff from his time as Physics Chair at McGill—the apparatus not cannibalized for newer setups—sat in storage for half a century until someone decided to do something proper with it. It took until 1967 for this to actually open, if I recall."

"My goodness. . . . This has been sitting for an awfully long time, then. I'm sure it won't work anymore, eh?"

"Well, you'd be surprised at how hardy a lot of this old equipment can be. Things used to be built to last, unlike nowadays. I wouldn't be surprised if we could fire up one of these bad boys and burn some radium," William says, eyes alight with excitement only a physicist would feel at that prospect.

I laugh with honesty this time. "Yes, he did have things built with quality in mind. No use making something if it's going to break on the way to the lab," I joke; I could be quoting Father himself.

William chuckles as well. "That's happened to me actually. . . . Anyway, here's some more of his, er, personal effects, in this case here if you want to see them. This is just photos, mostly of his assistants but one or two of his family too."

He's turned away from me now, facing the second low case with the photos. His hand points where his body is headed, toward a photo I instantly recognize and hope he'll turn away from.

It's of our whole family, with some friends of my parents, on holiday in Scotland when I was about nine.

Please don't let William recognize me, oh please God!

"Here's one of him and Soddy, a graduate student under him who was pretty smart. And here's one with his wife Mary and daughter Eileen and their family. . . ." He turns to me, amused. "Wow, your name is the same as his daughter's. Humph; I'd forgotten that was her name."

I'd laugh again, but I'm too shocked to move a single muscle of my face, so I only nod stupidly. A chill wholly opposite to the season wracks my limbs, and I swear I can hear my grey cotton skirt rustling along with it.

"Funny, you even look a little like her," he continues, more seriously this time. "Your high cheekbones are the same, just like Rutherford's too. And your hair parts that way from your forehead too, like the top of a heart. You could almost be related."

"Augh—" I say, or rather groan. It's obvious to me, and I can't believe William to be daft enough not to realize the truth. I need to steer him away, to continue our tour of the museum, anything, but my feet are nailed to the oak planks beneath me.

"And look!" William is pointing to a caption below another photo, one of Mother and Father. His head is close to the display case, studying the photos intently though he'd dismissed them earlier. "This one says, 'Mary Rutherford, née Mary Newton.' Your last name is the same as hers!"

"Mmm, yes."

He turns to me, curiosity circling his eyes. I can see his brain—no less intelligent than my father's students', at least—has come to the conclusion I dread to hear. "Are you, are you—"

My head spinning, my brain reeling from one thing to another to say to him to distract him from the obvious truth. The jig is up, as Father's beloved detective novels would say. There's no use keeping up the charade any longer, especially to him. He'd have found out eventually anyway.

"Yes. I am." There, it's done. Said. Out loud.

William's eyes widen to his ears, then narrow back in confusion. "A relative? A granddaughter? No, great-granddaughter?" He's mentally calculating what generation from the great Ernest Rutherford my age would place me in.

But I'm the one who miscalculated. He didn't come to the right conclusion, and now I've given myself away!

My face pales as my eyes crimp shut, but not before I see him turn back to the photograph from Scotland so he can study the girl's—my—face.

"But you, you look *just* like his daughter. It's uncanny, really, the more I look at her. She's half your age, probably, but I swear this could be you in this picture."

I lift my eyelids. Fear and resignation course through me. I see, finally, incredulity laced with a touch of fear on William's face.

This time it's him who can barely squeak out a word. "Are you—? Can it be? Eileen? Elie?" He turns back and forth from the photograph to me, unable to believe what his eyes tell him is true.

Almost apologetically I say, "I didn't think a photograph of me would be here. I thought it would only have Father's experiments. I didn't think—"

William takes two quick steps backward and bumps into a wall cabinet, rattling a set of glass vacuum tubes and the case doors themselves. Recovering with agility, he steadies his feet below his hips while reaching outstretched arms toward my shoulders. "No, no. That's, that's not quite possible. It's been a hundred years. . . ."

I half cough, half laugh. "Yes, exactly, hasn't it." The anvil has mercifully been removed from my person, and suddenly I realize I can speak cogently again. "I don't know how it's possible, but I am Eileen. *That* Eileen. In the flesh."

Reaching my hands to grasp his, which are now gently covering my shoulders, apparently testing their existence, I then pull them down between us.

"Oh, my God. I'm hallucinating, aren't I?" he asks, looking pale himself.

I shake my head, smiling with a tinge of sadness. "No, and neither am I. Why don't we get some fresh air? It's awfully stale in here, and I owe you an explanation."

* * *

Ten minutes later, we're sitting side by side on a minimalist teak bench nestled in a primly attended garden down the hill from the Rutherford Physics Building. We could be two people discussing our day's classes, or debating politics perhaps, but instead I've revealed a set of circumstances to him that would seem inconceivable if William hadn't the photographic proof to corroborate what sounds like a Jules Verne tale come to life.

I've described every moment from that fateful Friday afternoon to how I've come to collect my new classes, job, and way of life. William has sat silently through it all, looking only at my face while listening intently. His expression tells me he believes every word I say, yet the scientist in him can't understand how it was possible. Once I finish and fall silent myself, he opens his mouth to comment.

"Putting aside for the moment why and how you arrived here, I have to say that I can't believe you're holding up as well as you are. I don't get how you're not catatonic at the shock of a hundred years' change. No wonder you seemed a bit . . . I don't know, *confused* about some really commonplace things over the last few days. I chalked it up to you being a foreigner."

I incline my head in appreciation. "Thanks for understanding. It's been a big shock, yes. And then. . . ." I can't quite put this into words. "And then going to the museum today was harder. I don't know what I expected—to see Father's things as I remember them from a week ago, new and crisp and clean—but everything there looked like it was pulled from an ancient archeology dig. Dirty, dusty, disused—so *dead*." I scrunch my eyes, then lower my head to clear those images from my memory.

"I'm so sorry, Elie. I didn't quite realize until now that you're all you have from that time, and that everyone else is . . . gone."

I swallow with effort, fighting the emotion that surged back in those rooms. "I don't know how seeing those letters and that photo affected me so severely, but it's as if the past week and a half are compressing into this one moment. I've put aside some of the anxiety and fear that peaked when I first arrived here while I've been trying to put together a substitute life in the meantime—trying to pretend, I suppose, that everything is all right—until I can figure out how to get back home. But seeing my father's present now so clearly in the past smacks me in the face; I can't hide behind my ersatz life forever. And now you know the truth too."

"I guess you're not alone now—that's the one bonus."

"Yes, and I thank you for not thinking I'm a crazy ranting lady claiming to be from the past."

"Crazy? Are you kidding, Elie? This is incredible! It's amazing and ridiculously fantastic! I've met someone who's traveled in time!" William's eyes are practically glittering emeralds now.

"Ha—a time traveler. I don't even know how it happened."

"No, me neither. . . . You can guess I have a million questions for you about that moment in your dad's lab, and I want to explore the basement of the library, but for now I need to just absorb this."

I sigh, sensing I can share this burden with him but still weighed down by the sure sense of loss of my life as I've always known it. I must be showing this clearly on my face because William immediately swings one leg over the bench to completely face me, takes my near hand in both of his, and says earnestly, "But you're the one who needs help adjusting, not me. And I want to be the one to help you do that. If you don't mind, of course. I mean, I'd like to help you with anything you need."

His intimate gesture, his touch to my hand, is more forward than I'm accustomed to, but instead of recoiling, I let the sensation flow through me. I like it. Sharing this revelation with William has made me feel closer to him than I've ever felt to anyone except my parents.

Oddly, this sentiment brings up thoughts of Ralph. Why I want William to know about him, I'm not sure, but my ingrained propriety compels me to be upfront with him about more than just my immediate past.

"There's a few more things you should know about me, William."

He cocks one eyebrow up, then studies the daisies in front of us. "More?"

"I'm slated to marry someone. At least, that's the impression both of my parents have given me, and the man's hinted at it quite strongly himself."

William looks up sharply, a look of recognition flickering in his eyes.

"Already?"

"Yes, quite. Well, I know twenty can be a bit young to get married in this day and age, but in . . . *my time* . . . it's quite normal." I hesitate to let my true feelings show through to this man whom I barely know, yet know I can pour my whole heart out to. "Not that I'm keen to marry him, but it seems already set in a way—well, that is to say it *was* set, until I landed myself here!"

We both chuckle at that truth, me a bit more sadly than him. William's expression is still a bit quizzical, however.

"No, I wasn't thinking you're too young to get married. There are plenty of people who get married around twenty, sometimes because they have to, if you know what I mean. It's just that. . . ." Now it's him who hesitates, holding something back from me. He closes his mouth and twists his torso in apparent discomfort. *What is bothering him?*

"What is it? Please, tell me."

"It's just that I know a little more about your life than you do—your future, that is. This is too weird, like I'm reading tea leaves or something."

"What?!" I demand again, dying to know what my future holds—*held*—in store for me.

William sputters out: "I know about Ralph Fowler. I know all about him."

Every muscle in my body stops moving. *Does my future involve Ralph more than I hoped?*

"You did marry him. Or, rather, you *will* marry him. Or . . . you would have married him if you were still in your past," William attempts to explain my future, clearly getting confused the more he speaks. "Okay, I'll put it this way. According to what I've read about Ralph Fowler, you married him in 1909. I researched his life a bit for an undergraduate paper I wrote on a math theory a few years ago. I can't remember all the details, but I do know that you both lived in Cambridge for a while because he published a few papers while at Trinity College."

These revelations about my life, which I have yet to live, of course, shake every fiber of my being. *I married Ralph?! How did I allow that to happen? Did I have no choice, in the end? Could I no longer avoid him? Or did Mother and Father force me?* I stare off into the distance beyond William, my face probably contorted into disbelief and panic. *No, they wouldn't have forced me. I must have made the decision—but how? Could I really have had no other option? Or was the pressure too great to put it off? Oh my goodness, to have been unable to escape that. . . .* Suddenly I wonder what else William knows about my life.

"What else can you recall? Where did we go after Cambridge? Why did we leave here?" My mind starts spinning with more questions, and possibilities about my life sprout out into too many directions at once for me to make sense of them all.

William narrows his eyes at me in concern. "Are you sure you're feeling okay enough to hear about this now, Elie? You look kind of pale. If I make you go into shock. . . ." He reaches out to take my hands, perhaps trying to steady my shaking nerves.

It works; I'm surprisingly comforted, and know I have the strength to hear more. "Please—I want to know—it *is* shocking, to hear one's future with no doubt as to its veracity, but I can handle it."

He takes a deep breath before speaking again. He squeezes my hands gently; it makes me even more ready to hear the rest.

"Well, your father became the chair of physics at Manchester University in 1907, and Ralph took a post in Cambridge—maybe to be in the same country as you, I don't know. You'd lived there for a while, and Ralph fought as an officer in the First World War—"

This elicits instant confusion from me. I cock my head and open my mouth to ask a question. William holds up his hand and continues speaking.

"I'll explain to you later; I forgot there's so much you don't know about the last hundred years' history. Needless to say it was a very big and very bloody war in Europe from 1914 to 1918. Well, Ralph fought for the British and was in a battle in Gallipoli, Turkey, in early 1915. He was wounded pretty badly and sent home to you to recover. Soon after he started out of Portsmouth doing ballistics work—huge advances, actually. Anyway, a few years later, right after the war ended, Ralph moved back to Cambridge. He contributed a lot to the study of mathematics and astronomy, as it turned out. Actually, your father returned to Cambridge as well, the next year, to the Cavendish Laboratory so Ralph wouldn't be alone." He paused, wide-eyed, guilty, then started talking again at double speed. "Your father made an incredible run of discoveries; you wouldn't believe it—well, you probably would, given your father's an absolute genius. . . ."

"Yes, quite. . . ." I answer absently, my eyes staring deep in William's. My brain zeroes into his phrase "so Ralph wouldn't be alone." "Father couldn't be anything *but* successful. . . . Yet what did you say a moment ago, about Ralph moving back to Cambridge? And I . . .?"

William twists uncomfortably again and looks down at his hands, still clasped around mine. A moment of painful silence echoes between us while he seems to struggle to find a way to answer me. Slowly looking up to meet my gaze again, his eyes and mouth droop regretfully as he grips me almost as if trying to hold me together. Cautiously, deliberately, he finally replies.

"Ralph... returned alone to Trinity. Well, almost alone. Your four children were with him and their caretaker."

Four children! But where was I? I can't fathom a reason why I wouldn't have been with my own children. Four!

"Elie, you didn't make it. . . ." William is definitely pained when delivering those words.

"What do you mean, I 'didn't make it?' Why would I abandon my own children? And my husband, little as I probably loved him," I ask, still not comprehending a possible explanation. That last sentence, of course, I merely hope is true.

"You . . . had *died* at that point, Elie." My heart stops, as do William's words. His eyes are wide as he continues telling the past—my future—and probably the most gut-wrenching truths he's ever had to give someone in his life. It certainly is the most gut-wrenching news I've ever heard, worse than the news that I'd actually had to marry Ralph—in one year.

But I'm still not sure I'd heard William correctly. "I had died?" I repeat what he had said very distinctly not ten seconds previously.

"Yes . . . all very unexpected, of course, because you were still young. I don't think you were thirty yet." He did half a second of mental math. "No, you were still twenty-nine. It was a complication from childbirth."

I have only nine years to live. . . .

My father will be devastated. . . .

Four children and not living to see them grow up. . . .

I have nine years to live . . . that is, of course, if you get back to your life and let it play out like that, silly girl.

It's too much to take in, too many painful thoughts slamming my skull from all directions like my father's alpha particles shooting around his vacuum tubes. I can't comprehend the truth anymore; my brain is on overload and my vision zigzags.

I must have started swaying because William is off the bench in milliseconds and reaching forward to catch me from collapsing. His arms are suddenly around my shoulders, then one hand picks my head up as another is at my waist and pushing me carefully upright again. I moan ever so softly, not out of faintness but due to the truth finally registering in my body. All at the same time I want to hear more—every detail, in fact. I didn't envision my future being too difficult to handle, but evidently it is.

"Elie, Elie, I'm really sorry," William pleads. "I didn't mean to put you through this so bluntly. I should have eased you into the truth. I didn't realize—I didn't think—" He almost chokes on his words; his concern for me is surprising and pulls me, slightly, out of my own pain and shock. His caring touches me, and I wonder why a near stranger, if I can still consider him as such, would indeed be troubled so much for me.

"It's . . . okay, I'm okay," I reassure him, and I believe my own words. His holding me comforts me enough to be sure of my own vitality, even if I know what my future holds in a mere nine years. "Really, William, I'll be all right."

"Are you sure? I'm sure I just took years off your life telling you that." He stops and shakes his head, aware of the irony of what he said and surely berating himself.

I laugh and nod, a smile finally returning to my face. "You sure know how to make a girl laugh."

He offers a rueful grin of his own and reaches up to push my fallen hair out of my face. I shiver, tickled by a current of energy electrifying the air between us. "Anytime, my lady." He chuckles, then pretends to clock the side of his head.

"But seriously, Elie, I've probably stressed you out more than you need right now. As if you don't have a million other things to worry about."

I stay silent for a few moments, not to make him feel guilty but more to gather my own thoughts. The entire situation is incredible—my transplantation, getting acclimated to a new century, and hearing my own future told to me over one hundred years after it occurred but before I lived it. But would I live it out?

"William, do you think that's still my future?"

"What else would it be?"

"I'm not sure—I'm not an expert on fortune-telling or time-travelling—but I wonder if your research brought up any stories of me traveling back and forth in time."

Slowly his solemn face turns into an amused grin. "Now you know how to make someone laugh, Elie! Of course I didn't read about you time-traveling. People don't do that."

"Except me."

"Well, yes, except you. And you might be the only one in the world to have done so, unless this is as big a secret as Roswell."

I pause, trying to match that reference to some sort of physics achievement I'd heard about from Father.

"Never mind," he says, laughing again. "It's from the fifties. It was a supposed secret the US Government hid about an alien spacecraft, more a conspiracy theory than anything."

My mind can't take many more fantastical stories, so I let that sail over my head and continue my theory.

"Well, if you didn't read anything about me disappearing for God-only-knows how long into the future and reappearing in time to marry Ralph, maybe it didn't happen. In that history, I mean. What if I've now changed that history, and my life won't happen like that?" *And I won't die so young.*

"Maybe, maybe. . . . Is it possible to change the course of history?"

"How should I know, really? How could either of us know? But I do suppose there's a way to find out."

"Research your life again?"

"Why not? If my life happened about a hundred years ago, technically—or at least started about a hundred years ago—certainly books would reflect that change in course." I'm hopeful as I say this; I want it to say I lived, that I returned home to my parents, that I died when I was ninety-two instead of twenty-nine, but not that I married Ralph. Certainly not that. And as I stare into the eyes of my amazingly kind acquaintance—a friend, a dear friend, a handsome, dear friend—I think I'd rather stay here a bit longer to get to know him. More than anything, my curiosity about how the history of my altered life might read has woken my senses back up and brought me back into the present.

22

Wednesday, September 6, 2006
William

I know I'll be tired all day tomorrow if I don't fall back asleep, but my mind won't shut down. God only knows what the clock reads—3 a.m., maybe 4 a.m.—but my brain has been whirring like it's midday for a good hour or more. After I got home last night from my universe-bending rendezvous with Elie, I daydreamed all the way through dinner and the rest of the evening before dropping asleep at eleven, but I awoke from a Chagall-esque dream which has left my neurons firing at Mach 5.

The bizarre reality that is Elie won't stop swirling through my brain. She was a normal, albeit odd-acting, foreigner as of yesterday morning. Intriguing, yes. A tad beguiling, yes. Even the slightly strange, puzzled reactions she had to everyday words didn't tip me off she's a one-of-a-kind time traveler. Now that I know the truth . . . I can't believe it, and I saw it and heard her story with my own eyes and ears.

It all makes sense, and I do believe her, but my rational physicist brain doesn't understand how it could be possible. How is it a mere girl can accidentally be transported through a century when treasure seekers, crazies, and serious scientists have been trying to do just that for ages?

Of course, Elie isn't a "mere girl." She's the great Ernest Rutherford's daughter, I remind myself. She's more intelligent than she lets on.

The more I think about what happened, the more my brain slows with exhaustion. I need to sleep. I pull my light cotton blanket over my face to block the moonlit skies. It could be daytime in here with that damned reflected light burning my eyeballs.

But there's so much to this new truth that I need to sort out the problems and figure out a solution to them. I guess that's the engineer in me: collect the data, analyze the data, and formulate a solution. In Elie's case, she needs about sixteen solutions. She needs the obvious things like food, clothing, and shelter, but between her, me, and Jeanne she miraculously has that taken care of. She can survive from day to day, but how can she make a life for herself?

I give into my thoughts and prop up my down pillow behind me. Locking my hands behind my head, I wonder how she can complete her education. How can she get credit for the classes she's taking? She's not registered! She's basically ghosting the classes, which is interesting for her but potentially problematic come time to hand in assignments and take tests. Someone—probably very soon—is going to catch on and call her out. And then what? What will she say? Would they merely kick her out of class or call in the police? Once they question her, surely they'll call her bonkers and throw her into an institution.

Literally shuddering at the thought, I close my eyes and rack my brain for a way to make her legit and prevent that nightmare.

Can I register her? Won't she need a Social Insurance Number? Is it too late?

And on and on my mind runs. . . .

* * *

Finally dawn breaks and I can straggle from my mess of sheets. I stumble like a zombie and probably look like one too.

"Will! Watch it!" Evan mumbles loudly as he rubs his shoulder. I must have body-checked him on my way to the bathroom.

"Ugh, my bad. Where are my glasses?"

"Uh, where every man of the dead keeps them? On the nightstand?"

"Mmm, must be." I turn back to my room for them before I do more damage.

"Dude, Will—did you not sleep last night? Up thinking about that girl?" This time it's him elbowing me.

"Ha, ha. Funny." Too true.

"Better be careful or you'll end up in worse shape than you were with the last girl, man. . ."

I don't hear the rest of what Evan says once I reach my nightstand. *But good God—he's right, isn't he? This girl and her time traveling madness certainly have a grip on me already.*

* * *

It's twenty minutes past ten and pure mayhem in front of the McConnell auditorium where Elie's class is held. Two thoughts repeat through my head like a set of perpetually swinging Newton's balls: first, will I actually see her in the mass of students pouring out of the previous class and in for hers, and second, will she be freaked out that I went online to time out her schedule based on what classes she said she's taking?

"William, hi!" a quietly surprised voice sounds behind me. Elie.

"Elie, hello. And hello, hello," I add, nodding a greeting to three other girls—at least two I notice blushing a bit. God, how embarrassing.

"What are you doing here?"

"Not much." *Idiot.* "I was passing through the building on my way to a tutorial I teach and knew you're in one of these classes, so I thought I'd say hi."

"Aha, well, it's nice to see you." Elie is eminently polite, but her eyes say this impromptu meeting isn't something she enjoys. "Pardon me—these are my friends Lindsey, Natalya, and Isabelle. We're all taking Twentieth Century Novel right now. Ladies, this is William Hertz."

After a few shy waves toward me, I face Elie again.

"Look, I was wondering if you're free later. You, er—you mentioned you're taking a physics class that my friend is the TA for, and I thought I'd give you a hand if you need to get caught up on the material." She of all people, I know, needs no help for an intro physics course.

A pause, then an imperceptibly small shrug. "All right, yes. Thank you for offering. I'm free after lunch, but only until one thirty. Perhaps we can meet after my last class in the Arts Building? At two thirty?"

"I can meet you up there, outside the front doors, by the small garden."

"Sounds lovely, William. See you then."

I can't help but grin, a bit wider than intended.

"See you, Elie. And, nice to meet you guys." I almost forget to acknowledge them.

They wave me goodbye, and as they turn to walk into the classroom, I see the two next to Elie give her playful elbow nudges.

* * *

I get to our meeting place a few minutes before Elie's class is due to end, so I take the opportunity to relax and people watch. I'm immediately struck by how easy it is to pick an arts student from an engineer, who I'm used to being surrounded by. Most engineers and physicists are nerdy looking, myself included—there's no denying it. Arts students manage to have a slightly hip, chic, and sometimes hippy look to them. My best guess is they take more care in their appearance to look current than we do because we have to spend more time draped over books and keyboards.

When Elie dismounts the Arts Building steps, however, she's like a gazelle walking through a herd of zebras. She's obviously taken pains to look more modern, but I'd pick her out of a crowd in an instant. Her posture is like that of a master yogi, she seems to glide rather than walk, and her curls are like a golden waterfall. There's no doubt she's been bred a Victorian, now that I know the truth.

She says goodbye to Natalya, walking at her side, and continues down the steps to meet me.

"We meet again, Ms. Newton."

"Hello, Mr. Hertz. Did you have a fine tutoring session earlier?"

"Meh, it was all right. It's always a mixed bag at the beginning of a semester: half-filled with bored people who are showing up out of politeness and the other half genuinely lost."

"I see. Well, are you ready to give me a physics lesson?" She winks.

"Ha, yes—the daughter of Ernest Rutherford must be completely flummoxed by a simple Mechanics and Waves class!"

She laughs, those high cheeks turning into pale cherries. "Well, it isn't complex yet, though I won't pretend that we've already covered knowledge ten times that which was known during my time. It follows logically though, and I'm not having difficulty. I may at some point though."

"If you do, you know who you can turn to for help."

"Your friend Alain?"

I turn my head sharply to her as we're walking down the front walk through campus.

"I believe, William, he was excited about there being, and I quote, 'a hot froshie I can tutor?'"

My jaw drops with a thud. "What!" I scramble to remember when he might have said it, and then I remember—it was when we were coming down the library steps the first time I saw Elie. I was barely listening to Alain then, focused as I was on Elie, but sure as anything that sounds like something he'd say. "Elie, do you even know what that means?"

"I made an inquiry as to the nature of the phrase, yes."

"Uhh. . . ."

"Don't worry; I was only joking. I'll depend on you if I have class troubles."

"Phew! I'm smarter than he is anyway," I tease. "Plus, I don't have an accent to get in the way."

She laughs, tipping her head back. I guess some humor transcends centuries.

"Speaking of class troubles, Elie, have you thought about the fact you're not formally registered?"

"Of course! It weighs me down along with every other facet of my illegal life here. I'm really surviving on both the generosity of others and relative anonymity thanks to McGill being an enormous university now—oh, and pure luck, of course." She tugs at a low-hanging maple leaf cluster from the tree we're walking under. "I'm keenly aware I'm attending classes *gratis*, though paying for my classes hasn't been my highest priority thought lately."

"Honestly, paying for them can be pushed down the road. There are plenty of scholarships available, especially for women. You can apply to those, plus you can get federal aid, plus you can negotiate a payment plan with the university. Trust me, I know multiple people who did that and still completed the semester."

Elie raises her eyebrows, unsure. More than that, her mind seems elsewhere.

"Trust me, Elie. The big thing is registering, and for that you need a bit of documentation, especially a Social Insurance Number." Another surprised look. "It's a unique number assigned to citizens and residents, which is used for things like employment and education. Basically you need it to apply here."

"But how would I ever get one? I appeared with nary a scrap of documentation, remember."

"It's not easy, but you can apply. I had to a few years ago when I came from the States; I can show you. With that you can register for the classes you're taking. People mistakenly think you need to register before the semester starts, but McGill lets you do it through the first three weeks. So you still have time."

"I thought this was going to be difficult, but now it sounds very complicated. I assume everything administrative is different now too. I'd probably act as stupid as a two bob watch when I do it, stick out like I'm from another era, and end up in a mental institution!" Her fists are balled up, and her face is more angry than worried.

"Elie, Elie, don't worry. I can help you. I'll do everything to do with computers now. This might end up being a bit unorthodox, maybe stretching the bands of legality, but I bet we can swing it."

She stops walking and turns to face me, eyes clear and boring straight into mine. "Look, William, I understand your reasoning for wanting to help me become an official member of society here, and I do thank you for offering to use your time to do it. But . . . that isn't exactly how I see my time here unfolding. I wonder if there's a better use of my time, so to speak."

"Elie, what do you mean? There'll come a point, maybe sooner than we think, and probably when you're unprepared, when you'll be busted. No one will believe you time traveled, and they'll send you to a loony bin to rot for the rest of your life."

"And that's the last thing I wish to happen, believe me. But my thoughts have been running a bit differently than yours. I've been approaching this a wee less pragmatically and more emotionally."

She wrings her hands gently, a bit guiltily. Suddenly I realize I've been attacking her problems like they're a science experiment whereas she's been riding an emotional tidal wave.

"I'm sorry—I'm only trying to get you adjusted to 2006 and to fit you in. What's your plan of attack?" I ask this with genuine curiosity, and I hope it doesn't come across accusatorily.

"Well, it's more that I keep going over how I appeared here that Friday, trying to figure out how it happened."

"Fair enough. If I'd been sent to 2106, I bet I'd be doing the same thing."

"The thing is, for days I thought I'd surely see Father around the next corner—in the Macdonald basement, outside under our favorite picnicking tree, coming out of our old house on Rue Ste-Famille—but he was never there. I can't understand how I was the only one transported to 2006 when we were both in his lab that Friday. He was only a few feet away from me. Why was he left behind?"

"I'm not sure yet why it was only you, but logically if he was transported too, he would've appeared in the basement at the same time you did. That assumes there was enough physical space in the basement; I guess we could go back and do a sort of reenactment. But anyway, we know he definitely didn't time travel because we went to the Rutherford Museum and read his biography there. Nothing changed to indicate he left 1906 for another time period, else he wouldn't have discovered everything he did later in his life."

"I suppose that *is* logical." She sighs and wrings her hands in her lap. "It was . . . wishful thinking on my part. Perhaps my subconscious held onto hope because it would be much easier to . . . deal with this . . . with someone else's help."

As she looks up at me, those blue eyes heavy with sadness and something weightier—*loneliness*—I realize how alone she must have felt. Disoriented, yes, and probably confused and overwhelmed, but clearly lonely.

At least now she has me.

I reach out to pat her arm, but stop short. "You've confided in me, Elie. You're not completely alone. I can help you get through this—adjustment—and acclimate you to another century."

She smiles, the sadness lifting somewhat. "And I thank you, truly I do. It has been quite a load off me to have someone else know the truth. And having someplace to stay and kind people like you, Jeanne, and my girlfriends are a boon."

"Good." I can't help but be a bit ecstatic to be number one in that list.

"It's just. . . ."

"Yes?"

Elie lets an eternal pause hang.

"Obviously I've time traveled once, right?"

"Yeah. . . ."

"And I survived."

"Physically, yes."

"So . . . what's to stop me from time traveling again?"

I've been looking into her eyes this whole conversation, but now I have to shake my head and readjust my focus. "Come again?"

Now Elie's eyes are shyly brightening. "I've moved through time once, in one direction—forward one hundred years, let's say. What's to stop me from constructing the same contraption that got me here so I can time travel again, only this time backward one hundred years?"

This shocks me almost more than her news that she was from the past. *She wants to leave here? Forever?*

"I guess, yeah, it's theoretically possible." My mouth is so dry I can't believe it can actually form words. "Though we have no idea how your father's equipment moved you here. It's got to be the proverbial needle in a haystack to isolate the circumstances and setup that did the trick. Not to mention it'd be incredibly risky—you could end up another hundred years in the future, or multiple hundreds of years in either direction, or worse, dead."

"I thought you'd say that."

"But why would you want to leave?" I ask quietly. "You just got here."

She lowers her head, pushes down on her legs, and out tumbles, "I'm from then, don't you see? I never thought I'd be here permanently. And my family must be distraught. They probably think I'm dead by now! How can I do that to them?"

"But we have no idea what happened to you in your time, Elie."

"No, we don't—yet. But we can find out!"

Minutes later we're on the fourth floor of Schulich Library, and I'm pulling a book I well know the location of.

"This is *Famous Physicists of McGill*," I explain. "I was actually reading this a few days ago. It happened to catch my eye, probably since I'd researched Rutherford—sorry, your father, I should say—before. I read into his chapter but skipped right over his personal life."

"Oh, I can't wait to read this! Does it say anything about me in there?" Elie can barely keep from pouncing on the volume.

"Hold on, let me flip to his chapter . . . early life in New Zealand . . . marriage to Mary Newton . . . bingo! 'Family Life and Tragedy!'"

"Tragedy?" Her already pale skin fades nearly to white.

"The author is probably referring to your unfortunate and early passing," I say, as kindly as I can while I scan the page for her name.

"Oh, God, life is already horrible for him. . . ." Elie's head is cupped in her delicate hands.

"It'll be okay," I say distractedly. "Wait!"

"What is it? Let me see the page too!"

"Here, look! This is different from everything I've read on him! It says, 'Rutherford's only daughter, Eileen, inexplicably disappeared from Montreal at age twenty. Authorities suspected the young Donalda student was abducted or possibly died of natural causes in the Saint Lawrence River, as her remains were never found. Rutherford, whose wife Mary was as distraught as he in later years and died in poor spirits two years after Eileen disappeared, entered a melancholy state from which he never emerged. Rutherford continued his work and went on to mark numerous discoveries and achievements, but friends and colleagues noted he did so with a dulled spirit. It is often wondered what else Rutherford could have contributed to physics if his health had been better.'"

We both sit back on the window-backed benches, stunned. I reread the section in its entirety, then mentally review my old research on Rutherford. "Nowhere, Elie—I swear it—did I ever read before that you just disappeared. It was all about marrying Ralph and the children. This is new, this has to be."

I turn the book over in my hands, but sure enough the pages are flakey and aged. This is not a book printed last week.

"William, I've changed history, don't you see? And for the worse." With a barely quivering mouth, steadied only by her will, I'm sure, she whispers those words. Her small hands are now balled up, knuckles bone-white.

"Yes, you've really meddled with things, as every scientist has always worried about. That's the biggest pitfall of time travel. You know that, right? The so-called butterfly effect of a tiny change in history ripples to cause enormous changes down the line."

"I see what you mean, but this is terrible! I can't let this happen to Mother and Father. Don't you see? This is the very reason I have to return to them, to fix what's been messed up. I want Mother to live to whatever age she's supposed to, and I want Father to be happy. I don't want him to be depressed. And me not able to say goodbye to them. . . . It's too much!"

Elie's fortitude fails her, and the quivering degenerates into gently rocking sobs while a few lonely tears fall down her ivory cheeks.

I'm not very good with women, I'll admit, and even worse with emotional people as a whole, but it's hard not to sympathize with her. I lean into her and lay my right arm lightly around her tiny shoulders. "Ssh, please don't cry, Elie. You can't change what happened, and I'm sure they still loved you 'til the end. Don't blame yourself for their sadness."

"But I *can* change what happened, William! I need to go back and fix things! It won't be meddling with the future, it'll be setting things right. This book proves it to me. I can't let this stay the reality."

"But you're going to die in less than a decade if you do!"

"Yes, but they'll be happy. And who knows—maybe I'll be able to convince Ralph to stop at three children."

My stomach turns unexpectedly. I'm not a fan of this Ralph Fowler guy, suddenly.

"Or maybe I'll find a way to marry someone else, now that I know what happens."

Hmm, maybe he's not that bad after all. But. *But.*

"But Elie, that *would* be changing the future! Not having one of your children? Not having *any* of your children? You don't know what effect that will have!"

"No, but suppose we now research what Ralph's altered past is and see if he had any bad effects from me 'disappearing.' Maybe not marrying me won't turn out badly for him. Maybe he's already slated to marry someone new."

"And have her kick the bucket at twenty-nine?" I ask, sarcasm ringing the question—coldly, too, I realize too late.

"'Kick the bucket,' William? That's harsh. Die, you mean? I certainly hope that doesn't happen to anybody. But, sadly, death during childbirth is more common than you think."

"Not anymore, Elie. Good God, medicine is much better now—you have no idea. People live into their seventies and eighties on average now—seriously," I say, seeing utter shock color her face. "Yeah—you'd do much better living here. It's safer, healthier."

She shrugs. "Maybe. I really don't know yet. Goodness, there's so much I don't know; actually, there's a hundred years' worth of history I don't know. But William, please—understand what I'm going through. My fault or not, I seem to have ruined my parents' lives. I need to remedy that. I need to at least try to go back. It's worth a try, right?"

I can't believe we're considering doing this—hell, I can't believe, as intelligent as Elie is, that she believes we can actually build a time machine and successfully get her back to 1906.

But then again, if it happened once, it can happen again.

And I see the force behind her pleas. Here's a woman who loves her family and is thrown into a new world she feels she doesn't fit into, and all she wants is a chance to go home. How can I, the one person she's confided in, for whatever reason she did, deny her help in doing that? How can I say no to that face, that silky voice?

Even if I do say no, a little voice inside tells me, she'll do it anyway. But if I help her, I could help her do it safely? Use my modern physics knowledge? *What a justification, Will.*

"Okay," I respond after a long pause. "We'll give it a try. There's no use stopping you anyway, is there? But let me caveat that it'll be hard to do, dangerous, and even harder to hide from people. We wouldn't be the first people to fail at building a time machine."

"I know it's a shot in the bloody dark, William—I truly do understand. But what an exciting shot, eh?"

"That probably doesn't begin to describe it. But in the meantime, Elie, let's try to get you registered officially here. Think of it as a backup in case Plan A doesn't pan out—which has a high probability of failing, I'll point out. We'll do our best, but just in case."

My reasoning is met with a placating dismissal of a nod. She's convinced we can do this! It makes me wonder if, despite the positive attitude, she really isn't perhaps a bit crazy.

No, it's just desperation, Will.

"Fine, William, fine. Let's do both things, and I suppose it'll be a race to see what we can complete first."

"I can already tell you what'll be done first, Elie," I say with a rueful grin. "Building a workable time machine has been El Dorado to people for centuries. If we can get this to work, we'll have to rename you H.G. Wells."

23

Saturday, September 9, 2006
William

With so many thoughts working their way around my brain, I use the only way I know to really relax: jogging. My steady thump on the sidewalk drowns out the city's sleepy weekend morning rumbles and quiets my inner monologue. I don't know why, but I've always been instantly able to concentrate fully on running without any cranial interruption; whenever I try to use this time to mentally work through a problem, I find I stop mid-thought as my ears fill with *thud-thud* over and over.

Not so today.

Not only have I been ruminating about Elie's situation, but since my VERITAS work has been speeding up, as have my classes, that's been taking up the rest of my spare cerebral time. Already I have an intimidating High Energy Physics assignment and over a chapter and a half of the text to go over. Good thing I practically live on campus. But while the schoolwork is relatively easily solved, I'm totally lost on where to begin building a time machine to take Elie home.

Seriously, who am I, Doc Brown?

So I've started to work on her relatively easier problems. Signing her up for a Social Insurance Number turned out to be simple, thanks to the open online world existing today. Registering for classes was also fairly quick—and also online, of course—but applying for status as a student itself was a bit trickier. I contacted a friend working in Administration and sweet-talked my way into getting an application for Elie. It's amazing what you can do last-minute at a university even if the semester has already started. It helps to know people, for a peon like me.

Today requires a long run, and an hour after I start out I've looped up the Plateau and through as many parks as I could manage. I'm depleted when I return to our apartment and dripping molten September sweat onto my sneakers.

"Will!" Evan calls from his bedroom when he hears me swing the front door shut. "Jeanne called and invited you to tea later, at seven thirty, and said not to call if you can't come, but that you can't refuse her, yadda, yadda, yadda. . . . Basically she yapped on for a while and said she'll see you later."

"Nice," I say as I shove my head into his doorframe. "It sounds like you love talking on the phone with her."

"She's a peach, Will, but she rambles like both my grandmothers combined. She must really like you, dude." He raises his eyebrows suggestively.

"Ha! She has a soft spot for good-looking American guys who drink her tea and eat her cookies."

"Alain was saying that Aussie girl is living with her now. Must have something to do with it, eh?"

"She's from New Zealand," I snap back, then more lightly add, "But we're just friends. Don't believe everything Alain tells you. You know he's got one thing on his mind at all times, right?"

"Two," he corrects.

"Two?"

"Use your imagination."

* * *

"Will, dear, let me pour the rest of this tea into your mug. Our cups are still full." More than the black vanilla tea itself, I particularly enjoy how Jeanne gives me mine in a manly mug while she and Elie drink theirs from porcelain cups.

"Thanks, Jeanne. I'll take another Naniamo bar too."

"Take two, dear. If you're still doing those long jogs of yours, you can stand the extra calories."

"I did run for an hour this afternoon," I admit as she walks her pot back to the kitchen.

"An hour!" Elie exclaims. "Why so long? Where were you running to? Or what from?"

I can't help but laugh at her astonished expression. I've forgotten recreational running wasn't exactly the sport of choice in the 1900s.

"It was for exercise, Elie. I like to jog, mostly in parks, but around here I end up just going block after block."

"Sounds exhilarating." Her eyes betray her true thoughts, which amuses me further.

"Yeah, it's a bit crazy, but it helps clear my mind. It's a way of recharging, I suppose."

"Sure. Not something I'd fancy doing, but I do enjoy a long promenade around town. I love going up to Mont Royal." As her expression softens, I make a mental note to visit there with her.

Jeanne returns and stands with her now-empty hands on the back of her armchair, a scheming smile on her lips. "Well, kids, I suppose I ought to leave you two alone so you can chat without an old rock yammering into your free ear."

"God, Jeanne, this is your apartment!" I laugh. "I won't kick you out of your own living room."

"Me neither, Jeanne. Please, sit back down. It's a pleasure talking with you," Elie adds.

"No, no, you two have plenty to talk about, and I've sat with you forty-five minutes already. I know youth needs youth."

"Jeanne, I'd actually love some fresh air. Mind if Elie and I take our tea out to the balcony? Then you can stay in here." I get up and replace her back pillow which had fallen off her chair when she got up.

"That's a lovely idea, Will. It should be rather refreshing out there by now."

Once alone and seated on Jeanne's wicker settee next to Elie, I can finally tell her my news and give her a surprise.

"Why did you bring your knapsack, William? You're not planning on doing school work here tonight, are you?"

I'm not sure if she's teasing me or not. "No way, Jose. . . . I make it a rule not to do work on a Saturday night, unless I need to study for an exam. Actually, I brought you a little surprise—a gift really."

"What! William, no—I don't need a thing. What is it?" Her ladylike admonishment barely masks her curiosity.

"It's not a big deal; don't feel bad or guilty or anything. I know you haven't bought your course packs for your Arts classes—and I know how expensive those are—and that you've been borrowing your friends' copies to do your readings," I say as I pull four softbound letter-sized books from my bag. "I know you can't afford these, but you need your own copies—"

"Oh, William!"

"—so I went to the school bookstore and picked these up for you. And here's the physics textbook you need, the one I used for that same class five years ago. You're lucky the edition hasn't changed."

"That's too good of you, thank you! Oh, how will I ever repay you?"

"Don't look so despaired, Elie. You don't have to repay me, honestly. Think of me as a good Samaritan who wants to help out a destitute time traveler."

"That I am, and these I need. I won't pretend I'm not excited, and extremely grateful."

"And I have some news. I was researching how to enroll you, and I went online—"

Blank stare from Elie, as expected.

"—and filled in an application for a Social Insurance Number, which you'll get in a few weeks. Then I registered you for your classes online, once I got you a student number. That was the hardest part of the whole process, and I had to work carefully with a friend of mine in Administration. She explained how you can apply late and still be registered for class."

By this point Elie's eyes are as big as her teacup and her breath intake has stopped.

"It's sort of a concurrent procedure," I continue, "but all these things are in-process. I took the liberty of filling out your application, and here are copies of everything for you."

"This is unbelievable, William! I'm astounded it was possible and so quickly accomplished!"

"Well, it's not approved yet, but it's worth a shot to apply anyway. I filled in everything to the best I could, with the birth date you gave me, your address here, and a made-up address in New Zealand. I really hope they won't check up on that."

"Good God, with a wave of your wand, it's all sprung to life! It's a complete forgery, in a way, but still lifelike."

"Yeah, I thought that at first too, but then I realized hey, you're actually Elie Newton—or so you say—and if you want to become a Canadian resident, you'd have to do this, so it's legit in that respect. The only thing we're fudging here is your past. And we have to—you can't put your last known address of 1906 in there. Honesty like that will put you right in the ward of mental patients at Montreal General Hospital."

Elie shudders. "Yes, let's avoid that, please. But, gah! I could hug you. I'm awfully thankful for everything you're doing for me!"

I laugh uncomfortably. "You can hug me when it's approved. Anyway, you should know in a few weeks about the insurance number and in a few days about the application. They have no backlog this time of year on that, of course. As for the classes, you're in according to the website—that's the place where the class listing is—so you're free to act like you belong there."

Elie adjusts her position to sit straight forward, staring out at the city glowing its own twilight in front of us. She sighs slowly. "Goodness, William. To think where I was two weeks ago, and here I am with some solidity underneath me. I'm much more settled—though I'll feel better when I know I'm safe from a mental institution."

I nod, then turn to stare at the same scenery. I never tire of this view, which is slightly better than that from my apartment; I see the western side of the city, dominated by Mont Royal. And to enjoy it while sitting with her, this mysterious woman from a hundred years ago . . . it's an understatement to call this surreal. Next to me is a time traveler who has changed my life from routine to revolutionary. Instead of concentrating on my next VERITAS task, I'm making plans to build a time machine. A *time machine*, for Chrissake!

A few minutes pass in silence, but it seems she, like me, doesn't feel the need to fill it with chatter. Eventually I break the spell by broaching the topic of the time machine.

"Elie, have you thought about how we should go about building this thing?"

She knows exactly what I'm referring to. "A bit."

"I mean, what makes passage through the space-time continuum possible? A high-energy source? A certain magnetic field? A high gravitational force?"

"I'm not sure. I'm certain I can't explain how it can theoretically happen any better than you, and I lived through the experience."

"Maybe you can remember what your dad was working on that day in his lab, and we'll go from there. Perhaps once we get some puzzle pieces laid out we can arrange them and try to figure out what the magic combination was that did this."

"That sounds like an awful lot of trial and error."

"We won't be doing live trials, if that's what you're fearing."

"Oh! I was merely thinking what a long process this is going to be."

I chuckle and do my best not to respond with sarcasm, knowing she probably doesn't use that type of humor much.

"They say Rome wasn't built in a day, Elie. But it'll be easier if we take it one step at a time."

"You're right. And this was my idea, after all, so I'm prepared for this to take a while."

"Do you remember what your father was working on in the lab that day, where he was in the room, and what he was doing exactly?" As I speak, I pull a fresh, spiral-bound notebook from my bag and get ready to take notes.

"Well," Elie begins, concentration lining the edges of her narrowing eyes, "I heard from Soddy—one of his research assistants, well, you know—that they'd been running scattering experiments earlier that day. When I walked into the lab, Father was standing at the far end of the room, bent over the opened lead box, though I assume they removed the radium sample inside."

"Okay, good start. Where was the radium stored if it was removed?"

"Oh, Father's pocket, probably. He usually takes it home at night and puts it on his dresser for safekeeping."

I nearly spit out the last dregs of tea I'd been sipping.

"Are you kidding, Elie? His pocket?! Didn't he know radioactive substances cause cancer?"

Her shocked expression tells me everything.

"Of course he didn't know," I continue, trying to calm her. "It was years until Marie Curie died of complications from ionizing radiation. No one really knew the dangers back then." I pat her arm. "I'll explain more later, but suffice it to say you need to take precautions around that stuff."

"My goodness, I can't fathom. . . . But that wasn't the focus of what was in the lab that day." Elie describes an electronic buzzing she heard from the enormous power supply, the looping wires attached to it from all ends of the lab, and how there were tables of smaller experiments lining the walls.

"I remember the buzz clearly because it stopped abruptly when I landed in the basement in 2006. It was quiet, cold, and smelled of metal." She shudders. "The air was ionized, that I'm sure about; I've experienced it enough from being around after Father ran an experiment."

I'm scribbling with a speed my right hand never knew in class lectures. Her words with my side comments—"ionized air from creating radium isotopes? Or power supply overheating and charging the air?"—have already filled half a page. "Do you remember what exactly was on the tables? If you concentrate on one section at a time, could you recall it?"

"I might be able to, if I can separate the equipment well enough in my mind. Father was never too messy, but he did have a tendency to leave anything important lying around in case he could use it again. He often did exactly that, mostly out of budgetary necessities, but also due to his natural country thrift. I never saw anything go to waste in his labs. That day, though, there were an awful lot of wires running out and about," Elie trails off, eyes miles away. "Oh! Do you think this may have all been brought about by a series of experiments interacting, going badly maybe, or a sort of scientific garbage contaminating electrical fields?"

"I hadn't followed that train of thought," I reply with surprise. "I'm planning to draw out what he had at his workstation according to when it got added or discarded. Maybe then we can see what might have interacted."

"I have an excellent visual memory, but I'm not sure I'll be able to remember everything—only the most important bits, sod it all. I suppose it's as a good a place as any to start, right?"

"Absolutely. Anything's worth a shot right now. But," I trail off. My mind is burning double time to decode something critical. "But that was a good thought a minute ago. There had to have been an interaction that caused some kind of disturbance. What if there really was too much on that table? Too much energy? Magnetic or electric fields being multiplied because things were too close or shorted together?"

"Perhaps. You're the physicist, so I'm hoping you'll be able to figure that out." Elie's hopeful, pleading look is almost too much to bear, like a homeless puppy begging to be bought from the pet store.

"I'll do my best, Miss Rutherford! Well, go ahead and start from the table nearest your father and work your way to the door where you were standing."

She describes setups actually like what we saw in the Rutherford museum: a detector for electromagnetic waves, glass tubes filled with ionized gases and connected to high-energy light sources, and a gold-leaf electroscope. Metal coils were supposed to be stored neatly in one area of the lab, but they had been moved around haphazardly in the weeks before. But the biggest mess was due to the wires connecting the large power supply across various setups to the alpha particle scattering experiment.

"They were draped everywhere—carelessly, really," Elie explained. "I don't think they could move the power supply, which was near the door, but the scattering setup was on the other side of the room. So the wires ran right . . . over . . . the-the . . . tables. . . ."

"Elie, what's wrong?"

"The last thing I remember from 1906 was worrying that the wires were going to get tangled, so I reached to move wires off his experiment to measure time intervals. I didn't want the wire to get wrapped around the copper coil. I touched it, and. . . ."

"Yes?" Everything up to my hair tingles with anticipation.

"And . . . then I felt a sort of energy pulse go through me. *That's* when it happened. *That's* when I was transported! I can't believe I didn't remember until now, but I must have forgotten in the confusion I felt. How could I forget something so crucial?"

"Wow! Were you electrocuted?"

"I didn't feel hurt or singed—"

"You didn't smell any burnt hair?" I ask with a wink and crooked smile.

"No! I arrived here in exactly the same shape as I left 1906. And all I smelled was that ionized air. You know what that smells like, right?"

I nod.

"And it was chilly. Maybe it was because I was in a basement without the added heat of any running equipment, or maybe it was cooler on that day in 2006 than in 1906. But I had a definite sense that something had *happened.* I just felt it, you know what I mean?"

I stare at Elie, unsure what to say. I really don't know what she had felt. Heck, probably no one knows. "Not really, I'm sorry. I guess if you felt the energy pulse, you felt something happen, but it must have been slight enough not to have harmed you."

"Unless . . . the energy didn't go through me—like I was a conducting wire—but rather moved me instead."

This girl is smarter than I thought! That never crossed my mind. But of course—Elie wasn't a typical shock victim when she accidentally touched the wire coil. She may have somehow become part of the coil itself—maybe like just another electron conducting electricity. But instead of her doing the conducting, she was the thing being conducted. "It makes no sense, scientifically speaking, but that's brilliant. Your father must've rubbed off on you."

Elie smiles a relaxed, genuine grin. "It's good to hear that. Thanks, William."

"You're welcome. I meant it. It's almost as if you got in the way of whatever energy was flowing through that jumble of equipment. Instead of frying you, the energy moved you. But what amplified that energy? And what components were involved and which were innocent bystanders?"

Elie sighs along with me, leaning back in her chair to peer through the window at Jeanne's mahogany grandfather clock. "Goodness, it's late! I didn't mean to keep you up so long working on this. You probably want to get going, eh?"

I crack up; I can't help it. "Are you kidding, Elie? It's only nine-thirty! The night is young—like us. Are you on Jeanne's schedule?"

"It's okay to be out at this time? I mean, it's proper?" Her skeptical eyes are no doubt wondering if I'm being gentlemanly with her.

"Yes, it's okay. In fact, why don't you come up to my apartment for a while? Evan's home and we can hang out," I suggest. "In fact, we can press him for ideas about time travel."

"Isn't that risky? He'll surely catch on to our project."

"No, it'll be hypothetical, of course—or at least we'll couch it as such. No one's seriously thinking about making a time machine, Elie," I laugh. "Well, except us."

That seems to convince her.

"Just 'hanging out,' Will? Just for a little bit?"

"Yes, innocently, with both of us. I'll have you back well before midnight, I promise."

As we're walking through the apartment on our way to the door, Jeanne pops out of the kitchen and pulls me aside, out of Elie's earshot.

"Will, that's a very good thing you did out there, giving her those books."

I shrug. "She needs them."

"She must be poorer than I realize."

"I think so. She won't have a paycheck from the bookstore for a while, but she needs her books now, so. . . ."

She rubs the top of my back gently. "It's a good thing she has you as a friend, Will, but be careful if you head down that road, okay?"

It takes me a moment to get what road she's referring to.

"I will. Good thing she has you to protect her," I joke.

"Well, I worry about her. She's very . . . naïve. And maybe a bit . . . odd . . . though I don't say that disparagingly, you understand."

I almost choke. If Jeanne, an aging, with-it-most-of-the-time lady thinks Elie is odd, how long before everyone else sees through Elie's charade? But I force a small grin on my face.

"Yeah, I know what you mean. But don't worry; I'll be good." I mark an "x" over my heart. "See you later, Jeanne. Thanks for the tea."

Now that I have a scientific quest—a ridiculously impossible fool's errand, I don't kid myself—I'm too distracted to try anything with Elie. Besides, why would I risk heartbreak for a girl who's so desperate to leave?

So, Will . . . why are you so willing to help her then?

24

Saturday, September 9, 2006
Elie

William and Evan chat in the kitchen as Evan washes an enormous pile of dishes in the sink, each arguing a point about a story I'm wholly unfamiliar with—something set in the future called a "star trek." As I really can't follow what they're saying, except something about warp speed and whale calls, incongruously, I amuse myself until they're done by surreptitiously examining the twenty-first century objects filling the apartment's living room.

A pair of rainbow-hued shoes good for sports only, seemingly, assaults my eyes. A large television—which I learned about from Jeanne, embarrassingly—competes for space with a window. A pair of small television-looking monitors, as William has told me about, dominate a paper-strewn long desk, and I imagine the boys do homework here.

When I look over at William, I can tell he has something on the tip of his tongue but is waiting for the right moment to say it. His eyes are a tad squinty, focused, and he keeps rearranging his lips as if to speak. It seems the boys' conversation has paused.

Finally, he leans casually onto the counter and says, "So how *do* you think they traveled through the space-time continuum? What kind of equipment must their ship have needed?"

Evan furrows his eyes and replies, with a slightly curious grin, "Uh, dude—that was a movie. Time travel isn't actually possible."

"No kidding—I'm just saying, *hypothetically speaking*, how do you suppose they could do that?"

I know what William's getting at—and I hope Evan isn't reading as much into his hopeful expression as I can—and I'm as curious as he is to hear what Evan might say.

"Well. . . ." Evan, clearly intrigued by this scientific holy grail, rests his soapy hands on the edge of the sink. "There's a way it *could* happen, but I bet it wouldn't be survivable by a human."

"What do you mean?" I ask, stepping toward the half wall splitting our two rooms.

"I mean Einstein theorized how it could happen, so to speak. You need a really strong energy source—I mean, *gigantic* wattage, terawattage, who knows—and a super-high velocity, and—*boom*—you're in the next decade or wherever you want to be."

William waves his hand as if to push away Evan's answer. "Sure, sure, relativity—we all know about that."

We do?

"But surely there's more to it than that, right?" he adds.

"Well, maybe. But the laws of physics put that envelope around time travel. I suppose you could make an argument about ripping the space-time continuum apart with a wicked strong gravity field, or blasting something with radioactivity and shooting it off somewhere . . . but that's sci-fi stuff."

"Yeah, sci-fi. . . ." William muses quietly. "But how awesome would it be to pull that off?"

"Hmm, maybe if we could figure out how to make our own time machine, we could send Elie back to the 1800s!"

Evan's joking, clearly, but I know for satire to be good there must be an element of truth in it. I didn't quite realize before now my hopeful attempt to pass myself off as just another modern student was so unsuccessful.

While my brain digests this tease, William's face shows the shock immediately; his eyes are wide, incredulous.

Thankfully, Evan is looking at me and doesn't notice William. To give him a chance to recover, I blurt out, "I'm from *New Zealand,* Evan, not the 1800s. I know we seem like aliens to you, but it would help you every once in a while to put down the calculator and pick up a history book."

I reach across the wall to punch his arm playfully to sell my point—and then marvel at how easily I can lie now.

"Yeah, *nerd,*" William reinforces, recovering.

"Hey, look who's talking, book-man! The only time you're not reading a textbook is when you're reading science fiction or running—when you're probably thinking about a book you've read. Am I wrong?"

"Humph. . . ."

"Thought so."

"Anyway, back to the subject," I say, trying to mete out any more time-travel hints from Evan. "That's your conclusion, gentlemen? High energy, a strong gravity source, or decay from a radioactive material?"

Evan shrugs. "I guess. I really have no idea. Maybe there's an alternate universe somewhere that you flip into when you time travel. But you couldn't return very easily through the worm hole. Maybe Scotty's waiting in 2306 to beam us up—I don't know. Oops." A soapy plate slips into the sink. "Say, Elie, you sound like a physics student. Didn't Will say you're in Arts?"

Now I've binned it! "Oh, I'm used to your lingo, that's all. My father's a physics professor back home," I say with a wave of my hand and as light an air as I can manage.

"No wonder you're hanging around this dork!" A shower of suds hits William square in the face.

As a small soap fight breaks out, I laugh—*boys*—and return to the living room to thumb through a textbook for High Energy Physics lying on the coffee table. *Some light reading, I suppose.* It makes me wonder if Evan's point about a high energy source could be right. After all, that's what powered Father's equipment. But how high is high? And would DC versus AC current matter? I sigh heavily. Evan's brief suggestions breed more questions. It only reinforces how enormous this task is. I start to lose heart . . .

. . . and then William turns the corner into the living room and says, "Elie, let's go onto the balcony and chat for a bit." Suddenly, I know he'll help me through this; we'll figure it out.

* * *

As William later leads me to the front door, us having decided to call it a night, I say quietly to him, in case Evan can hear us through his closed bedroom door, "Would it be a good idea to make up a name for this . . . project . . . we're doing? So we don't have to worry about someone accidentally hearing the words 'time machine?'"

"You mean a code name?"

"Yes! Something practical, though, of course."

"That's a good idea. But what project could we possibly be working on together?"

I'm stumped at that. "Ugh . . . right. I don't want to build a big, confusing cover story. I've done enough of that already, thank you very much."

"I bet. Well, we could say 'the project.' It could refer to anything that way. The less we have to explain, the better."

"Hmm, not bad. Okay, we'll see if it works out."

William turns to face me, opens his eyes wide, caringly, and gives my shoulders a squeeze. "Elie, please try not to think about this nonstop. We'll figure this out and make it work for you—trust me. As you said, it's worked once, therefore it can work again—theoretically."

"That's easy for you to say, but thank you for saying it. I have little else to ponder. . . ." My shoulders droop though his hand pressure is light.

"I know, I know. I can't imagine. . . . Well, if you're going to think about it anyway, why don't you flip to the end parts of that physics textbook, say, around page 1275. You'll find the chapter on relativity rather . . . enlightening."

"Relativity? What?"

"Just read it," he laughs, winking, "and remember what Evan said earlier. We'll talk about it later this week when we meet. Why don't you stop by the Macdonald basement labs some afternoon this week?"

I nod slowly, already replaying Evan's words for the fourth or fifth time tonight. "Okay, sure. I'll see you then."

"Good. Remember, relativity. And enjoy it!"

* * *

The third week of my Introduction to Physics class has started, and it's so comfortable to me now to take a science course I've stopped noticing it's not a

Donalda-type course. Oh, I'm enjoying my literature and architecture courses here immensely as well—also because I'm surrounded by a group of sociable friends—but there's something satisfying and familiar about learning physics while having an air of being forbidden for me. I am very much the minority gender here, though far from the only girl in the auditorium. I may not have any friends in this class—and at times it has felt a bit lonely—but it may now be my favorite time of the week, these Tuesday and Thursday morning classes.

I'm seated in the rear right area, and today a boy—named David, I learned last Thursday—is on my left and an unknown boy is on my other side. David is from the United States and hasn't taken physics before, as his furious note-taking style supports.

"Today we'll be working through constant acceleration equations of motion. These are the basics of motion in terms of solving for simple circumstances of motion—your typical ball thrown at an angle and how far does it fly problem, et cetera," Professor Nagar says as he picks up a piece of chalk and starts to write symbols on the board.

"You probably won't ever need to derive these equations to solve anything, but it's useful to do it once to understand them, so we'll do that. So, let's start with the position *x* of our particle."

As he writes several terms and works through the derivation of the four equations, I write them down cleanly in a new notebook bought yesterday at the university supplies store. Though I've never seen Father run through these derivations before, they make perfect sense to me, thankfully, and in my head I can supply the key words he's working toward before he says them aloud.

"Now, we also want a formula that gives us position as a function of time using its initial velocity and acceleration, and to do this we can take the equation for velocity we wrote and . . ." Professor Nagar trails off expectantly, waiting for the class to fill in the blank.

"Integrate with respect to *t*," I whisper.

David's head flicks toward me, his eyes narrowed. At first I think he's annoyed I spoke aloud, but then I read surprise in his eyes—surprise, I suppose, I have the answer.

Professor Nagar, hearing only incoherent murmurs and whispers like my own, supplies, "we can integrate!" A few chalk-strokes later, "And now we have a similar equation, but instead of initial velocity, we have . . ."

I pause timidly. "Final velocity. . . ." I whisper again.

Again, David stares at me in shock. "How do you know the answers to these? It looks like you're not even thinking hard!"

I blush. "It just makes sense, I suppose. It is just math after all, right?"

"I guess. Are you a math major, then?"

"Me? No. I'm in Arts, actually." I try not to sound nonchalant, but as I'm concentrating on taking down notes as I reply, I realize I may have come off that way.

David's eyes are wider than the black-rimmed glasses overpowering his face. "What? Why—Why are you taking this class?"

My cheeks redden further. "I just like physics. Anyway, it's only the beginning of the course. I'm sure I'll be as lost as a lamb in the ocean in a few weeks."

"Sure, sure. . . . You seem to know what you're doing though. I couldn't do these derivations by myself. Maybe *you* should be a physics major, and I can be an Arts student. . . ."

Now it's my turn to spin my head in surprise. "It never occurred to me to be in physics," I say, realizing how true that is. Regaining my concentration on the class, I continue, "Anyway, let's get on with this, shall we? If you're lost, pay attention to the professor and take notes."

David slowly returns his gaze to the chalkboard, where mine already is. While my ears are listening to the lecture, my brain is churning David's last remark.

Later, as the professor wraps up his lecture and writes our homework problems on the chalkboard, I sit still and take down the assigned numbers. David shoves his still-open notebook into a stained backpack, knocking into my left foot in the process—without noticing or even apologizing. He gets up and nearly walks into my crossed legs in his attempt to get to the side doors to our right.

I look up at him with indignant irritation. Some manners! "Excuse me!"

"Can you let me by?" His head bobs forward like a chicken.

"The class isn't finished yet," I whisper. "What are you doing? Sit down!"

"He's done teaching. Why should I stick around for babble?" With that rude remark, David manages to slide in between my knees and the seat in front of me. All around me I hear paper rustling, zippers chirping, and feet shuffling, all the while Professor Nagar is still talking to us, though admittedly only administrative points regarding homework formatting. Still, the lack of respect these students show him astonishes me. After three weeks, I cannot get used to the way kids apparently can't sit quietly through an entire class. In my time, the professor would be so chuffed by a student like that he'd kick him out of the class.

"I say. . . ." I huff quietly after Professor Nagar finishes, then pack up my satchel.

***

After our Renaissance Literature lecture ends at half past two that afternoon, Natalya and I stroll lazily along the paths in front of the Arts Building, happy to be out in the sunshine again.

"Goodness, I love Montreal at the end of summer," I say, breathing in the scent of freshly mown grass with closed eyes. "No matter what, it makes me feel good." I'm reminiscing of being in Montreal as I know it in 1906 and the many enjoyable summers I've passed under this very campus' trees, and how it's just as soul warming now.

"You mean, despite the scads of readings and essays to write, it's still great to be here rather than some dump college in our own hometowns?"

"Er, yes. No matter that. We'll get all that done; I'm not worried about that." And I'm not.

"Ha! I wish I had your brain—or your speed in writing, Elie. This all seems too easy for you. All I can think about is the work I need to finish today."

In moments like these, I wish I could tell my new friends I'm actually two years older than them with that much more college experience already earned.

"You'll finish it, don't fret. You're not too slow yourself, but thanks."

"Well, all the same I'd better get on all this work. Are you headed back home as well?"

I shake my head, then gaze down to the Macdonald Building. "Nah, I'll start it later. I'm going to pop into one of the labs in Macdonald and see what my friend William is up to. He asked me to come by sometime this week, and . . . I guess I can spare some time this afternoon."

Natalya lets out a short whistle. "Ooh-la-la! Hot date already? Nice work!"

"Hardly! We're friends, really. I'm just interested in physics—you know—so I'm going to see what his group is doing." And hopefully, I don't add, work on a physics project of my own.

"Mmm-hmm. I'm sure his primary goal is to tell you all about his lab work," she teases, throwing her head side to side as she speaks; I avert her eyes. "Say, Elie, when do we get to meet this William guy?"

"Anytime! Do you want to come by also? There are probably a few other men in the lab too—oh, and women too, I understand."

Suddenly Natalya loses her playfulness and turns shy, her shoulders curling forward. "Umm, no, not today. Thanks, but maybe some other time. Maybe, maybe when the other girls can meet him too."

I consider how she, Isabelle, and Lindsey *could* meet William. It'd be a lot easier if his friends were there too. Perhaps he'll have an idea.

"Well, suit yourself. I'm sure there'll be plenty of opportunities to stop by." Despite my effort to portray us as strictly friends, I realize how that statement leads otherwise.

"Sure. . . ." Natalya winks at me and waves goodbye as she turns north toward the dormitories.

With a laugh and a wry smile cracking across my shaking head, I walk in the opposite direction.

Though it's not sweltering outside, thanks to a cooling breeze off the St. Lawrence River, the lobby of Macdonald is stuffy and stale. I glance over to the right, where my little broom closet lies down the hall and up a short staircase, and it occurs to me I haven't been there for two weeks. Time does fly, and much has already changed since then; I swear time actually moves faster in this century.

I remember William saying the office he works in is off that hall as well, and I'm tempted to stop by there first, in case he's not in the basement labs yet, but he did say to meet him in the lab. I'd never want to show up somewhere unannounced.

The basement, thankfully, is cool, but the air is heavy with old machine oil vapors, ancient dust, and a hint of sawdust. I'm familiar with the labs thanks to my jaunts through them my first weekend here, but it takes me a few minutes to find William, crouched under a table and unscrewing a vise from below.

"Well, the top jobs go to the smartest people on campus, I see."

"Oomph! Ach, not so much," he says, rubbing the top of his head where it smacked the table in surprise, then waves my help away. "No, I'm all right."

"Sorry to surprise you like that!"

"It's okay. This job cleaning up the labs is no picnic."

"This hardly seems work fit for graduate students paid to make groundbreaking discoveries," I observe.

"No, but when the people paying you ask you to do something, you do it. . . . Anyway, I can take a break from that. I want to show you around the lab—*and show you the equipment*," he adds in a whisper with his head cocked downward.

I nod in the same manner, as if we're two crooks colluding to rob a bank.

William leads me through the main room—which he doesn't know I'm rather familiar with already—and into each room, pretending to neaten up the areas as he goes for the benefit of the few other people in the basement.

"Here's the stores of wires, which are already pretty well organized by gauge, and wire snips and strippers and such. In this closet are a bunch of ammeters and power supplies." The last two words are spoken at a dropped volume. "There are two which are the highest voltage available, at least in our labs."

"How high?"

He laughs. "As high as your father's, and then some."

That gives me reassurance, and I smile in return. In a voice barely above the rustle of my clothes, I ask, "Will anyone notice one missing?"

"I'm betting not. This closet is full now, but as the semester wears on, things move to various labs to support all the experiments going on, the graduate work, and to run some undergraduate mechanical labs. It's always in flux, and there's no formal inventory of this old stuff."

"Good. I was worried we wouldn't be able to borrow something as important as a power supply for as long a period as I'm assuming we'll need one. I'm being realistic, I assure you, in thinking we'll take more than a fortnight to get this working."

William arrests any lingering hope that could indeed be a possibility by a look of complete incredulity. "Not a chance, Elie, that this will be done quicker than that. We need to gather everything and recreate each setup of Rutherford's down to minute detail, then array them together in their jumbled state, and *then* do some sort of testing of the machine—on mice or something, I don't know. Then it'll be considered working—*if* we can get it working."

"Yes, yes, I know, *if*. And I know all the intricate workings of Father's experiments will be difficult to remake—"

"Although," William cuts in with excited hand gestures, "We have the exact blueprints for nearly all of his work, thanks to the Rutherford Museum. The guide for the place has notes for everything he used, down to the smallest tube and wire. But that's not to say it'll be easy."

"Aye, yes, I recall thumbing through that booklet when we went. You think that's all we'll need to put it together?" I ask with excitement tingling down my neck.

"I think it's an excellent head start. We'll probably hit a hiccup or two—that's unavoidable—but I have another idea too. It's slightly dangerous, though, and actually kind of illegal."

My eyes widen like inflated balloons. William, do something illegal?

"Don't be too worried, Elie." He places a calming hand on my arm. "It occurred to me last night that we can use your father's actual equipment—if we can get it out of the storeroom attached to the museum . . . and if the old curator doesn't notice something's gone."

"Goodness! Wouldn't he notice?"

"Again, I'm guessing not. There is of course a formal inventory for something so valuable, but since they never leave the storage area—and I'm referring to his lesser-known setups, not those on display in the actual museum—I doubt he checks up on them. Why would he, really?"

"Indeed. Well, that's certainly very gutsy. I don't know if I condone it . . ."

"But . . ."

". . . but I suppose it would make things easier, quicker, and more accurate. I like the idea of using Father's own things to recreate something that happened with them to begin with. Is there enough equipment there to make it worthwhile?"

"There's a fair bit, yes. I've seen it, since the curator took me on a special tour that included that—and only because I requested it. Usually no one sees it. I actually don't know why they're still keeping it all, but then again there's junk down here that's probably as old."

"'*Junk?*'" I should feel insulted, but in the midst of our good progress I chuckle along with him. "Well, that's a start. That makes me feel a bit more optimistic, William."

"Good! So let's keep going around here and see what else we can scare up."

Over the next half hour we dig into dusty heaps and ordered shelves of items in all the Macdonald engineering labs, the architecture labs below Macdonald-Harrington, and the small area underneath FDA, though those are newer, cleaner labs. Along our trek, we ponder where to put everything we will collect; it has to be somewhere no one else will find, but we also need a large enough area for work tables to fit—and we need some power outlets.

A light bulb flickers to life inside my head. "Say, let's use my little broom closet!" I explain, to his bewilderment, my temporary home from my first days here.

"Crazy—that's not far down the hall from my office. That'll give me some cover when I go down there, but it's shielded enough from our office door that no one will see me or you if we're careful. Getting the equipment in will be a bit more difficult, but we'll figure that out. Might have to do it at night. We'll see."

"It's like I was meant to discover that little room, eh?"

"It's served its purpose and then some."

Having been reassured this afternoon of a few key things which had been gnawing at me, a happy lightness washes over me, and I fairly float after William as we weave our way upstairs through the basement labyrinth.

***

I'm lounging in Jeanne's greenhouse, as I'm calling it, relaxing in one of her padded wicker chairs with my legs curled loosely in the seat's ample base. A small lamp fights back the night's darkness. My hands clutch the Twentieth Century Novel course pack which William bought for me. The reading on Steinbeck is gripping, more so for its account of a history I'm learning for the first time than its analysis of his social perceptiveness.

Into my ears suddenly floats the delicate notes of classical music from Jeanne's record player at the end of the front hall. It's Chopin, I digest immediately—my favorite. His lively *Polonaise* curves my lips into a smile, and my eyes close. Instantly I'm transported back home. I could be listening to Mother's record and sitting in our parlor instead of here. She could be tinkering with tea in the kitchen, humming along; Father could be writing a paper at his desk in his library. I could almost open my eyes and see it all. . . .

"I thought we could use some nice music to brighten the evening," Jeanne says as she enters the greenhouse, stooping even her short frame below a tall, gangly false aralia.

"Mmm, yes. It's beautiful."

"Oh, I didn't see that you're reading. Do you want me to turn it off so it doesn't disturb you?"

"No, no," I answer, opening my eyes. "I love Chopin. I'm actually surprised people listen to him still."

"Oh? Why not? He's famous."

"Oh—sure. But it isn't . . . old-fashioned?"

She laughs. "I'm sure I could be accused of being old-fashioned, but classical music is timeless. People still buy records for Beethoven, Rossini, even that wretched Wagner—well, they buy CDs and digital albums, not these old records. I suppose I'm one of the last hangers-on to run one of these ancient phonographs, but I do like their pure sound."

"What else *would* you use to play music?"

"What else indeed?" Jeanne's tone is airy, almost flippant.

A minute deeper into the song, the phone's metallic notes fracture Chopin's piano staccato.

"Elie, dear, it's for you. It's William." She brings the phone to me. "I'll be in the other room until you're done."

"Oh, please—stay right here," I insist, then into the phone's handset say, "Hello? William?"

"Elie! How's it going?"

"Fine, thank you. And you?"

"Great. What's that music blaring? You and Jeanne holding a dance party down there?"

I tease him back. "A ball, you mean? Surely one can't do anything but waltz to a fine Chopin piece like this!"

"Chopin? I suppose you would like classical music, wouldn't you?"

"Yes—well, what else would one listen to?" I can't fathom an alternative, save folk songs, but that's not widely popular music. "Besides, I love Chopin. It reminds me of home. Mother wears out his recordings. . . . I should stop rambling, I'm sorry—"

"Don't be; it's fine—"

"—and you must have called for some reason, I presume, since I saw you a few hours ago. . . ."

At the other end of the line, William laughs. "All formality, eh, Elie? I was wondering if you're free tomorrow night. Evan'll be out, so we can have some privacy to start detailed planning of the project."

I sharply breathe in, my lips pursing, eyes flicking toward Jeanne. "I don't know, William. That's a bit . . . improper, you know."

More laughs. "Oops, you'd like a chaperone, wouldn't you? Should I invite Jeanne too? Maybe she'll have some time-traveling tips."

I can't help but giggle myself. "I see your point."

"Come on, I promise it's okay. This is 2006! It's all right to visit by yourself. It wouldn't be a scandal, even if we were more than friends." He pauses as I myself am momentarily dry-mouthed. "Err, besides, it's business only, right?"

"I suppose you're right." A corner of my brain acknowledges the tiny disappointment it will be just business. "Okay, I'll stop by after dinner."

"Good! See you then."

I hear the pleasure in his voice and am pleased myself.

Jeanne clears her throat with a squeak. "You two seem to be getting along quite well."

"Oh!" I shift my legs to cross them like a lady, aware of a slight warmth on my cheeks. "He's been a wonderful friend, really. I'm enormously grateful for his help."

"A wonderful friend, eh? Yes. . . ."

25

Wednesday, September 27, 2006
William

Shavash and Nico are entering the latest gamma ray data from Arizona into our analysis program, bopping their heads to the latest Muse album, when I barely hear a timid knock from the doorway.

"Hello? Can we come in?" It's Elie with Natalya, Isabelle, and Lindsey behind her.

"Hey! *Entrez-vous,*" I say, reaching over to my iPod dock to lower the volume.

"We came from class in McConnell. I thought I'd say hello before lunch, and the girls wanted to meet you guys," Elie says as explanation of her pack; it's always only Elie who meets me at my office. When I peer around her at her friends, I see they're shyly but curiously stealing glances at the older guys in the office, and I know why they're here.

"Well ladies, this is Alain, Julien, Jean-Philippe, Shavash, and Nico." When I introduce the girls to my friends and coworkers, the guys let their eyes linger an extra moment on the young undergraduates.

Her friends step forward to see what the guys are doing—though I'm sure only Elie would understand, and only because I've explained things like gamma radiation to her—while Elie rolls her eyes at me behind their backs. I shrug.

She leans in to me and whispers faintly, "Did you slip in the wire coils last night?" After I finished my work here yesterday, I gathered some loose wire and exposed coils we put together in the lab and hid them away in Elie's old closet, free from prying eyes. I nod discreetly.

Isabelle gestures to a detailed three-foot-by-two-foot poster of VERITAS detector array, asking with wide eyes, "Did you guys build this?"

"Yeah—well, some of it. Well, we contributed to the design and machined some of the parts. Now we process the data when they send it back and verify its fidelity, modifying some of the algorithms from time to time," Nico says as he runs his hands through his tousled hair.

"Huh?" she asks, prompting Julien to jump in with a further explanation.

Before he gets too far, Kevin and Anna interrupt with a generous clap on our open door.

"Quite the crowd here," Anna says with amusement, her blue eyes jumping from boy to girl. "Why didn't anyone invite us to the physics party?"

"Because we're old, Anna, and clearly of the wrong set," Kevin quips, keenly aware the young women in the room aren't physics students; I'm pretty sure since he teaches the intro physics course he can recognize the dozen girls in the class, of which Elie is one.

"Professor Nagar, Professor Davidson, the girls are friends of Will. This is Natalya, Lindsey, Isabelle, and Elie," Alain says, laying the blame on my desk.

Kevin's gaze stops on Elie as her face registers. "Ah, yes. Eileen Newton, is it? You're in my PHY131 class, aren't you?"

Startled at being plucked from her obscurity, she nods faintly.

"You did an excellent job on yesterday's quiz, Ms. Newton. Notably so, and on the homework. Either you're the next Marie Curie or Will here does your work," he says with an obvious wink at me.

Elie, however, reacts with horror, not catching the tease. "No . . . no, I wouldn't. . . ."

"Oh now, I was only joking. Will would've had to have taken the quiz yesterday for you too!" He cracks one of his hearty, bellowing laughs rippling his loose beard.

"Say," Anna adds with a playful tease of her own, "is this *the* Elie that Alain and Nico keep telling me you're with in the lab when I call down here for you, Will?"

Now it's my turn to be startled. "Uh . . . yeah, er . . . maybe. . . ."

She laughs at my squirming. "If you weren't so damn smart and did so much work for me so quickly, Will, I'd tell you to ease off the, ahem, extracurriculars and get back to the books." She passes an approving smile to Elie.

At this point I don't know who's blushing more, me or Elie, though as I look at her friends, they're starting to redden for her sake as well. To steer away the attention I ask, "So . . . what brings you both here, anyway? Did we accidentally blow up the detector array or something?"

"Don't even joke about that, Will," Kevin says. "The Americans just called and need to move up our teleconference with them to Friday. We'll have to parse that data and get that prototype gripper piece machined ASAP and discuss. When can you gentlemen and lady be ready for us all to sit together? Tomorrow morning?"

We all nod in agreement and set a time. When they leave, the rest except for me, Elie, and poor Shavash are in deep, intimate conversations. Shavash sighs in slight disgust and returns to her computer, which gives me a chance to talk to Elie privately.

"Meet me in the basement after lunch. I do need to work on that gripper piece Professor Nagar mentioned, but I can finish it tonight."

"I only have until one thirty. And won't the basement be crawling with people then?"

"No, that's good timing. That's the most popular hour for classes, and these guys will all be up here. I'm the one slated to be working down there today."

"Fine. I'll drag these ladies away for a bite of lunch, then fly right down there."

"Great—see you in a bit."

"Wait!" She grabs my left arm as I start toward my desk chair. "Did she mean what she said a few minutes ago? That you're always with me? If she feels that way, then everyone must. . . ."

I admit I wasn't aware it's that obvious. "Yes, I guess so. Maybe we should meet up later instead, when your friends have gone home and I'm supposed to be downstairs working anyway. No one will suspect anything then. Let's say, four o'clock?"

"Yes, that's a better solution. Better to play it safe and not let anyone know we're spending time together."

I hate to tell her that ship has probably already sailed—and that people think we're together for a romantic rather than a working relationship—but I don't want to send her Victorian mind into a whirl of worry.

* * *

Later that evening, when everyone else seems to have left for dinner, Elie and I are the only people in the entire basement of the adjoined engineering and architecture buildings except for a small group of architecture students in their wood lab, absorbed in model-making. We're bent over a small but well-lit table, assembling a gold leaf electroscope. It looks like a plain metal box, but inside are parallel metal plates and a sensitive rod that moves at a rate according to the alpha radiation. A strong electromagnet and a battery are still to be inserted. Next to us lies my actual work, complete save a few rough edges that need filing.

"How is everything going overall? I realized today how long you've been here. We've been so into the deep with this setup that I hadn't noticed," I say as I strip the sheathing off one end of a wire I intend to connect to the battery.

"Yes, quite," Elie says slowly, staring at her hands while she contemplates. "I'm actually quite busy between my classes, the homework for them, working at Odyssey, helping Jeanne at home, and of course working on this."

"You're still doing the homework, eh? Planning to return home yet diligently not falling behind in this century? Model student."

"It would be odd to do otherwise. Why bother taking the classes if I don't do the homework or readings? I'd be lost if I didn't, and I wouldn't be able to chat with the girls. Plus, I suppose it is sort of enjoyable, though it is work. And . . . what else would I do with my time here?"

I shrug. "I guess you'd be awfully bored if you didn't. And would you be able to work on this all day long? Unlikely, since I can't be free all day to help."

"Help? You're doing most of this, William. I'm providing the data, so to speak, on what was in his lab, but you're doing the hard work of finding the parts and putting them together."

"We're both putting it together. I'm not doing all the work."

"Okay, fine. Let's say we're moving like a finely tuned orchestra," she says with a flourish of her tool-wielding hands.

"Something like that." I laugh. "Say, speaking of orchestra, I completely forgot I picked up an album for you so we can listen to it while we work. Thought you'd enjoy it."

I plug my iPod into its speaker dock and thumb through my collection until I find the album I added last night. I'm eager to see her reaction and hope she's pleased.

I tap the play button and a soft "Prelude" begins. The notes, mild but clear, pick at the air and fill first this spot and then the next, until the entire lab is a cloud of flickering sharps and flats.

Elie revolves her face toward me and inhales slowly. Her breath, when let out, blows cool against my forearms. Slowly her mouth breaks into a smile, content and dreamy.

"You look happy."

"I am. I love Chopin." Elie's eyes close slowly, as if drifting asleep. "And you never forget what you love, no matter how far away it goes from you."

"Good thing he was a hit," I whisper as I lean in to gently poke her—first aiming for the ribs but then redacting my hand before actually touching her.

She chuckles but stays in her musical reverie. We sit silently for a few minutes as the Prelude turns into "Nocturne No.2" in E flat. The rhythm is slower, the notes even quieter, and I start to see the music as an exact mirror of Elie's personality.

"You know," she says, her words barely above a whisper, "when I close my eyes, I can imagine myself back home. With this music playing, I could be sitting on my parents' green velvet sofa and Father could be in his study next door, writing a letter to Eve or Grandmother. It's almost. . . ."

"What?"

She's silent for a moment.

"It's almost . . . it's almost as if I'm home, but then I open my eyes and the wall is bricked over. It's so far. . . ." Her voice is tiny now, the smallest chord in the mellow din.

I turn my gaze away from her, not trusting my face to hide the tinge of sadness that remark brought. As if it's the first time I realize it, I say, "You really miss home, don't you? No, you really belong there."

She's looking down at her hands too. "I do. Of course I miss it. I think about Father and Mother so often every day. That's not to say my time here isn't pleasant as well," she continues in a rush, keeping her propriety and politeness. "I like my classes immensely, and despite the gravity of what we're undertaking here, I'm enjoying spending this time working here with you too."

"Mmm." I absolutely cannot let myself get more interested in Elie. I cannot let myself get attached, whether she's "enjoying spending this time with me"—which I am too, since what am I, a monk?—or not. I slap my hands on my thighs and stand up, breaking the moment. "Well! Get you the right music and I make you melt right into the floor. I'm sorry for having distracted you, Elie. Let's get back to building this thing so you can get back home, right?"

She looks curiously at me and nods, then returns to her task of fitting the charging wire onto the electroscope terminal.

Soon we're back acting as our orchestra, grabbing materials and fixing them together as if we've been doing this for years. And despite the ancient-looking designs of this equipment, I'm really appreciating its simplicity and efficiency in design. I doubt any of us graduate students could've done this as elegantly, remembering Rutherford was in his mid-twenties when he was working on much of this apparatus.

Our own elegant movements break down, however, when, as I return to the table with a cleaning cloth, I bump full-on into Elie as she's standing up from her stool.

"Oomph!" She reaches for the stool to steady her, but I've dropped the cloth and grabbed her thin frame before she can topple. For a moment the lower halves of our bodies are intermingled, and I'm craned over her arched figure like a hero saving a woman from falling over a cliff. The moment could've stretched half a minute, but a second later I'm setting her back down on her stool and breaking our locked stare. Those sky blue eyes, wide with shock. . . .

"So sorry, Elie. I'm usually not a klutz like that. You okay?"

"A what? No matter, I'm fine. Great balance there, William." Her countenance returns to default, and I hope my own isn't as crimson as my violently beating heart.

"Nice recovery, you mean."

She laughs. "Yes, quite. So . . . changing the subject—"

"Thank you—"

"—I got an interesting comment a few weeks ago from a bloke in my physics class. We were sort of talking quietly while Professor Nagar was teaching, and I was answering the questions the professor was asking. Well, this bloke was struggling to answer them, and he said I should be the physics major, not him." She's twisting her hands around and around as she recounts this conversation.

"Uh-huh," I say while getting back to my work. "What did you say back?"

"Well, nothing out loud, but I've been thinking about it since then. I do love physics so, but I don't know about actually majoring in it."

"Why not, Elie? It's in your blood, and apparently you have an aptitude for it."

She turns to me, mouth silently forming words while her eyes convey confusion only.

"Elie, are you okay? Did I say something wrong?"

"Yes, I didn't think you'd say that. Could I really, a female, major in physics?"

I burst out laughing. "Elie, is that what this is about? You being a girl? This isn't 1906! You've met Shavash—she's a graduate physics student. Of course you could do it. You'd be a tad behind since you're taking your arts courses this semester, but intellectually and officially you could definitely do it if you wanted to."

She still looks stunned. "I-I guess I could. It's odd to think so. I'm not used to women being on equal footing as men, William."

I stare at her hard for several seconds, trying to understand her perspective. To me, it's perfectly natural, if not as common, for a girl to consider a physics degree—or a medical degree or engineering or anything else male-dominated. But to her. . . . I keep forgetting how few opportunities women like her had in her era. I know her schooling situation as a Donalda and how she was limited in what she could pursue. When I explain this to her, she nods and thanks me for the support.

"I'm more shocked that you take this all in stride and have so little reaction, really. I can't imagine, say . . . Ralph Fowler supporting me taking *one* physics class, let alone going for a physics degree. He had little time even for my Donalda classes. The contrast is severe, William. I should be saying thank you."

I'm unprepared to be compared to Ralph.

"Elie, um, you're welcome. I wouldn't react any other way, really. You should do what you want in anything you do. If it takes us six months to get this thing working, by all means take a physics track if you want to. If you get back to 1906 next month, see what you can do to get into McGill's physics program. At least you know it's allowed eventually," I say with a wink.

"Thanks, William, really." She clasps my forearm and squeezes it lightly.

I stiffen instinctively and resist the urge to pull away. With forced calm I try to smile a little, then turn back toward finishing the electroscope.

Time passes, and before we know it, we're done and it's past time for us to get back to our apartments and have dinner. As we walk, we decide to do test runs on our amalgamated setup in the closet once everything is ready and set up on tables there. Neither of us has any idea how we'll do a test run, or what we'll test the time machine on. As usual, we're shooting into the dark with this wild experiment.

* * *

A warm breeze from the open windows in our apartment flushes my face when I open the front door. Though it's evening, by now our Indian summer keeps steaming on.

"Were you out with Elie?" The pungent pepper of Chinese take-out reaches me a second after Evan's question does.

"Yeah. Just got back now."

"Wow. Hot and heavy, eh? She's really replaced your old girlfriend."

"Who? She was a long time ago," I say while waving my hand away.

"Yeah, I know. As in, it's about time you found someone else."

"No, you don't understand. Elie and I are just friends."

"Right—friends that are of the opposite sex and hang out exclusively—and pretty much all the time. Hey, that's what JP and Elise are, just friends," he says with a wink as he hands me a container of chicken and broccoli. "Here, I got this for you."

I thank him while pouting. "No, really, it's not like that." There's really no way to explain our real relationship, so I leave it at that.

He pauses, eying me sideways. "Will, are you . . . you're not . . . are you?"

"Are you trying to ask if I'm gay, Evan?" I can barely say the words for the laughs pouring out of my mouth.

"Yeah, I mean, are you? Who could just be friends with Elie? She's—okay, she's maybe a bit weird in a way—but she's smart and pretty smokin' hot. The rest of us think so. Thought you'd noticed too."

I'm trying so hard not to blush or show any hint of how those words made my insides a mass of twirling spaghetti. Of course I think Elie is—well, I'd word it as beautiful—but I can't admit that and tell Evan how hard it is to tamp down those feelings every time I see her . . . and, really, any time I daydream of her. But if I were to get irrevocably attached to her . . . *ugh*, the spaghetti sinks heavier in my gut . . . and then when—if—she goes back home. *God, what a shattered mess I'd be.*

I shake my thoughts back to Evan. "Of course I see it. Maybe now's not the time for a relationship, that's all."

Evan looks like he doesn't believe me. Who would?

"Look, Evan, she just moved here from New Zealand and is still adjusting. I'd like to let her settle in before I get involved like that."

"You mean before you work your all-powerful Will Hertz love magic?"

We laugh. That "magic" is about as effective as making the philosopher's stone. If only Evan knew my magic is wiring physics experiments on our "dates." If I weren't so focused on that, I might have let myself fixate a bit more on her—and who knows how we might instead be spending our evenings.

26

Thursday, October 12, 2006
Elie

While I wait for William to finish his class up in the Rutherford Physics Building—I love hearing that name—I enjoy the month's likely last warm day out on the Commons. My physics class ended a few minutes early, and I have a bit of time to relax before we picnic together for lunch. Behind me sits the regal Grecian façade of the Redpath Museum, but in front of me extends a still-perky emerald carpet dotted with a few crisped, fallen leaves among many pockets of fellow sunbathers. I'm lucky to find a free patch to sit on; while near the top edge of the grass, it does give me a wide perspective to surreptitiously watch people.

At first it looks like groups of friends sitting together—some reading books, others sharing lunch, most chatting and laughing—but the longer I look, the more couples I see, all looking as if their opposite is the only other person on the Commons. To my embarrassment, some are embracing, lying close to one another, even kissing—out in the open! As soon as I spot a couple with lips pressed together I avert my eyes. Are they not aware they're not in private? Do they care that everyone else here can see them—see them acting how couples should act only when in their own homes?

As I'm scanning other people's gazes, it seems no one is watching any other group besides their own. No one except me is paying any attention to what these couples are doing. It doesn't seem to discomfit them. Suddenly, I'm embarrassed for them as well as for me—a voyeur if ever there was one.

Yet, if no one else cares, should I? If this is how people in this century carry on in their relationships, I suppose I should view this as normal and accept it. It's awkward and uncomfortable, but, surprisingly, a bit freeing as well. No one seems uptight; those couples are smiling and enjoying their other's presence, lost in their intimate moments of love. It's actually curious to watch. The longer I—subtly—watch them, the more I see how happy they are. One girl is twirling her long blond hair around a finger, looking up now and then at her beau while he seems to be telling her a story—yet when he stops to bend forward and kiss her twirling hand again and again, her face erupts into a wide smile with velvety eyes that say *I love you* more clearly than her words could. Those few gestures say so much. . . . I can see how in love they are, no matter how foreign those feelings are to my own heart.

Instantly a vision of Ralph Fowler crosses my sight. It's a cordial view and nothing more. Never with him did I imagine having emotions evoked such as that blond girl has right now. What a contrast! Even taking into account the reserved, relatively platonic courting rules of my time, I can see in hindsight how ill-suited Ralph and I are. I could never, ever feel toward him how rapturous that girl feels toward her date.

It strikes me forcefully how self-absorbed I was by my inward struggle against Ralph's overtures. In hindsight those thoughts filled most of my waking minutes, and it was trivial compared to the immense hurdles I'm facing now. So what if I would've been pressed into marrying a man—a man who's smart, mostly kind, successful, and friendly to my family—even if he doesn't incite a vague stirring, let alone ecstasy? Weighed against trying to survive in a foreign century with no money or connections, that's utterly trifling. I'd give anything to have that simple sort of life back—which is why William and I are working so hard to get the time machine alive.

Yet, as I continue to stare ashamedly at the couple, I must admit this era does have its pull. It would be nice to have someone close to me in that way.

With a pang of jealousy—accompanied a tick later by emptiness—I take one last look at the two lovers, then turn my study to the groups of friends. Now they all look familiar to me. Why, they could be transported—with an era-appropriate clothes change—to 1906 and fit right in! Just like I used to do with Emma and my other girlfriends, they're reading and talking in a fashion that's timeless. Friends bond in the same way no matter when they're living, and a laugh is a laugh. These people I'm not jealous of, realizing I've fit into my own pack of lovely friends here already.

"Hello? *Bonjour*? Elie?"

"William! I didn't see you walk up." A bit startled, I stand up to greet him.

"Yeah, I know. Ten mile stare," he says with a wink and a grin. He hands me a paper cup with a lid. "Cup o' tea for your thoughts?"

"Mmm, thank you." A wave of dull-scented steam fills my nostrils, but it's welcome nevertheless. I don't like to miss my daily tea.

"So . . .?"

"I was observing, that's all."

"Looked like you were thinking hard about all these people, Elie. Do they pass the test?"

"Hmm? What test? Oh—very funny. It struck me a moment ago that while I'm shocked repeatedly by what's on the outside of people—what they look like, of course, and also some of their actions—they're still about the same now as they are in my time."

William's face reads confusion mixed with curiosity.

"I mean, I see some couples being very . . . open . . . in their relationship, right in front of everybody else, but when you watch their emotions, it's the same as a couple in love in any time period. And it's the same with a group of friends spending an afternoon in the sun—now, then, it doesn't matter—people are people. That's comforting to me."

"Wow," he says, impressed with my revelation. "That's deep, Elie. And true, I hope; you're really the one who can judge that. Does that mean you're comfortable here amongst all of us ogres and heathens after all?"

I laugh, mock-crashing my shoulder into his. "It means I can understand people here a bit more, I suppose, and not assume there's so much difference between us all."

"Just a bit of immorality and overexposure?" William gestures at a couple nearby who are playfully—and sensually—feeding each other berries.

"William! They'll see you!"

"Don't worry; they don't see anyone besides each other."

"Yes, but. . . ." I turn away from them to face the engineering buildings to the east.

"Elie, I know it's a huge adjustment for you to see all this—really I do. But don't think you're seeing anything you're not meant to see. That's how people are nowadays. If they didn't want you to see them . . . they wouldn't do it. Simple as that."

"Simple as that. . . ."

"Yeah, it is. Things aren't very proper anymore, I guess you could say, but that doesn't mean they don't have to be." His deep green eyes are boring into mine.

"Oh?"

He nods, then looks down into his own paper cup, undoubtedly filled with black coffee. Clearing his throat, he adds, "Anyway, uh, should we find a private spot of grass for lunch before we go to the lab?"

For the briefest of moments the thought passes through my head that he was about to put his hand to the small of my back to press me along with him. Pausing for that thought to vanish like a whisper, I nod and follow into step beside him, arms at my sides just like his.

* * *

"Why did Professor Rand give us *so long* of a reading to do when he knows we have a midterm coming up? He's torturous!" Lindsey wails as she flips through forty pages of our Twentieth Century Novel course pack. "This is the length of a novella, for God's sake!"

"He's sadistic," Isabelle agrees. "Obviously it'll be included on our midterm, so we have to read it."

"That and we have to complete those questions at the end of the reading *and* write that mini essay," I add. "Well, we'll just have to give it heaps."

"Give it what?"

"Heaps," I answer, "as in, 'a lot of effort.' I forget you all don't say that, sorry."

"We love your sayings, Elie! Don't ever apologize," Lindsey says, and the other two girls nod.

We've decided to spend our Sunday afternoon in a joint work session in Isabelle and Lindsey's dorm room. I have an off day from the bookshop, and William is working on a particularly difficult homework assignment for his high-energy physics class. Though I'm loathe to "waste" a long available day not working on the time machine, it was William who convinced me to take a break—we were in the lab and closet until late last night—and spend some time with my girlfriends.

"So let's get on with it," Natalya says with her usual Russian pragmatism. "Since we've all read far enough to answer the first two questions, let's do those and then read the rest and finish the questions, then plan the essay. *Da?*"

"*Da, da,*" we all parrot back to her, nodding in mock earnest.

Joking aside, we work as if under threat of a whip for an hour and a half, then take a break for tea and strawberry scones which Jeanne and I baked this morning. Soon, the conversation moves from Hemingway to our futures.

"I keep hearing people say if we have a degree in English, then we'll only be able to get a job teaching about English," Isabelle complains. "But I don't want to be a professor my whole life!"

"You don't have to be," I say. "You could become a writer—"

"Or an editor—" Lindsey interjects.

"Yes, or get a graduate degree in something else—"

"Like Law, or get an MBA—" Lindsey adds again. "Sorry to keep interrupting, Elie; I guess I'm used to defending our choice of major."

"It's all right. I didn't know there were so many options, actually. I hope women can pursue some of those too. A lawyer, imagine that!"

My comment is met with blank, unbelieving looks.

"Uh, of course we can do those, Elie. Maybe New Zealand doesn't have many women lawyers, or CEOs or whatever, but here in Canada that happens all the time. It's not a fifty-fifty split, but it's getting closer every year," Isabelle says.

Saving me from sputtering a face-saving remark, Natalya replies, "That's all good if that's what you want to do, but I plan on getting married and raising children, so why do I want a graduate degree now? I'm only going to work for a few years and then stay home with my kids. If I want to work a fancy job later, I'll get a graduate degree then."

I'm stunned, as it appears her view is somewhat of a deviant path nowadays, and Isabelle and Lindsey are as well—but for the opposite reason as me.

"So why are you bothering going to university, Natalya?" the latter asks.

"Because I like learning," she answers simply. "I like the classes, and I do want to teach for a few years—maybe high school or middle school, not in university—but I don't want to embark on a big career."

We're all quiet for a minute, each pondering her and Isabelle's strong views while wondering who will speak next.

It's Lindsey who breaks the silence, saying, "That's perfectly fine if that's what you want to do, Natalya. What's great about where women are in society right now is that we have a choice. We can embark on a mountain-topping career if we want and go all the way, so to speak. Or we can have a family and focus on their life instead of our job. But we can also do both, just at different points in our life. There isn't only one path."

Isabelle turns to her with arched eyebrows and slightly rose cheeks, if I'm not mistaken. "Wow, that was . . . eloquent. Really! I've never heard anyone, especially not my hippie, women's-lib mother, describe things that way."

"But you have to make what you're doing count, and you have to believe in it. Becoming the president of a company would make certain people happy but would drive others mad. Raising four kids would fulfill one woman's life dream but crush another's," Natalya says.

The three girls banter about for several more minutes and debate both sides, but I stay mute, just listening to the conversation. Never would any of my friends from back home hold such opinions—yet never would we have the opportunities these girls are speaking of. In truth, I'm not chiming into the conversation because I'm a bit in awe. In the weeks when I've been in classes at McGill, it's only been for the moment, not a means to an end as these girls are describing it. I hadn't realized there was a way other than what being a Donalda graduate offers.

"What do you think, Elie?" Lindsey asks. "You're awfully quiet."

"I . . . I agree with all of you. We have it so good right now, you have no idea."

"You'd be the type I'd expect to build a big career, Elie," she says in earnest. "You're smart enough to top our class, and you could do a science degree if you wanted."

"Yeah, I wouldn't be surprised if you did a double major or something," Isabelle says.

"A double major in literature and physics? Each is hard enough, especially physics!" I say, actually more stunned they'd suggest me doing physics than having two majors.

"Maybe," Lindsey concedes. "But I could totally see you becoming a physicist. You're smart enough to practically teach our literature class, and it sounds like physics is a breeze for you. You could seriously do it, Elie."

I thank her and smile, a bit embarrassed by the praise, then shrug my shoulders noncommittally. The conversation moves back to potential jobs after graduation, and I'm left to muse what that would hold for me if I *were* in fact to switch to physics.

In the end, William was right; taking a few hours to enjoy the wonderful ladies I have as friends here is worth it, both for the pleasure of their company and the temporary mental release from the stress of getting our time machine together. In the trying weeks that are to test both of us, I know I should appreciate these moments now while I still can.

27

Saturday, November 4, 2006
William

"This is it," I say with a nervous tickle of excitement. "It's all laid out how you described it. Solenoids, wires, electroscope, mica sheets, power supply, battery, magnets, charging plates, and so on . . . and I think that's about it!"

Elie looks with pride at our careful setup. It looks like an old storage closet spit up on our work table, but to her it looks perfect. To me . . . well, I have to trust her that this is what we're aiming for.

"It's it, William. Now we have to connect the battery to the electroscope, and when we turn on the power supply, it should excite the circuit. If I close my eyes, this is precisely how I picture things in Father's lab that fateful, frightful Friday."

"Are we ready for a test run? Is this it—*the* moment?"

"Yes," she says with solemnity. "It's time we try it."

"Are you ready? Are you sure?"

"Of course I am. What are we waiting for?"

I give her a half-smile, hoping to convey my best wishes this works as we planned. "Okay, Miss Rutherford, switching on power supply in three, two, one!"

Click! A quiet crescendo of electronic whirring as the circuit comes to life. A few gentle cracks as loose connections spark and dust fries. But neither of us moves an inch.

We, for safety's sake, are standing behind the heavy door, ajar to Elie's secret closet. When we peer in to look for our test subject, a fat, brown caterpillar, we both groan with disappointment that it's still squirming on the floor.

"Drat!" Elie cries. "Something must be wonky!"

"Don't worry," I say as I relax her waving arms. "I heard some loose wires move. We'll fix it and retry. Just a minute. . . ."

Forty minutes and two dozen test attempts later, our caterpillar is still on the linoleum. It's as I've feared it: this jumble of crap is just that—crap. Immobile, unworkable crap. It's a disparate Pollock-esque collection of junk we've found and cobbled together, and I've known it all along. Elie swears this will work, somehow, but I can't see this amounting to anything.

"William, please, let's take a short break. I can see you're frustrated, and frankly so am I."

"Humph." I agree to walk outside and breathe some head-clearing fresh air. We stroll side by side on the grass and below trees in front of the engineering buildings. Dusk has shaded the campus, but the very top of Mont Royal still glows golden.

Elie clasps her hands behind her back and looks up at the moon, newly risen and full. "So bright," she says. "It makes me think of home."

"How so?"

"I used to see the moon rise outside my bedroom window when I laid there before bed. I sort of marked time by the lunar phase, in a way."

"You were in bed when the moon rose? That's so early!"

"Well, I wasn't in bed the second the moon rose, but soon after. Remember, in 1906 people don't stay awake as late as they do now. We have gas and oil lamps at home, but we don't keep them lit late into the night. And I actually used to read by candlelight in the evenings. Mother says it'll ruin my eyesight. . . ."

Sometimes it takes something like this to remind me how far removed she is from my time.

"Elie, that's crazy. You actually fit in so well now that when you say things like that it kind of shocks me."

"Thank you. But the conveniences are easy for me to adjust to, in a way. I can imagine you'd have a bit of a start trying to read by candlelight—and survive without a computer or cell phone." She wears a devious smile, half her mouth curved up and eyes flickering.

"Sadly, yes. Anyway. . . . Nice moon. Good thing it is full, since VERITAS is a little slow right now because of it. Gives me less analysis work and more time to work on our project."

"There's sunshine after every cloud, William. Perfect, since it's taking a long time to get this going."

"That's a nice way of saying we're currently crashing and burning."

"So what if we're not making progress right now? That's alright! Father never solved anything in one day either." She's standing with her hands on her jean-clad hips and face as relaxed as mine is furrowed. "We'll think about it, work on it, fix it up, and Bob's your uncle!"

"Wha-What?" *Literally, what the hell did she just say?*

"That's the Kiwi version of '*voilà*,'" she says dismissively. "Look, William, we've only just begun the hard part. But we'll get this to work, really, we will. I can *feel* it. We need to persevere. Maybe we're overlooking something here."

"We've gone over the layout, Elie. It's laid out exactly as you remember it, so unless there's a connection somewhere here that's missing but that you remember now. . . ."

"It has to work. It has to send this little guy backward. . . ."

Ugh—I slap my forehead comically. *How could I be so stupid?!* "Elie! We've hooked this up forward, not backward. Remember how we talked about reversing everything—the polarity of the connections—so it works opposite of how it did for you?"

"Oh, right. . . ."

"Not that it'll make this magically work," I add, "but I'd rather find this out now before accidentally sending you to 2106."

We both laugh.

"Well, genius, let's switch everything," Elie says. Once we're back into the closet, she immediately gets to work unhooking the main wires from the power supply terminals. "Wait a moment, do you know what else we've neglected? Connecting our time-travelling critter to the same apparatus I touched—we have to make him touch the time measurement device!"

"Oh, God. How tired are we that we missed these two fundamental aspects of the setup?" As a scientist I'm appalled at my own lack of quality and follow-through.

"Very. How about we make these two fixes, do one more test run, and then call it a night? Perhaps we need to step away from it a bit."

"Good idea, Elie. Okay, lemme find a conductive plate for the little guy to crawl on, and I'll use an alligator clip wire to connect it to the time interval device."

Several minutes later, we're back behind the door and ready to turn on the power supply, which I'm doing remotely. I see Elie's fingers crossed at her sides, and I'm fighting the urge to do the same.

"Ready? One, two, three!"

Fzzt! A sizzle and a small pop. Not a good sign.

"Eww, he's been cooked! William, we killed him!"

My whole body wants to melt into the floor. This is a terrible sign, and she knows it too. We're both quiet for a minute.

"Well, at least we know the circuit did something this time, William."

"Always looking on the bright side!"

"Of course! Look, we'll make this work. We're definitely going to need more insects though."

"I'll collect a jar full of them tomorrow morning and we'll get back at it. Do you want to meet back here before your shift at the bookstore tomorrow?"

"I think we ought to, if you want to spend the time. I have a feeling we'll be doing an awful lot of test runs."

"What else am I gonna do?" I ask, truthfully and a bit pathetically. My life is completely wrapped up in hers. Does she know that? She's replying with an excited smile, intent only on getting a successful test run. "What am I going to do with my time when you're gone?" I murmur.

But Elie, oblivious to my wistful question, is already packing up her bag to leave.

* * *

"What are you up to, Will? *Mon dieu*, it's Sunday morning! What's so important that you're always running out and working on instead of hanging out with us?" Alain bangs one of our cheap mugs on the counter in protest of me leaving during our weekly hangout; coffee sloshes dangerously up the side.

I freeze, arm midway through my jacket sleeve, and turn around. True, none of us miss our Sunday morning hangouts unless it's absolutely necessary. But I didn't realize my absences otherwise, mostly late nights, were noticed. Maybe it's because my lack of sleep has caught up with me, but a snippy response comes out of my mouth.

"So you're hurt I'm not with you guys as much anymore, is that it?"

"Man, I could care less if you wanted to ditch me and the guys if you said you were studying for a midterm or banging Elie, but it's not that. You won't say what you're doing. You're always sneaking around. It's off, Will; it's just off."

I have no idea how to play this next. There's no way to explain this. *Why does he have to be so inquisitive now*?

"Alain, it's not what you think. I'm not sneaking around to anywhere. I swear to you."

"Right. *Merde*, you're probably working double time on the project to score extra points with Kevin and Anna."

"No, I'm not spending extra time on the project—"

"That's it, isn't it?" Alain's glaring eyes could singe my face. He's so angry he doesn't notice he's gnawing his lips aggressively. "That's it—you're trying to do more on the project to impress them, and then impress the guys in Arizona while you're at it. You're trying to push me off the project, big shot!"

I'm flabbergasted; this isn't going well at all. I don't want to cause a permanent rift with him no matter how much I need to hide something. Odd, though, the conclusion he's jumping to.

"Alain, honestly, I'm not trying to cut you or anyone else out. I'm not going back to the lab to work on VERITAS, I swear to you. And you see my laptop is here—I'm not working. You can see that."

"I don't believe you, Will. *Osti d'tabernak*, there's something still not right. Where the hell are you off to then?"

I hesitate—a mistake.

"I am off to bang Elie—you were right." It's the first plausible story that pops into my head.

He snorts. "*Bien sûr*. Right, you've been screwing her for weeks now—and I've got a date with Scarlett Johansson Friday night. We'd know if you were, Will, and you're not."

"Ouch, man. What makes you say that? I'm always with her." At least that part is true. "How do you know we're not screwing?"

"She'd be all over you. Girls turn emotional and clingy when you screw 'em, and Elie isn't like that, man. And Evan said you told him you guys are just friends. Nice try. So what are you up to? Admit it's the project."

"Honest to God I'm not. I told you the truth—I'm going to see Elie."

"Liar." The anger is still there, chased by a little disgust. I wonder if he's thinking about spitting in my face.

"I'm not lying!"

"*Putain de mec. . . .*" he mutters as he shoves past me and back to his apartment.

Evan's squeezing through the door with a grocery bag just as Alain is leaving in a huff, swearing at me further.

"Did he call you a—"

"Yeah."

"What did you do to him? I've never seen him that pissed off before," Evan asks.

I sigh. "He says I'm gone all the time. Needless to say he's jumping to the wrong conclusions and thinks I'm working extra on VERITAS to push him out."

"Wow . . . that's pretty crazy."

"Irrational, really."

"Why on Earth would he think that? He's with you all the time you're working on that, and he locks up the damn door every night!"

"I know—it makes no sense. Anyway, let's forget about that. He'll come back to his senses." Really, I'm just desperate to change the subject rather than open myself up to the same questions from Evan. "What are you up to today?"

"Dunno," Evan shrugs. "I *was* going to hang out with you guys like usual—I bought breakfast—but I guess that's off. Maybe we can hang out instead."

"How about a little later? I'm off to see Elie for a few hours before she has to go to work." At least this isn't a lie.

"He *was* right that you're going off a lot, Will—"

I snap back to look at him as I grab my coat by the front door.

"—but I trust you. Have fun with her." He winks.

* * *

In the lab on Monday night there's literally no sound except the dull hum of the power supply, wastefully pumping out electrons, and the occasional rustling of our clothes as we shift thoughtfully, restlessly, in our chairs. The lack of noise echoes our recent lack of progress. In every single test we've tried, today's caterpillars have been zapped or worse.

"Do you know what times like these need? Music," Elie says, determined to change the emotion of the room. In the absence of my iPod dock, she's left to humming—strong notes of a familiar song.

I cock my head and regard her with narrow eyes. "What are you humming?"

"'Onward Christian Soldier.'"

I relax my eyes, which develop a thousand-foot stare. "You really are Ernest Rutherford's daughter. That he loved that song is an obscure fact about him—no casual reader of his work would know that."

Her expression turns crooked and questioning.

"You're you, Elie, but there have been times I've thought myself to be crazy to believe it. Look at what we're doing—a fool's errand! It's practically modern alchemy! Yet, yet. . . ."

"Yes. Yet, it has to happen. It *has* to work. It did once, it bloody well will again. We're just . . . missing something."

"Clearly. But what? What other damned piece of junk can we add to this?"

"Hey! It's not junk. It's not orderly, that's all," she adds, looking at our array of odds and ends with motherly pride. We both take our time examining each piece of equipment with our eyes. Finally, she draws hers up and says in an almost reluctant whisper, "Say . . . there is one big thing we're missing, one we dismissed as irrelevant long ago."

"What's that?"

"Radioactivity. Alpha particles." Barely a whisper.

"That has nothing to do with any of this setup, though. Radioactivity and electricity don't mix."

She nods slowly, probably realizing what theoretical nonsense she's suggesting but showing conviction for her hypothesis. "That's what we thought, yes—and I agree they *shouldn't* affect each other when interacting *normally*—but the scattering experiment *was* in the lab that day. Maybe the radium was still there. Maybe it altered the state of the energy in the room somehow, I don't know how, and is the key to it all."

"That's absurd—but possibly brilliant."

"Thank you."

I smile. "You *are* brilliant. But you're also not playing by the laws of physics I am. Maybe that's how you can see this. But you're right; it's the only thing we haven't recreated."

"It could be worth a shot, as you say."

"Worth a shot," I agree. "But do you know how hard it is to get a sample of radioactive material for approved research projects? How are we going to sneak a sample for our time machine?"

"Don't any of the physics labs use radioactive sources? Can't we borrow some like we've borrowed the rest of this equipment?"

I laugh a single, ironic chuckle. "If only it were that easy in this day and age. Radioactive materials are very, very closely guarded. If they get into the wrong hands, however small a sample, it could be dangerous. No, there's no way we could take any from a lab. That's a sure ticket to getting kicked out of McGill, Elie."

"Ugh," she sighs. "There's *nothing* that uses a radioactive element that we can procure, somehow, from someone?"

I start shaking my head, dreading that we've come this far and are hitting the end of the trail. There's no way to get thorium or polonium without this being an official research request, let alone uranium or plutonium ... but there are radium, used in watch faces, and americium, used in smoke detectors, I realize. It's a small amount, granted, but now I remember Alain telling me about a guy in New Jersey who recreated the gold foil experiment using polonium as his alpha particle source but hypothesized the possibility of using americium.

When I tell this to Elie, she glows brighter than a nuclear reaction. "That's it! *Voilà*—we have our source!"

"Yes, I suppose it'll do. It'll be easy enough to buy a smoke detector and open it up, and when we're ready to use it, we'll set up a directional lead box."

"Will it be dangerous to us, William?"

I stare directly into her eyes for a long, long moment; I doubt she knows the stories of even a few of the countless souls dead to radiation poisoning over the last century. "You've already been exposed once, Elie. But . . . I doubt it was a large dose, and not for a long period of time. But we'll do some test runs on something other than you, don't worry."

"Like lab rats?"

"Exactly like lab rats."

28

Friday, November 10, 2006
Elie

By the time my Friday shift at the bookshop rolls around, I'm quite drained. I've been thinking of reorganizing the entire philosophy section, and this afternoon's dearth of customers is the perfect time to do so. Yet I can't stop my legs from walking over to my recent obsession: the twentieth-century history bookshelves.

I can't help myself. I know I shouldn't, but when I'm not helping customers, neatening up the shop, or doing schoolwork I find myself drawn to catching up on a century's worth of news and progress. My reasoning—justification—is *how can I blend into 2006 if I don't know what the past three generations have lived through?* But as I bring William Shirer's *The Rise and Fall of the Third Reich* back to the desk, something William said to me this week replays in my head for the forty-fifth time.

"The less you know about the last century the better, to be honest, Elie. If you do get back to 1906 and you end up telling someone about a part of history that could end up changing things for worse . . . oh my God, it would be terrible," he had told me in horror. "Hell, you might make me nonexistent!"

"Well, it's already a bit too late for that. Before I had much to do here, all I could think of doing was to read. I was too nervous to walk around much downtown, you see. So I spent many, many, *many* hours in the history section of the Redpath Library. I read several condensed versions of twentieth century history."

"Oh, God. . . ." he had moaned, hands pulling his tightly curled hair.

I had guiltily told him what I did, but he had to know I did it without trying to endanger the present. It was out of boredom and curiosity. Besides, at that point I didn't conceive of possibly returning home. If, God willing, I'm able to, I'll try my best to forget every piece of modern history I've read. If I were to alter history, even if by accident. . . . My teeth clench to steady my shivering. I know that going home to 1906 is perilous enough, but I'll have to be constantly on guard for the rest of my life, forever watching my tongue and reactions when such a subject comes up.

Two hours and six customers later, I've browsed through enough of the tome on Germany's darkest years to feel at once the deepest sadness for all the wretched destruction and queasiness from what people can do to one another. The descriptions of everyday citizens turning on each other and the squalor so many were forced to endure. . . . It makes me weep onto the ivory pages. I know from previous readings the Second World War was cataclysmic in many senses, but these words shock my core until I break down weakly.

With regrettable timing, the store phone rings. Wiping my tears and clearing my throat of emotion, I greet the caller professionally.

"Elie? It's Will. Are you okay? You don't sound right."

I clear my throat again. "I'm fine. Just caught me deep in a book. What can I help you with?"

"Nothing, ma'am," he says in a formal tone. "I only wanted to say hi. I'm back from McGill and bored here, waiting for you to be done so we can get together tonight and plan our next test runs."

With heavy guilt I sigh into the phone. There's still *so much* to do on our project—we're at the most difficult and dangerous stage of our entire endeavor, and here I am essentially wasting time at a job. Yet my common sense reminds me, reluctantly, of my need to survive here before we can return me. I must have money to live. Despite Jeanne's graciousness, I still must purchase groceries and small things like notebooks and pencils.

That doesn't mean I can't be irritated at the circumstances.

"William, I'm sorry you're bored, but my shift will be over soon. I'd rather be making the project work instead of getting older in this smelly old shop."

"I thought you like working there?"

I sigh, yet again. "I do. I mean, it's a fine job and pays me what I need to survive. I want to be in two places at once, you know?"

"Yeah . . . listen, I'll let you go. Try not to get discouraged, Elie—we're making good progress. I'll see you later."

After we hang up, I wish I hadn't been short with him. Him, the only one who knows the truth of my life here, and the one person I need on my side.

By the time I lock up the bookshop at night, William is still in my thoughts. As I begin my long evening walk east, I spy the thick waxing moon barely risen in the east, my internal cue that night has begun. I ruminate on my luck to have a place to live, a source of income, security, classes in a renowned university I quite enjoy taking, kind friends who are splendid company, and one very wonderful friend who's working his darnedest to help get me home.

And that last, I know, is the most amazing.

Here I am, worrying about not spending every free moment constructing the time machine, when poor William has a life of his own and probably doesn't *want* to spend every moment working on it. Unlike me, his life is to be spent here, and I'm sure he wants to enjoy that life and his very bright career.

Yet . . . he does spend an awful lot of time with me. He has plenty of friends, yes, though I gather he's with them considerably less now. And he has no girlfriend—proven by Evan, who takes me aside every time I go to their apartment and asks me if William and I are dating—only me as a girl friend—two separate words, firmly, no connection. He's been undeniably kind to me, astonishingly generous to me in every way. I stop mid-step and wonder, *Why is he helping me return home to 1906? If he enjoys my company, why would he want to see me go? If he doesn't like me at all—which I'm pretty sure is wrong—why would he bother wasting his time? Does he want it to work and send me home or fail and keep me here?*

Confused yet having no answer, I can only keep walking. But all my brain does is focus on my difficulties, not the positives.

* * *

"I'm starting to really pity these caterpillars," I moan the next evening. I gingerly coax another little green crawler onto the conductive plate and whisper an apology to him.

"Yeah . . . It might be less than ethical, but better them than you," William says. "The electricity, the radiation . . . I'm glad they're testing it until we get it right for your run."

I nod solemnly, looking with reverence at our mock scattering setup with our americium source inside. It's taken two weeks since we decided to procure it for us to gather enough without arousing suspicion.

William has more than once warned me that using americium is a double edged sword; it has a relatively low emission rate of alpha particles—so it's safer than the radium Father used—but it may be too weak to be a comparable imitator of his experiments. In other words, using it here may be, for the purposes of getting our time machine to work, moot.

"Okay, ready," I say, almost shaking with nervousness as I walk outside the closet door to stand next to William. This is our first test run using the alpha particle source, and we're both completely unsure what the result will be. I know he thinks we'll keep sizzling our critters, and I can't say I foresee a different outcome. I hope, however, for something different.

With a fervent hope such as my whole being could not summon more, I reach out in the darkness to squeeze his hand, but I stop before I reach it. *Keep this professional, Elie.* I shake my head to clear it; in this very early hour of the morning, I must be becoming delirious.

"Here we go . . . one, two, three!"

A brief moment after the power enlivens the circuit, we hear an odd, tiny thud—like a small footstep.

"What the—" William exclaims when we peer into the room. Our poor caterpillar has not succumbed à la Joan of Arc but rather looks like an elephant of Hannibal has trampled it. He is a confusing mass of green goo; I physically feel a bit sick for him.

"Ugh, poor little thing. He's been squashed!"

William is grounded to the floor with a shocked face of horror. "Elie! Do you understand what just happened?" His voice is low and steady, but sounds a wee scared.

"Our caterpillar died gruesomely, but beyond that, no. Do you?"

"Not exactly, except this kind of death is not . . . natural. Nothing stepped on or fell on him. It's as if space itself crushed him."

Now my face mirrors his. "Oh, God! You're right—I was so concerned with how gross it is. Goodness . . . this means it . . . it w—"

"It works, sort of. We've done something here which isn't the result of a normal electrical circuit. He's been bent by the space-time continuum, you could say."

I can't help but shudder from my abdomen outward. "It's ghastly. Can you imagine if this was me? Oh! What if Father's lab did this to someone else after I was transported?"

William looks at me with pity that quickly turns composed. "No, it couldn't have. We'd have known about it—it'd have been in his history or something. 'A death at McGill's laboratory,' or something like that. This place would be infamous. No, don't worry."

"I suppose. . . ."

"At any rate, this is infamous enough. I'm seriously astounded, Elie. Up until now I really didn't believe we could do something like this."

"You didn't? Where's your faith, William? I thought we could!"

"Of course you did. The physicist in me doubted, okay?" He exhales sharply. "But this doesn't work fully yet, though it's more promising than it was two minutes ago. There must be something off with the voltage. We haven't turned it up to the maximum yet."

"I thought it was. Why don't we crank it up to full power?"

He hesitates. "I think we should increment the power gradually."

"Okay. Let's go up ten percent and see what happens, and so on."

Five minutes and more power later, our new caterpillar is also dead. He's not as flat as his unfortunate cousin, though still definitely dead.

"It's progress," I say with confidence. "More voltage."

The next three insects are also squished to death, but the third one is curiously missing half his legs when we inspect him.

William's shaking his head slowly, the picture of distress. "This is madness. Unbelievable. Where . . . what?"

I'm equally concerned, but I try to sound confident. "More progress, William. Look—where could his limbs have gone?"

He scans the floor of the closet, dimly lit as it is.

"You don't see them, do you?"

He shakes his head even slower than before.

"They're gone, William, gone back. Maybe they're in 1906. . . ."

* * *

Over an hour later we've made scant advancement. Though we're tired from lack of sleep, we're energized by what we've done so far. But we've hit a brick wall, and we're frustrated. Every caterpillar, every little insect, has lost limbs or sections of their bodies. We can't deny there's something eerie going on, and our conclusion—however hopeful—is that those missing parts are ending up somewhere else in time, since they sure aren't here right now.

"So we've got two things right, or going right," William says. "We must be moving in the right direction with the voltage increases, because more and more of the insect's body is disappearing each time. And you were certainly right about using alpha particles, because that's completely changed the outcome to something other than outright electrocution."

"But where do we go from here, besides increasing the voltage? They're obviously still dying during the process."

"I don't know," he says with a hint of pout. "I guess alter the scattering experiment setup? Perhaps the orientation of the alpha particles exiting the lead box matters. Do you remember where it was pointing? Where was your father standing in relation to it? Could you see directly into the box?"

I close my eyes to visualize, once again, that fateful afternoon. I saw Father mostly bent over the box, but I think about other times when I saw the setup, since he didn't move it once it was assembled.

"I'm not completely sure. I'm sorry, but it was oriented somewhere to the left, toward the table of equipment in general."

"That's a start." He adjusts the box, sitting on its own table and cranks up the power supply voltage a tick more. "Okay, we'll give that a shot. This is the maximum voltage possible, per your dad's own records. Next specimen, please."

The result surprises us more than anything else so far.

The caterpillar is legless—but still flattened. Dead. Yet . . . my nose detects the same notes of ionized air I smelled when I time traveled.

"God, this is disgusting, but we must be on the right track now. Elie, we've got to refine the alpha particles' direction. That must be it! Think, where exactly was it pointing?"

William's excitement is contagious. I try to remember Father and Soddy working on the setup and where they stood in the lab. I turn a page in our "project notebook" and start re-sketching the layout. He's patient while I draw and several minutes later is rewarded with my answer.

"It was pointing at the time interval measurement device, actually—of course."

"Of course what?"

I can't quite describe what I know instinctively to be the key. "I think it was more than coincidence that I touched that device. Maybe it was the intersection of it, the alpha particles, and electricity, but it makes sense that the americium emission points toward it. I don't know . . . perhaps it scaled my time travel when I contacted it, eh?"

"You've lost me. Sorry, Elie."

"Look, Father built it so it can measure with an accuracy of hundred-thousandth of a second. I was sent *one hundred* years into the future. Was there a connection? Maybe, maybe not, but it's more than possible."

With a nod of agreement, William says, "Could be. I say let's move the device in line with the emission stream and see what happens."

It takes a couple of ladybugs and several more caterpillars, which increasingly lose more and more body parts until, when the power supply voltage is about at its maximum, the entire caterpillar vanishes.

Finally. . . .

"He's—he's gone!" I exclaim.

But in its place is a mash of bloody gore. He's gone, mostly, but obviously still died in the process. I groan in disgust and frustration.

"But he didn't survive, clearly. I think we're missing something fundamental here," William says, sitting down on the mildewed couch slowly. I've never seen his forehead so creased.

"How? We're so close to this working. Shouldn't it be a tweak of something? More voltage, something?" It has to be something simple, I think, more out of hope than with belief.

"If there was an incremental change, I'd say yes. But this. . . . There's a roadblock."

William mutters to himself as if speed reading a textbook while staring unseeing at the jumbled apparatus. I'm afraid to interrupt him, so I simply sit next to him and try to be patient.

Finally he stands up, rubbing his eyes, then lays a hand on my shoulder.

"Elie, it's late. I can't think straight. I don't know what to do next. And these things dying. . . . It could be you. . . . We need to figure this out with a clear head."

Sod it all, we're so close!

But we're not, if I'm honest with myself. Looking into William's bloodshot eyes, I know he's right. Like him, I have no clue what we're doing wrong. "Fine, we'll take a break," I say. "A few days, maybe. I'll search my memory again, sketch the setup again, and you—you should spend some time doing something else. Be with your friends. Or go jogging, which I still think is pointless, but there you go."

He laughs. "Yeah, maybe I will. Okay, a break. Tonight's Saturday, so maybe next Saturday we'll have something to go on."

Will we? Will I ever see Father again? Three hours ago I could see him when I closed my eyes, but now. . . . Now I'm struggling. He's as far away as ever.

Elie, how could you possibly think you could build a time machine?

29

Thursday, November 16, 2006
William

When I walk into our office, I expect Alain still to be angry. He has been for weeks, ever since he accused me of working overtime on VERITAS. I worried earlier he might blow up at me again, but this time in front of everyone. But I didn't expect the silent treatment.

As I set down my backpack and start unpacking my laptop, I greet the group as a whole. Everyone answers with a "Hey, Will," except for Nico, who isn't in yet. But Alain continues staring at his computer screen. I catch JP's eye, who gives me a face that says "what's with him?"

I glance briefly at the ceiling, expressionless, and continue getting settled for the day.

This is going to be fun. . . .

I've got to finish an assignment for my High Energy Astrophysics class before getting to some VERITAS work, which I'm embarrassed to be behind on. In fact, Alain and I are supposed to be collaborating on it, and I'm pretty sure he started without me. All I've done since getting home early Sunday morning—well, after getting some sorely-needed sleep—is research Rutherford's experimental setups during his McGill years.

Five minutes later, Kevin walks in.

"Gentlemen," he booms, looking at Alain and I. "Did you see my email? What's the status of the part drawings?"

"Done," Alain says smoothly before I can mutter an excuse. "Just waiting on Will for his part."

He hasn't glanced at me yet. *Wow, he's still more pissed at me than I thought.*

"Will?" Kevin asks, his eyes shifting between us. "How far are you? And weren't you two going to do this together?"

I clear my throat. "Umm, I got tied up with homework, Kevin. Not done yet, but—"

"You, late with work?"

"Sorry, sir, I know. I have time today. I'll get it done, and we'll send it all over to you." I hate being late; I hate disappointing Kevin more.

Alain shows more surprise than Kevin and looks around his monitor at me for the first time. After Kevin leaves, he asks, "You're not finished? What have you been doing?"

"I haven't started my drawing yet. Haven't even completed the calculations," I admit.

"You haven't been . . .?"

"No."

"I thought you . . ."

"Did all the drawings myself or something?" I have to stop myself from laughing at what would've been something I'd never have done.

Alain makes a sheepish half-shrug. "I'm . . . sorry, man. I don't know why I—"

"Forget it," I say, smiling. "We're good."

"Maybe I'll give you a hand with those calculations?" he suggests.

I thank him and pass a notebook with what I've done so far over to him. Forty minutes later I've finished my homework and started sketching the part drawing with Alain.

After a while I start listening to JP's conversation with Nico, who's since come into the office. He tends to tell the best stories out of all of us, distracting though they may be.

"And so Morgan—you know him, dark blond hair, like ten hairs above his lip he thinks make a mustache—he raises his hand—and this is in Nuclear Physics, a fifth year class, *tabernacle*—and asks Professor Nagar, 'Sir, what's the difference between alpha, beta, and gamma rays again?'" JP's mouth hangs open at the end, as if to say "Can you believe him?"

Nico cracks up. "What a dope! Isn't he the guy who asked last year who came up with relativity first?"

"That's him!" JP cackles.

I can't stop myself from joining in and laugh so hard my eyes water. "Wonder how he got in this program. Can't define a gamma ray. . . ."

Then I stop laughing.

You might be the bigger idiot, Will.

Gamma rays, of course—how could I have missed it?

"Not so funny?" Alain asks, wiping his eyes.

"Oh, it's funny all right," I answer dryly. "Biggest dope in our year, no question."

I sure am.

Sighing, I scan our progress. I figure Alain and I can finish the drawing by the end of the day between our classes. My heart is now beating fast, as if I've been jogging. I need to see Elie. To hell with our "break from the project."

I think I figured it out.

***

Tonight I'm battling excited anticipation and cautious thinking. I've been running over my hypotheses for hours, anxious to try them out, but now I'm worried if this will be safe in the end, for Elie. Earlier in the evening before dinner, I had stopped by Jeanne and Elie's apartment and had asked if she could stop by my apartment later to do homework together. That's been our code in front of others; Jeanne thinks Elie's at my place doing homework, and I tell Evan I'm down at Elie's apartment, but really we both meet downstairs and walk to our secret closet.

After telling Elie I had a major realization today, I've spent the last five minutes simply looking at this messy set-up from all angles, especially from the conductive insect plate, the site of so many recent tiny murders. Elie is sitting on the dank couch, alternately watching me and lost in her own thoughts.

"The thing about alpha particles," I finally say, still looking at our setup, "is that they have low penetration power."

"Which means what?"

"Alpha particles only penetrate a few centimeters through the air or the skin. While the alpha rays are hitting the time measurement device, they're not hitting the insects. And they probably didn't hit you back in September, no matter how close you were standing to it."

"About an arm's length away, no closer."

"I thought as much. If we move the insect so it's hit with the alpha particles, it still won't solve the problem, if I'm thinking correctly."

"So . . . no ray penetrates that little caterpillar to make him go back in time?"

"No, I didn't say that. But there is something we've completely neglected."

Elie looks at me expectantly. "What?"

"It couldn't be more obvious. I of all people should've realized; it's what I've studied for years now. . . ." I sit down on the couch, closing my eyes and feeling as stupid as humanly possible.

"William, tell me!"

"Gamma radiation."

"From space?"

I shake my head. "There are really two kinds of gamma radiation, and both are deeply penetrating, unlike alpha radiation. There's the high energy type that I deal with in the VERITAS program and a lower energy type that's Earth-based. Less than 100 keV, more like x-rays than gamma rays. Materials like the radon gas your father used emit it. . . ."

But that radon gas emitted far more energetic gamma radiation than this americium does. We'll be lucky if it will spit out enough. Don't get her hopes up, Will.

Before I can stop my brain, it wanders down the path of what will happen if I let Elie down. I stare at the setup, frozen. But now Elie's no longer patient. She scoots closer to me. "But what does that mean? We need radon? X-rays?"

I shake my head and clear my throat. "X-rays and gamma rays overlap on the electromagnetic spectrum, so yeah, either radon or radium—no chance we'd get either, as I told you before—or an x-ray would do it. But I can't get an x-ray machine here, no chance."

"But the americium is radioactive! Doesn't it . . .?"

I nod morosely. "After alpha decay, the americium does emit gamma radiation by gamma decay, but it's not as strong as from radon. But if . . . but if— "

Elie turns toward me and places her hands on my knees, unable to stand the suspense as I work out the problem. "If what?"

Instinctively, I lean my torso backward and close my legs, suddenly very aware how close Elie is to me.

I've never seen her commit such an impropriety, as she'd say. She puts her hands back in her own lap, looking aware of her reddening cheeks.

"If," I say, clearing my throat again, "we put the caterpillar close enough to the radioactive source, directly in line with it, the gamma rays will penetrate him. I don't know if they'll be strong enough to do whatever your father's radium did to you, or if this is even part of the equation."

"It's the best guess we have."

"Yeah," I mutter, resting my head in my hands.

"Chin up, William," Elie says. "I'm lucky you work on gamma radiation."

I lift my head and say, dimples blazing, "And here I was thinking you're doing all the intellectual heavy lifting on this project."

30

Thursday, November 16, 2006
Elie

"It's the best guess we have," I say to William, trying to impart some positivity.

"Yeah," he mutters, resting his head in his hands. He looks like an exhausted Atlas holding the world upon his shoulders.

"Chin up, William. I'm lucky you work on gamma radiation."

He lifts his head and says, dimples blazing, "And here I was thinking you're doing all the intellectual heavy lifting on this project."

I laugh at his absurdity, then together we alter the setup. Where before the caterpillar's plate, the lead box containing americium, and the time measurement device formed an L-shape on the table, now we place them all in a straight line with the americium pointing very clearly at the other objects.

When we're satisfied, William steps back and mutters, "And now for the proof."

"A test run?" I ask.

He digs into his knapsack and withdraws a device I've never seen before. It's more buttons and screens than anything. He's holding it reverently.

"A gamma ray detector," he says. "We use it in the physics labs. It's just a handheld thing. Actually Alain and I took this one apart at the start of last year, to see how it works, you know, sort of a lab version of the VERITAS array of detectors."

When I smile, I try not to not be in awe of him so I don't embarrass him. "Did I mention how lucky I am to have befriended someone on that project?"

It takes a moment, but he blushes. "Good for something. And hey—it's reading the americium! Low levels, but it's there."

William is holding his detector an inch above the caterpillar's plate. He moves it backward off the table, but still in line with the beam of gamma rays. "It reads here too. That means if this works, you can stand here and touch the time measurement device while absorbing some of the radiation. Good God, that sounds horrible. . . ."

His expression is nothing short of revulsion.

"William, I know. Gamma rays are dangerous. But you said yourself the dosage is light. And it'll only be for an instant."

"You're sure you want to risk future cancer?"

I close my eyes and think of my home, of Father, of Mother. To be so close to them again. . . . With a firm voice I say, "I understand the risk, William. I accept it.

But please, let's test that little caterpillar first, okay? Before I die of curiosity?"

He nods, though still looks unsure. We double check everything again, place the critter on his metal plate, and step outside to turn the power on.

A whir of power supply boxes coming to life, a buzz, a flash of yellow light, and then—nothing.

The metal plate is empty. And clean.

It works!

In a moment of elation I let out a celebratory shriek, and William hugs me from the side. "We've done it, Elie! This is seriously beyond belief!"

I stiffen from the shock of the embrace, but I'm too pleased to let my old-fashioned propriety stop him. Not at any time since I've been in 2006, not during the enjoyable work times with my girlfriends nor working side-by-side with William, have I been so joyous. My throat constricts, and my insides are bubbling up and trying to push through it. Unable to contain my excitement, I loop my right arm behind his back and gently squeeze.

"It's. . . . It's the happiest I've felt in quite some time, William. This is amazing progress we've made in only one day. I can finally, really, hope I can go home. I really feel it's possible."

"Wait, you didn't believe it all along?" he teases.

I can't help but smile. "Oh, I allowed myself to hope, but I didn't believe it, lest I be devastated if we failed."

"Well, you're not home yet. We don't know yet where that caterpillar is in time, Elie, and can't know. Unless . . ."

I might collapse in the time it takes for him to finish his sentence.

". . . Unless we change the settings of the time interval device and change it to sometime in the very near past. I guess we'll know it works if the specimen is still here when we complete the test."

"That's brilliant, William!"

"Thanks. But maybe we should use something bigger, like a mouse. Then we'll also know for sure if this setup will scale up to something more massive. We know it works for different sized bugs, at least."

"That's a good point, but do you have a mouse?"

"Call me crazy, but I do. I was thinking we'd want to test this on a mammal. Yesterday I caught the one who's been nibbling electrical cords in the McDonald-Harrington basement. It's hidden in the basement labs, in a shoebox, marked with a dab of blue paint on his head."

In ten minutes of tinkering and mouse placing—putting him on the conductive plate with the open shoebox over him—we have our answer. Beneath the box, after we let the circuit run to ten minutes in the past, there is silence. But under the musty couch, my onetime bed, we hear the telltale squeaks of a tiny mouse, then see a flash of blue and fur scurry across the floor with all four of its legs and a tail sticking straight up—none the worse for wear.

* * *

On the walk back to du Parc, the very early morning air is crisp and silently biting at my hands, ears, and cheeks. I curse the coming winter, which I'll face either in this century or the last. Ahead of us, the moon is about to drop over the western skyline. We walk next to each other, as quietly as the city is still, whether from fatigue or because we're both replaying in our heads what we've just done.

We walk on a little farther until he breaks the silence. "Say, Elie, you know what this reminds me of?"

"Tell me."

"There's a song, an old one. . . ." he trails off, leaving me with silence again.

"And? What song?"

"You're going to think this is really sappy. . . . I'm not usually a mushy guy—you can tell that."

"I won't judge you, William. I barely understand modern social conventions, anyway."

"Mmm, true—sorry. Well, this—us, walking here—and you going back to your family . . . it reminds me of an old Billie Holiday song my dad used to play. It says, 'I'll be looking at the moon, but I'll be seeing you.'" He stops short of reciting more of the lyrics, evidently embarrassed.

"That's not sappy at all. It's kind," I say right away, not knowing what he's implying but not wanting him to feel awkward. "The next time I see a thick waning moon, I'm sure I'll think about this night—or morning, rather."

"Yeah," he says slowly. "There's more to the song, but . . . I-I don't remember all the words. Every time I see the moon, or walk past the Rutherford Museum, or God, go into the basement labs, or walk past your broom closet, I'll be looking right at those things but only be seeing you. You'll be . . . *there* . . . and I'll be *here* . . . same city, same roads, but in a time that's already come and gone. It'll be as if I've read a book until it got snatched away from me after I've only read the first half."

He sped up there at the end, the words tumbling out faster than he probably intended, if he wanted them to at all.

"I . . . I didn't realize that . . . that you felt that way," I say, clutching his left arm and angling my face up to his. "I hadn't really thought about your future that way."

"I don't mean to dump that on you. You just want to get home to your father and your old life; I can't fault you for that. Only it's a bit sad for me, having gotten to know you over the past three months and then getting you ready to leave . . . forever. I always knew that was supposed to be the outcome, of course, but it doesn't make it any easier now—for me." He stops; the darkness doesn't hide his apple-red cheeks. "I don't know why I'm telling you this."

I'm quiet as I try to feel things from his side, but he continues.

"It's always harder to be left than leave, that's all. It maybe didn't hit me until that song popped into my head."

"I'm sorry, William. I didn't consider things—it's just that my family. . . ." I don't know how to finish; I really have been thinking of myself the entire time.

"Please, don't think about it. I'm happy for you to go back. But I'll want to know how you'll be—that you made it okay and are happy."

I'm still unsure what to say.

"Maybe," he considers, drawing the word out, "you could write me a letter."

"I don't understand. How would you ever get it?"

"There's got to be a way. After all, a hundred years isn't that long; people still write letters, after all. You could leave it somewhere."

"I could surely write you as soon as I get home and have paper and ink, but where can I put it that no one will take it?"

"Well, you could always bury it, like a time capsule."

"That's brilliant, William! I could write you a letter and place it in a metal box, then bury it somewhere on campus that won't be disturbed through the century."

"You can bury it next to James McGill's tomb, on the southeast corner. No one would dare dig around there. Make it deep enough, maybe two feet." His voice sounds as excited as I feel.

"But what if someone else opens it before then?"

"Write on it 'For William Hertz, to open in November 2006,' just in case."

"William, if someone else finds an old letter addressed to a specific person a hundred years in the future, then opens it and reads about me knowing you in the future but living in the past. . . ." My head begins to ache. "Oh goodness, the ramifications of someone else finding out time travel is possible—we have no idea how horrible that could be!"

The horror on William's face echoes how I feel. We stare at each other for a minute, then consider ways to make the letter ambiguous enough an accidental discovery wouldn't reveal anything dangerous to mankind.

"I'll simply write your name on the envelope, nothing else. And I won't refer to any kind of time in the space-time sort of way, I promise." It makes my chest hurt, strangely, to say this, but I add, "And I shall keep the letter brief, or try to at least, so it won't raise questions."

"Good. That should work," he says with airy relief. He flashes me a flat smile holding none of the impishness I first found so . . . fascinating. "Well, I suppose that sort of takes care of me worrying about you—and history."

I smile back at him, but by now I can read his face fairly well. His mouth is tight with apprehension and his eyes droop with sadness. Guilt over leaving is starting to overcome my excitement, but I try to smother it.

"I suppose we should decide when to send me back."

"I'd say tomorrow night—or tonight, I mean. Now that we have the time machine working, we should use it before we bump something and mess it up. It's probably smart not to have it lying around too long anyway, in case someone sees us."

I honestly thought he'd say I should get ready to go next week sometime; though I've been pushing and pushing to go back, the event is steaming like a train at me. "So soon? As in, twelve hours from now? Eighteen?"

"Yeah. You are ready to go, right? It's not like you need to pack an overnight bag," he teases.

"You're right—tomorrow it is." I nod sharply, girding myself for another shock while tamping my excitement to see my family in such a short time.

But I don't forget what he said earlier while we walk the rest of the way home.

31

Friday, November 17, 2006
Elie

Friday's lunch comes much too soon and passes almost too quickly for me to enjoy living it. Natalya and I join the rest of our girlfriends in the Shatner Building's lunch hall after our Twentieth Century Novel class finished.

"I'm glad you came, Elie," Isabelle says. "Lately you've been having lunch with William on Fridays. Is he busy today?"

"No, I wanted to spend more time with you all. I like you ladies very much, and . . . I value the friendships we've made."

From their bewildered faces I can tell my overt pronouncement of affection for them has caught them off guard. Without telling them I'll never see them again after today and will miss spending time with them, this is the best I can do.

"Well, yes, I think we all feel the same way," Natalya agrees. "We really have formed a good group of friends, haven't we?"

"It's made starting our university life easier, that's for sure—and it's fun to be close enough to share secrets," Lindsey says. Then in a whisper she adds, "And now for something we're all dying to know, Elie: are you . . . you know . . . sleeping with William?"

Embarrassed shock drops my jaw with a thud, and in the time it takes to draw it back up, I recover enough to reply. "How could you think I would do that? I'm not that kind of girl!"

The others giggle like schoolchildren, and after a few moments, I find myself joining in.

"I can't believe you're not. He comes across as a nerd, sure, but those eyes . . . and I just want to run my hands through his hair and—"

"Stop, just stop, please. Let's change the subject, shall we?" I don't know what's come over me that I can't stand Lindsey to continue—my sense of propriety being shocked at her forwardness of speech, the strangeness of William being anything other than a friend to anyone, or a pierce of jealousy at the thought of anyone but me being close to him—something I haven't felt since I met him.

"Okay, okay." She holds up her hands as if giving up. "But if you don't move on him soon, Elie, someone else will."

"And as a good friend of his, I wish him the best of luck with that," I force myself to say.

Before we part, I give them all a long hug and tell them I'll be away visiting family for a week. I receive shocked, confused hugs in return, but none of them want to let go and make me promise to call them straightaway once I return.

I promise, robotically, because to show any emotion might break my resolve. My intention of spending my last quality time with my friends in a happy state before I leave is fading, and as time advances, I'm nearly overcome by how much I'll miss these girls—as well as William.

32

Friday, November 17, 2006
William

If ever I've spent with my mind less on my work, it's been today. No classes to keep me busy, only some VERITAS work from Kevin and a pile of assignments from his Quantum Physics class to grade. Shavash offered to grade half of them, but I refused, knowing less time on my own to think would be a good thing. Every moment I don't have something to distract my brain, it keeps turning to Elie, to how she's going home tonight. *If* this bizarre time machine works, which it did, as long as it does scale up properly to a human.

But it did once, Will, so it'll do it again. Then she'll be gone.

"Stop reminding me," I scold myself.

I forgot I'm at home now, as is Evan. *You couldn't be more lost in thought.*

"Reminding you of what?" he calls from the living room to me in the kitchen.

"Nothing," I mutter. I pour myself a cup of coffee—since I'll need the caffeine come midnight—and walk in to sit with him.

He eyes me analytically. "You haven't been yourself at all today."

I sip my coffee, stalling. Elie had come up with a cover story for us, but I had hoped to only have to use it if she actually does go.

Which she's going to do.

But since I'm not operating with a full shell of electrons, I can't think of anything else to say but, "Yeah, it's . . . it's Elie."

"Did you guys split?"

"We're not dating, for the millionth time!" The usual amusement I have in providing this answer to my friends is this time replaced with snappy irritation. Maybe even misery.

Evan raises his hands in surrender. "Okay, okay, I believe you."

I stare at my mug.

"Not."

"Evan, for real! It's that she's flying home tonight. To . . . New Zealand. For a week."

He frowns. "Not waiting until Christmas? Is she going back again in a month?"

I shrug. Honestly, I wish I'd gone into my room instead of the living room. There's nothing I'd less like to discuss right now.

"Man, you're gonna miss her. What're you going to do without your not-girlfriend?" There's no trace of teasing in his voice, only genuine concern. "I guess you'll be here Sunday morning for our hangout again."

Without her . . . lots of free time again . . . full sleep again, that'll be nice . . . but no Elie . . . none of that prim but passionate attitude in every word she says . . . in that rather adorable accent I'm so used to hearing practically every day . . . without her . . . none of that golden hair that smells like a summer garden when she's leaning over the work table, next to me . . . not next to me again . . . never a flight of stairs away again. . . . Poor Jeanne, left alone again too. . . .

"Will? Buddy? You okay? You look like you're gonna be sick." Evan puts down the magazine he was reading and eyes me like I'm his patient.

I feel a weird constriction in my throat and nausea forming in my gut, but I try to act like I'm fine—*You realize you're not fine, right, Will? That you're devastated and you really have no idea how much you're gonna miss her*—by forcing my lips upward in a smile. "Maybe JP will finally corral me into playing Call of Duty. That's what I'll do with myself."

He laughs. "Uh huh. I better line up a bar crawl or something for Saturday night, before you find some hemlock."

I laugh too at his poor joke, trying to at least act more cheerful, but he knows me too well. I give him a sad half-smile and get up, heading for my room. You better get used to being lonely now, I tell myself.

It's too late to stop Elie from traveling back home tonight. Anyway, I promised her. As nuts as it seemed initially, and I was pretty sure then we'd fail, I gave her my word. We've gone this far. We've proven it works.

And it's what she wants.

For her sake, not mine, we put together this time machine. And now, no matter what I feel for her—*don't kid yourself, Will, you fell hard*—she's going back. And I can't let her see how I feel. I won't complicate this for her.

It's what she wants.

33

Friday, November 17, 2006
Elie

"Are you sure you want to take this risk? You're absolutely sure? Because there . . . there isn't any going back on this, Elie."

"Yes, I'm sure. This is what we've been working toward for months, right? I do miss my family ever so much—Father especially, but Mother also. They must be sick with grief by now. I couldn't live with myself if I didn't go back."

"Elie, if something goes wrong. . . ."

"It won't, William. We've tested this, right? And . . . and even so, I'm accepting the risk."

"But Elie, I'll be responsible. You know that, right? I didn't think about it before now, but I'm a full accomplice in this whole expedition. God, Elie, what if it kills you somehow? What if you die somewhere along your space-time path?"

"I won't. None of our latest tests killed anything. I'll be safe, and you'll be safe. And I'll be happy, William. And you too. . . . You'll be . . .. happy, right?"

He pauses, mouth open, for several seconds. "Will I? I'll be happy for you, Elie, because this is what you want. I can't say I won't miss you though. What a time this has been—like some sort of fantasy."

"Yes . . . believe me, yes."

"Tell me though. Are you absolutely sure this is what you want? That you'll be happier there than here?"

I don't answer right away. I'm absolutely sure I want to go back home, that I should because I don't belong in this century no matter how much I've enjoyed the last few months. Finally, I nod. "Yes. I must, William. But I'll miss you also. I can't . . . I can't describe how wonderful it's been to have you help me. I'm truly not sure what I would have done here without you."

Both of us shyly smile; neither of us are comfortable with big displays of affection.

"It'd have been the loony bin for sure," I say with a wink.

"Well, if you're ready, I guess we should get on with it. But . . . promise me you'll write to me, okay? You have to let me know how you are."

"I will, I promise—though I know you'll read an updated biography of Father straightaway."

"Of course I will. But those books won't have your account of time travel in it."

"And you're the only soul I'll tell, William."

"You won't tell your father what happened, will you? Remember, he can't know about the future. No one can."

I hadn't really thought of how I'll explain my absence without telling Father the truth. I only figure that if William believed me, Father surely will.

I pat his left arm with light, short strokes. "Don't worry, William. I won't let anything slip. I'm prepared to keep my head down."

"I hope this isn't a disaster," he mutters.

I have nothing to say back to that, only my promise to be careful. So I look over our setup in the broom closet one last time and make sure, with William's eyes also, that the voltage and time interval settings are tuned correctly.

We do one last test run with a caterpillar to make sure the time machine is working correctly, then I ready myself. I'm wearing my old black skirt, the white shirt I modified when I first got here, and the most traditional-looking coat I could find in Jeanne's granddaughter's old closet. Over my shoulders sits my satchel, heavy as granite with my course packs—their printing date removed, and not the one for Twentieth Century Literature, of course—and notebooks, a sandwich and two apples in case of emergency, my old cardigan sweater, leather gloves, and a scarf. Since I assume I'll be home in less than an hour, there can't be anything else I'll need.

I turn around, standing in the middle of the tiny room, and face William. His face is completely neutral, but his hands are tightly balled.

"Are you sure you want to be hit directly with radiation—again?"

"William, you said yourself this is a low dose. Besides, I've probably been exposed to a hundred times this by being in Father's lab." I pause to consider his train of questions. "Are you trying to convince me not to leave?"

He pauses just as long. "Maybe."

I wonder what exactly he means, whether it's because he's truly worried about my safety or if he really will miss me. My chest squeezes in on itself as it considers about both possibilities, but I can't dwell on either. I need to accomplish my goal. I need to go home.

"I'm ready."

He stands still for several seconds, then swallows, nods quickly, and steps toward me, arms out.

"Good luck, Elie Rutherford," he whispers as he pulls me into a gentle, slow hug. He holds on for two seconds, then steps back. "Okay, I'll step out. I'll turn the power supply on, then you touch the time measurement device, exactly like you did before. If anything looks or feels wrong, shout out. Okay?"

I nod, my throat unable to open to allow words to come out. Anticipation is freezing my limbs. Finally, I nod again and whisper back, "Good luck to you also, Will."

He smiles until his dimples show, chuckles a little, and slowly walks out of the room. As I was when I first got to 2006, I'm all alone again.

"Ready for power on three—one, two, three!"

The power supply purrs to life, the circuit is energized, and I reach out right away to touch the time measurement device. With a strong ripple of energy my body pulses painlessly, and this time, I'm yanked in a direction I can't determine, though my body hasn't changed orientation. In the quickest of moments, it's all over, and I feel as normal as I always have, except chilled and breathing in sharp, ionized air. Old air—the air from a century ago.

My century—and I'm back home.

34

Friday, November 17, 2006
William

Once our setup—or "time machine," as Elie calls it, though that's too bizarrely hokey a term for me to use—is ready, Elie turns to me. She's standing straight up, clutching her bag and looking more Victorian than I've ever seen her. The dull clothes have yards too much fabric and her hair is spun up and piled atop her head like a furry bird's nest. Looking like this, I can more easily picture her not fitting in here; it almost makes it easier to think of her leaving in a few minutes. For her sake, I'm trying to look like this is just another day, that I'm not nervous or sad. *I have lots of friends—why would I need another? She wants to go home, silly Will.*

But I can't stop myself from asking, one more time, if she's sure. "Are you sure you want to be hit directly with radiation—again?"

"William, you said yourself this is a low dose. Besides, I've probably been exposed to a hundred times this by going to Father's lab." She pauses; I know she's reading exactly what I'm thinking. "Are you trying to convince me not to leave?"

I hesitate—*should I tell her or not*? "Maybe."

"I'm ready."

I shouldn't—I won't—stand between her and her home. But before she goes, I have to let her know there's someone here who cares about her too. Taking a chance against her proper manners, I walk toward her and gingerly circle my arms around her narrow frame. Her hair smells like lavender.

"Good luck, Elie Rutherford," I whisper. Only without looking into her eyes can I pull myself together. "Okay, I'll step out. I'll turn the power supply on, then you touch the time measurement device, exactly like you did before. If anything looks or feels wrong, shout out. Okay?"

She nods, looking now like she's nervous too. A moment later she whispers back, "Good luck to you also, Will."

That's the first time she's said that—and it sounds so off, coming from her. It makes me smile—finally, something does. Not wanting my time with her to end, I have to force my legs to walk my body into the hall. I move the heavy door to slightly ajar and hover my right thumb over the remote switch for the power supply.

It's go time.

"Ready for power on three—one, two, three!"

And suddenly, literally with the press of a button, Elie is gone. I know without looking she touched the device and is gone. The room is dead silent when I switch off the power supply five seconds later. I know something extraordinary has happened, but only a sudden loneliness fills me, and then sharp fear. Now that we actually accomplished the time travel, a tsunami of questions I hadn't paused to consider before flood my brain, and I can't process any of them.

What if the time interval measurement device isn't exact and she's sent 110 or 95 years into the past?

What if she ended up squished to death somewhere on the way to 1906?

What if she was electrocuted instead of transported?

What the hell was I thinking trying to send someone in time—and why didn't I stop to consider what I'd do if it all went wrong?

Did I contemplate going to jail if I'd accidentally killed her?

Or what if someone finds this setup and sees the stolen equipment and—God forbid—the americium? What if I get kicked out of McGill? Or arrested?

But most importantly, *how could I be so reckless with someone else's life?*

Suddenly, I'm terrified of what's happened to her and what can happen to me. My whole body is shaking as if it were negative twenty degrees in here. The answers to all of these horrible questions scare the hell out of me—and more than that, I'm really, really scared for Elie. All I want to know is where she is, to know she not only survived but is okay.

I realize it's Elie herself that made me go along with her wild idea to go back in time. I can't blame her, but it was easy to say yes to someone as charming as Elie. And sure, the thought of achieving something as miraculous as time travel is one of the biggest temptations for a scientist. To actually have done it makes my limbs quiver as if held together with linguini. But it's the fear over Elie's safety that's making me shake.

I need to check Rutherford's biography before I have a heart attack. The library is closed at this hour, but I have a key to our office. I close up the lead box with the americium sample, unplug the power supply, shut the closet door, and sprint down the hall to my desk. My computer is still on from this afternoon. I browse to a search engine, right foot tapping a staccato on the floor, and a moment later I'm reading an online bio of Elie's father.

Scrolling, scrolling... Nobel prizes, collaborations, wartime effort, family life! There—"daughter Eileen was born March 30, 1888. A bright but rebellious woman, Eileen was known for her independent thoughts and a nearly three-month adventure trip to the United States she took while a student at McGill's Donalda Department. Despite an expected engagement to mathematician Ralph Fowler, Eileen instead eloped to New Zealand with an unknown suitor. Nothing is known of her later life."

I slump back into my chair. So few details in that summary. At least she didn't end up marrying Ralph and dying before she reached thirty, but to have such an obscure, quiet life is . . . disappointing. Of course I want to know why she fled to New Zealand—*to escape Ralph?*—and what happened to her after that. For all of her complaining about being pushed onto Ralph and being pestered by her mother, I'm glad she hasn't lived the life previously in the history books, though I fear what she did live might have been worse.

But she must have survived the time travel to change her history. She's alive!

As soon as I think those words, I realize she has actually already died by now—and my relief fades like dim moonlight.

Being alone in the office, exhausted from lack of sleep, left behind, glad she at least survived yet depressed I'll never again see her or talk to her, I do something I haven't done in years.

I cry.

* * *

Before I know it, I've spent at least the last hour walking aimless circles around our apartment. To the living room couch, to the kitchen counter, to the table by the front door, to the bathroom cabinet, to my bedroom closet, to the coffee table, to my computer desk, to a stack of magazines next to a chair—all with no reason for visiting and no task accomplished. I realize I'm merely trying to fill my time while not thinking of one particular thing: Elie. It being a Saturday, I have no classes, no work to do, no papers to grade, and only a bit of homework to do, which I find I can't concentrate on.

She's gone—I know she is—but I can't yet accept it. Twelve hours ago I was talking to her; from now on, I'll never talk to her again. There is one way I will "hear" her voice, through the letter she wrote me, but I'm not ready to read it yet. Once I read it, that'll be my last moment with her, and I don't want that yet. Maybe it's savoring the anticipation of the letter, maybe it's denial, but I can't yet—I just can't.

Paradoxically, not knowing how she's feeling is the worst part of all. At least I know she ended up safe with her family, explaining as soon as she walked to her house a far-fetched story of a US adventure to them—thank goodness she's well-practiced at making cover stories believable. It pains me not to be able to pick up the phone to talk to her and have her reassure me everything is okay and her family is taking care of her again. I'm physically anxious about Elie's well-being; my chest hurts, my fists are tense, and my diaphragm pushes air out of my lungs in short, quick bursts.

I have to keep myself busy. I have to keep from letting my imagination create a chain of possible catastrophic events. *She's okay.* I breathe deeper. *She survived.* I breathe slower. *She's happy and not in danger.* My breath is growing shallow and rapid again. I need to do something to channel my emotions before I have a nervous breakdown, both for my own sanity and to keep other people from becoming suspicious. The last thing I need is for someone to wonder if Elie's gone for some nefarious reason and pin me as the guilty culprit because I look like a twitching, guilty freak.

I still can't calm my breathing or relax my muscles, try as I might by lounging now in bed. My last thought plays over and over in my head. *She's happy and not in danger. She's happy and not in danger. She's happy. . . .* The last bit puts me at ease, but the first bit tears at me. If she's happy at home, that means she's contented with her family and familiar surroundings, which is of course a good thing.

But it also means she's happy without me. Without me.

So this is what's bothering me. It's taken me this long to realize how much I care about Elie. No, I more than care for her. I adore her. I love her company; I'm almost lost right now without it, like the proverbial ship without a rudder. Everything about her—the velvet voice, the silken hair, the silly, naïve comments, her endearing determination to work hard every day—is missing, and it's already left quite a hole in my life. Reflecting on this, I almost can't believe what a void she's left.

Despite vehemently proclaiming a platonic relationship with Elie during the teasing I've gotten from Evan, Alain, JP, Kevin, and Anna, I suddenly wish for the opposite, almost out of nowhere. Okay, it might have been simmering in the very, very far recesses of my mind. I've been concentrating on the time machine for too many weeks to think about getting close romantically with Elie. Who would want to fall in love with someone who's planning to exit your life as soon as she can?

As hard as this is for me right now, I assume she's not having an ideal time of it either. My head is filled with images of her; mostly of the past months but also peppered with flashes of her being grounded by her father, berated by her mother, and hounded by Ralph and her mystery suitor. Not pretty mental pictures, those last. What I need to do is push out those thoughts and concentrate on the happier moments her life must have had—that'll get me through this until my time with her is a far, far memory.

Love. Is it? That the word came so swiftly to my thoughts surprises me. In this instant I know exactly what I need to do: write Elie a love letter. She won't ever read it, but it's the only way I'll ever be able to express those ideas outside of my head. Maybe that's the closure I need, to finally say goodbye to her in a way I couldn't say in person.

"Dear Elie," I begin, dully. And then, I'm stumped; if only I could write this in equations instead of words. I try again, setting an appropriate tone—nothing as dopey sweet as poetry—that's measured and sincere but which "her generation" would still call a love letter. Maybe this letter is sappy, I don't know, but it's straight from my heart. I know Elie wouldn't want it any other way. Once finished, I sigh deeply with eyes closed, remembering her happy and excited walking around the Mont Royal Overlook with me, sharing lunch on the grass outside the engineering buildings, and busy at work on the time machine. I fold the letter up, mark it with "For Elie," and leave it on the corner of my desk. Back in my bedroom, I recline on my bed and allow myself to slip into a nap. . . .

***

Three days and six letters to Elie later, I'm deep in a funk—a lonely, depressed funk. Evan is worried about me, Alain has stopped teasing me about Elie, and I can barely function in class and during work. It's finally hit me I'm as alone now as I was busy with Elie since early September. The abandonment is unbearable. When I can't take it anymore and have to break down and read Elie's letter, I take a small shovel to James McGill's tomb on the lawn in front of the Arts Building near midnight on Wednesday.

A part of me is expecting to find newly mussed grass; I have to remind myself that while I think Elie should have just buried the letter, her past is still a hundred years ago. I hope I can find the burial spot quickly. I scan the nearby grounds and see no one, and thankfully I'm not illuminated by a streetlamp.

It takes ten minutes for my shovel to sound a hard "thump." Right at the southeast corner of the stone tomb, roughly two feet below the grass, is a small steel box the size of a modern shoebox. I stare at its auburn rusted lid and shiver with anticipation.

Here she is!

To avoid lingering and risk being seen digging around the founder's grave, I lift out the box and replace the dirt and sod lump I removed. There—it looks undisturbed.

With the cold box under one arm and the shovel in my other hand, I walk east toward the Prince Arthur gates, toward home, intending to read the letter there. But I can't wait until then. Twenty paces on, I stop at a limestone bench and open the box's creaking clasp. Under the lid is a large zip-top bag—filched from Jeanne's kitchen before Elie left, for the purpose of sealing the letter from water, I'm sure—with a folded ivory paper inside.

And now I can't wait. I grab the bag and half-fumble, half-rip it in a rush to unfold the letter. Across the sheets is Elie's neat, pencil-straight cursive, looking much too fancy and old-fashioned for a twenty-year-old.

My eyes can barely believe these are her words. I force myself to read it one word at a time instead of barreling through it.

Dear William,

As I promised, here is a letter to you, which is one of the hardest things I've ever had to write. . . .

35

Sunday, November 18, 1906
Elie

As before, it's over before I really know what's happened. Only a slight chill and a tickle of ionized air in my nostrils alert my senses that something occurred. My eyes, shocked from the sudden thrust into darkness, search about for something to focus on. I stand still and wave my arms in an arc to touch something, anything. I take tiny steps until they brush a doorknob. A fierce arc of static flies from my left hand. I draw it back and massage the tingling fingertips, remembering the same pain from months ago. But I reach for the doorknob again.

Please be open.

With a twist and pull, I'm out into the hallway—I've made it! There's only faint light coming from a few windows in the large front lobby, but I follow the familiar steps and halls out to the front door. I hug my coat closer and start the short walk to my real home, taking in all the small details of my old life—now, just *my life*—that stand out now: short buildings, more trees, darkness at night touched only by a quilt of stars above, and the warm light of the occasional gas lamppost. It feels like home—an almost eerily dark, quiet home.

"Where have you *been*, Elie?!" Mother comes to the door first, and instead of a smile and a hug, she gives me her best shocked face, examining me from head to toe. Her eyes slow at my collar-less shirt and odd coat.

I give her no answer. I'm not ready to tell them the truth, if I decide to tell them at all. I'm not sure if they'll believe me or think I'm loony. Is it safer to use the lie I've prepared? I need to read them first.

Father steps behind Mother before I can say anything, and his expression breaks from concern to happy relief. "You're home!" He eases past Mother and pulls me up into the bear hug I've been missing for months. I lay my turned head onto his shoulder and squeeze his chest as best I can.

"Elie, you've lost weight," he says as he sets me back down. "Are you okay? Are you sick?"

I laugh. "No, Father, I'm fine. It's an illusion from this shirt—I took it in, so it's a bit tighter than it used to be."

Mother clucks. "I'll say."

"Well, come in out of the cold, dear. Thank God above you're alive, Elie!" Father moves aside, his robe flapping around his ankles. "Though I must say you've chosen an odd hour to return."

"I'm sorry, Father. I forgot you'd be sleeping. I'm quite exhausted as well. I'm really looking forward to collapsing in bed."

"Don't you think you owe us an explanation for your disappearance, Eileen? We can all wait to sleep once we've heard what you have to say. Goodness, we feared you were dead!"

No matter how wide the differences between my mother and I at times, those words sting; guilt the weight of a boulder fills my bones—not that disappearing was my fault, I remind myself.

"I really, truly am sorry, Mother. I don't know what else to say right now, but in the morning, we'll sit down and talk for however long we need to. But it *is* after midnight, and I can see you're both tired."

Father steps in. "She's right, Mary. Let's get our rest, now that we know she's safe. But Elie—I will lock your bedroom door."

"Fine," Mother says. "But I won't sleep a wink."

I sigh, then step forward to hug both her and Father. "I love you both, and I've been waiting so long to see you again. You have no idea."

Surprisingly, I get as warm a hug in return.

As I tiptoe through the house, up the stairs, and into my bedroom, I see our home as the yin to Jeanne's apartment's yang. Everything is fresh and clean, but jarringly old-fashioned. As familiar and heavenly as my old quilt is, though, I fall asleep only after running through multiple stories to explain my absence.

* * *

The air in our parlor is icier than outside. Instead of going to church, my parents are asking for answers. At least a steaming cup of tea warms me.

"Alone? Unchaperoned? Eileen, you *know* how unrespectable that is! Were you seen?!"

"Of course I was seen, Mother. But I posed as a widow of the Boer War—I was wearing mostly black anyway—so I could be alone."

"And you were in the States all this time? Where on Earth were you staying? How did you survive? Elie, were you hurt by anyone? Are you . . ."

"Am I what?"

". . . with child?"

"No! Mother! Good gracious, no. What do you think I was doing?"

"That's what we're trying to find out! I'm sorry—Elie dear, we trust you, but it's the other people we don't trust. Anything could have happened to you all alone."

"Nothing happened to me, Mother."

I take my time answering her questions, giving the words I carefully rehearsed last night. I try to use as few details as possible, saying I merely stayed in a home for single women in Buffalo, New York, and worked as a secretary for money. Thank goodness our family visited Buffalo a few winters ago so I can provide some specificity. Yet they send question after question my way.

Finally Father asks the most important question. "Why did you leave?" His voice is level, quiet, and pained.

I let my breath out slowly. "Truthfully, I felt cornered into marrying Ralph. It seemed my only option in life, but I can't stand him; I don't love him and didn't want to spend any more time with him. The thought of marriage to him was too much to handle. I just couldn't do it. So I escaped."

"Why didn't you say anything?"

"I guess I thought my reactions were enough. Did I ever seem enthused to be with him? But everyone was for the match, and it felt so far along. . . . It couldn't end well if I said no—I couldn't say no."

"Why would you not like Ralph Fowler?" Mother interjects. "He's a wonderful man. And you didn't act like your world was going to end if you were going to go on an outing with him. You weren't jumping for joy, but you weren't clinging to us."

"I was trying to behave like a lady, Mother, as I was taught to do. But inside . . . I couldn't do the same."

"Elie, dear, your father and I could have worked something out if you truly didn't care for Ralph."

"Could you have? It seemed a *fait accompli* to me."

I'm exaggerating here—and of course I know my parents would have backed off if I'd had my chance to tell Father how I felt that fateful Friday instead of being shipped away in time—and I wish I could be fully honest with them. For another hour we go back and forth, me answering questions from a curious father and a concerned mother. Both are hurt, but both are being more kind than I thought they'd be, considering—for what they know—I ran away from home.

After lunch, they send me upstairs to my room, locked again behind me, while they talk downstairs in private. Despite gluing my ear to the door, all I hear is a low mumble. I'm sure they're debating whether I'm sane, whether I'm telling them the whole truth, and what to do from here. After a while a beautiful Schubert record muffles their escalating voices.

I never expected my return to be so calamitous. It's wonderful to be here, but definitely not a smooth ride.

Before dinner, the three of us take a walk around our streets, Mother insisting I wear a low-brimmed hat to cover my face from curious neighbors. We don't talk about the last three months, and I barely add a word at all. Father describes some staffing changes at McGill while Mother tells him about some of her upcoming Women's Circle events. On the whole, we could be back in mid-August; if my mind blocks out my time in 2006, I'd feel no change at all. Only the coming frost of winter signals the advance of time.

Late Sunday evening, since I'm still largely confined to the house and not conversing with my parents, I decide to write my letter to William. I wish I had more to tell him, but mostly I want to let him know I survived and am home safe; I know that's what he wants to hear, anyway. Truly, I owe everything to him, but I'm unsure how to say that to him.

The more I think about William, the more he rests on my mind, and it seems incongruous with our old house. I'm strangely split when writing to him—more than because I'm secretly writing a letter to someone whom no one else here knows exists. I find myself wondering how he's getting on. His words to me early Friday morning won't stop echoing; the hurt in his voice which I couldn't hear clearly then is stinging my heart now. Though I'm trying hard to enjoy my old life, I can't suppress the small part of me that wishes I could talk with him again.

* * *

On Monday morning the conversation has picked up where we left off yesterday but with a more belligerent tone from Mother. She persuades Father to stay home from work to help "deal with me."

"Elie, I still do not understand why you were protesting being with Ralph," she says.

"I told you, Mother, I didn't want to end up marrying him."

"Well, what did you imagine was going to happen with Ralph after you spent time together, Elie? That's what young, eligible women your age do—they get married, especially to intelligent, successful, and may I add kind—men like Ralph Fowler. He's a very good match for you—and may be the best option you'll ever have now."

"Come now, Mother—surely I can find an intelligent, kind man whom I actually love."

"Elie, you don't fully grasp what the result of your jaunt is. Ralph, bless him, hasn't dismissed you—yet. He obviously cares for you a great deal because he's risked his own reputation by sticking by you while you were gone."

"He has? He *still* wants to court me?" My stomach clenches. I thought by now he would have moved on. *Dear Lord, does my ill-fated future with him still hold?*

"Yes, miraculously. That shows what kind of character he has—and that's rare, Elie. If you choose to rekindle your romance with him—"

"Romance?" My stomach is an iron ball now.

"Yes, romance—then we can probably convince people you were perhaps in the States to recover from an illness, and in a few months to a year it'll be like it never happened. But if you shun him, people will be sure you ran away, and I daresay you'll not recover your reputation. Who do you think will want to take a chance with a woman who spurned a prime match—and God only knows what people's imaginations will come up with for your activities in Buffalo, no matter what you tell them. Gossip is impossible to correct once it starts twisting."

I didn't realize my choice of a path forward was that bleak in either direction. Frankly, I haven't given much thought to having a different future since I didn't purposely leave, no matter what my cover story is. I never stopped to consider my reputation; I naively thought I'd be welcomed back with open arms and pick up my life from August, sans Ralph. But neither of my mother's choices are palatable; I'll suffer either way, though maybe I'll live longer if I don't marry Ralph.

"Elie, do you want to see Ralph again? Or do you want to forever be ruined?" Mother has always had a way with bluntness.

"I don't know, Mother. I didn't intend to sully my reputation, honestly."

"Well, again, what did you think would happen?" Her voice has now turned shrill, her cheeks a dark rose, and her eyes a deadly combination of hurt and fire.

"Mary, let's not berate her. She's just returned home, after all. She's come home to us because she wants to be here. We shall deal with any sordid mess of reputation later, when we have to. After all, no one but us knows she ran away; others may have suspected it, but the social circles have nothing firm to bite into yet."

"Perhaps not, Ernest, but the other alternative was that Elie was abducted, so what is better?"

Here I can't help but interrupt.

"What is better? What is *better*? You ask if it would be better if I were abducted instead of run away because you're worried what people will say? My God, Mother!"

Her face is now nearly all red, and I've made the mistake of angering her further and embarrassing her. I'm in for it now.

"You *know* I would never want you abducted, Eileen. That is *not* what I'm implying."

"Then why did you say that, *Mother*?"

Father jumps up from his wingback chair and stands between us, palms raised. "I will not listen to this arguing in my household. Elie, your mother and I were worried sick you were actually abducted, and we've had friends and the police on the lookout for you ever since August twenty-fourth. She was speaking of your reputation only, and you cannot deny it will be more difficult for you to find a husband if it's known you ran away when you were on the cusp of an engagement."

I sigh. Suddenly I'm cornered. My rosy life seems dingy brown now.

"Furthermore," Father continues, "you do need to decide soon what you plan to do in that, ahem, department as well as with your studies."

"Actually," I say immediately, without knowing what my response would be, "I'd like to become a physicist, like you."

Their stunned faces say it all. Mother looks like I suggested shaving my hair and parading down Ste-Famille Street, and Father looks part amused, part intrigued.

"I'm serious. Why can't I? Lise Meitner and Marie Curie are physicists."

"The world already has a Marie Curie. Besides, you're brilliant when it comes to literature. Why throw that away?" Mother asks.

"I won't be throwing it away. I'll still enjoy reading literature during my life, but just because I'm good at something doesn't mean I have to spend my life doing it. I also happen to really enjoy physics. It intrigues me."

"She does show an aptitude for it, Mary," Father says. "More than some of my students!"

"It's a difficult subject for women though, dear. And she needs to settle down, not pursue a career like an old maid."

"So what if I want to become a physicist? Can't I get married, too? Why can't I have both? And I know it's hard, but maybe that's what makes it a bit fun for me. Physics is a challenge; there's a lot to discover still."

Father holds up his hand to calm me down. "Elie, it's more complicated than that for a female in the field. There's a bias against women scientists—you know that."

"It's easy in some places," I mutter.

"If you mean Germany, remember that Lise Meitner is treated like an assistant rather than an accomplished physicist in her own right. Her laboratory never lists her as the lead on a published paper she's written."

"No, I don't mean Germany!" I flee to my room, wishing I hadn't alluded to the next century, not that they'd understand. It seems they won't ever understand either.

* * *

Half an hour after I stormed upstairs, I hear Father's heavy knock on my door. He enters, closes the door behind him, and drops with a tired sigh into my desk chair. "Elie, tell me—where were you? Honestly, please."

How does he not believe my story? I stay silent, trying to read his eyes.

"I know you trust me enough to tell me the truth."

"You wouldn't believe me."

"Maybe not, but try me." He leans forward and raises one eyebrow. "I may know more than you think."

I can only squeak out one word: "How?"

"I heard you that Friday, Elie, the last day you were here. You cried out, just a little. I turned and thought I saw you in the doorway, near the table. I couldn't be sure. It was so quick, like a flash. You were gone an instant later. I thought I was hallucinating perhaps. I went into the hall, asked the other men if they'd seen you. Soddy had but a few minutes prior and said you were coming to my lab."

I can only nod slowly as he accurately recounts the events.

"So," he continues, "I could only conclude that you were in my lab but ran off or were taken. The more I talked to people, though, I realized you couldn't have left the building by the stairs—someone was coming down and would have seen you—and there were people in the hall that would have seen you also. Well, they saw you walk toward my lab, but no one saw you leave."

My mouth is too dry to respond.

"I couldn't tell anyone that I saw you, lest they suspect funny business from me—not that anyone would assign me any motive, for they all know how I love you—so it was left to assume you'd told Soddy you'd come to my lab, walked toward it to fool people, and then left the building instead—ran away. Or you might have innocently gone outdoors and been abducted there. But I had a strange feeling something odd happened. I couldn't say it, of course, but I really thought you had vanished from space. Vaporized yourself on my equipment or something." His head falls into his big bear palms and twists back and forth. "I thought I'd killed you, Elie. . . . You don't know how I've been tortured since then!"

I pop off my bed and settle onto the floor below him, then reach up to steady his head and hands. Staring at his mop of mussed hair, I hesitate to tell him the truth. He knows most of the story anyway, I rationalize. I'll try revealing what happened without telling him exactly how—and certainly not any details of the future—to protect all of us.

"As usual, Father, your instincts are correct. I did vaporize myself on your equipment, only I didn't die, obviously. I stayed in Montreal even; I just traveled . . . to the future."

36

November 22, 2006
William

I have to reread the beginning of Elie's letter; I was so excited to read it the first time the words flew right past my open eyes.

Dear William,

As I promised, here is a letter to you, which is one of the hardest things I've ever had to write. I hope it finds you healthy and happy.

Firstly, I survived! I knew I would, though you had a bit of doubt. There was no problem physically in the travel, and I walked home in relative comfort, if chilly. It seems we are having an early winter here.

It's Sunday evening now and finally quiet enough in the house to compose my thoughts. There's a candle burning next to my writing desk, and the light is so spare my eyes are straining already. I took electric lighting for granted when I was with you.

Anyway, I was saying this letter is difficult to write. Once I sat down, I realized I didn't know how to word it—and despite your words Friday morning, I didn't know if you would care once I left. A few hours ago it dawned on me that as I write this, you haven't been born yet—not even close. Yet I feel like you're still living to me and are as real as anyone on the Earth with me now. You, Evan, Jeanne, Natalya, Isabelle, Professor Nagar—everyone—is still bone and blood to me. It's difficult to reconcile the reality of where I am with who is alive with me. That sounds like I'm losing my mind, and perhaps I am. Perhaps this adjustment is simply still in its difficult beginning stage.

I am, however, very happy to be home. Father and Mother held me close when I came back, no doubt fearing I'd disappear from their eyes again; I can't blame them. Since then, I've felt more loved, certainly by Mother, than I had felt here for quite some time. Oh, Mother did berate me for leaving on a whim and not saying goodbye—my cover story is a spur-of-the-moment trip to the States—but that was short-lived, surprisingly. I seem to have escaped the severe punishment I expected from her. That may be merely delayed, however; they were talking privately earlier, and I feared they were going to keep me locked in my room. Worse, they might have discussed sending me to a private boarding college—or worse yet, forced me to marry right away.

On the subject of that, I don't know how Ralph Fowler has taken my disappearance. Mother has only alluded to him briefly, and in a positive light. She may have been suggesting he still wants to see me, but I didn't press her. I'm sure I'll find out very soon whether he took the hint that I'm not interested. The cover story of my leaving is, I suppose, the worst form of rejection, and I'm awfully sorry for him on that account.

Besides the touchy business of Mr. Fowler and the possibility of a forthcoming punishment from my parents, things are quite fine here. I can understand all the phrases people are using here. Getting dressed in the morning doesn't require careful review and suppression of a panic attack, though it does require more layers, lace, and ribbons. I can play music on the phonograph by myself instead of fumbling through your "high-tech" music player. The familiar and comfortable surrounds me again, and that's . . . comforting. No surprises. It does seem a bit old-fashioned, though, as I'm looking at life through the eyes of one who's seen twenty-first century modernity. But that's probably nothing but an initial shock, and I'll get over it; things will feel normal again soon.

I had a good laugh this afternoon when talking to Father about how his work is going. You

> would get a kick out of it, as you like to say. It seems that on Thursday he was disturbed by the janitor of the engineering buildings, Mr. Roget. He complained that someone was setting insects into his storage closet in the Macdonald engineering building. You will know exactly which closet I'm referring to. It seems Mr. Roget thought lab assistants such as Mr. Soddy or Father himself were playing a trick on him by putting caterpillars and ladybugs and such in the room. Apparently most of them were dismembered or just legs or wings! Now we know what happened to those poor guys we tested with. Mr. Roget is quite the entomophobe, it seems, and let loose a series of female-esque shrieks when he found them throughout the day.
>
> Lucky for me he was home when I appeared in his closet!

Oh, Elie! I can't hold the letter still enough to read further until I stop laughing so hard and shaking my hands. We really did a number on those insects! I thought they might have been sent off in time, but I didn't think they'd reach their intended destination in time. I can imagine Elie trying to keep a straight face as her father told her this story.

This tidbit lightens up the mood for me; I was increasingly hunched lower over the letter. Reading about her being mostly contented to be back at home makes my loneliness sharper. *If I want her to be happy there, why is it not what I want to read?*

Now I've gotten that out of the way—hopefully I've reassured you that I not only am in fine shape but in high spirits as well. We together achieved my goal of returning home, and I really do not know how to properly thank you. This letter does not do it justice, and I'm not sure I said it eloquently before I left. I truly owe you everything, William, for sacrificing your time—and possibly your legal record—for me . . . someone you barely knew but protected and helped survive nonetheless. You were wonderful, *et merci mille fois.* That is the only way I can express my gratitude: in two languages.

With that said I have some regret in saying what I'm about to say, but I would fail you if I did not say it. I owe you the full truth, if for no other reason than because you were always honest with me, you believed me when few others would have, and I want you to know how this whole experience feels and ends—for both of us. So here it is. The truth is, I've been home less than a day—and perhaps the shock of returning is the sole culprit—but I have a strange tugging in my heart that I do not fit in here like I used to. Though everything's familiar, homelike, I know I'm not familiar to myself here. Does that make any sense at all? I can hear differences in my speech—and I know Father's heard them too—and my reactions. I now see this era, my era, as one a bit touched by over-gentleness of the female sex, too much separation of the sexes, and a heavy weighting of propriety versus freedom of thought. All the improvements in your last hundred years have done a lot of good there. Oh, there's plenty of security in how I'm living here, and in a way I'm relieved to be back in a role that's relatively easier to live than one I would've had to build for myself in 2006, but the lack of independence is nothing less than stifling.

But that's quite harsh of me to say of my own family and friends, as this is all they know to be. I cannot fault them for that. It's just that I have seen another way, and that has made all the difference, to paraphrase Frost. Living here is much less complicated. Well, perhaps I should say there are *different* expectations for females here, but it's also much slower. It's too slow at times. Like a flood my memories came to me in full clarity once I returned, and I see my Donalda classes were dull in comparison to what I was taking at McGill this fall. I used to accomplish in a week around the house what I can do in two days in your era.

I know I'm an utter blighter to be complaining as I have. I truly am grateful to be home; I suppose it was naïve of me to think it wouldn't be without struggle. All of a sudden this home of mine feels like a step backward, that's all. Perhaps I merely need a new start here, and to forget what I have seen.

My mouth, hanging open for the flies to nest in, is as dry as the fallen leaves around me. A small part of me is skipping inside to read that she doesn't love home 100 percent—possibly regrets going home—but my heart is also wringing itself for her. I really don't want her to suffer there, really, I don't. With all that we both went through these last few months, I want her to stay home and love it again.

Maybe that's why she ended up moving to New Zealand—to get her fresh start there? I would hate myself if the reason she felt she had to abandon her family is because she saw the future.

I suppose I have little else to tell you, being back for a short bit so far. I wish I could tell Father about you and what amazing parts of the universe you're researching. He'd be doubly as interested as I was, and I was enthralled. But I'll keep my mouth closed.

So I will thank you once again, William, and hope you're enjoying your life—a life free of this crazy lady from the past. Now I'm part of your past, as you are part of mine. I must confess that you've filled my thoughts ever since I returned. I want to know where you are and what you're doing; mostly I want to know that you're well. There is one cruel aspect of me being the one from the past: while you can dig up this letter from me and read my history long after I'm dead, I shall never know how you are. You might achieve world recognition—you might win a Nobel Prize in physics!—and I'll be ignorant of it. You might be the one to marry and have four children, and I won't be there to know. You'll live on only in my thoughts, and those thoughts will no doubt become dreams, until I no longer recall how William Hertz's brown hair curls. No one here will ever know you, but I'll remember everything since the end of August: that other reality whose end I shall never see, but it satisfies me enough to know that, like me, you will go on.

Kindest regards, with all my heart,
Elie

And then it's over, and she's completely gone. My little sun is finally snatched away from me, an ephemeral star sent back to its own galaxy. The last paragraph makes me shake almost as much as the insect story, but this time it's more a shiver starting from below my ribcage. Elie didn't come out and say it, but I can't be reading too much into it by saying she misses me. *Missed me.* That I was as important to her as she was to me . . . and that was exactly what I hoped to read. It wasn't every word, but as much as I could hope for from my Victorian lady.

I reach down to put the letter back in the metal box, then I freeze; there is a second letter! This one looks like a single sheet and only has "William | Elie" scrawled on its folded front in hurried cursive.

I tear into this faster than I did the first.

> Dear William,
>
> So much has changed since I wrote to you; I fear writing this letter may jinx what I'm about to do. With Father's blessing, I may have made the riskiest decision of my life a few hours ago, but I'm sure it's not only the right decision but possibly the sole one to give me a chance at happiness. You should know very soon if I've succeeded. . . .

37

Monday, November 19, 1906
Elie

"But Elie, it's dangerous to meddle with time! Any number of things could've gone wrong! It's a miracle your physical form survived to come back here to us! And to think how dangerous the world could be one hundred years from now!" Father falls lost in thought, then demands to know, with a curiosity I haven't seen since he began his gold foil experiment, how it felt to appear in 2006 and what that century was like.

With enthusiasm to match his, despite my reservations, I describe the sensation and assure him 2006 was safe.

"McGill is still standing—it's huge, in fact. I turned up in an actual room, though it wasn't a lab anymore. But—" I stop myself right before mentioning the Rutherford physics building. *God, it'll be harder than I thought to avoid referencing the future.*

"Well of course it is. The university will always be a pillar for Canadian education," he says proudly. "But tell me, how did it actually work? I assume you know how since you've returned. You must have duplicated the situation."

I sigh; I'll never be able to keep much from my intuitive father. "I shouldn't tell you, Father. This kind of knowledge is dangerous, like you said. But . . . if you're asking that, it means you believe me, right?"

He stares hard at me, intensely, with faith and sorrow. "I do believe you, Elie. I don't know if it's because there's no other explanation or because what you've said so far proves it, but I do. It's unfortunate for you, however, because you won't be able to tell anyone else the truth—perhaps including your mother—unless you want to live out your life in a sanitarium."

That's exactly the reaction William had, I realize. They're more alike than I thought; though I'm with Father, I suddenly miss William. I remember the letter to him hidden upstairs and start plotting when I can escape to the McGill campus to bury it.

"Elie, did you hear me? I do believe you."

"Yes, yes, thank you. I knew you would, Father. I hated lying to you, but I had to gauge everyone's reaction to me leaving. And I suppose I'm used to lying now. I've never lied so much in my life, and I fear I'll go to hell for it. All I did in 2006 was lie—about who I was, where I came from, why I had no money or place to live. You know that wasn't how I was brought up."

"Don't dwell on that, dear. If it was deceit, it was only for survival. If you hadn't, you would have been locked up and never able to come back home—I'm sure of that."

"Me too. Thank you, Father."

"So . . . did you touch anything in my lab that made you travel? Or was it a force field?"

I try to deflect his questions with more description of life in the next century, but he's not fooled. He continues to gently but persistently pester me—I'm sure purely out of scientific curiosity—about how the time machine worked. It'll slowly eat away at his brain if he never finds out.

Remembering William's stern warning not to tell anyone else how to make our time machine lest they alter history, I hesitate. I know guilt is all over my face, though I want Father to know the miracle we've managed—what I've managed to go through twice.

"Father, it's best if you just believe me. . . . Think of how dangerous the knowledge is if it falls into the wrong hands. . . . It's better if no one else knows how this can work. . . ."

"But Elie, it's science! I must know! I'm your father! This is, this is enormous!"

After several more minutes back and forth, he finally breaks me down; after all, I've never been able to say no to Father. And I suppose it's better he hears it from me than embark on a secret project of his own to build one. So I tell him a little bit, just enough for him to understand. I vaguely describe the principle of relativity without calling it by name, mention most of the equipment we needed without specifying the exact layout, and say how long it took for us to replicate how his lab was set up that day.

"The key to it all, though, was radioactivity. An alpha particle and gamma rays! Who would've thought?" I muse, then add, "That's the one thing Einstein missed when he thought he had this all figured out."

Father's head immediately cocks to the side, his face aghast. "Einstein? What the devil has Albert Einstein got to do with this?"

Oh, God, how did I let that slip?

"Nothing, Father, nothing. I never met the man. Forget I ever mentioned him, please."

He straightens his head, but his expression is still screwed into one of intense reckoning.

"Please, Father—I really have told you much more than I should've. I can't tell you anything that might change the future. Besides, I don't know that much about the next hundred years—I didn't want to know, in case I would spill a secret to the wrong person back here." That's more than a small lie, but I know it's up to me to protect us. The apple didn't fall far from the tree; I'm as curious as Father.

***

By late Tuesday afternoon, I'm in much the same position as I've been. Father and I have talked on and off about why I time traveled and why the "secret ingredients" worked the way they did—as if I'm his equal. He's also been pressing me more about what I was doing in 2006 and why I suddenly want to be a physicist.

"Father, in 2006 if I wanted to sign up to be a physics major, I could just do it—with no questions from anyone! I met a female who was working on her master's degree in physics, and she wasn't an oddity at all. That's what amazed me. All that time when I was trying so hard to come back, there was such a draw to study more physics. It would have been very easy there—then. I had one foot in already. And now I want to have that same opportunity here, now."

"I'm not sure if you will—not for a while at least."

"I know . . . and it didn't hit me what I left behind until I had already come back home."

Father raises his eyebrows.

"I didn't mean that I don't want to be here," I say quickly. "It's more that since I know what's possible eventually, can't I push it a little bit now?"

"I'm not sure. Even if I use my clout, getting you into the all-male classes at McGill would be nigh impossible. If perchance you did, they'd treat you like you were an ignoramus, and you'd have a devil of a time finding a husband—assuming you would want that."

"Yes, I do. I want both—I want it all."

"Tall order."

"Here, I know." I sigh. I seem to be doing that a lot the last few days. I know the expression about grass being greener elsewhere, and it seems true now. Even Father can see I'm trying to fit myself into a space that isn't suitable for me yet.

Father tries to cheer me up by describing some of the new classes the Donalda Department is starting up, but I feign excitement. But those pale in comparison to my McGill Arts classes, like Medieval Art and Architecture.

"Elie, I can see I'm not doing a very good job of persuading you of the wonderful education you're already enrolled in. Why don't you help your mother with the tea while I do a bit of work in my study? I need to make some plans for cleaning up the basement labs in the physics building."

"Cleaning the labs? What happened to them?"

"Nothing, but I haven't let my lab with the scintillator be touched since you left. I didn't want anyone moving anything in case your disappearance was linked to it. Now that you're back, I want to move all that old junk into proper storage so we have more room to conduct our scattering experiments."

"Oh, sure," I say. "I'll go help Mother." I do walk toward the kitchen, but my mind stays fixed on Father's lab.

* * *

"Elie, dear, can you pull the sugar out of the pantry, please?" Mother asks.

As I bring the tin to the table, I ask, "I suppose I can't simply rejoin my classes as a Donalda, right?" It's better than doing nothing, I reason.

"We told you—you were kicked out because you missed too many classes. It'll take a strong plea from your father to get you reinstated for the winter semester. And if he can't . . ."

"He didn't say that to me. I was under the impression I can restart without a problem."

"He didn't want to worry you, dear. But you know they have a strong policy against bad behavior."

"And what I did was bad behavior," I say with more snide than I intended. *If only you knew I didn't leave intentionally!*

She stops fussing with the kettle to press both hands on her hips. "Yes, Elie. You showed very bad behavior and poor judgment too. You're bound to be punished for that, don't you realize?"

I hadn't really thought about it, but Mother's arched eyebrows seal my fate.

"I can't wait to find out what other punishments are in store, Mother."

"Don't you give me that tone, not after the worry you put your father and I through!"

"Oh, you don't understand a *thing*, Mother!"

When I'm not sighing, I'm fleeing, it seems; this time it's to the backyard. Despite my long skirt I can still climb a tree, and it's my only escape at the moment. I huff repeatedly to quell my blood pressure.

Only after I sit in my perch for those few moments do I notice a sharp wind icing my ankles. I can't stay out here, but I don't want to go back inside.

What choice do I have? There's only one person here at the moment I can talk to openly. I reenter the house, march through the kitchen, and step unannounced into Father's study. He takes a one-second glance at my distress and says, "Close the door."

"Father, I've really binned it, haven't I?"

"Well . . . in many ways, yes. I heard you two just now. She wasn't exaggerating, I'm afraid."

"Wonderful," I exhale. "A slim chance for a fair education, choice between a man I don't love or a rotten reputation, with which I'll never find a man I do love, and a mother who will never trust me again."

"We can at least fix the last. You could tell your mother what you told me. If I believe you, she'll believe you. At least you won't have to live housebound for the next year—or more—as she would like."

"Oh does she? Fantastic. I'm going to love the next year," I moan. "I'll surely need your help convincing her of the truth, Father."

"You know I will."

"But that won't help my life beyond these walls. If I can't study what I want to—goodness, if I can't study at all—and I will repel a quality man who I could possibly be happy with in marriage, then my life is certainly doomed."

"You could always go back to Ralph, Elie," he says gently. "You could love him, in time."

"Perhaps, Father, but . . . there's more to consider than love when it comes to my future." I weigh telling him; when William warned me not to alter history, but surely he didn't want me to lock myself into only nine more years of life. "Initially I didn't want to continue seeing him because I didn't want to end up marrying him—that's why I was going to your lab that Friday, actually, to tell you I couldn't see him anymore—but now I know I'll doom myself to an early death if I marry him."

Father's face becomes as pale and hard as marble while I tell him what I learned from William about my future. My despair is echoed as pain on his face.

"And you're sure your future will repeat if you end up having a family with him, even after your time travelling?"

"I never discussed it with William, and we can't know for sure, but I can't see why not."

"Then it's settled, Elie. I don't want you to be unhappy with your life choice, but above that I sure as God's love itself don't want you to die before me."

He reaches over to squeeze my arm. My stomach is clenched in torment. I've just done what I swore I would not do: tell someone in 1906 about the future. If I don't marry him, what about those four children I won't have? Will Ralph have them with another woman? Will that portion of the future stay the same?

Or is killing the lives of four unborn children the price of saving my own?

But Father is oblivious to my selfish, unanswered thoughts. "Now, tell me who William is. You didn't mention a gentleman you met there. . . ."

"Oh! He's a physicist also, a graduate student, and I happened to meet him while in the library one day." With those words, my stomach unknots and my heart begins to pick up speed. "I couldn't tell you why, but I immediately trusted him. I was in a terrible position at that time—no place to stay, no income, just sitting in classes to keep busy, really—and he helped me establish a life. He even enrolled me in classes! Without him I would've been sleeping in a broom closet until I returned here."

"He must have been extremely kind and generous to you."

"I can't convey just how much, Father. I was so despondent at the point I told him who I was, but instead of thinking me crazy, he believed me, as easily as you believed I time travelled. He knew who you were—"

Father's eyebrows raise to his hairline.

"—and who I was too. He was amazed at my journey, you could say, and went along with my wild idea to recreate the time machine in order to return here."

"Aha. So you had help coming back. And you say this chap helped you assimilate into a new life there yet also helped you leave to come home?"

"Y-Yes. The former was a contingency in case the latter failed, although having a regular routine of school, work, home, and friends was very pleasant."

"Did he help you adjust to the culture as well? I imagine it was as jarring as if Napoleon came to our century."

"Yes, he did, though my cover as a Kiwi came in handy. I could pretend to be shocked at their rather open society from a foreigner's perspective. So much is accepted in that era, Father! Their licentious manners hurt my eyes and ears at the beginning, but I got used to it. I had to. The biggest changes are that people are open to independent thought, and social conventions are much more relaxed. It's very laid back in that regard, though the pace of life is tiring."

"It must've driven you mad to put up with that. You're not a prude, Elie—you've always leaned toward being rather progressive—but still you've been raised as a proper lady."

"Quite. It was awkward and rather embarrassing to witness. But eventually I realized people then are the same as now—people with friends and family and goals as ever. Their core doesn't change, though the dressing does, but that can be looked beyond. I made several wonderful friends there."

"Elie, I can't help but notice how your expression brightens when you talk of 2006—and especially of your friend William." I blush, despite all my prior friendly feelings toward him. "You're more animated than I've seen in quite some time. Surely you aren't implying you were actually happy there, are you?"

I pause to honestly answer him. "You know, Father, I wasn't unhappy, despite missing my home here. It was excruciatingly painful and lonely at times. But I enjoyed the friendships and learning there. Certainly at the moment when my future here seems to have taken a dark turn, I had a comparatively rosy future there. Knowing one's death date . . ."

He leans back in his desk chair and wears his calculating face I know so well. After a series of head cocks and ceiling stares, he faces me with sad, droopy eyes. "You do have a third choice, Elie. You don't have to stay in Montreal forever. You could start fresh anywhere, somewhere they wouldn't know what happened. You could leave this all behind." His eyes bore deep into me, and I cannot believe he's suggesting this. Once it's into the air, I realize it's what I haven't acknowledged myself as being what I might want.

"And leave you? And Mother? I'm not sure I could leave you again, Father. You mean more to me than anyone else in the world. You've taught me everything that's important in life. A girl is always her daddy's girl, no matter her age."

Father steps around his desk to pull me into a hug and kisses the top of my head. "My dear Elie, I have given you my heart and soul, and together with your mother have helped you mature into an intelligent and kind woman. I will always be right here and here—" he taps my heart and my head, "—no matter where you are. I want you to be happy, even if that's not here with me. When you have children of your own, you'll understand."

"I want you to be happy"... I've heard those words recently....

I hug Father tighter. I have more to say to him—I must make sure he knows how much I love him—but for now I have another letter to write. I need to write to William, and then I need to bury the letters for him, and then I need to prepare for what's coming next.

38

Sunday, November 26
Elie

I can hear birds tweeting through the brick walls, but the only sounds inside are my footsteps. Around me are piles of papers here, a couple of stacked physics textbooks on an armchair there. The remaining drips of last night's tea, as cold as the chill on the window-panes, lie in cups on the coffee table.

Advancing with soft, measured steps, I approach the desk I know well. With nostalgia I examine the neatly organized pens, papers, and books. My eyes stop at a family photo I never appreciated before. A stack of envelopes below tilts the frame. When I reach its level, I see two unexpected words on the top envelope: "For Elie."

Though this isn't my desk, I can't be trespassing if this is marked for me, I reason. So I pick up the envelope and make to open it—and see the envelope below is also addressed to me, and the next, and all the rest after that. Now in a rush I pull them all to my chest and move to the couch to read them. My greeting, interrupted by this surprise distraction, can wait a few more minutes.

The lined paper, crisp and cloud-white, unfolds briskly in my hands. The handwriting, scraggly as an old man's beard, is such a welcome sight it draws my cheeks and lips into a smile. Reading the first words alone speeds my heart more than any exercise could.

> Dear Elie,
>
> The past two days have been nonstop suffering for me. Since the moment you left me on Friday night, I've been nearly convulsing with worry about you. As I write this letter to you, I know you survived this crazy attempt of ours at time travel because I read the updated biography of your father. I know you're safe, but I really know nothing about your life except that you moved to New Zealand. But I don't know why you moved, and visualizing you living some obscure life there really hurts—maybe it's because I don't know the whole story of your life and why you went, but probably because I'm fearing you had to go there to escape something; I can't think of any other reason why you would. I just wish I could know the details of your life.
>
> Even though you got home okay, the pain of sending you on such a perilous, hair-brained journey has me so sick. . . . Elie, how could I have ever thought of putting you in such danger, of throwing you into unknown physical forces that

could've possibly destroyed you? Despite you wanting to go back so badly to see your family—and not stopping for anything to get there—you probably think I'm an absolutely heartless bastard for consenting so readily. Please forgive me. You'll never read this letter, so I guess I'll have to trust God to forgive me.

The reason I'm writing to you is because of the past two days' agony, actually. All 172,800 seconds have been filled with thoughts and worries and dreams of you. I can't concentrate. I'm only thinking about your security and how you're doing with your family. The only way I can think of to help me deal with my misery while you're gone is to write you letters. You'll never read them, but putting this on paper is removing the pain and worry. Only a little though.

Another reason why I'm such a crazed wreck is that I'm having trouble functioning without you. We've spent so much time together since you came that I don't remember how to be alone; it's hard to walk around with half of me shipped off to a previous century. I miss you, Elie. I miss you more than I thought possible. The pain of considering the possibility of you suffering a dull life somewhere might be more than matched by this solitude. The absence of you makes my life miserable and so pale, I wonder how I lived before August of this year.

It's ridiculous to daydream that I'll run into you again, through some weird twist of fate or the cosmos, but still I dream that. How a brain can allow a body's heart to suffer by letting these daydreams happen is almost criminal. Maybe this is penance for risking your life by building that time machine.

William

I bend down to pick up the second letter. Not bothering to be careful, I rip open the envelope this time to get to the letter faster. This one has more white space, and its paragraphs are divided into short sections:

Dear Elie,

I was walking to the lab today and saw a thin waxing moon setting. The last time I noticed the moon was when we were walking home from the lab the day before you went home. All that really mattered that morning was making sure you knew what you were getting into and were ready to leave. I was also getting myself ready for my last time with you. I wasn't admitting it at the time, but it wasn't enough to hear your voice and laugh with you. I may have ruined that walk by mentioning the Billie Holiday song about the moon, but at least I didn't share the lyrics with you then, because all they made me think of was how miserable I'd be once you left. I hear it in my head now when I imagine you without me. Despite this, though, it keeps me warm in a way and makes me smile as I remember your beautiful eyes gleaming in the moonlight that night.

I'm a little sad I never played the song for you, because it really is a great song. I find myself humming it when I pass by all of our favorite places. Here are the words—your one chance to hear them, or read them, or whatever this letter is.

The rest of the letter are the words to the song, all the beautiful words I too wish I had heard. How he'll see me when he passes everywhere we went together—the cafés, the parks, the trees—and when he looks at the moon. Just like I thought of home when I used to see the moon.

My eyes don't move from his signature as tears crest my cheeks and fall onto the oak planked floor with a *splat, splat-splat.*

Like a child pulling candy from a jar, I reach hungrily for another letter. This one is shorter.

Elie,

Right now I'm picturing you in your living room with your mom and dad, sipping tea while you explain everything you've seen here with me. The late afternoon sunlight is warming my apartment, so I know it's tea time for you. I'm comforted in knowing that you're with your family, and I'm sure the relief you're feeling right now is like a hundred-pound weight lifting off your shoulders. I hold onto a glimmer of hope that you're missing me as much as I'm missing you; however, I'm certain I'm the last thing on your mind.

What I'm going through right now is what I always imagined drug or alcohol withdrawal to be like: a steady, deadening force slowly sucking the breath right out of me. You've left a hole where my heart should be, and my insides are whooshing out through it. God, that sounds embarrassingly dramatic. But I've finally admitted how much I like you. Adore you. I fooled myself into believing I could detach myself from you and only help you get home—then I'd wipe my hands and move on. I thought I'd suppressed any feelings for you; well, I did suppress them while you were here, but they've sure surfaced now. I was so damned naïve to think I could forget you that easily. I spent too much time with you for that to have happened, but you were also unforgettable. You were fascinating to be with and always left me wanting more. Now you've left me for good, and I can't ever have more.

Evan and Nico are doing a good job of distracting me, but that only works so well and for so long before mirages of you saunter into the room and break what little concentration I can muster.

I can't even talk to them properly because they believe you're on a trip with your family, as does Jeanne, and I haven't reached the point where I can "break the news" that you've decided to quit McGill and go back home to New Zealand. So for now I suffer without the tiny comfort any phony closure could give.

My lovely Elie, you're all I can think about when I'm not forced to do otherwise—like putting one foot in front of the other and remembering to eat and sleep. I try to remind myself how happy you must be at home, but I can't stop asking myself, "is it over yet?" I'm counting down the days until I really can forget you—so this emptiness will go away—but I also don't want to let those memories go because I loved our time together. I don't want to forget. I guess I'm doomed to suffer.

I just want to look at your pretty face one more time and tell you how much I love you.

Your William.

"You can," I whisper. "You can see me more than one more time."

But it's his last words that still me the most.

The top of my throat driving hard upward, I'm trying not to break down. His words certainly push me. Instead I plow through the rest of the letters. They are each delightful to read, yet no others are as emotionally electric—or romantically direct—as the one I just read; either William had released his emotions at that point, or that last letter was the final one he wrote and jumbled into the pile. None are dated.

When at last I've read them all, I can only sit and stare at the landscape of missives on the coffee table. I can't stand or talk; I can barely think about the wonderful words within them. All I can do is run my hands over the papers and catch a few words over again.

A shuffling from the hallway leading to the bedrooms draws my eyes as William turns the corner into the living room. My gaze meets his, a meld of sleepiness, incomprehension, bewilderment, and surprise. He stares with a dropped jaw and compressed brow while moving his eyes from me to the opened letters to his flannel pants. He twists his pajamas between his thumb and fingers as if testing to see he's awake.

I, being far more prepared for this moment than he, stay in my seat and wait for him to adjust. I let him speak first.

Before long it's clear he can't quite form words yet, so I say, "Yes, I'm here. You're awake."

"You're . . ."

"Yes."

He waves his head side to side.

"William, you can step closer. I won't vanish."

"You came back."

"I couldn't not."

"For . . .?"

"For good."

One eyebrow lifts halfway up his forehead, and all of a sudden he's regained his ability to move. As he bounds toward the couch, I stand up to meet him, and he pulls me into his chest in the closest imitation of Father's bear hug I'm sure I'll ever get. I wrap my arms around him and turn my head; my cheek instantly warms. He holds me tight for a very long minute, doing nothing but breathing evenly and occasionally running a finger through the ends of my hair.

"You've survived three time travels," he finally says. "Too bad we can't submit that to the *Guinness Book of World Records*."

"You're always quick with a quip, William."

"It's a defense mechanism against revealing how I really feel."

"It's okay—I already read the letters."

He groans and pulls out of the hug. His chin falls to his sternum, eyes closed and ears red. "Ugh, I didn't mean for you to ever read those. I just wrote them as a cathartic thing; I've been a little, um, sad since you left."

"I'm sorry! I didn't mean to invade your privacy. It's only that they were addressed to me, so naturally I thought. . . ."

"Don't worry. You're allowed to know, I guess. Someone has to."

In a slow, arcing movement—perhaps ringed with hesitation—he closes in again and points his mouth first directly toward mine, then turns his head and touches his lips, soft as a butterfly's landing, to my waiting cheeks. They stay there for a long second, then he straightens up. "I forgot for a minute I was coming onto a proper Victorian."

I can cling to my upbringing forever, or I can start blending into my new century's culture right now.

I lay my hands on his forearms and ease my own mouth toward him, then I bravely touch my lips to his, just barely, just enough for a charge nearly as strong as an electrical shock to zip from his lips straight to my heart. I hold them there a long moment. I stand back and look into William's eyes, not sure if I did this right.

By his smile I'm guessing I did.

"Are you sure the Elie I know came back to 2006? You sure left behind a lot last century."

I shrug as if I do this all the time. "I have to adopt a modern attitude sometime."

"Works for me," he murmurs, then leans forward to return the gesture.

Ten minutes later we both have warm mugs in our hands, coffee for him and earl grey for me, and William has changed into day clothes. My legs are curled under me with my knees barely touching his as we sit on the couch, now cleared of his letters, which he folded up and allowed me to put in my satchel.

"Are you sure we won't wake Evan if we talk here?" I ask.

"Nah, we'd have to shout into his bedroom to wake him. So tell me how you got here—well, I guess I know the how—and why you decided to return."

Between steaming sips I describe my unexpectedly morose return home and gloomy prospects. I don't hold back, figuring I owe him since I've read his bared heart.

"It was actually Father who suggested I leave the Montreal I came home to. I know it pained him, but it would be worse to see me wither away unhappily. He knew I have potential to become a physicist, for example."

William's expression lifts.

"Yes! I told him it was easier for me to pursue that here. Sans stigma. That excited him more than me avoiding a soiled reputation."

"You could've moved to a new city, though, to fix that. Or to New Zealand. . . ."

"Of course—and that was the cover story he gave for me leaving. It seemed logical to tell people that. But in reality he knew I'd be as miserable anywhere else, career-wise, life-wise, and just as far from him and Mother. So he wanted me someplace where I could 'have it all,' he said." Half my mouth smiles at the memory of our last days together.

"He must have loved you more than anything to let you leave when he'd just gotten you back."

"It was just as hard for me to leave, William. It took me awhile to realize that's what I wanted."

He stares at me for a few beats. "We too often realize what we want only after it's gone."

I nod, then see his earnest, pleading eyes and grasp what he means. I look down shyly.

"After that it was a matter of getting Father's lab working like we had things here, which was easy since he hadn't touched that lab since I left. But I had the blueprints with me anyway."

"Aha! Now it makes sense—when I cleaned up the closet I couldn't find the final sketch you made of the setup. I wanted to destroy the evidence, so to speak, but without knowing that page's whereabouts, I panicked a bit."

"Yes, I put it in my bag, on impulse really, right after you stepped into the hall before I left. It came in handy."

"Insurance?"

"Not exactly. I was never planning on returning here, of course. I took with me only an instinct that I would want it, if only for the memories."

He breathes deeply and exhales as if to cool his coffee. "Well, what do we do now?"

"I suppose the first thing to do is look at my father's biography. I'd like to know he ended up all right after all this."

"Of course! I have a book on him in my room. Hold on. . . ."

When he walks back he's laughing at an open page.

"What? What does it say?"

He shakes his head and laughs some more. "It says exactly what it said over a week ago when I looked at it because nothing's changed in your futures for a hundred years."

"I don't get it."

"By the time I read your Father's updated future—which I did pretty much right after you left—you'd already decided to come back here because it had happened a hundred years minus a week ago."

"Of course. The future was the same to you here then and now—it just took me the extra ten days to come back here."

"Yes. In other words, your cover story worked. No one suspects you of being a rogue time traveler, Elie."

"Well, thank God for that. Father and I were both worried something would go wrong, but of course there was no way to let him know it all went well besides my ardent assurances."

"I'm sure he felt he could trust you in that. After all, you came back and forth already without a problem."

"That's what I told him. And I told him to believe in his equipment, as I did." I chuckle a bit when I think of how I barely held back at revealing his future museum chock-a-block with his old apparatus.

"You didn't tell him exactly how we got a lot of the pieces, did you? About his old stuff?"

"No, no, don't worry. I was quite vague. But he knew by then that some of his things would be preserved for a long time, and by that point some of it was."

"I guess it's safe to say you came and left without a trace."

"Except to my father and mother, and to Ralph to tell him I was leaving."

William groans. "I'm sure that was a pleasant conversation."

"It was smoother than I anticipated, given how my mother especially was adamant he still was in love with me. The months apart actually cooled him, or maybe he saw a change in me that he didn't like. But regardless, he agreed to say we mutually cancelled our relationship and wished me the best in my new life in New Zealand."

"He's a better gentleman than I gave him credit for."

"He always was, for that time. He just wasn't the gentleman for me." I give that last word an extra syllable, then pause, turning on the cushion to face William. The guilt I felt when I spoke to Ralph last week bubbles up again. "Though I do wonder what happened to him."

William's face brightens. "Incidentally, so did I, once I read that you didn't end up marrying him. I looked up his history, and he married a woman named Emma. They had four children—she survived, you can relax—who ended up being the same children you would've had with Ralph, as far as I can tell. Different names, if I recall, but same professions and achievements."

I can almost hear my heart beating as loudly as the birds' twittering outside.

"I know, I know. It's like a kind of fate, or the universe settling down. I was feeling so crappy at that point I couldn't properly digest that as being pretty dang miraculous. But now . . . wow, right? All that worry about a butterfly effect, but we didn't mess up history," William says, smiling until his dimples show.

It was always hard for me to imagine the children I would've had with Ralph, but knowing they still lived on calms a worry I'd hidden in my heart ever since William told me about them. And now they lived with a mother, to boot.

"Well," I say with a smile that matches his, "it seems I have officially moved on from him, with no consequences to history. I have my whole life ahead of me here. So . . . I'm available for a date, as you all say here."

"Do you mean I can court you?" he teases.

"Whatever you want to call it."

"Maybe I'll ask you out sometime, Ms. Rutherford."

My smile vanishes. "It's Ms. Newton, remember. I can't change my name now to Rutherford, no matter how much I wish I could."

"Right. Well, that unfortunately can't be helped." He smooths the cotton wrinkles of my shirt sleeve.

"No. But at any rate, I am available, that is unless I'm too busy with my physics classes, which I do intend to take full tilt next semester."

"Good! You really should. Oh—you would laugh that Professor Nagar asked about you this week."

"What? How does he remember who I am in that big class?"

"He knows you mostly because of me. When I saw him at a meeting on Thursday afternoon, he asked if I convinced you to drop his class because he's such a bad teacher—jokingly, of course. He must've noticed you gone. But he also saw I was a bit of a wreck and asked if we had fought. He assumes we've been dating for months, you realize."

"I'm not surprised. Apparently everyone has. That's awfully nice of him to be concerned though. And you were in such a state, weren't you?" Now I'm the one stroking his arm.

"A bit. And now you're back and everything is strangely and wonderfully back to normal—except that we don't have to spend hours locked in a dank closet. It's really fantastic to just look at you, Elie. This is the definition of surreal, I swear."

"Believe me, I know." We sit in silence for a few minutes, closer together than we've ever sat before. Our mugs have long since been drained. "You know who else I'd like to see? Jeanne. I haven't stopped by home yet."

"Home?"

I freeze. "Yes—it is home now."

We stand up and he hugs me again. "Can I come with you? If I let you leave again, my brain might convince me I'll never see you again."

***

In the now-familiar rooms of Jeanne's apartment, I'm warmed by her kindness and another mug of tea. Jeanne has welcomed me back from a long family trip to New Zealand, or so I explained to her before I left. I won't ever tell her the truth, no matter how close we are by now. She's a mother and grandmother figure to me now, I realize.

"You've been sorely missed, Elie. I've managed without you, yes, but it's much easier with you here to help me. Though it's the company I've been without. The tea actually felt colder, you know? Oh, that's a silly thing to say," Jeanne says as she waves her fingers.

I blush and grin at her. "It's good to be back, Jeanne. I was gone longer than I intended, but the trip didn't exactly go as planned."

My eyes shoot sideways at William, hoping I'm being ambiguous while still answering her.

"Well, it's a good thing you weren't gone longer, else I'd have to hire a secretary to answer the phone for your calls."

"What? Who's been calling?"

"Mostly Bernard from the bookstore, ever since the second day you were gone. The first time he was polite, then he became agitated, then he asked me to take down messages." She points to a paper next to the phone. "He was begging you over and over to come back to work there. He sounds desperate, Elie. But I didn't know you had quit on him, so I didn't know what to tell him."

My face burns rouge, and my guilt matches it. "I had quit before I left for the trip," I say truthfully, "On Friday morning I called him. I thought I was working too many hours there—"

"And you were!"

"—and thought now was a good time to cut back. But then I knew I would be gone for a bit, and I thought I should quit and let him hire someone else. It was frightfully rude, I know, to leave so quickly. I should call and apologize."

"But don't you need the money, Elie?" William asks.

"Yes, to an extent—though I enjoyed the job for more than money. But my father finally set up a bank account that shares money with me."

"When did he do that?"

"Last week."

"It took this long? In this day and age, it takes months for our banks to get money from New Zealand?" Jeanne looks positively bewildered.

"Oh, it was slightly more complicated than that," I say dismissively. "Foreign currency, me being somewhat young. . . . I don't know. I let Father do it. Anyway, I need to go to the bank and make sure it works—that is, that I can withdraw the funds I need."

"Elie," William whispers to me, "did your dad name you as a beneficiary of the account or put Eileen Newton as a co-owner of it?"

"He left me the money, actually. He hired a lawyer to set it up that an heir with my name, a descendent on my mother's side, he said, would be able to open the account."

"Has it been . . . accruing interest ever since then?"

"That was the plan. I know, I know," I say in response to his gaping mouth. "His bills would be worthless today, so this was his only way of taking care of me. I'll wait and make sure it works before I get excited."

"But that's a lot of money, potentially!"

"It could be," I whisper back. I turn my head back to Jeanne. "So it's not critical that I work as many hours now that my family is helping me out a little bit financially. And that means I can pay you a decent rent."

She waves her fingers again as if trying to rid the air of gnats. "Don't you worry about that, Elie. Our arrangement is suiting me fine. You use your money to buy books." She eyes William over her delicate bifocals.

I lean over to her on the couch and embrace her. "Thank you ever so much, Jeanne. You're truly a Godsend."

"I'm happy to help—you know that. And speaking of help, your girlfriends have been calling this week as well. Isabelle called just yesterday afternoon asking if were back yet, something about doing catch-up work you missed. They seem to really care about you, Elie."

"That's so kind of them. I did take my course packs with me and have been reading while I was away, but I don't know what assignments I missed. I should call them soon."

"Why don't you call now, dear? They were a bit worried about you falling behind, so probably best not to delay that."

Once the phone is ringing, I see that it's a small yet not insignificant task to get acclimated to my new life in 2006. My way of saying goodbye to my friends,

Bernard, and Jeanne was to tell them I'd simply be going on a trip—and then never return. Now I actually have to pick that life back up. However, instead of being challenged, I'm excited to accelerate back to where I was.

"Elie? You're home!" Isabelle shrieks.

"Yes, hi!" My energy level peaks to match hers.

"Hold on, lemme put you on speakerphone. Everyone else is here. We're lounging in the common room delaying working on homework."

After the rest exchange hellos with me and briefly fill me in on what I missed, both academically and socially, they ask when I can meet.

"I guess this afternoon or evening, if you're all free."

"Yes," says Lindsey, "But we don't know what you missed in physics."

"That's all right. I can find out this week from the professor. But speaking of physics, I have some news I can't wait to share with you. I'm switching to a physics major next semester."

The girls clog the phone with excited cries and congratulations.

"We'll miss you in our classes," Natalya says, "but physics is a better challenge for you."

"But who'll provide expert analysis on the classic nineteenth-century work? Only you know about that kind of stuff," Lindsey adds.

"You guys will do fine without my blabbering. Besides, you'll learn about that next semester, I'm sure. You won't need me after that."

"Maybe," she concedes, "though we'll miss seeing you so often. But maybe we could all rent an apartment together next year!"

"That would be fun," I say, though I know I would miss Jeanne. "Maybe there'll be one with a couple of bedrooms opening up in my building here."

"Ooh, keep your eyes open, Elie! That would be *so* much fun. We'd be able to hang out a lot more. You'll meet some new friends in your physics classes, of course, but still make time for us!" Isabelle pleads.

"Of course I will. That's a great idea." I then make plans to go over to their dorm after lunch for a long study session.

"How wonderful that you've made friends like that," Jeanne says when I mention Lindsey's suggestion.

"You'd be okay if I left?"

"Well, I'd be as sad as when you were gone this past time, but I would adjust. One can't expect the little bird to stay in the nest her whole life."

"Thanks, Jeanne. I'll try to grow my wings well. But I'd like to stay in this building if I could—for a number of reasons."

Jeanne giggles as if she were fifty years younger, and William coughs to cover his excited grin.

"Needless to say I think I made the right decision to come here." My chin clicks up and my shoulders straighten a bit more.

"I'll leave you two to chat while I get some sandwiches ready in the kitchen," Jeanne says. She gives me a mischievous look.

"You're right, Elie," William says quietly. "I didn't think you'd be happy here, but I'm glad you came back. Even if you didn't come back for me necessarily, it's nice to be part of your life. I'm a bit stuck on you, you know."

"Yes, I gather. The feeling's mutual. You're definitely a part of my new life here, a new life which I can make into anything I wish. I have so much freedom."

"You've definitely changed. When you first came here, you seemed to try to shirk from everything, and all you wanted was to go home. Now you want to take every opportunity. I just hope you won't have any second thoughts about leaving home for good."

"Not a chance, William. I said my goodbyes and meant them. My father and mother were at peace with my decision, and so am I. Now you're stuck with me."

"Well, my little H.G. Wells, if everything turns out terrible for you here after all, I suppose we can always ship you back home."

"What?! I meant it—I'm here forever. This is my life now."

"Don't worry, Elie," He moves closer so his thigh is touching mine and loops his arm around my shoulders. With a soft kiss on my hair, he continues, "I don't want you to be anywhere but here."

"Me too, William."

AUTHOR'S NOTE

This book is a work of fiction, but as those readers who love science or foggily recall details of high-school physics and chemistry know, Ernest Rutherford was a real physicist—one of the best and most prolific ever to set foot in a laboratory. His most acclaimed achievement was describing an atom as having a very small, positively charged nucleus surrounded mostly by empty space populated by negative charges. This revelation was indeed the result of the scattering experiments he and his team conducted at McGill University with thin sheets of mica and continued at the University of Manchester with even thinner gold foil. His remarkable career—topped by a Nobel Prize in 1908—boasts extensive work on radium and thorium radioactivity, discovery of the element radon, alpha and beta ray descriptions, and transmutation of elements due to radioactivity, as well as contributions to sonar, radar, wireless communications, and the splitting of the atom. It's difficult to overstate

Rutherford's contributions to the field of physics, and for that matter chemistry, though in a dig to the latter field he once said, "All science is either physics or stamp collecting."

He began his studies in New Zealand's Canterbury College, then in 1895 studied further under the famed J.J. Thomson at Cavendish Laboratory, University of Cambridge. Rutherford became the Chair of Physics at McGill in 1898, which he left nine years later for Manchester. It was during his years in Montreal that Rutherford married Mary Newton and raised his daughter Eileen, who was actually born in 1901, not 1886 as my story states; I suppose I made her time travel twice essentially. I tweaked her birth date in order to place her in 1906 Montreal so this story could take place in Montreal, not Manchester.

Eileen did end up marrying Ralph Fowler in real life, and there's no evidence she had any hesitation in doing so. My apologies to history and her descendants, as Mr. Fowler was truly a fine man by all accounts, but a happy marriage makes for a rather boring plot. Sadly, she did die at the age of twenty-nine, soon after the birth of their fourth child in 1930; William was unfortunately telling Elie the truth about her doomed future. Little is known about her life or character, but I hope I did her memory justice in these pages. She was indeed known to be a rebel in her time, such as taking wine to a picnic—*say it isn't so!*—but, though adored by him, didn't share her father's "spirit or scientific interest," according to David Wilson, author of *Rutherford: Simple Genius*.

While the majority of this book, save the two details mentioned above, stays true to the Rutherford family's history, I did make small changes here and there for the sake of adding interesting experiments and people. The device capable of measuring time to the nearest hundred thousandth of a second was Rutherford's invention, for example, but it was for the purposes of measuring the rise time of magnetizing current—and did not enable any kind of time travel events . . . that we know of.

As for William, he is a complete work of fiction, but physicists like him at McGill University do actually work on the VERITAS (Very Energetic Radiation Imaging Telescope Array System) project—a gamma ray observatory in Arizona—as part of a collaboration with dozens of universities. However, McGill's partnership began in 2008. If you are at all interested in astrophysics, check out what VERITAS has seen since its first detection in 2004. Thank you to those at McGill who unwittingly lent me their roles so William could have a career. I really enjoy that he's focused on gamma radiation since the term "gamma radiation" was first coined by Rutherford.

To those interested in the social history of Elie's era, the concept of women in science was not unknown, but it was not an easy course for women. Those who did pursue it not only faced objection from some of their male peers and, shall we say, lack of support from their supervisors—Rutherford being a rare exception who encouraged, celebrated, and gave credit to his female students and colleagues—but also suffered from markedly lower marriage rates. It *was* actually possible for women at McGill to take math and science courses in the early 1900s, but in female-only classes until the uppermost levels. Few women braved this life. Owing to Mary Rutherford's strict traditional conventions, I cannot imagine her wanting that life for her own daughter.

Montreal and McGill University are described as I knew them when I lived there from 2002-2006 while completing my own degree in mechanical engineering. I fell in love with the city and the university's buildings, with their nooks, crannies, and mazes of hallways. If ever there was a "hidden" place to live, it's the engineering buildings Elie found so labyrinthine. As much as Elie adored the campus—its buildings, people, and academics—I did as well, and I encourage everyone considering secondary education to put McGill on your list.

I would like to thank several people who helped me with the scientific details of this book. First, thank you to Jean Barrette, Emeritus Professor of Physics at McGill, who is the curator of The Rutherford Museum in McGill's Rutherford Physics Building. He kindly gave me a tour of the displays and the storage room—from which William so shamelessly filched—while indulging my numerous questions. I highly recommend any fan of Rutherford to visit the museum and take advantage of Professor Barrette's special knowledge. Second, thank you to my former colleague, physicist extraordinaire, and possible muse for the character of Jean-Phillippe, Damien Marianucci. Turns out Damien was one of those New Jersians at Stevens Institute of Technology who built a copy of the gold foil scattering experiment, as featured in Richard Reeves' excellent book, *A Force of Nature: The Frontier Genius of Ernest Rutherford (Great Discoveries)*. Damien, thank you for giving me a copy of your materials and research for that project. Finally, thank you to my engineer and physicist-in-a-different-lifetime husband, Aaron. Not only were you an intelligent and entertaining sounding board for my irrational question, "So how do you think one could travel in time?" you read my drafts and gave me the honest feedback I needed to improve this book. You helped me navigate Eileen's jumps through time and her effects on history when I doubted and re-doubted I got her hypothetical moves and countermoves correct. You "have has had been" the best ally.

Thank you to my publisher Silversmith Press, who brought *Scattered* into the world. Joanna, thanks for believing in my story and my voice. I'm proud to be part of Silversmith's published family.

My appreciation also extends to those who helped polish this book. Thank you to Kim Lajevardi, Kelly

Burke, Chris Dorian, Sharon Forrester, and Rachel Kelly, and also to my editors, for your feedback and revisions. Any errors—and *erreurs*—are mine alone. All writers are fed by a supportive writing community—and plenty of coffee—and I am grateful to be part of the Wordsmiths group, with whom I share this amazing craft. Thanks for your encouragement and inspiration, now and years to come. Finally, thank you to my family for encouraging me to finish this manuscript and not give up on it—and for accepting my hours engrossed in my laptop and my brain in Elie's and William's worlds instead of in the present. Thank you, Mom, for loving the characters as much as I have and not allowing me to let them go. To my daughters who also love writing stories: let the words out onto the paper, and they'll find their way out into the world.

Photos from Rutherford's Life

Credit: Science Museum London.

Ernest Rutherford's apparatus in the Cavendish Laboratory at Cambridge University, where he was director from 1919 to his death in 1937. To Rutherford, this was orderly, but this displays the sort of mess of equipment and wires which a fictionalized, young Elie could've happened upon in Rutherford's McGill laboratory.

https://en.wikipedia.org/wiki/McGill_University#/media/File:Sir_Ernest_Rutherfords_laboratory,_early_20th_century._(9660575343).jpg

Credit: Robin Marshall, Manchester Particle Physics Group, University of Manchester.

Ten-year-old Eileen Rutherford (front row, second from left) on holiday to Scotland with her father Ernest (far right) and family friends in 1911.

Credit: McGill University Archives

Ernest Rutherford in his Macdonald Physics Building laboratory at McGill University in 1905. Rutherford had to borrow a research student's cuffs for this formal photo to make Rutherford look distinguished enough for the photographer's taste.

https://en.wikipedia.org/wiki/File:Ernest_Rutherford_1905.jpg#file

Credit: McCord Stewart Museum

Young women like these, the graduating class of the Trafalgar Institute in 1907, were contemporaries of a fictionalized Elie. The Trafalgar Institute was a Protestant secondary school for girls in downtown Montreal.

Printed in the USA
CPSIA information can be obtained
at www.ICGtesting.com
LVHW031621250823
756278LV00006B/264